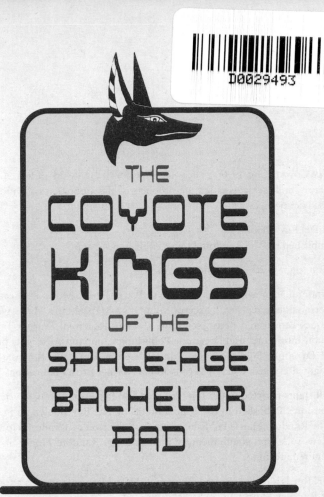

THE COYOTE KINGS OF THE SPACE-AGE BACHELOR PAD

Minister Faust

BALLANTINE BOOKS
NEW YORK

A Del Rey® Book
Published by The Random House Publishing Group

www.delreydigital.com

Library of Congress Cataloging-in-Publication Data is available upon request from the publisher.

ISBN 0-345-46635-7

Manufactured in the United States of America

9 8 7 6 5 4 3 2

First Edition: August 2004

Text design by Susan Turner

With eternal love for my first and finest teacher, my mum

THE COYOTE KINGS OF THE SPACE-AGE BACHELOR PAD

Epilogue

IN ADVANCE, SHUT UP. I KNOW EPILOGUES GO AT THE END. MY point here, which should have been obvious already in my opinion, is that I am telling you some of the end of this story so as to get you to comprehend the mind-set under which I am currently operating and during which I am escaping.

I think that made sense.

The point *is*, is that this summer has been really, well . . . it has included an unexpected series of events.

"Events."

That doesn't quite . . . *episodes? Adventures? Harrowing escapades?* Whaddaya want me to say? *Things.*

Basically, what? I'm supposed to make *sense* of this? Okay, in the space of, like, a week, I find out, well, confirm, really, ten years after the fact, that two of my best friends from high school are scumbags on a scale that will take me the rest of this space to divulge in full vulgarity and horror . . .

. . . that my roommate is a brilliant antisocial son of a gun (damn near literally) who abandoned me at the moment of my greatest epiphany and my most supreme terror . . .

. . . that washing dishes at the preppy-restaurant equivalent of a roach motel *is not and was never supposed to be* my destiny . . .

. . . that a gang of crack criminals in a ninja van from hell were in league with (who else?) Satan . . .

. . . that the woman of my dreams—strong, smart, beautiful, who can accurately and appropriately quote *Star Wars* and *2001*—has fins, and her pursuit of a seven-thousand-year-old vendetta would almost get me killed about a million times in the Wednesday-to-Wednesday space of the middle of July. That she could both rebuild my heart *and* break it. And I still don't know if that's the correct order . . .

. . . and, of course, *that magic is real.*

It was the worst week that summer.

And the greatest seven days of my life.

CHARACTER DATA:

Hamza Achmed Qebhsennuf Senesert

INTELLIGENCE: High.

STRENGTH: Unkillable.

WEAKNESS: See *Intelligence* and *Strength*.

SHIT POINTS, TAKE/GIVE: 50/100+.

BITTERNESS, RANGE/DURATION: Unlimited/unlimited.

WISDOM: Fortune cookie +8, experiential −2.

CHARISMA, WORK/LEISURE: −19/+23.

ARMOR TYPE: Hipster leather coat (secondhand), kaffiyeh, goatee.

SCENT: Questionable due to age and condition of coat.

FIND-DETECT UNAIDED: Uncharted.

BRAGGADOCIO/IMPROVISIO: Legendary.

REPUTATION, BELIEVERS/INFIDELS: +100/−23.

BLADDER/COLON CARRYING CAPACITY: Ultraminimal/average.

TRIVIA DEXTERITY: General TV +10, superhero comics +49 (see *Genre alignment*).

GENRE ALIGNMENT: SF (general), *ST* (original series), *SW*, Marvel, Alan Moore +79.

IMPAIRMENT: The Box.

AKA: "Specs" Muhammad, the Dark Fantastic, Warlock, the Maaan, the Coyote King.

SLOGAN: (Attributed to Marshal Law.) "They say I don't pray for my enemies. They're wrong. I pray they go to hell."

I Wash Dishes for Scumbags

You will never find a more wretched hive of scum and villainy.
—B. KENOBI, failed tour guide

CUE THEME MUSIC: "FE FE NAA EFE" BY FELA ANIKULAPO KUTI. Badass Nigerian horns and Afrobeat drumming funk—James Brown's Jurassic DNA blasted balls first into the future. That's *my* song, damnit, and I pity the fool who forgets it.

It's Wednesday night again, which it always is after Wednesday afternoon, which it always is after Wednesday morning.

*Wenzz*day.

This is what my life has become as I stand in front of this stinking sink in the colostomy zone of the Brightest-Lil-Preppy-Joint-in-Town™, called ShabbadabbaDoo's. Can you believe that name? Temple of freaking jerks. Here's a haiku for you:

> *ShabbadabbaDoo's:*
> *Frolicking fashion fascists*
> *Wealthy swines dining*

Yes, while mentally composing happy poems just to keep my soul from falling into the deep fryer, I get both to scrape AND wash the crud off of the shingles they slide in front of a bunch of rich kids' maws night after succulent night in this Tex-Mex-Cali-cocktail cesspit, before, during, and after they drain pitcher after pitcher of *Can't Believe It's Not Urine!*

Why pick on Wednesday? *Wednesday* is the day that says it all. See, in Norse mythology that'd've been Woden's Day, or Odin's Day. Odin was the supreme god, kind of like Zeus but with one eye and icicles hanging off his ass (the eye wasn't hanging off his ass—I mean he had only one eye, which you knew what I meant anyway).

And what day gets named after him? The middle of the freaking week. As in, week's not young enough for freshness and vitality, and week's not old enough for the hopeful release of the week*end*.

I work Mondays to Fridays here at Castle Scumulus, way down in the kitchen, the lower intestine, if you will, scraping and swearing and stacking and dreaming of leaving for Star Fleet Academy, and the day that gets me worst is always Wednesday.

Mondays I can actually take, which is because of an aggressive policy of Weekendventurism that gives me some holdover. Tuesdays I'm okay cuz if I work during the day I might catch a flick on account of it being cheapskate night. Thursday is practically Friday and Friday *is* Friday. But W—

Don't make me say the name again.

There's this one zitsack here, a freaking blond puffball who looks like a sissy-sized Ken doll with really, really, really tiny teeth (I swear, they look like someone glued rows of white corn niblets into a denture), who for some bizarre reason unknown to me *doesn't like me*. The little bastard.

Anyway, every time this busboy—DID I MENTION HE'S A BUSBOY?—drops off stuff for us to wash, if he sees *me* at the sinks, he always arranges to take a big pot or frying pan from one of the cooks and slams it in my sink to splash me sudsy, so my goatee looks like an ice-cream bar hanging off my chin.

I warned him that if he wanted his gonads to remain in their handy travel pouch, he'd better back off, but every night he keeps coming back with more kitchen meteors.

Now this *busboy* aspect is significant because the pecking order here is vicious. Out on the deck you got all the hostesses and managers and waitstaff who're mid-twenties, usually blond, and therefore White. The cooks are usually cooking-college Whites, with the prep cooks uneducated Whites or Browns. The dishwashers are all Brown. Most of these poor freaks don't speak much English and none of them has an education.

Except me. Honors BA in English literature.

Well.

Okay.

Actually I'm missing one course.

Actually I'm not likely to get that course.

Actually I'll never be allowed back to do that course.

I don't wanna talk about it.

So I'm here in this freaking swinetopia taking orders from a bunch of spray-ons in rayon. Sometimes I try to liven it up a bit here in the dish pit, put on some music the boys'll like. I've brought CDs by the great oud player Hamza El Din, my namesake and fellow Nubian (although he's Egyptian and my dad's Sudanese), and of course Fela Anikulapo Kuti, king of Afrobeat. Sometimes I've slammed in some Nusrat remixes by Bally Sagoo and Massive Attack, or some Apache Indian or Hot Hindi Hits for my boys, here—

You know . . . two weeks ago I brought in Public Enemy's latest album, *Muse Sick-N-Hour Mess Age*. Angry, super bad, and a Brother's best pain relief in this freaking joint.

So it's late night, I'm playing the music and washing pots, when the damn head cook comes in off his break—it's like one in the freaking morning and he's basically done anyway— and he tears my disc out of his box and in his ear-splittingest Australian accent yells at us (actually at me), "Keep yoh fakkin *ands* off moi radio!"

And to tell you the truth that mess is still burning up my guts.

(The sink-swamp in front of me is now completely aswim with filth, and I figure I'm gonna cut my hand against a sunken X-Wing if I don't drain it.)

I'm a grown man. And this Outbacks tool who probably hasn't read a book since the warden sent him a hygiene manual in solitary yells at me not to touch his stereo like I was *infecting* it or something.

Bad enough having to do this crummy job in the first place. Bad enough having to put up with the Zitsack. But getting sworn at? If my dad knew I was letting scumwads treat me like this, he would cry. I mean he would actually *cry*.

The sink's empty now—I got it washed out again, blasting it free of crud with the water jet. And now while I'm filling it up with scalding hot, the steam is billowing out of the depths like a spell from beyond time, a formula of hiding to keep me from going completely nuts in this stenchorium.

I'm wearing a Walkman-style belt jobby but without headphones. . . . My madman roommate, Yehat, who I'll be seeing in a couple of hours after I get off work—he's a genius with gadgets and whatnot—anyway, he rigged this baby up for me. An antidote to Captain Kangaroo's tirades and musical censorship. Got super-slim speakers sewn right onto my belt so I can play music for me and my South Asian dishwash posse.

I put in a Vangelis score, *Opera Sauvage*. It's for quiet times, melancholy, you know? And with the steam swirling around me and blanking out Dante's Ristorante, and Vangelis's lonesome strains chiming like death's bells . . .

. . . I'm suddenly on the cliff.

I don't know how long ago it was that I saw the cliff for the first time.

I guess it was way back maybe even before high school, before Yehat and me met. Might've even been the first time I heard this Vangelis piece, "Irlande," as in *Ireland*.

Hm. Never thought of that before. Ireland: *the Angry Country*.

Anyway, house was empty, which it basically always was by then, and me at all of fourteen years old listening to this gaunt, rib cage echo piece in the basement and probably, being the melodramatic kid I was, maybe even thinking about how lonely I felt and my eyes welling up with water. Poor little boy.

And suddenly I see myself on the side of a cliff, in a little carved-out portion, with the angry sea way below all cold and clutching, and me way too high up to climb to the top and walk to safety. No trees, not even the cries of seagulls.

And then . . . in this vision . . . I realize I'm not alone.

She's with me.

I don't know who she is, but her skin is like fired bronze, dark and glowing, and her hair is midnight and curly and wet-heavy, like soft, black chain mail draping round her shoulders. We're holding on to each other, and, I suddenly realize, we're both naked.

But it's not sexual. I don't know what it is, in the vision. . . . Maybe it's . . . survival.

With the swirling ocean mists cutting off the world and killing the skies, we're clutching each other for sweet life, like if we let go, the seas and rocks below will shred us apart like the teeth of some grim leviathan from those cold, cold waters.

I don't know her name. I can't even say for sure I see her face. But for more than a decade, whenever I see fog or overcast, or maybe just a wall of steam, I'm back on that cliff.

And the feeling it carries with it is of a loneliness and yet a sense of, well, *completion*, so intense it's like a mouthful of fresh blackberries, bitter and gritty-seeded and intensely, intensely *there*.

Ah, hell's bells, now you're thinking I'm pretentious and flowery and navel-gazing. Guess you want me to apologize.

Get used to it.

In two interminable hours I'm off. Until tomorrow. Until the next day.

Until the next Wednesday.

Maybe when we walk home Ye can pull me outta these Wednesday freaking mist gray blues.

I swear, I'm starting to feel so freaking trapped by the wrong stuff *in* my life and the right stuff being *out* of my life . . . so pinned down and pissed on and pissed off and pining for something, *any*thing to tear me outta here. . . . I'm so damn desperate I sometimes feel like I should just find the cliff in my dreams and jump the hell off it.

CHARACTER DATA:

Yehat Bartholomew Gerbles

REAL NAME: Ulysses Hatori Bartholomew Gerbles.

STRENGTH: Unshatterable self-esteem.

WEAKNESS: Mule-ass stubbornness +22.

TECHNOLOGICAL INTELLIGENCE: +99 A-Team/MacGyver.

DOESN'T-GIVE-A-SHIT POINTS: +25.

COME-ONS, FREQUENCY/RANGE/SUCCESS: +32/unlimited/+1.

SOCIAL APPROPRIATENESS: −1.

AFRO: Close-clipped.

EYES: Four.

ARMOR TYPE: R-Mer, class-10 Gundamoid somatic unit.

SMIRK: Pronounced.

MECHANICAL, INVENT/IMPROVE: +89.

VENGEANCE: Unchartable.

ENCUMBRANCE: Spotswood Persimmon Gerbles, brother.

BLADDER/COLON CARRYING CAPACITY: Superior drought/superior famine.

TRIVIA DEXTERITY: Scientific +379, mote in neighbor's eye +100.

GENRE ALIGNMENT: Hard SF text (Clarke/Asimov +122), PKD +79.

AKA: Scotty, Tony Stark, Supreme Love Doctor, the Coyote King.

SLOGAN: "One day I will rule them all. I will be MASTER OF THE UNIVERSE."

Kingdom of the Jimps

I'LL BE CLEAR. THE CUSTOMER ENTERS AT 1:13 A.M. TO GET A video. So far it's by the book.

I'm in the first third of *The Right Stuff*, where LBJ is talking with Wernher von Braun, rocketry genius and formerly my hero (until Hamza spoiled that for me by informing me Braun was an unreconstructed Nazi in league with myriad other Reichists on the Kennedy assassination [sidebar: the Kennedys *were* 1930s liquor drug barons, but the point stands]).

(Second sidebar: *The Right Stuff* is still, nevertheless, my twelfth favorite film [it was the eleventh, but as I upgraded into the architecture of adulthood, I reconsidered *Silent Running*], even if written by that Tom Wolfe [synthesis of Intellivision pusher George Plimpton and hockey cultist Don Cherry] bastard, self-satisfied "Radical Chic/Mau-Mau" cutie pie guff and so forth [I was *really* pleased when *Bonfire of the Vanities* bombed at the box office, with the added bonus that that smirky-jerk Bruce Willis also got smeared by its failure]).

I digress. In this scene, LBJ is trying to get his post-*Sputnik* (it should be pronounced "spootnik," BTW) cabinet cabal to rally around the flag and beat "the COMm'nists" in the space race.

Braun explains that the US should send up a pod, but LBJ hears "pot" due to Braun's screen-German shtick, followed by a verbal slapstick romp that lasts well over a minute.

Braun presses on, declaring that NASA should send up a chimp, which LBJ hears as "jimp," demanding, like Foghorn Leghorn (only missing the "what's a, I SAY, what's a—"), "What the HELL's a *JIMP?*"

Now, at ex*actly* this moment, buddy comes into the store, White, mid-forties, startling resemblance to a prairie dog (somewhat, but not substantially, larger). I am about to be annoyed. He's a #5. Allow me to explain.

Having endured interminable night shifts at Super Video 82 for thirty-seven months, I can assure you with empirical clarity that I have classified five subspecies of the life-form called Customer:

1. *the loving*
2. *the lusting*
3. *the lonely*
4. *the librarians*
5. *the losers*

Note: Subtype #5 usually covers the previous four, but they do vary.

Subtype #1, the loving, probably means couples looking for chick flicks. It's always painful for me to see a guy so obviously and obliviously whipped that he should, in fact, be bottled and labeled "Lite Dressing."

(Addendum: In general, no video-seeking male except a true movie buff is happy without at least one prolonged experience with SCERBS: *spies, cars, explosions, robots, breasts,* or *sports.* But I'll give you, any guy looking for chick flicks with his girlfriend is still giving her the groceries, so at least our gender has *that* victory.)

Subtype #2, the lusting, is fairly clear. Sometimes this includes couples, but it's usually single men looking really ashamed and when you give them their change they avoid your eyes and you avoid their palms.

Category #3 is huge, likely subsuming #2, but these jimps are pathetic in a paleolithically painful way. These demicretins like to watch movies about lonely people or dying people or doomed romances and the like.

(This practice strikes me as paralleling that of a man dying of starvation who rents documentaries on the Ethiopian famine while whistling "Food, Glorious Food," but in fairness, these customers aren't me.)

Subtype #4, the librarians, are film freaks such as myself who genuinely want to see everything worth seeing—"Watch all that is watchable," to paraphrase V'Ger of the vastly underrated *Star Trek: The Motion Picture* (aside from the flat, featureless Ilia-Decker romance and the fact that the series' supporting cast gets almost no lines, the Kirk-Spock stuff is touching, funny, and fresh, without camp, and the SF is some of the screen's best ever, as screen SF goes. I still get misty when Ilia says that "carbon units are not true life-forms," and then later when V'Ger explodes in earth orbit from the Ilia-Decker cosmic orgasm).

Subtype #5, the losers, brings us to the jimp in question. Tragic, weird loners who don't know what they want . . . these guys, they say they want your help, but actually they don't want your help—they just want somebody, *any*body, to talk to, or *at,* forever. *Which,* sadly, is usually me.

These jimps, presumably lost on their way to or from the thirteenth circle of hell with just enough film trivia and mistaken information to make a team full of Young Life Christian teenagers seek out Dr. Kevorkian, are the worst part of my Super Video 82 splendid isolation.

So that brings us back to the initial moment of this story,

the big bang, if you will, of cosmic jimpdom at the moment the jimp emerges from the celestial darkness into the brightness of the Videopolis.

Once again: I'm watching *The Right Stuff* while filling out an application for a local business needing a network jockey. John Shannon, my overlord and paymaster, bumbles towards me in all his glorious, towering baldness and orders, "Yehat!"

"Yes, Captain?" (He's never asked me once why I call him "captain," "milord," "quartermaster," or any of my galaxy of false titles. He is a truly uncurious being.)

"Yehat, hurry up with whatever y'r doing there and get over to the pornos. Alphabetize all of em between *Dirty Harriet* and *Robocock*. Somebody's got em all screwed around slipperier'n bat shit."

His turns of phrase are uncharacteristically comprehensible tonight, believe it or not. While he's talking, of course, I'm hiding my job application, and I tell him I'll get to it.

That's when the jimp comes in, wearing, no lie, one of those black-and-red, square-shouldered jackets from Michael Jackson's *Thriller* video, except this guy looks like a postal worker or a middle-aged ex-Hutterite from outside Red Deer.

"I'm looking for something in a good De Niro, maybe," he says. "Got any recommendations?"

A promising start: like all men my age, I burn offerings of goat and herbs at the Temple De Niro. "*Goodfellas,*" I say instantly. "All-time greatest—"

"Aw, yeah," he says, "just saw it last week."

"Okay, *Once Upon a Time in Amer*—"

"Actually, I'm not really into gangster movies."

This remark strikes me as somewhat peanuty. How the hell can a jimp say he likes De Niro but doesn't like gangster movies? That's like saying you love swimming but you hate the water, or you like sex, but hate spanking.

"Okay, guy," I sigh. "*Awakenings*? Subtle and startling performances with a touching story of tragedy and transformation." Between the movie boxes and living with Hamza, I've enjoyed learning to talk in *copy*.

"Oh, I can't *stand* Robin Williams. . . ."

"Okay, okay, I can grok that. *King of Comedy*?"

"*Yeah!*" he snorts and sneers. "Sandra *Bern*hard? Right! She's like a big, y'know, screeching, annoying . . . hoot . . . uh . . ."

"Owl?"

"Yeah, Sandra Hoot Owl!"

"Well-spoken." This charade of human interchange grows wearying for me. Irritation is building up in my facial muscles like nitroglycerin. Unless I can ditch this guy ASAP . . . "*Last Tycoon*?"

The Jimp: "I don't like period pictures."

Me: "*Taxi Driver*."

Jimpotron: "I want something . . . fun. Funny!"

Human: "*Midnight Run*."

Jimpimple: "Oh, that Charles Grodin drives me crazy!"

Increasingly angry sentient being: "*DEER HUNTER*."

Jimpussy: "I don'like *war* pictures—"

Premeditating premurderer: "*MAD DOG AND GLORY!*"

Jimpuke: (*Pause.*) "Y'know, that Bill Murray is such a scamp!"

I'm on the edge of the counter. Is this fruit fly actually going to land?

"Sounds good," he says.

I'm ecstatic. I tap away frantically at my computer, but— *wait for it—*

"It's . . . out," I whisper. I'm a Roman centurion . . . at Masada.

And then he does it.

The Bad Year Jimp, looking very dismayed, chirps, "Hey, do you have Madonna's *Truth or Dare*?"

"GET OUTTA HERE!" I scream. "*GET THE HELL OUTTA HERE!*"

The guy bolts out the door in his *Thriller* coat, running like Michael J. away from all those zombies. Considering how the neighborhood's changed here on Whyte Ave, that's not a bad idea, given the proliferation of drunks and punks.

But I'm stalling, as I'm sure you realize. Because Grand Moff John Shannon is running up from the back room like I've just shot the secretary general.

"YEHAT! WHAT IN THE DONKEY'S BALLS IS GOING ON OUT HERE?"

Yes, he actually talks like that.

Fortunately, my comrade-in-arms, my brother-in-dashiki, dishwasher and imagineer supreme Hamza Senesert is slipping through the door right now and he knows what to do.

Hamza: "And STAY out, you damn pedophile!"

John is huffing and puffing, glancing, with eyes dancing. "What'd . . . what just—who—"

"Don't worry, John. It's all under control," I say.

"Ye, it's *Mum*," pleads Hamza. "She's really sick! We gotta get some medicine fast!"

John looks like we're either trying to steal candy or steal the very concept of candy.

"John, my shift's over"—I point to the clock—"and Mum's real sick. How sick is she, Hamza?"

"She's speaking in tongues again, and her gums are really, really puffy."

"But what about restacking the *pornos?*" demands John, arms akimbo, actually whining.

"Well, jeez, John, you shoulda asked me with more than four minutes left in my shift! You heard my brother—Mum's gums are puffy! You wanna live with that on your conscience?"

John's pupils flick between us like two tiny cataracted tennis balls.

"Okay." I decide to stop waiting. "We gotta go!" I grab my duffel from beneath the counter. "John, I'll overhaul the 'baters section tomorrow, all right?"

"But—"

And we're out the door, standing on a sign-lit Whyte Ave

night with drunks and weirdos and losers and nutcases, and
each other. Me and Hamza. Brothers without a womb between us (read that how you like). Soul men. Champions of a
new age. Together at last.

    The Coyote Kings.

The Coyote Kings in "Feet of Fury"

OF COURSE, THE FIRST THING YE DOES IS PULL A CAPE OUT OF HIS sports bag, unfurl it grandiosely by snapping it out not once but *twice,* then swirl it around his shoulders.

Throughout this I pretend I'm watching the street for cars, freaks, really hungry gulls—*any*thing but feed him the attention he lives off like lampreys live off fish guts.

I start to walk, notice Ye isn't budging. I stop, wait for him to say something. I know he won't, but I have to hope.

He's not moving.

I wait, keep pretending to be on the lookout.

He's still not moving.

Me: waiting. Fake watching.

Him: not moving.

Crap.

Eventually: "What's with the cape?" I wheeze.

Ye, with his usual chipperness: "It's my July idiosyncrasy. Like it?"

"Ehn." I wonder when the hell he *made* it? "When the helldja *make* it?"

"Couple of weeks ago, when you were out getting comics, I whipped out the old Singer and started click-clackety-clicking along. It's okay, y'know? Maybe . . . forty percent what I wanted it to be."

He's modest, actually. I hate to admit it, but the cape is *smoking:* black on the outside, emerald, I think, on the inside (it's hard to tell under the fluorescents), with two Kirbyesque star medallions at the shoulders, gold braid ringing the collar, and fancy gold vine trim down the edges.

I'm jealous.

"The cape is dope, Ye."

"You like? You're not just saying that?"

"Naw, it's dope."

"Well"—he shrugs—"it was either this or a red leather diaper and a hat with moose antlers."

"Well, far be it from you to fly in the face of convention. Maybe next month."

"Exactly."

Satisfied, Ye lights a cigarette, which he doesn't usually do around me, as he knows just how much I despise cigarettes, the tobacco industry, and everything else associated with them (at home he only smokes outside).

I don't conceal my irritation, but he's so busy shooting out spumes of fumes and making grand gestures to make the cape flutter, all the while listing, numbering, and detailing the observable contents of the known universe, that he doesn't notice my antismoke grimacing and groaning.

Walking, on the avenue. At night.

Whyte Ave this time on a Wednesday night is usually okay. Most of the way-too-many bars have already shut down and their scum have filtered away to their various petri dishes. Still, I keep my eyes out, and so does Ye. His eyes, that is. *He* keeps *his* eyes out.

You know something? This bastard only started to smoke last year—twenty-four years old at the time and he *starts* smoking—and *that* was to get a chick, can you believe it? She was a dancer and Ye said, "It'll give us something to do together." See, that's just *sad*.

I've never understood the whole thing with guys and dancers anyway. Singers—now *they're* what puts the fire in my dragon. A singer, damn, she can coo in your ear with perfect pitch, sing you a love ballad or a sultry smokified seduction that'll have you vibrating like a tuning fork. She can sing in a bar, she can sing in a car. She can sing at a lake, she can sing with a rake. She aint space-dependent to bring dreams to life.

But a dancer needs room to do her thing! What's a dancer sposta do in your room, is she gonna—okay, scratch that. I'm not naive. I just . . .

Singers. Yeah.

One time I was at this restaurant in Kush and was sung to by (stung by) a be-*you*-tiful Ethiopian waitress wearing a sequined gown that glittered like a mountain river beneath moonlight.

She was singing during some special dance night the manager set up to showcase his talented waitress so she could launch a CD or get an agent or maybe just so he could give her the groceries. Actually, I'm being unfair—I think he really was trying to help her out.

Now, see, she sang to *me*—I think she was kinda sweet on me. And she had me in her gravity the entire night—I couldn't take my eyes off her. Her voice echoed in my brain for a week, set my steps to syncopated polyrhythms, even though she was singing in Amharic and I couldn't understand word one. But damn! Gorgeous.

Ye never forgave me for not asking her out. He wouldn't let it lie for like a year, every time I was home on a Friday or Saturday night. But hey, we had no future. She *sang* beautifully, she *was* beautiful, but she barely spoke English. We had nothing in common.

"Do your parts fit?" asked Ye, ever the one for elegant speech.

"I need more than me*chan*ical congruence, guy," I told him.

He's an engineer, though, so I'm sure he found my remark completely indecipherable.

(In the interest of full disclosure, this one time I actually did try to ask her out. I gummed up my courage one Thursday afternoon and went down to the restaurant to ask her to a movie. But when I got there, she was talking with a guy I knew had to be a new boyfriend. I think she knew why I was there, cuz when she saw me all awkward she looked awkward, too, like she was at the airport holding a ticket she'd just paid for, but now she didn't wanna get on the plane anymore. [Melancholic pause. Sound effect: sigh.] I guess I'll never know.)

Now, I may not have a cape as we stroll down Whyte, but I aint so bad to look at, myself. Not every day do I feel like this. Sometimes I look at myself in the mirror and feel like a colorized Quasimodo.

But Ye doesn't fret like I do. He's short and, to me, kinda crazy-looking (I love him, but seriously, he actually is weird-looking. It's his eyes: his irises are really small, so you can see their entire circle, like he's in a permanent state of delighted surprise, which really jars with his actual attitude).

But it's his self-confidence, see. I never could understand just how successful the guy is with women.

One day he says to me, "Hamz, you're like most guys. You ask out ten women a year, you have a ten percent success ratio, so most of the time you're lonely and you got no momentum.

"Me, I ask out ten a *night*. Same success ratio. But *fulfillment* is in *frequency*, G."

Now, see, I disagree with that. To me, fulfillment is in quality, not quantity. But even I gotta admit, my depression over my *in*frequency has become a freaking tornado warning hanging over my head, a yellow prairie sky announcing hail to any woman with her gynosensors on at even half gain.

I just can't seem to shake it. Nothing I do works. I've been a Creature from the Loser Lagoon who can't even raise himself *up* to the level of basket case, ever since the incident with—

Forget it. Nothing.

I was saying I don't look so bad myself, tonight. Got on my hipster's black leather thigh-length coat (got it for twenty-nine bucks at a half-price night at Value Village). It's well-worn, but I call it the battle-scarred look.

And, of course, my kaffiyeh. My dad gave it to me—he wore it when he went on hajj—and it's still in great shape. And it's no Saudi scarf, either—it's the original Palestinian black and white. And sometimes, I wear this dope fez I bought at the Ghanaian pavilion during Heritage Days Festival, purple and gold, and Ye says I look like a sheikh when I wear it. I like that: Sheikh Hamza el-Coyote.

So despite working at Shit Hog's on a Wednesday night, with me and Ye dressed as we are, I feel good. We're all right, outta sight . . . and the kot-tam masters of the funktacular night.

We're passing Army & Navy Surplus on Whyte and 104th when a punk kid sitting on the sidewalk (not on a bench or anything, you understand, this is some kind of grunge shtick, to sit on the actual cold and dirty sidewalk, and half the time these Cobainoids don't even wear *socks*) calls out to us, "Hey, soul brothers."

Ye shoots me a look. We both hate that "soul brother" shit these guys try to pull. They try to soul-shake with you, or like one time, I went into one store here and the clerk says to me, "Whassup?" Or they call out "Respek!" like they're Rastafarians or something. Kot-TAM—do I *look* Jamaican?

*Any*way, kid calls out, "Hey, Brothers, kick a punk for a buck?"

Ye and me share more eyes and eyebrows.

Me: "Excuse me?"

"Kick a punk for a buck, homey?"

Homey?

Yehat: "How hard?"

"Hard's you like, man."

"For a buck."

"That's right, one shiny loonie," he says. He's maybe nine-teen, wearing expensive boots and he's got a pack of cigarettes rolled up in his sleeve. Kids like this bus in from the suburbs, Millwoods or Blue Quill, then pose on Whyte Ave begging for money, like being poor is a freaking fashion statement. Subur-ban Whitekids begging Blackfolks for money—what the hell is this world coming to?

Yehat shrugs, then kicks the kid in the thigh. Not too hard, but I'm glad it wasn't me. The kid yelps, his face is torn for a second, and then he holds out his hand.

Yehat deadpans the kid, "That'll be a buck."

The punk looks like he's gonna freaking cry and Yehat bursts out laughing. I think it's cruel, but I can't help myself and I start laughing, too, while Ye walks away. I fish out a dol-lar coin, throw the loonie to the little freak, catch up to my best friend, the Cadillac of jerks.

The Coyote Kings vs.
the Whyte Wolves

WE CUT ACROSS WHYTE TO THE NORTH SIDE OF THE AVE AND pass an electronics store with banks of TVs in the window set to an all-news network. It's more footage from last year's genocide in Rwanda, what with the new investigation into who knew what, when, and how much outside parties are actually guilty.

The sound is piped out into the street, with twenty-four pristine Sonys and Hitachis beaming aerial photography and interview close-ups about butcheries to round out the heavyweight century of blood.

At two A.M.

To an empty street.

Who's watching? Who cares?

This is who we are.

Yehat sees me staring. He knows I'm about to blow.

"Rwanda again?" he asks rhetorically.

I nod anyway.

"I hear they're saying now," he mumbles, "that France and Belgium knew it was gonna happen."

"Aw, hell, Ye, all these freaks knew it was gonna happen. The French were the ones who *armed* the Interahamwe—"

"Who?"

"The 'Hutu SS.' "

"Oh."

"*Ev*eryone's dirty in this. They say even UN officials were ignoring reports when they *knew* what was gonna happen. Course, the US could spend billions to kill two hundred thousand in Iraq over oil, but not spend dime one to save nearly a million in Rwanda."

I can see Ye tense up. He hates it when I start talking about this subject. Last year I taped all the coverage on this—I've still got about forty tapes lying around. He said it was my Dealey Plaza, my Grassy Knoll. My Nuremberg.

"People scrambling all over this mess of planet Earth, freaks just tryinna get paid, tryinna *eat,*" I breathe, "while, while *scum*bags in offices wearing neckties an Gucci suits an, an, an *stars* on their shoulders an *brass* on their chests . . . deciding how half a million people're gonna die.

"Is it gonna be rifles 'n' grenades 'n' machetes, like in Rwanda? Or stealth bombers, like in Iraq? Or, or, how bout slower? Yeah, IMF-style! Force the freaks to cut every dollar they spend on medicine or education. So they can freakin starve to death while they're ex*por*ting avo*ca*dos an-an-an *MANGOES*—"

"Hamz, c'mon—"

"—or mining diamonds'r bauxite and diggin their own graves AT THE SAME TIME!"

I turn my back on Ye, spin face-to-face with Whyte Ave and its cold streetlights and its empty night sidewalks, throw up my arms like I'm threatening the beanstalk giant.

"It's a *SICK* FUCKIN WORLD!"

The street doesn't say anything. Not even an echo.

Ye puts his hand on my shoulder.

I lower my arms; breath trails out of my lungs, spills onto the asphalt.

"Man, Hamz," he says softly. "You can't . . . it's gonna kill you, switching like this, happy-sad, laughin-yellin. Manic-depressive."

I'm still again. I wait.

Finally I speak, softly.

"This is who I am."

Ye's quiet, too.

Then he says, "I know."

The newscast switches audio. Ye turns and I do, too, trying to smooth out this moment.

The TVs are showing something I didn't even know happened. Some kinda earthquake in southern Alberta and all over Montana, happened only yesterday.

Images: smashed houses and stores and burst sewers and snapped power lines. It's not like in the cartoons . . . no giant cracks in the earth forming newborn cliffs. But it still looks like hell booked a luxury suite at the inn. Like maybe the first stop on the Judgment Day tour.

The choir of TVs sings, ". . . epicenter at Kalispell, Montana, but at seven-point-two on the Richter scale this is by far the largest earthquake to hit this part of North America in recorded history—"

"Man!" I snap. "I feel like a freakin mope. How could this've happened and we not even know about it? Did *you* know about this, Ye?"

"Nope. Must be our jet-setting schedules."

"Damn, Ye, the whole freakin planet is crumbling! And what were we doing so we didn't know about this? We were watching crap on TV! How come we didn't—"

"We weren't watching TV."

"Oh no? Then what were we—"

"We were watching videos—Carpenter's *The Thing* and the original 1950s dumb version with the evil scientist and the man-carrot from space—"

"Well, what the hell's wrong with us, then? Do we have our heads so far up our genre asses we don't even know it when the earth is splitting open? We're like fifties housewives hopped up on goofballs, makin SPAM meat loaf an putting our hair in curlers while Kennedy's threatenin to start World War Three!"

"You even know what goofballs are, or you just steal that from *Seinfeld*?"

"From William S. Burroughs. Okay, not goofballs. Prozac and soap operas!"

I scowl, flail, rage on: "Ye, didn't you think that by the time we were twenty-five we'd've done something important, be having ad*ven*tures or something, not working shit jobs and watching PAL copies of *Space: 1999* while the world is flushing itself down a black hole?"

"Hamza, re*lax,* guy—"

"Y'know, we always thought that if *we* were Luke, when Ben offered the chance to go to Alderaan and become Jedis, we'd jump up and say, 'When do we leave?'"

"But naw, we'd just be a couple of pussies whinin about not havin enough money to pay the utilities an then go back to playin with our own light sabers."

I gather up the muck in my mouth, spit in the gutter. I hate public spitting, but my mouth is dry and I'm sick of this goo.

"Are we even *men,* Ye?"

"*I'm* a man."

"Then why didn't you know about this earthquake, either?"

"Listen, insteada getting your dick all outta joint, see this another way. There's a positive—"

"To us being ignorant?"

"No, the earthquake! Think of all the things they might find now, with the earth shaken up. Fossils of undiscovered dinosaurs! Ancient settlements from the Cree or the Blackfoot. You ever see the petroglyphs they got down near Milk River, at Writing-on-Stone? They could find new ones now! And don't forget, the Cree are related to, like, the Maya, the Aztecs, the Olmecs—"

"*Pretty* distantly—"

"Okay, okay, but still—and the Olmecs might even've gotten their start from the Egyptians! That was even in that UNESCO survey! Maybe they'll find some buried pyramid here in the badlands!"

"That's bullshit. That's *bull*shit. You're talkin *fantasy*—I'm tryinna talk human rights abuses, here, getting real, bein *men*—"

"You gotta keep hope *alive,* Hamza!" Then Yehat goes off with his Jesse imitation, eyes bugging, jowls shaking, arms gesticulating: "Keep—hope—ALIVE! Keep—hope—ALIVE! *I AM*—"

"You sound more like Shatner—"

"*—SOMEBODY!* I AM—"

"—an idiot."

"I AM—"

"A freak!"

He's punching me in the shoulder now, yelling, actually *yelling:* "I AM—"

Aw, what the hell. "SOMEBODY!"

"I *AM*—"

"*SOMEBODY!*"

"DOWN with DOPE!"

"*UP with HOPE!*"

"MAY THE FORCE—"

"*—FEED YOUR HORSE!*"

Ye's got me laughing again. He's smiling; he's done his trick.

But it doesn't last long, cuz we walk right in front of the Wolves' Den.

Ye shakes his head when he sees my expression.

Look, I don't like being like this, always angry and everything. I know he's trying to make me feel better, but for freaking out loud!

Light and music blare through the picture window, the

neon sign featuring planet Earth held inside an upstretched hand, and the name of the joint:

THE MODEUS ZOKOLO

Now, I don't hate this place cuz it's a yuppy import joint catering to dilettante cappuccino-snorting rich freaking rectaloids. I don't hate this place because they thrive off yak-wool Colombian hand-knitted sweaters and other exotica stolen and swindled from around the world for pennies, then sold here at jacked-up prices for a bunch of jack-offs.

I don't even hate the place cuz it took over the space a conscious bookstore used to occupy until they were chased outta this newly upscale block by the new landlords to make way for woolly-mammon stores like this.

I mean, those are all good reasons—they're just not the reasons I have in this case.

My reason is who *owns* this store.

I don't know what the hell's going on in there at this hour. This place's been open for a year already, so it's not their grand opening. . . .

Awwwwwww! Hell's bells. I can't be*lieve* it!

"Hell's bells," I say out loud. "I can't be*lieve* it!"

"What now?" wheezes Ye. "Why the hell d'we have to walk past this place every night if you're gonna react like—oh."

Ye sees it.

A poster in the window says what these freaks must be celebrating. A book launch, on campus, Friday. This is the PRE-launch party.

A book written by one of the co-owners of the Modeus Zokolo, with photographic essays by the other co-owner of the Modeus Zokolo.

How very freaking nice for them.

"You didn't know?"

"Naw," I say, "I had no idea."

"Shoulda been you, Hamz."

Ye pauses. I know what he's gonna say.

"*Coulda* been you."

At that exact moment, the private party inside, squirming with all its canapés and martinis and makeup and platform shoes and cigars and designer glasses, squeezes two faces into view. Two siblings, one White, one Black, our old high school chums. They're looking at me. I'm looking right back at them so they know I know they know I'm watching them.

Heinz and Kevlar Meaney.

The Wolves.

"That joint," I growl to Ye, my thumb jerking towards them like a stiletto blade, "is packed with wimmen and munney, while we walk home from, from dirty dishes and stacking VHS *por*no racks . . . like a couple of low-ticket jerks."

"Well, Hamza, you coulda had that if you wanted it, right? But how low are you willing to go, huh?" he barks. "Everything has a price. Sure they get a book published, sure they own a store, sure they have all-you-can-eat women, but do *you* wanna be like the Wolves?

"We're Coyotes, man! That's who *we* are. And we don't play *that* shit," he nails the point, using his chin to drive it in. "We don'use hairspray and we don'kiss ass. We don'sell out. *We* do what *we* do. Now let's get the hell outta here."

I pause a second longer, seeing White Heinz with his spectacular South Asian ho and Black Kevlar with his glamorous White ho. The hos have "classy" glasses: real flat, narrow frames, to make them look intelligent. Probably grad students, or escorts—or both.

Women.

"You ever meet either of their mothers?" I ask Ye.

"What, the Wolves'? I met their dad a coupla times, way back in the day. Screwy guy. Half Howard Hughes, half John Wayne. C'mon, let's roll."

I'm still looking through the window. Maybe Heinz isn't really looking at me. Maybe he never was. But Kevlar tips his glass towards me after a phony squint of *Oh, is that really you?*

I'm nothing to them.

Ye: "Let's freakin *go*."

I reach into my jacket pocket, pull out a decal I printed up at home just for these guys, then step away. Crouching from the side, I stick it on their store window.

WE SUPPORT THE THEFT
OF INDIGENOUS CULTURE

We take off.

Ye lights *another* cigarette.

"How can you freakin do that?"

Yehat ignores me. We keep walking. Traffic's slim, but a car slows down, stops across the street. Hey, so long as it isn't a cop car, I'm okay.

"How much one of those packs cost you?" I ask.

"Five twenty-five."

"Plus tax?"

"Five sixty-two."

"How many packs you smoke a day?"

"One-point-five."

Ye. I'm telling you, only he could use decimals in conversation. Not "pack-anna-half," but "one-point-five."

Me: "An in a week?"

"*Ten*-point-five."

"In the last year?"

Ye pauses for just a second, looking up, but even if I had a calculator I still wouldn't be able to beat him.

"Five hundred forty-six."

Me: "That's insane! So at five sixty a pack—"

"Five sixty-two a pack times five hundred forty-six equals . . . three thousand sixty-eight dollars and fifty-two cents."

"Three thousand dollars?" I choke. "Three thousand dollars? Shit, Ye, for that kind of money you could buy a car! You should be driving us home insteada us freakin *walkin* every freakin night!"

Yehat takes a long drag, then spills smoke out of his mouth like a bored Smaug chatting up Bilbo. He looks me dead in the eye.

"So where's *your* freakin car?"

Good point.

"I think you owe me a 'touché.' "

I curtsy. "Touché."

"Hey, Hamz, look over there."

I turn back to the street. The car that pulled up is still there. Gorgeous old fifties machine, all fins and chrome, black and shiny, more spaceship than automobile. And the window is down. The driver is staring at us.

It's a *she.*

Thick braids . . . cut features like shadow on stone, chocolate-milk skin . . . and purple plum lips I can practically sniff from here.

"Hamz," Ye whispers, "she's starin at *you.*"

I pray to Allah she's gonna ask us for directions.

Her window closes. She drives away.

"Man! You get a look at her?"

"Whoah-yeah," says Ye. "*Damn.*"

"Car wasn't bad, either," I say.

"Indeed."

"Now, why can't I meet a woman like that?"

"This is that singing Ethiopian waitress all over again—"

"Don't start—"

"You shoulda said something."

"Like what? 'Hey, baby?' Or 'You drive around here often?' "

"Ham on rye, when you gonna learn, when opportunity knocks, get up off the damn couch!"

We walk towards the High Level Bridge, and Kush beyond, towards the Coyote Cave, laughing and talking trash and feeling alive in the warm, dry summer darkness and E-Town's

Lite-Brite cityscape and the formula of my existence, my joyous, angry, bitter-succulent Hamzatude.

I look up into endless depths of space, see something that
burns into my memory like a searing arc. In three days' time I
will open the journal I haven't written in for three years and
write:

> In sky-dark indigo shimmer
> City lights strike and ignite night clouds
> And they swim
>   Silently
> White-bellied whales
> In a sea of stars.

I have no way of knowing it at the time, but as I am almost
immediately going to find out, the dark woman in the dark car
in the darkness is going to introduce me to a world of wonder
beyond anything comics or genre films or garish-covered pa-
perbacks have prepared me for.

That woman is going to make my most fantastic imagin-
ings into a touchable, tasteable reality, and shatter my understanding of what is real and what I really am.

And she's going to drag me to palaces of knives and into the
hands of murderers.

CHARACTER DATA:

Digaestus Caesar

REAL NAME: Wilbur Hamish Guelph II.

STRENGTH: Observation.

WEAKNESS: Social interaction.

EATS: Contents of discarded fast-food containers.

MEMORY: +18.

WISDOM, FALTERINGLY QUOTED/ACTUAL: +2/−8.

PRIDE (DESPITE REALITY): +23.

SLEEP CAPACITY, DURING NOISE/WHILE STANDING/WITH EYES OPEN: +8/+9/+10.

ARMOR TYPE: Tweed, ratty.

FIND-DETECT, UNAIDED/AIDED: Extensive +9/superlative +76.

TRIVIA DEXTERITY: Uncharted.

GENRE ALIGNMENT: Victorian scientific adventure fantasy.

IMPAIRMENT: Verbal circumambulation.

SLOGAN (EDITED FOR STAMMER): "Gentlemen, given the opportunity and the inclination, I'm confident we can comprehend the elegant simplicity of a quasi-late-Victorian serenity that allows for libertine solutions such as those articulated by—" (Defect in tape destroys remainder of slogan.)

The FanBoys and the Lord of the Inferno

Punch him in the throat! Kick him in the nards!
—Children's chant

PERHAPS A LESSER MAN WOULD BE PERSPIRING NOW, GENTLE reader, but allow me to assure you that I, delightfully, am not. I'd estimate tonight's temperature at a more than balmy twenty-six degrees Celsius, even with the breeze high atop this Rice Howard Way downtown skyscraping parkade.

Yet my brow is dry and my underarm regions are models of Saharan decorum. My clothes are humble, yet defiantly gentlemanly in this age of trend-driven *"grooviness"* and *"hipness."* I remain what I have always been.

Civilized.

A tie, a jacket, a clean white shirt, and a handkerchief. Ah, the decline of both the handkerchief and even the pronunciation of the word itself ("hangk'rchiff" . . . good heavens, what is a "chiff," and why does it hanker?) seems a strong metaphor for what is wrong with this world.

My colleagues, on the other palm, are of a decidedly differ-ent species. It's hard for me to believe, at times, that we're all the same age, plus or minus a year or two.

The mid-twenties have not been equally kind to our clan, least of all in the Bureau of Maturity and Cultivation. As my fellow merry men dance and strut atop this concrete aerie, bil-lowing their chests with clouds of high-octane cannabis smoke and reptilian-brain testosterone vapor, the nighttime distant scents of gasoline and eleven different brands of high-speed hamburger "food products" whirl about us and mingle with downtown tower lights.

We are face-to-knee with titans. And I sigh, realizing that such a fact means that we are merely gnats.

Were I to start a file folder (not that I have need—my memory is nigh . . . dare I say . . . holographic?) of my young comrades, I suppose the title bar would read BIZARRELY GROOMED YOUNG MEN. At the edge of the wall, beyond which lies six stories of air and the abyss, is our vehicle, lovingly named the FanVan.

Did I mention that my shag-tag team, my Magnificent Molochs, my Fantastic Five, is called the FanBoys? Perhaps that would better justify our vessel's nimble moniker (or our nimble vessel's moniker).

They are arguing, again, as they do incessantly. Mr. Alpha Cat is wearing his absurd giant shiny red gauchos and absurd giant shiny red shirt, with his absurd fuzzy red hat turned ab-surdly backward and declaring the word *Kangol* to any who would look. He looks like a gigantic little boy.

Mr. Cat is as pale as a subterranean cave crab, yet for what-ever reason has chosen to ape the "style" and even the dialect of the West Indian negroes. It is *his* portable stereo, roughly the size of a navy refrigerator, that is blaring the collected "Mr. Loverman" arias of one Mr. S. Ranks to the moon and the stars; my eardrums ceased their agonies some time ago, having finally shattered.

Yet somehow I manage to hear his argument with Mr. Zenko.

". . . all mi sayin, all mi sayin, is yu don'introduce an den SOLVE di main charAKter's mos'imPOtant CRISis in di damn PIlot, an expec fi geneREETE an entire SERIAL's wort' of epiSODES afta dat. DAT'S why *Dyeep Speece Nine* is raas. . . ."

Why they continue to descant upon this topic exceeds my comprehension and my patience. Mr. Zenko, after all, is a dyed-in-the-rayon Next-Generation Trekker, who will defend any Paramount product until the end of our galaxy, and is very much the foe of Alpha Cat's defection to the very much newer and as-yet-unproven *Babylon 5*.

Of all the FanBoys, Mr. Zenko is the only one whose sartorial imperatives even approximate mine; he, too, wears crisp white shirts, although he contents himself with a white T-shirt underneath rather than a tie above; his dress slacks boast pleats sharp enough to lathe wood; his shoes are always polished enough to reflect laser light with only minimal refraction.

And zounds! His hair—it's so lovingly coiffed it seems carved by Michelangelo.

"Yeah, basically," says Mr. Zenko, "it's better to just drag out the 'mysteries' for five years with aliens who can't speak in sentences—"

"What, yu talkin bout Kosh? Kosh can speak. E juss doesn'NEED to—"

"Plus those sophomoric computer graphics? It's basically friggin Intellivision, dude! It's an em*bar*rassment! You're *never* gonna upstage model photography on a *Roger Corman* budget—"

Then dear Frosty Gorkovski ceases fondling his ever-precious Minolta to enter the fray, frayed shutterbug cyberthug that he is. You'll note him for his hair, which he bleaches to a cocaine white, then gels stiff into upright icicles. Frankly, it's quite striking, if you're a Jotar frost giant from Norse mythology. But it's his argot, though, that is most strikingly *him*.

"Fer fuck's sakes, Zenk, man, *Babylon 5* does NOT look like Intellivision, man! Now you're just talkin outta your crap chute. That's the best goddam effects on TV, man—Caesar, back me up here, all right?"

At last my squadron of subcutaneous subcretins seeks out the sole voice of reason. I clear my throat from demure noblesse oblige, and begin.

"I'm . . . afraid, Mr. Zenko, I must, well, that is to say . . . agree . . . with Mr. Frosty, insofar as . . . that, ah . . . you're a little, uh, too quick, to . . . DISMISS, what is, well, surely—"

Frosty throws up his hands as if he is nutcracker to the moon. For a moment I fear he is set upon hurtling down his Minolta to bash in my tender brains.

"Caesar, shit! I know you're on my side and everything, but d'you *think* you could finish your sentence this millennium, ya lil creep-fuck beaver-bot?"

"C'MON, Frossee . . . ," booms a Mack truck engine retarder voice, "lee Caesar *lone.*"

No one turns to look. It is the final and furriest member of our band, a coelacanth of sorts, or perhaps that's inaccurate. A Sasquatch, then, the missing link between apes and even larger apes. He is an adequate driver and a surprisingly effective cook, but unfortunately, diction and enunciation were not among the components when he was sewn together in Dr. Frankenstein's discount surgery sweatshop.

Despite my astonishing memory, even *I* cannot recall his real name. He is called what he apparently has always been. The Mugatu. He continues: "'S jss tryin to HELP—"

"Moog, did anyone ask you?"

"Frossee, c'mon, Fros*see*—"

"Moog, that's Fros*ty,* Fros-TY, not 'FROSS SEA.' Where'dja learn ta speak, Caveman School?"

I must intercede. "Now, uh, Mr. Frosty, ah . . . my good fellow—"

"SHUT UP, anyway, the point *is* is that *B5*'s CGI makes *DS9* effects look like dick grease. They got space battles better'n

Jedi! Whadda *you* got—freakin *Star Trash: Voyager*? I mean, what tha fuck is that?"

"*Loss in Speece,*" lilts Alpha Cat.

"*Lost in My Anus* is closer. 'Where's the Federation?' " Frosty whimpers. " 'I don't know—let's just fly in a straight line until we run into some writers—' "

"*Heyyyy* . . . don'put down *VOY-JER*—"

"Or what?" begs Frosty. "You'll eat me?"

"Shuh DUP—"

"You shut up, ya fuckin no-talkin man-ape—"

"*YOO* SHUH DUP—"

Any fear that fisticuffs will erupt are shattered by the bone-snapping sound of a certain car door opening and slamming shut on a certain car, and certain footfalls approaching us.

The SUV has been there all along. Its pilot, however, has apparently lost patience with my compatriots' behavior.

The FanBoys shut up and stand down.

While not the equal of the Mugatu's six-foot-seven-inch musclery, the stature of our patron is nonetheless not to be trifled with. Long ago he was once halfback teammate to one of our former premiers on the once-great Edmonton Eskimos. Arguably his own success, though, has been greater, if more secret. And more terrible.

He glowers at us from across the tarmac. I am suddenly aware of my testicles slinking inside my nether regions, like snails retreating into their shells from an avalanche of salt.

In one hand he holds his cellular telephone; in the other, a bottle of Tums. He rattles the bottle, and again. And again. His lips twist into a cosine wave of revulsion as he uncaps the bottle, shakes out a handful of stomach balms, lifts his pot-roast-sized paw to his maw, and crunches them down. I have no idea how he does it, but the grinding of his teeth sounds distinctly like the *pop* a knee makes when it dislocates.

His expression is terrifying.

He must *hate* Tums.

He takes another step towards us. We all quiver, as if imagining our finger bones on the killing floor of his mouth.

He clears his throat with a rifle-cocking clank. "I . . . am trying . . . to conduct . . . *business,* you hellish geeks—"

His eyes stab us each. I examine the quality of work in my shoes and the floor that supports them.

"—which," he resumes, "is very *diff*icult when you are screaming, and yelling. It is *now* quiet time."

Frosty jumps up, ever the schoolchild too sadly devoid of impulse control.

"Yeah, but Mr. Allen, *the Moog* here—"

"WHAT PART of 'SHUT UP' did that Yugo brain of yours fail to PROCESS, ASS-PARTS?"

The Mugatu gloats; at least, I assume that is the reason for his smile; perhaps he has just consumed a hedgehog. Or perhaps he's simply happy because the Master has just made another addition to his legendary "ass lexicon."

Frosty leans against the railing, surrendered. Perhaps he realizes that arguing is contraindicated to preserving the structural integrity of his buttocks.

The Master turns back to his ambulatory telephone, and turns his back to us. "You *sure* it's comin in tomorrow?" Pause. "You sure *he* doesn't know *we* know?"

And far too quickly, my relatively quiet FanBoys forget their fear, teacher-out-of-the-room junior high reprobates that they are. The Mugatu starts to snicker-laugh at Frosty, who in turn starts to "huck" refuse at him. Immediately each fellow selects rubbish for an impending throw of his own.

Alpha Cat pleadingly whispers, "Frosty, c'mon," but is ignored as Mr. Zenko begins collaborating on ensuring our imminent punishment. "Zenk!" Alpha Cat begs again.

There is a pause.

Then there is an explosion of throwing. The last image I see is Frosty's face behind his Minolta recording the FanBoy-to-Fanboy missile fracas, and then I become aware of sudden blindness; there is, I believe, a day-old Tim Hortons cherry-filled powdered doughnut lodged in the region of my face I usually employ for sight.

Sudden silence. I attempt to restore my dignity. As I scoop cherry jam from my eye wells, like the blind man healed by Christ's spittle and mud, Mr. Dulles Allen, our master, who has been dismissed pithily but unfairly as one-third Archie Bunker, one-third Oliver North, and one-third the Incredible Hulk, with his *"Rush Is Right"* gold lapel pin reflecting light like a torch in the mines of Mordor, commands our attention.

"Alpha Cat."

"Yes, *suh*, Mistah Allen, suh!"

"You sure Digaestus Caesar saw what you said he said he saw?"

Alpha Cat looks at me, beaming pride. "Mi'd *steek* iz *liyfe* on it, suh."

"Then it's time to get your little crew of ass-tongs in gear. You got a job. If the item's going to Target Zero, I want the place cased and you ready. If it's not, I wanna know where it's going first. I want it in our hands before any of these other ass-lips can get it. And definitely before Mr. Fancy, understand?"

"Yes, *SUH*!"

Mr. Allen hands Alpha Cat a folded piece of paper, returns to his SUV, starts the engine.

Alpha Cat: "FaanBWOYYS, assemble!"

Mr. Allen puts down his telephone, opens a briefcase on the passenger side. I am standing close enough to him to see his wedding ring glitter from reflected Scotia Place lights as he sorts through his equipment: vials, zippered plastic bags, spoons, razors. An iron attachment for his fist, featuring reverse shark fins atop each of the knuckles. Pliers. A small ice pick. A book whose title I cannot read in this light. A handheld steel device I believe should be classified as a light cannon, or perhaps a rib remover.

While I dawdle dangerously, my comrades are obeying Alpha Cat's command, clanking open their own equipment cases and arsenals. Their demeanor is transformed utterly; they have become a *M*A*S*H* unit of grand theft. What a splendid description, like a Victorian tea, or a tour of the Forbidden City: *Grand* theft. And when the time necessitates it, the object of such theft is life.

My only preparation is internal; the focusing of the mechanism of my mind. Me—the human spectroscope, the living MRI.

Mr. Allen beckons me with a grunt; I trot over, accept my demi-vial.

"Buncha slacker sociopaths from hell," he grumbles. "But at least you're *my* sociopaths, ya lil shits."

"Uh, yes, sir, ah, Mister, ah, Allen . . ."

I drink my white eucharist.

My mouth releases a moan.

I sigh . . . as the chalkiness assaults my throat . . .

. . . shudder as my stomach accepts the agonizing entrance . . .

. . . the villi of my intestines puckering in anticipation—my artcrics throbbing to, to, to STRIKE

to STRIKE the parietal regions of my brain with the ten thousand, thousand

thousand ousand sand nd d . . .

GONGS ongs gs

of neurochemical

rape.

When my REM finally stills and I've wiped the tears from my eyes and the drool from my chin, I see Mr. Allen staring at me, disgust as stark upon his face as a soak of urine upon a plush white carpet.

He closes his briefcase of pain.

I don't think he is talking to me, but he states clearly as he starts his engine, "If that lousy fuck . . . thinks he can CHEAT ME . . . after all I've done for him . . . and all he's done *to me* . . . then he'd better lick his nuts good-bye."

He drives off.

We begin our mission for the night.

Passing through the Belly
of the Whale

MAYBE ME AND YE WERE FATED TO LIVE TOGETHER, EVER SINCE we met in high school. We were like anode and cathode, and we've been a reaction of one sort or another ever since.

Sometimes we talk a lot on the way home, shooting the skeet, hyucking it up. Other times, like tonight, I'm in one of these funks and Ye figures it's easier just to let me be. Two guys been together this long (not like *that*), it's easy. You know the echo of each other's heartbeats. You know the creak of each other's hinges.

This damn walk home, however many nights a week since life turned to manure, this is salvation here on nightdark streets. So quiet out, city light sentinels and a chorus of stars above, yelling their whispers at us, talking up dreams we forgot we had. Me and Ye, and the long walk, slapping souls on E-Town concrete.

(And it's E-*Town*, by the way. Super deejay Grandmaster and General Overseer T.E.D.D.Y. *created* that phrase. Not E-*ville* like some of these cooler-than-thou/alt-hip/fake indie shitbacks are trying to promote. Yeah. "Evil" is cool. Should

go Vader on these punks. See how well they can type their
arty-cles and wipe their arty asses with one hand.)

We cross the North Saskatchewan River via the High Level
Bridge, one of the few remaining black metal girder bridges
left, like the spine of some midnight cosmosaur. We walk it,
walk the decommissioned train tracks on top of it, ghost
lights flickering off and on beneath our feet as the occasional
car drives below, the last nerve cell messages from a time before time.

Can I read that primeval code? Or that prime evil code?
How many sins from the past are we made to suffer for?

Aw, forget it, and don't go calling me self-important, self-
indulgent, or self-whatever. Twenty-five, alive, but washing
dishes . . . ? Brain rot transmitted through yellow gloves,
wrinkled fingers, and an aching back? I'm al*lowed.* I'll indulge myself if I kot-tam feel like it.

You know, in the summer, they turn on taps on the east side
of this crazy bridge, and suddenly E-Town has an artificial
waterfall. I remember when the city first installed it, damn
near everybody turned out for the show.

Now nobody cares.

You make some magic, and freaks don't care. If a magician
pulls a rabbit out of a hat, and nobody's watching, does it still
eat carrots? (Not the hat. You know what I'm saying, freak.)

We're over the bridge, past the west side of downtown up
109th street, past Ibex Ethiopian Restaurant and through an
underpass everyone calls the Rat Hole. Not my dad, though—
he always calls it the Belly of the Whale. Which is more lyri-
cal, eh?

When we were kids, Dad'd drive us through it, this long
skinny tunnel, and he'd tell us stories Mum'd later tell us to
forget in case we got nightmares, all about being swallowed by
Monstro the Whale, or how Jonah the foolish prophet ended
up as fish bait.

Mum was good at that, undermining Dad's magic. But *she*
showed *him,* when she did her own disappearing act.

Speaking of Jonah, you know, back when I was doing my English degree, I remember a real conservative Calvinist professor in King James Bible class (it was an English course, understand), who nevertheless always gave us solid academic explanations of biblical amazements.

He said the ancient Hebrews were never intended to take the Jonah story seriously. Said it was satire, and the ancient Jews all recognized it, how some fools are so damn full of themselves and their own pain that they won't listen to God, and even if God drops a freaking whale on em, they still maybe don't wake up and climb outta their own peat bog of misery and self-pity.

Reminds me of so many freaks I've known over the years, beach fleas who can't read the neon billboards a million miles tall: STAND UP AND STOP CRYING, TURD-BOY.

Outta the Belly of the Whale. Me and Ye are careful coming out, eyes and fists ready. It's creepy down there, cold even in the summer. If you aren't careful, you could easily get jumped, cuz anybody on the lookout could signal guys on either side to come after you, and there's only two traffic lanes, so if you hadda leap into the road to avoid some freaking tigers, you'd get completely skwushed under a cab.

I guess we could just walk another way, but we take the Belly every single night we walk home.

E-Town doesn't have much graffiti, but, like, half of it is down there in the Belly. Somebody scrawled *Indian Police* on the north entrance. I never did figure that one out.

My dad told me that in Egypt, at the Step Pyramid, which was the first pyramid, on the inside wall of the outer complex, is graffiti, as in *So-and-so wuz here,* but in hieroglyphics. Like, they had tourists three thousand years ago, when this pyramid was already almost two thousand years old. I mean, that is simultaneously amazing and depressing. Monuments defaced by fossils.

Now we're up on 107th Ave and 107th Street, grid middle for our neighborhood, home since I was old enough to pee.

You got more Somalis, Ethiopians, Eritreans, and Sudanese here than any other place in E-Town. Some people call it the Horn. We call it Kush.

In the skin-baking heat of a July day you got merchants and bazaars and the gut-puckeringly delicious aromas of roasting lamb, and squadrons of flies near the grills and men in white desert robes with kaffiyehs and women in silk scarves and sashes and dresses more colorful than sunset over canola fields and the music of a dozen different languages and a hundred different dialects and people going to mosque with the echo of the *mueddhin* calling them to prayer and the laughing-sparkle of kids romping and running after the Dickie Dee teenager pedaling his ice-cream bicycle cart of frozen-milk-fat-sugar-temptation.

But it's night now, and all the stores are shut, and there are no kids, and when you see somebody, you don'wanna meet their eyes. The Addis Ababa Obelisk is lit up, a massive stone finger pointing up to Andromeda and the Crab Nebula and black holes and quasars and every place other than here, a buried titan's last message to fools like me:

Leave Tatooine.

But there's no Academy, and no Alderaan. And no Ben.

We're here, at last.

The Coyote Cave.

The Coyote Cave, or The Space-Age Bachelor Pad

He who loses control, loses.
—DETECTIVE FRANK PEMBLETON

YE CLICKS A BUTTON ON HIS BELT, AND A MYLAR VOICE SINGS out to us, "*Welcome home, Coyotes. The Pod Bay Doors are now open.*" The front door clicks, swings forward a millimeter. We walk in. We're home.

We kick off shoes; Ye sheds his cape. I keep my jacket and kaffiyeh on. It's dark inside, but as we walk around, Ye's motion-activated illuminatrix lights up the hallways, rooms, closets. Sometimes it's fun, and guests (such as they are) usually love it. But I really feel like darkness right now.

"Ye, couldja . . . ?"

He nods, taps a wall keypad, and the lights shut off and switch back to manual.

Ye goes to the kitchen, opens the fridge, the light inside pouring out to inscribe him boldly out from the shadows. Then the light winks out and he opens the freezer door. He

gets what he wants—another one of my ice-cream sandwiches. That guy never stops. Class-7000 moochotronic mo-
bile unit.

I sit in the living room, sag, really, body heavy, like I'm on
Jupiter. Well, the air's thinner, of course. "Living room."
What the hell does that mean? We don't *live* in the *other*
rooms? We die there? Don't exist there? How about sitting
room? Drawing room? Parlor? Or how about—

I know, shut up.

Funny how some people talk when they don't feel like talking.

Ye walks back in, drinking a can of some mad grass jelly
juice he got in Chinatown. Guess he's already finished my ice-
cream sandwich. He kneels down in the corner, starts working
on the arm to his R-Mer. Is he ever gonna finish that thing?

"You want something?" he offers me suddenly. "Grass jelly?
There's another coupla cans—"

"Naw, thanks. 'Mgoinna bed."

"Kay. Gnight, Hamz."

I'm in my bedroom, too tired to go to bed. I shove a tape in
the box, hit play: Vangelis's "Le singe bleu" (doesn't that
mean "the blue monkey" or something?) plays . . . sax so
lonely and barren it's like a doomed whale moaning on some
gray, forsaken arctic beach.

I sit in my chair. Streetlight filters through trees, through
glass, spatters my coat, my scarf. My body is like wet concrete, and every breath is like trapped bubbles straining to
reach the surface.

I know I shouldn't.

But I look at the bookshelf.

I should look away, but I don't even have *that* much shame.
Or is it self-respect (that I'm lacking, that is)?

I extend an arm the weight of an iron beam, reach for the
Box.

The Box was a gift from my sister, made in India, hand-
carved. Beneath my nostrils it whispers to me in sandalwood

verse. Its hide is rough beneath my fingertips. Its door opens
too easily.

I look inside.

Ahhh . . .

After too long looking, I still my breathing, sniffle back my
nose, put palm to face and eyes to make them dry.

I close the door.

I put the Box back.

It's dark, and the heavy trees deny me full streetlight company.

My chin is heavy in my hands, my elbows feel sharp on my
knees.

I'm a lead marionette, and my iron cables have all rusted
and snapped away.

Thursday Mourning

Bitterness is like drinking poison, but
hoping that the other guy dies.
—DETECTIVE TIM BAYLISS

HAMZA'S NOT UP. MY TURN TO MAKE BREAKFAST.

Hamza and I have radically different kitchen styles. I would describe him as a culinary free radical, whereas I'm more like a carbon isotope, proceeding in its transformation (not decay) with dependable precision.

The H-man's "method" involves getting out *all:*

> *a.* fresh ingredients,
>
> *b.* leftovers,
>
> *c.* spices,
>
> *d.* crockery, and
>
> *e.* electrical appliances.

In short, all organic and nonorganic matter in the kitchen, to begin his restauranteurial regimen. (Sidebar: *Restaurant* comes from the Italian, meaning "restore"—which helps illuminate the vital role of chefs and cooks as alchemists, or, as I prefer, scientists.)

Hamza and I agree on the power of food, but it's *method* where we don't meet monacle to monacle. His mm-good Merlinry occasionally produces gastronomiracles, but almost never can he *replicate* his results, which is the tragedy.

I, on the other hand, employ precision methodology. Even when experimenting, I carefully mentally catalog ingredient vitality, the doses and synergistic potencies of various spices, energy levels, reaction times, gustatory activation levels, the psychological complements of serving dish and tablecloth colors, and so forth and so on.

Sure, Hamza's manic kitchenary flailing is entertaining in an *I Love Lucy*–esque sort of way and occasionally produces deliciosity, but my dignified, controlled approach is key to dietary stability, both in import and export biological functions.

This morning I'm making pancakes.

Hamza still isn't up. That jimp. It was *his* turn to clean up the kitchen and before I can even begin, I have to transform chaos to cosmos in this joint. This is the *eighty*-fourth time he's failed to fulfill his cleaning contract since I moved in. And that was only 1,421 days ago!

Cleaning is quick when you're as efficient as I am, but the problem here is the principle of the matter. I'll take my reparations in ice-cream sandwiches for Hambone's numerous infractions, but I shouldn't *have* to.

YEHAT'S PLANETQUAKES

241 mL *whole wheat or quadrotriticale flour*
253 mL *pure wheat bran*
18 mL *cumin*

1 *clove, crushed and abused*

1.5 mL *sodium chloride*

16 mL *baking powder*

2 *ripe bananas or* **4** *sweet Chinese small bananas, mashed*

1 *ripe mango, minced*

2 *brown egg whites (oh, the seeming contradiction . . . egg* clears, *then, in the non-Scientology sense)*

259 mL *goat milk, 1 degree Celsius*

Mix and cook as standard—beware burning due to thickness of cakes. Serve hot with creamy feta, dark honey, or red mung bean paste.

Hamza's still not up and usually the smell of breakfast has him trotting in here and nibbling and sampling.

His door's closed.

I overcome the urge to knock. I'm afraid I already know what's going on.

I open the door as silently as I can. He's there, in the chair, eyes closed, slumped over, drool crusted white at his mouth edges. The Box is on the shelf, but not where it was the day before, and I know, because I check every day and even place a hair there to see if he's opened the stupid thing.

And damnit, he's been into it again. If only his brain were a long string of code, I could go in and cut and paste. I could digitally divide and heal. But that stinking jimp refuses to be free.

I close the door as silently as snow falls.

I knock.

"Awake, snake?"

"Mm, AWAKE—" (Crashing sounds.)

"Hammy, breakfast's ready. Let's rock and roll."

"Mmupnnll bethere innasecnn—"

I open the door again. Hamza's thrashing around in his day clothes/sleep clothes, trying to change into a bathrobe to cover his tracks. Sunlight flashes on his thrashing limbs, gold on brown, like a strobe light inflicting a seizure. But I can't laugh, knowing he slept in that damn chair again, knowing what idiocy is in his head on account of the contents of that damn Box.

He chuckles artificially, nervously. "Musta drifted off *read*in rr somethin—"

"If you're working tonight, we'd better get some groceries during the day."

"Just lemme shower."

"An hurry up. Breakie's getting cold."

"Smells like . . . planetquakes?"

"Indeed."

"I'm hurryin, Top Hat."

Breakfast is done, so while I'm waiting for Hamza to scrape the crud off of himself, I tinker in the living room with the starboard brachial unit of my R-Mer.

Getting parts for this behemothra has been (*a*) expensive and (*b*) maddening. I trade services and spare parts for what I can, but getting the correct filament gauge and the weldable steel density for the plating—well, let's just say that when I began the R-Mer two years ago I never dreamed that I wouldn't be done by now. It's been a giant mechanical, exoskeletal anime albatross round my neck and body for twenty-six months, three weeks, and two and a half days.

Hamza's out of the shower, dressed, and twenty-seven percent less malodorous. He hauls mounds of comics off of the dining table so he can set the table for us to eat, stacking *Cerebus, The Big 4,* and *Slash Maraud* into neat Mylar-encased piles. Sound is coming from the R-Mer's exospeakers. . . . I must've forgotten to turn off its receiver. Some 740 AM goofus is droning on while I get up to deactivate him.

". . . most potent form of crack yet to hit the city. Police are offering no clues as to its source, and continue to deny rumors that the recently closed drug den 'the Catacombs' was the site of ritual amputation and *cannibalism—" (Click.)*

We eat.

Silently.

I clear my throat. At last.

"Naw, food's great, Ye. Sorry. Thank you."

"I wasn'doin it for that. But you're welcome."

He's silent.

I look at him.

He looks down, carves a planetquake with his fork. Moves the morsel mouthward.

I speak, despite his downward eyes.

"You've been in that damn Box again, haven't you?"

The food is on the fork, waiting for his mouth to open, like a dead soul waiting for Charon to shuttle him across Styx.

"This kinda bitterness's gonna kill you, Hamza."

He sniff-chuckles, munches his food. By his expression I'm guessing he can't taste anything. He's just moving tongue and teeth to distract himself.

"*I'm* bitter?" he finally says. Aint too quick on the come-back when he's like this. "You're, like, Peter Parker nibbled by a radioactive lemon."

"Exactly. You're muscling in on my action. *You're* supposed to be the dreamer keeping *my* eyes off the ground."

More silence.

Hamza doesn't finish his food.

He cleans up.

I don't bother going back to the R-Mer. It can wait. "C'mon, ya jimp. Let's buy some groceries."

Neither of us realizes that we'll end up with a hell of a lot more than Asiago cheese and tofu mock turkey. We don't know it, but we're about to meet Cinderella.

In Chinatown, Glittering Jackal Tantalizes Coyotes

MAYBE YE'S RIGHT. HELL'S BELLS, I KNOW HE'S RIGHT. I AM bitter.

But I can't stop it. It's like a freakin tumor. One day I'll wake up, go to the crapper, look in the mirror, and see my head all deformed, like the side of my skull is halfway through laying an egg. My bitterness-tumor-egg. Give me a big enough food processor, and I'll mix some more metaphors for you, smart-ass.

We're on the porch, ready to rock. Or at least walk.

Ye: "You okay?"

Me: "I'm tryin, Ye. Honest."

Silent seconds slip softly.

Ye, delicately, an arm around my shoulders, and then my waist. "Time to bury that Box, my friend."

I fish out a loonie and flip it. I pretend to look at it.

"Not today."

His hand slides off my gut, grabs the flesh of my upper arm.

"Make you a deal. *You* quit looking in that Box. *I'll* quit smoking."

Hell, now that *is* a deal. Man made me smile. We'll each give up our poison.

"Deal."

I can shake it all off now, a little. No matter how angry or sad I am, I got my best friend with me, and that bold E-Town summer blue sky beckons a new day. Inside the Coyote Cave I was some freaking shrunken apple carving of a man. Outside, I'm different.

Outside, I'm a Coyote King.

I'm wearing my portaspeakers, the slim ones Ye worked up for me to wear on my belt, playing a dynamite album by a Sudanese brother who played at the Sidetrack Café last summer. Sparkling Congolese-style guitars, muscly brass section, bass to make a statue boogie, a song called "Tour to Africa."

I'm glad Ye likes the album, too. Cuz today, it's our soundtrack.

Walking through Kush down 107th Ave on our way to Chinatown to buy groceries, we get a million greetings a minute. All on accounta our neighborhood presence. Our workshops. Our schemes. Our hijinks.

"Hey, Coyotes!"

"Cay-yo-TAZE . . . whassUP?"

"As-salaam walaikum, Coyotes!"

With what we do and we pull in this neighborhood, it's no surprise. It's the *prize*.

Summer morn, man. Fresh sweet air, still cool with getting-hot sun on skin, little kids and teenagers running and squealing and triking and biking, sipping Slurpees and tossing Frisbees and reading grab-bag cheapo comic books on the park picnic tables. When the sun's at zenith, they'll be dancing in lawn sprinklers in their Smurf bathing suits, eating halal hot dogs and *shwarmas* and "fudg-icals" and orange Revels.

I don't deny it. It's good to be alive.

"Coyote, baby!"

"Gimme some skin, two times, quick, Cay-yoats!"
"Good morning, Coyote, Coyote. . . ."

Soon we're in Chinatown, which isn't just Chinatown. That's what it's called, but that's not what it actually is. Think Little Italy, Tiny Kiev, Mini-Santiago, Bite-Sized Hanoi, Baby Lisbon. You look up, below the power line spiderwebs and traffic light flies caught on them, and there're signs in every language and script nestled among July-fat foliage. A giant turn-of-the-century redbrick schoolhouse way down 93rd Street and another one way up 97th, the crazy-named run-down edifice called "The Society of Oddfellows and Rebekahs," the giant, carved Slavic jewel called St. Josaphat's Ukrainian Basilica, Pagolac's restaurant where you can sip the best Vietnamese iced coffee and three-bean cocktail (nonalcoholic—it's got coconut milk and ice and jelly and three types of beans) in the city.

Inside the Chinese grocery on 106th Ave (not the rude one down the block where I once was hassled while trying to return a can of sweet mung bean paste that was all moldy inside when I opened it up—looked like three mice had died in there—and they made it seem like *I* was in the wrong, so *not* that one, the other big one), me and Ye go looking for all the exotic delights we love.

We challenge ourselves to try at least four new bizarrities in every week's groceries. I have to draw the line around any pork products, of course—I may not've been to mosque in long enough to make my dad feel bad, but at least I haven't sunk that far—although with Asian food, that really cuts into the selection. Like with dim sum, for instance, I can only have, like, a third of their smorg. Which is a drag. *Smells* good, anyway.

So we're horsing around with the octopus (mixed metaphor again, jerkface) when I get a crinkle in my nose. The good kind (of crinkle).

I look up, and standing over vats of preserved Chinese roots that look like the internal organs of Orcs, and near the omnipresent mound of chicken feet that looks like the carnage of an avian death camp, is a woman.

A Sister.

Wearing a cape.

Well, it's not a cape, exactly, but some kind of flowing garment, like a desert robe or something. She's got her back to me, but her hair is set in three huge braids and a series of smaller braidlets, like Jada Pinkett meets Medusa, but taller (than Jada).

I can't see her face, but she moves her head a moment and I can make out rich brown skin, glowing like sautéed butter and bananas. She's tall, my height at least, and elegant as she hefts a bag of crawly roots and one of graspy, poking-out chicken feet.

I turn to nudge Ye. "Ye, man, get a loada—"

But when I turn back, she's gone.

"What?"

"There was this Sister, man—" I still don't see her. Where the hell . . . ?

I walk towards the stuff she was sorting through. Ye tags along. I still can't see where she went.

Ye: "She was looking through the chicken feet?"

"Yeah—"

"See, now I draw the line at chicken feet. Something too ungood about chicken feet. And there aint much meat on the lil jimps, anyhow. Too much work. Long driveway to a small garage, you know what I'm saying?"

"Where'd she go?"

"Chicken feet, man, now, see, *this* is what's wrong with the world. All the Sisters've gone spacey—"

There she is—at the cash register, no, she's done—she's out the door—

I dump all my groceries into Ye's arms. "Pay for this—"

"HEY!"

I scramble outside, look this way and that on 97th, but she's gone.

Damn.

Yehat swaggers out, grocery bags swaying.

"Um, if it wouldn't be too much trouble, what, exactly, would you have done if she'd been out here?"

Hm. That's a good question.

"I . . . I just wanted to . . . you know, get a better look at her."

"Yeah. Like the singing Ethiopian waitress."

"Enough with the waitress, already!"

"Listen, how you gonna pick up a woman when you smell like that?"

"What are you talking about? I showered!"

"In what, piss? Are those clothes clean?"

The nerve of this freaking guy.

I sniff my shirt (defiantly, you understand).

Oh.

Me: "Maybe we should, uh, get some detergent or something."

Ye: "Uh, yeah."

Later on we're on the south side at the comics megastore (which shall remain nameless). From the outside, it's just a regular store, but inside, it's a two-story dinostore that about thirty million trees died to furnish with the latest *X-Fetuses* and *X-Pets*. If the great library at Alexandria were concerned with nothing but men in colorful tights who talk!!! like!!! THIS!!! it would still have nothing on this place.

(BTW, don't get me wrong about that "men in tights" line; I aint one of those insufferable self-loathing genre guys, the kind who you meet at work and you can swap *Trek* or Lucasfilm or Silver Age Marvel/DC trivia with, but then the second that Normals come around, they act like there's something wrong with *you*. I hate hypocrites.)

Ye flips through the latest (and late-ish) ish of *Love and Rockets*. He's griping, but that's ninety percent of the reason

we come here. Haven't really been any good comics since the
late Miller/Moore years. All this digital color, slick paper, ul-
traexpensive moose spew. Everything is a #1. Everything is a
"Collector's Item!!!"

"Man," says Ye, indicating the mag, "the Hernandezes've
fallen off. I mean, *not everybody* is *secretly* gay! It's that simple. Are *you* secretly gay?"

"No." Here we go again: Ye's "gay theories."

"Am *I* secretly gay?"

"Not that I'm aware, although—"

"Shut up. I'm just sayin, it's a realism thing. If only sixteen
percent of the population—"

"What about Langston Hughes? James Baldwin? Marlon
Riggs?"

"Those Brothers are cool with me. No problem with gay.
Gay's okay. The issue is *realism*. In real life not everybody's either hiding in the closet or 'outed'—"

"Realism? It's a comic book with aliens and superpowers.
You're griping about demographics?"

" 'Homographics.' "

"What about Peter Tosh?"

"PETER TOSH," he yells suddenly between racks of
Spawn and back issues of *Dazzler,* "WAS NOT GAY!"

I glare at him, speaking softly. "Time to use your 'inside
voice,' Ye." He de-angers, frumps up. I say, "You are *so* easy to
get."

"Fine, but Peter Tosh was *not* gay."

"No, but everyone else in reggae is, *especially* Shabba
Ranks."

He laughs and shuts up, goes back to his *Love and Rockets.*

Just then I overhear a woman customer talking with a clerk
about a bound edition of *Watchmen* (I have a good ear for
these things), and when I look across the wastelands, no lie,
it's *the same woman from the Chinese grocery*! (Well, it *is*. I
don't care if it's hard to believe—it really is her.)

(!!!)

I try to still my breathing, try putting down my copy of *Border Worlds*, try walking over softly from the other side of the store. But the place is packed—

"This looks great," she's saying faintly, I guess holding the book, which I can't see from my angle. "When'd this come out?"

Scott, the clerk: "'Eighty-five, 'eighty-six. You never heard of it?"

"I've been out of the country. I haven't really been keeping up—"

The guy's ringing up the sale, but there're about fifty grade-seven kids clogging up the aisles pawing AD&D and *Magick* junk. I don't wanna blow my cool (such as it is), but she's already got the thing in the bag, she's pushing open the door, damnit—

I struggle through more kids, parents, university kids—I'M OUT THE DOOR—

Crap—*again*!

Back inside I ask Scott, the clerk, if he's seen her before, but like I know he's gonna tell me, he says he never has, then adds that she's a real looker. Gee, thanks, guy, but I've still never even seen her face from the front! Barely even the side, actually.

Damn.

Yehat: "What the hell?"

I explain.

"Couldn't've been the same one, Hammy. You got chicks on the brain, Hamz. Different chick, I'm tellin you."

"I know what I saw."

"Well, then, why don't you just find her like you find everything else you're looking for, Captain Detecto?"

I shake my head. "I barely saw her. I didn't get a fix on her long enough to track her. But for crappin out loud, Yeek, she likes *comics*! Think of how *rare* that is—"

"The elusive Genre-Chick."

I correct him. "The far more elusive *good-looking* Genre-Chick."

"Hey, Coyotes." It's Scott T. Clerk talking.

Us: "Hey, Scott."

Scott: "We just got a complete collection of *Yummy Fur.* Wanna peek?"

Us: "No."

Scott: "Got the *X-Men* screenplay by Mamet, Hamm, and Schrader."

Us: "No."

Scott: "Got the latest issue of *Hate.*"

Us: "We'll take two."

But even the joy of *Hate* won't take my mind off this. This is too nuts. Twice in one day I see this woman? Good things happen in threes. It aint a question of *if.* Right now, it's only a question of *when*.

Hamza Senesert, Public Dick

WE'RE NOT BACK IN THE COYOTE CAVE EIGHT MINUTES AND fourteen seconds when the doorbell indicates that someone wants to see at least one of us. As Hamza is currently indisposed (with his microscopic bladder, the biggest shock is that he doesn't drive around in a motorized Porta Potti), I check the door monitor.

I know this woman: short, dark hair, mid-forties, Mayan or Aztec features. Why's she crying?

I open up. "Mrs. Itzel, what's wrong?" I try to usher her in, but she doesn't seem to want to move off of the porch, or maybe she can't see me through her tears. "Hey, what is it? Is something wrong with Sylvia?"

"She, she's missing, Mr. Yehat—I haven't seen her since this morning. . . . I thought maybe, you know, she come to your camp—"

"C'mon, Mrs. I., c'mon inside. Lemme getchu a glass of water. You want coffee? Come on—" I tug her gently until she finally relents. I guide her around piles of junk until I can get her to sit down. I hand her a few tissues for her tears.

"Hamza, c'mon out here—we got a situation!"

I hear the siren call of his flush, and he appears, a wandering knight returned from the crapsades, ready for a new mission. And for once, an important one.

"Ye, what is it? Oh, Mrs. I., hi! What's—what's . . . ? Are you—hey, is something wrong with Sylvia?"

In a second his whole posture's changed, and suddenly he's down beside her at her knee while I'm pouring water in the kitchen. He's taken her hand and is stroking it, his glance searching every part of her face as if his eyes were themselves a comforting embrace.

And I can see into those eyes myself, right into his imagination, see tiny little Sylvia, already ten but no bigger than a six-year-old, ultracute, features straight out of an ancient Mayan painting, no neck, looks like either the sweetest little girl you've ever seen or maybe an undernourished forty-year-old. Every day we hold Coyote Camp she's there, and every time she shows up I have to stop myself from hugging the stuffing out of her.

And I'm not only worried about Mrs. I. I'm worried about Hamza. He's emotional—he doesn't have my adamantium constitution. If she's missing, he could go to pieces like Sylvia's mum.

By the time I put the water down next to Mrs. I., Hamza's telling her not to worry, that everything's gonna be okay, and he starts repeating back to her everything she must've told him about (a) where Sylvia usually goes if we don't hold camp, (b) how she was dressed when she left, (c) where her friends and aunties live, and (d) where she'd go if she was upset or afraid or angry.

But I know Hamza doesn't care about any of that information. He must've just asked her to tell him so she'd feel better, so she'd feel like she was helping find her own girl after probably looking in vain for five or six hours, all the while wondering what *I'm* wondering, whether some sick fuck has stolen her, done things to her. Turned her . . . off.

"Don't worry, Mrs. I.," I tell her, helping her up. "We'll find her. As soon as we've got her, we'll bring her home."

I show her to the door, ask her if she needs someone to come pick her up, but she says she's going to keep looking, since the police won't help for another day and a half.

I lied when I said *we'd* find her.

Because, whether she's alive or . . . or . . . Hamza's the one who'll do the finding.

Once Mrs. Itzel is out of the door, I see Hamza go into his mode. I've seen him do this with a thousand things, do this for a thousand reasons, ever since I've known him. There was only one thing he lost that he never found again.

But that's a totally different case than this one here.

Wait, look at him! Standing near the door, saying nothing, not moving . . . his eyes bigger, bigger, staring into nowhere and nothing, and then fluttering shut . . . his breathing so slow, so still, so silent . . . and finally stopped.

Five seconds.

Ten seconds.

Fifteen.

"The armory!" he snaps, shoves his feet into his shoes, and bolts out the door.

"Hamza, wait up!" I yell, pulling my own sneakers on and jetting out after him. We run north up 108th Street, east down 106th Ave. After three blocks I'm barely keeping up and my lungs are burning (curse these jimpomatic death sticks I've been buying . . . and curse Hamza if he finds out I've cursed them) and I'm calling out, *"Wait up!"*

But he's going faster, pulling out ahead . . . aw, shit. I plow through my own lung-spiking agony and keep going. Hamza zips across the green field in front of the massive redbrick fortress called the Prince of Wales Armoury, streaks over the parking lot, scrambles all along the base of the building, left, right, looking, searching—

"Ye! YE!"

I finally catch up, my lungs feeling like they're inflated by a highwayful of diesel exhaust, and I look down where Hamza's looking. Down a stairwell.

On the wet litter-strewn concrete at the bottom of the stairwell is the crumpled body of a ten-year-old girl who looks either six or forty.

"Good God," I choke out.

Hamza's face: his eyes have hospital beds in them, mental wards, dark and rainy alleys, graveyards.

I haven't see his eyes like this since . . . well . . . since—

We descend the stairs.

Hamza touches the little girl's face tentatively, tenderly, tensely.

"She's alive!" he whispers. "SHE'S ALIVE!"

"SHE'S ALIVE!" I yell. "HEY! HEY! HELP! We got an injured girl, here! My God, she's ALIVE!"

"Should I pick her up?" he asks me.

"Better not," I say quickly, holding him back. "Could have a spinal cord injury—we don't know *what's* wrong with her yet. You go get an ambulance. Royal Alex is just across the street—Emergency's on the left! I'll watch over her."

"Why don'*you* go and *I'll* watch over her?"

"You c'n run faster!"

"Freakin cigarettes—I *told* you one day—"

"GO!"

Hamza dashes up the stairs.

I wipe my cheeks, my nose. "There, there, Sylvia. Everything's . . . everything's gonna be okay."

By the time the ambulance is here, Sylvia's woken up and has been crying and I've been holding her in my arms while she still has to sit on the concrete.

Her one leg's moving just fine, so she hasn't got any spinal problem, but apparently she'd been chasing after a cat she called a "mud-proof cat," whatever that is, stumbled over something, and fell down here and broke her leg and screamed and screamed, but no one could hear the poor little jimpette scream (she has a very quiet voice, even for a child). She finally must've passed out from the pain, but she woke up and whimpered some more, passed out, and so forth until we found her.

Until Hamza found her.

"I swear, Hamziana Jones," I tell him after I've given Sylvia the hug and kiss I always meant to when I hand her off to the EMT, "this time you amazed even me, and I've seen you do this before. How the hell do you do it? Howdja know where she was?"

"I'ont know. I just figure, like, where could she be? And then I realized here. It's no big deal. If you'd thought about it, you woulda hit on the stairwell, too."

"Not likely. Even with my superior brain, I wouldna thought of this place in six hundred and twelve years. I don'think I even knew it existed, actually."

I slap him on the back, squeeze his shoulder. "C'mon, let's go tell Mrs. I." We start across the field.

"Y'know, Hamz, you could be a professional adventurer. A detective. A private dick."

He chuckles.

"Scriously. You can find anything. Always have. Why not? You hate your job. You could really do it. You could earn a mint doing PI work."

"Oh, right . . . having beautiful daughters of missing scientists seducing me before they try to rob and kill me? Or spending the rest of my life spying on deadbeat cheating spouses and tracking down lost Elvis collectible plates? Forget it."

"Okay, then, a *public* dick. Finding kids, like today!"

"Where's the money in it?"

"Like *you* care about money. C'mon, Skywalker," I say, putting on my best James Earl Jones, "how far will you go . . . to avoid . . . your *des*tiny?"

"As far as the end of this alley if I don't get to a john right away."

Return to Paradise

All you need is love.
—THE BEATLES, played during thousand-bullet shoot-out at climax of final
episode of *The Prisoner*

BACK AT THE COYOTE CAVE AFTER A LONG SUMMER THURSDAY
(better than Wednesdays, of course, plus you've got the Thor
angle), much more eventful than most, and Ye's laughing
loudly in the crapper.

I gotta admit that I'm feeling pretty good. So many kids
come through our camp, and sometimes we get to know the
parents a bit. Some kids we know better than others, but like,
Sylvia, she's there every day we hold camp, me helping her
make her little papier-mâché donkeys and kangaroos and
dragons, and Ye helping her build a pair of walkie-talkies out
of old telephone guts and transistor radios. Such a sweet
freakin kid. Smart, too.

And when I heard she was missing, and then thought what
could've happened to her . . . and then when I think what

could've happened to her if we *hadn't* found her . . . ah, hell, no sense dwelling on what didn't happen. Score one for the freakin good guys!

And telling Mrs. I. she was all right, hey, that was pretty sweet, too. Maybe Ye's right. Maybe I should go into some sort of detective work. Find stuff, people. Have an office, a secretary, flash ID, break down doors, look through garbage, get a license, get paid.

Nah, that'd be stupid.

Ye is still in the freaking can. Disappeared into there about an hour ago with a copy of Philip K. Dick's *A Scanner Darkly* and another book called *How to Disappear Completely and Never Be Found*. He's a freak. He can read two books at a time, double-handed—no lie, I've seen him do it and even tested him on the contents.

Actually, that's pretty good as far as superpowers go, but the reason he's been in there so long is what drives me nuts. Ye has excretory powers, or more actually, he has anally retentive powers.

I don't mean that in any Freudian way. I mean that rectodroid can go three or more *days* without making southern exports. Now, I've known lots of women like that, what with all their hormones and gynostresses and whatnot, but one thing you can say about guys is that the gravy train runs on time.

But Ye, good ghosts. The man . . . this goes back to high school. We went camping with Venturers (don't ask) and our leader kept insisting on proper hygiene. Ye took insane delight in betting every guy in our unit that he could go the entire weekend without, well, going. He bet ten guys ten bucks apiece, and this was, like, in 1985 dollars.

Everyone watched him like some kind of butt buzzards, but seriously, no one caught him even *trying* to cheat. We went swimming the last day, in the lake, and two guys followed him with snorkels and masks just to make sure he wouldn't try anything sneaky.

But to be honest it drives me crazy. How can anyone keep

all that poison inside of them, all that filth, without it infecting them or something, backing up and clogging their hearts or brains? Hyperbole? Sure, thanks. But the point stands.

So, anyway, that fecal camel has not vacated the shitter in almost the time it's taken me to watch "The Savage Curtain" up to the parts where Lincoln calls Uhura a "Negress," and the most fascinating rock creature since the Horta plays mind games with Kirk.

And of course, when he finally *does* bug out of the throne room, it's going to smell like he's been hoarding zombies in there. Or turned it into a zombie smokehouse. I wonder what made me think of zombies?

(Speaking of zombies and toilets, Yehat's brother [and get this, no lie, his name is *Spotswood Persimmon Gerbles*—I'm not making this up—his parents must've really had it in for him at one day old or else the poor bastard was born during some kind of unholy hell of a Gerblian power struggle] is a whole other realm in nonviable life-forms. Imagine Steve Urkel meets Rain Man. Now imagine that, but also eating everything in your fridge, using your computer and TV, and sleeping in your bed if you can't find your plunger. And once a year *minimum,* Spotswood befalls our house like a scourge of locusts or toads. And when *he* leaves the bathroom, it's like Armageddon was made of a million pounds of chili, sulfur, and dynamite.)

I bang on the damn door. "Ye, hurry up, you freakin Colon-Powell! I gotta get in there before work!"

He just laughs to himself. "Barris, you old rascal," he wheezes in reference to his favorite character from the novel. He's read it, like, twelve times. I like Dick as much as the next guy (Philip K., smart-ass), but *come on.*

At last, the flush of victory.

Washing sounds.

The door swings open, and a draft from the crypt burns the power of taste off my tongue. I can *feel* my cilia singeing in my nostrils. Ye emerges, wiring swirled round his neck like jewelry, a circuit board or some damn thing forming a pendant stuffed into his breast pocket.

I shave while in agony from the atmosphere, change into dishwashing clothes, smear extra Vaseline on my neck to keep the rope from chafing too much before the trapdoor opens at ShabbadabbaDoo's.

In the living room, me: "Time to go to work."

Yehat's working on his R-Mer, and some smaller device I don't recognize, looks like a space-age handheld hairdryer. He stands, ready to roll. "Yuh-huh." Then his realization blossoms: "Wait . . . where's my e-key?"

This again. A guy who can organize the stuff he does, fix computers and build scale-model bridges and pyramids and simulation Marsbases in the backyard for our neighborhood summer Coyote Camps, and he still misplaces his zap-key nearly every freaking day.

I scan the room.

"Down there. Under the, the left boot of the, uh, R-Mer."

Yehat scoops it up, stands up, ready to go, but then: "Ah, my, uh, wallet . . ."

I scan.

"Side of the couch."

He digs. He wins.

"Oh . . . and my glasses."

"On your face."

"What would I do without you?"

"Be locked outside of the house blind and without money."

"Thanks, Magnum. I owe you one."

"You owe me a million."

We put on our shoes and turn out the lights.

July night outside, E-Town summer light, sky is glowing red-blue neon, framed with tree-leaf silhouettes and interrupted by twinkling towers, some of them flaring gold in the final good-bye kisses of the sun. Streetlights announce the sidewalk tiles beneath our feet, and off we go.

We walk through Kush, back to where we were having fun

earlier in the day, but not for fun do we go. But the walk, at least . . .

Two pretty Somali girls, one in jeans and a mango blouse boasting chocolate cleavage, the other in multicolored *hejab* and ankle-length formless dress with sneakers poking out girlishly at bottom: "Hey, Coyotes!"

Us: "Hey, Sisters."

They giggle. They're, like, eighteen or whatever. Way off-limits, even without the *hejab*. I think we met them cuz they brought their little cousins to our Coyote Camp. Nice smiles, damn.

As we walk, we talk about finding Sylvia, about Mrs. Itzel's expression when we told her we'd found her daughter, about whether we should pool our talents and do something and actually quit our moron jobs. Hell, we could do a thousand things. Thousand, hell—million!

But that'd involve . . . well, whatever you have to do to do all that. Maybe I could do some research, check the Net, go to a career counselor or something. Maybe next year or something. Or in a few years. And I could always go back to univ— no, of course not. Of course I can't.

West on 107th Ave, past the Addis Obelisk, down 109th Street and through the Belly of the Whale, across Jasper Ave's teeming thousands and stationary, sinless, *manga*-slick motorcycle club, past teenagers buying pizza by the slice and Popsicles and falafels from the cartmen, over the High Level blacksteel gantry, along Saskatchewan Drive to bear witness to the spectacular E-Town Legislature-downtown skyline (from ancient to modern, lit stone to electric glass), then head down 103rd and Whyte Ave.

Dead men walking.

I bid Ye good-bye at Video Losers, walk on down to Shabbadabbadork's.

I walk in, see Busboy McZitsack, glare at him while he lip-whispers curses at me, hit the sinks, blast filth off plates.

Wash pots.

Load the washers.
Unload the washers.
Wash pots.
Blast filth off plates.
Breathe steam.
Stifle screams.

After one hundred and eighteen minutes, I need to take a leak. I inform Ghalib (good guy—Pakistani, barely speaks English, likes Pharoah Sanders) so he can cover me (these Shabbadabbafreaks actually monitor your bathroom time. I swear, I should report these guys to the Alberta Federation of Labour).

I shake the dish suds off my hands, strip off my apron, walk over to the john door.

And then the awareness spikes my brain like I've jammed my fingers in a live socket.

Sitting alone at the window of ShabbadabbaDoo's drinking tea and eating onion rings with what must be her own pair of chopsticks (!) and wrapped in desert scarves as beautiful as the moon in a crèche of stars and reading a bound edition of *Watchmen* . . .

. . . is *Mystery Woman.*

CHARACTER DATA:

Dulles Allen

STRENGTH: Evil.

WEAKNESS: The place past Manning Freeway.

SHIT POINTS, GIVE/TAKE: +3000/0.

MAIM/TORTURE: +90/+91.

INVESTMENTS: Diversified.

CHAIRISMA: Steel or wooden, through windows, across rooms, into skulls, over spines and ribs.

HEALTH FOOD, DISCUSS/PREPARE: +22/+17.

LAUGHS AT: Ziggy, people falling down, Rich Little.

ARMOR TYPE: Hugo Boss, GWGs.

SCENT: Light curry/yogurt/peach-scented candle/lemon.

FAVORITE ANIMALS: Mongoose, anemone, ant lion.

TRIVIA DEXTERITY: NHL/CFL +100/+200.

ALIGNMENT: Son of a bitch (certified level 12).

IMPAIRMENT: Vocabulary.

MIND SHACKLE (ASSISTED): Adept +73.

SLOGAN: "How ya like summa *this,* hahn? And summa *this?* And *this!*"

The Inferno

*I could squash you with my bare hands, but that
would be messy. Gas is neater for bugs.*
—THE KINGPIN, from Ralph Bakshi's *Spider-Man*

SWIRLING LIGHTS AND EAR-STABBING MUSIC AND ENOUGH SMOKE
to kill a regiment of the king's troops. That's what my club is
on any given night. These little ass-bakes. I serve it up—they
shove their fucking faces in the trough.

Dolly the Waitress taps me on the shoulder, hands me my
usual, a tall glass of hot water and Metamucil. I inject it down
my throat. I hate Metamucil.

We have hip-hop night on Wednesdays for the niggers and
the white whores who'll pay their way for em. Niggers don't
treat their women well, not even their own women—and they
got some beautiful women, lemme tell you—and they won't
buy their own drinks, either. They'll just dance all night and
leave without one damn dime leaving their oversized pants.
But so long as their whores buy the drinks, I don't care. But

every once in a while I let my Freikorps at one or two of em just to keep em all on their toes. Even have a line of betting on the side. Got some suits who come just to watch that. You see, you gotta diversify, not have all your legs in one basket.

Tonight I got these "Goth" kids and their horror makeup. I saw that film of theirs, *The Crow*. Worst piece of ass-puke I ever saw. Except for that avenging-the-girlfriend thing. But other than that—I mean, this shitty little punk gets killed, and for some unexplained reason, he wakes up dead a year later tougher than Steve McQueen? Why wasn't his body rotten, with meat dripping off his bones like pus?

Me, if I woke up after being dead for a year, I'd want to know why I was alive, uhn? Plus I'd sell the story to every news outlet and publisher on the fuckin planet.

Fags are good, too, on Monday, which is fag night. They never cause fights, they spend a mint, and they're neat. No spills, except in the johns. That's the price you pay for an open club. Me, equal opportunity all around. I'll take anybody in here, anybody. Except dykes.

I walk on the second floor with white-faced, black-robed ghost teens shaking and bobbing to freak-show music droning I-don't-know-the-hell-what. Sounds like chanting Gregorian monks being run through an industrial saw. These ass-chalks part for me, like I'm Moses parting the white-pancake, black-cloth sea.

I like that. It's not only my size, you know. Sure, I used to be CFL. I was with the Eskimos for *three* Grey Cups. Used to be cheered by hundreds of thousands. When I was seventeen, or twenty-one, or thirty-five, it was a very good year, like the Chairman says.

But a man makes his own way. I get more respect now than any time out on that gridiron. And I was never quarterback in the old days. But now I got my own team, the little ass-scrapes. An lemme tell you, they work harder than any crew of thick-neck farm boys. Coach always wants players who'll die for him. I got that. In spades.

Enough of that. The Inferno's the finest fucking club in the city, I'm telling you. Best speakers, best sound systems, best deejays, best selection of drinks. These ass-rakes love the names we give the drinks—I swear that's what keeps em comin. Forget about "Blow Job" and "Sex on the Beach"—we got "Beaten to a Pulp," "Leather Mama," "Sweetballs," "Rimming," and my favorite, "Poon Tang."

And we actually use real Tang! Tang, Jamaican rum, and three drops of anchovy oil. Big seller, too. Must've laughed half an hour after coming up with that one. In the old days laughing like that would've made me hack up a lung. Not anymore. I'm a changed man.

I don't drink any of that puke anymore. Your body is like Solomon's Temple, you know? And most ass-horns are doing the shimmy at the Wailing Wall on accounta they don't take care of themselves. Me, I'm gonna live to be two hundred. If not older.

Wipe that fucking snicker off your face.

I'll see the year twenty-*three* hundred. I'll piss on your *great*-grandkids' graves.

Alpha Cat spots me above the mass of morons, crunches through. He yells, but he doesn't need to—I could hear a tooth hit the floor, even with all this screeching crap. Shit— whatever happened to the King, uhn? To the Righteous Brothers? To Tommy Hunter, for fuck's sakes?

"SUPA-DON MISTA ALLEN, DI EK*WIP*MAANT'S REDDY—SIGNAL COMIN TRU LOUD AN CLEAH—"

We get back to the office section, beep past fifteen security machines, visible and hidden. Inside the Situation Room, the Ass Crew is in full gear, filing their picks, calibratin all their electronic machines and countermachines, shovin dum-dum clinks into their magazines. Zenko and Frosty are sparrin, practicin the sixty-one excruciatin holds I taught em.

They all straighten up when we walk in, what with Alpha Cat yellin at the top of his rib cage, "MASTA'S ON DECK!"

"At ease, ya buncha ass-bones. How's everything going?"

Frosty hops over to the recording deck, hits buttons, slides dials. Red LED bars wave up and down. Voices slip through:

"It's coming in tomorrow? Are you sure?"

Tomorrow? When the fuck's it gonna be here already? Wait—

"By mail? . . . Oh, that's absolutely hilarious. . . . No, of course . . . who'd ever suspect Canada Post? That's priceless. . . ."

Using the ass-smoking regular mail? Never woulda thought. You're smart, all right, ya little ass-hairs. Which only makes fisting you like this even better. I goddam *gotcha*!

Whoever's on the other end mumblin suh'm . . . I think maybe "*time to celebrate.*" "*I'll say. We've only been waiting since—*" Then the mumblin, I think in the middle with "*ready soon,*" and "*Chinese silk panties,*" followed by laughin and mumblin. "*Of course I'll be here. Those cretins at customs have no idea—*" Mumblin into "*safest way, of course—*" and more mumblin and laughin.

"You ass-snakes did good work," I announce.

They're happy, smilin like I just complimented their coloring within the lines or suh'm. Whatever it takes. Positive reinforcement and all that puke.

They did good. But I want that package *yesterday*.

"Your gear went up just in the nick of time," I continue. "To think we almost missed it, that ass-fucker. Well, you guys can stand down tonight. You've all earned it. Go have fun. Go make some money for yourselves. Tonight you keep *thirteen percent*."

They cheer.

Before they leave, everyone takes their medicine.

When their seizures end and they wipe their mouths, they dance out the door, down the hall to the Goths in the strobing darkness. All except for Alpha Cat, who I snag.

"You'll have those ass-pins ready for tomorrow night?"

"Cose, Mista Allen, suh."

I nod. "Tonight you let the ass-balls do their thing. But you . . . I just got a hunch, Al. Take Digaestus with you. Something's coming. . . . I can *feel* it. You understand? I can feel something coming in the air tonight. . . ."

He nods, salutes. His face is blank—and his eyes are gold and tear-streaked.

"Now get the fuck outta here."

I like Al, I really do, but that Jafaikan wouldn't know Phil Collins if he bit *off* Al's ass.

Ah, well. Got my treasure. Got my castle. Got my knights. And I'm twenty-four hours closer to my ultimate prize, and bringing a three-year search to an end.

All my joints ache, all my bones feel like lead pipe. I can taste copper in my mouth. . . . My teeth are vibratin, and my jaw clicks. My sack is sagging, like I got bowlin balls.

After so long, so damn long waitin, not to mention listenin to my crew of ass-freaks and all their geek sci-fi fantasy bull-shit, well, still, it gets me thinkin about some of the stories *I* usedta read when I was a kid.

Specially that old King Arthur. I mean, after sloggin through all that mud and in all them swamps and through dark forests with wolves and robbers, and over mountains and bod-ies and skulls with arrows stickin outta their eye sockets and rats eatin their nuts off and silverfish livin in their ears . . . can you imagine the number of wounds Arthur musta had after all he went through? Freezin hands and feet, all chipped and chapped, scarred up and callused like leather, skin itchin and chafin under all that armor. Wouldn'even've been able to wash his hair. Woulda been all matted and greasy and filthy with dirt and sweat and stink underneath his helmet. Coupla old, tired legs like bulgin drumsticks off a game bird, just barely keepin him upright there on some damn peat bog. Lonely and miserable. He'd be breathin out hot breath, maybe just barely meltin the icicles forming in his mustache and beard, and it'd be night and the breath'd turn all white underneath the moon. And . . . and one of his own ass-porks'd already betrayed him over a woman. His own woman.

I wonder if this's how he felt? With tears and screamin and . . . and *howlin joy* all crammed and packed up inside him, the night before he finally got his hands on the thing he'd spent his whole life tryin to get?

Aw, to hell with it. That fucker's dead anyway.

Moth Seeks Advice on New Flame

VIDEO MORONS IS SHOCKINGLY EMPTY FOR A THURSDAY NIGHT. Usually jimps are massing, thronging—dare I say it?—*milling* here by this hour. Not that I mind, you understand. Still, it doesn't matter what (*a*) feature, (*b*) documentary, or (*c*) "Specialty Item" I put on the floor "Staff Pix" display, Chief Bellower John will immediately step in my path the second he sees me actually not unhappy.

That's why I'm so delighted when the phone rings. Something to do that isn't really doing anything but looks like it is.

"Video Reich, One Thousand Videos Über Alles, ask about our Sudetenland Special, how may I melt you?"

"Ye, it's me—"

Even better! My partner in grime.

"Yeah, what's going down, Hamz?"

Hamz, breathlessly: "It's her."

"Her? *Who* her?"

"The chick! The gorgeous Sister we've been seeing all day!"

"Where?"

"Here! *'Where?'* Where I'm at, where else?"

"No way!"

"It's her, I'm tellin ya! It's Mystery Woman!"

"No-o-o-o!"

"Coyote-certified!"

"Well, spam damn, Ham. Whatcha gon do?"

I hear a nasal voice in Hamza's background: "*This's a place of business, not a homeboy action pad, Hamster.*"

Hamza snaps back, "*Listen up, Yorkshire puddinboy, it's called 'a break.' It's called 'labor laws.' So why don't you make like a job and blow?*"

"Hamz, hold it together, now—never mind Zitty. What's happening?"

"Like I said, Ye, she's here. . . . I'm . . . I don'know what to . . . I don'know . . . I'm . . . I wanna—"

" 'In all history, no one's desired anything more than they've desired *a second chance*.' Quick, who said that?"

"King Arthur, *Camelot 3000*—"

"Excellent. And this is your *second* second chance. Mystery Woman! Use your find-o powers and find some balls! What the hell you waiting for?"

Silence. Shuffling with the phone.

"Are you *flipping a coin,* you super-turd?"

"No, no, I just—"

"Are you gonna do this or not?"

"Yes, yes, I'm gonna do it!"

"Then go to, young man—"

The line is dead. That bastard hung up on me.

After all this, she'd better be worth it. Or Hamza's gonna get himself all messed up again.

Jackal Descends, Coyote Rises

I am the woman who lighteth the darkness. . . .
It is lightened doubly. . . .
I have overthrown the destroyers,
I have adored those who are in the darkness.
I have made to stand those who weep,
  who hid their faces, who had sunk down.
—Per-em-Hru, LXXX

I'VE PUT THE PHONE DOWN, AND I REALIZE WITH BELLY-JELLYING exhilaration and terror that Mystery Woman's been watching me watch her. And now she *sees* me seeing her see me see her.

And now, for the first time, I can really get a good look at her face. She's as gorgeous as I thought she'd be, maybe even better looking . . . dark, her hair draped in that bizarre constellation of three major and several minor braids—not dreadlocks—and her nose and cheeks . . . I'm guessing she's Somalian, maybe Ethiopian.

And she's still got on those exotic silken scarves. . . . Beneath the restaurant lights and backlit by the streetscape, the material glimmers like the aurora borealis in the darkness.

And those eyes of hers fixed on me, black and shining, like mountain lakes beneath starshine.

Ye's right. No choice. Now or never.

I walk over.

My feet weigh billions of pounds.

I'm suddenly aware that the downward vector of gravity has shifted about seven degrees. I'm walking tiltedly to avoid crashing into the tables of our swinish customers. I have to collapse my left leg slightly to maintain my balance in this 3-D fun house mirror world.

She's still staring at me.

I'm at the table.

I want to do the conscious, respectful thing, call her "Sister," but I've seen too many situations where nose-ups and sellouts react negatively to that, not to mention the fact that I'm at work and she's a customer. So I'm completely hands-bare in the pretext and opening banter departments. This is not good.

Her eyes on me. My mouth moving, sound escaping.

"Excuse me, um, miss. . . ."

She's still looking at me. Silently. She aint making this any easier.

"I . . . uh . . ." I try to avoid visibly gulping, but I really need to swallow, and I can feel the spit welling up at the back of my throat. It's gonna be real embarrassing if I actually *drown* in the middle of a preppy restaurant while failing to style a woman.

I should've had a pretext, a *pre*text, damnit! Why didn't I think this through better? I'm freezing here, I'm freakin *freezing,* I'm choking. . . . "Well, this'll sound like some sort of, uh, fabri*ca*tion, I'm sure, but—"

The Mystery Woman: "—but we've seen each other three

times now, today—in Chinatown, at the comic store, and now, here."

Whoah.

This did *not* show up on my tricorder. And now it hits me—I should've just started talking about *Watchmen* with her, but aw, hell, now I'm committed: "Well . . . actually, yes. I didn'know if you'd actually seen me or what—"

"Of course I saw you. How could I *miss* you?" she hums, sliding aside her teapot and her empty onion ring plate, slipping her metal chopsticks into a breast pocket inside of her vest beneath one of her many iridescent scarves. "Sit down, Brother."

Good *gravy*. That *voice:* a damn three A.M. *waking-up-and-snuggling-again* voice. Dark and feminine and embracing . . . like, like . . . uh . . . like spandex. Gravelly enough to make a driveway. Okay, I'm *trying* here, at least, c'mon!

And she actually said *Brother*. Can this really be happening?

While I'll grant you that all this is great, the fact is that I'm not really on a break, even though I told the Zitsack that. I guess I could retroactively go on one, but then staff, especially dishwashers like me, aren't supposed to fraternize with customers.

But still, *she* asked *me,* so if anyone gets on my ass, at least I have an alibi, unless this is some elaborate practical joke, arranged by some cabal of telepathic androids and a subdivision of the RAND Corporation. . . .

I glance around anxiously, then sit.

"Thank you, Sister."

"What's your name, Brother?"

"Hamza. Hamza Senesert."

Now it's her turn to look startled. Is it my name? She squints, and so subtly I almost don't notice she does it, she checks over her shoulder and out the window. She hushes and says, "*Nuk Ur, se Ur, Nesert, se Nesert.*"

I have no idea what she just said, but I did catch my name in there somewhere. Must be a greeting. Dad'd be mad at me, seeing as how bad my Arabic is, assuming it's not Somali or Amharic. If only I'd spent summers in Sudan with him, like he wanted me to. Then I'd probably be able to understand what I hope was a very poetical come-on from Ms. Mystery.

As it is, I feel like a twat. I'm the most educated dishwasher in the city, and I don't have even a microbial idea of what to say.

"You've got me. My Arabic's pretty rusty . . . or, uh, was that—Amharic?"

"Ren-Kem. 'Hamza,' huh? As in Hamza El Din?"

Oh. My. *Gourd.*

"Yes! Yes, exactly, the oud master. My dad named me after him. We're both big fans. I, well . . . I haven't met many folks around here who know Nubian music—"

"You're . . . Sudanese?"

"*Yes.*"

Those giant dark eyes are still on me, the restaurant mood lights now nebulae in their blackness. I can just make out her scent. . . . It's like sun-baked sand. And mist . . . spray . . .

"You know," she intones, "I saw Hamza El Din once."

If she had my attention before, now she's planted a flag on it.

"Yeah. I *almost* saw him in Baghdad, but I missed the show. A few years later I saw him in Aswân, right there with all his people, all those people who'd lost their homes to the dam."

She runs her hands through her bizarre braids, as if she's comforting a brood of serpents. They seem to quiver and undulate more than hair actually should before they finally settle. Her hand pushes one of her scarves away from her neck, and the skin there is so lusciously smooth I'm almost aching with the abrupt thought of getting close enough to sniff her skin, there, or brush my lips inside the notch of her neck. But . . . is that a scar . . . at the edge? Rippling in the skin like the tail of a lizard disappearing beneath a dune?

She's still speaking, unaware, I hope, of all my madness.

"It was an open-air concert, you know?" Her teeth flash on the word "air." They're bright, perfectly shaped.

"You know what it's like there. . . . The leisure day doesn't really start until night in Aswân, and then you see families out, at midnight, even, walking around and buying spices from the street vendors, men slapping dominoes and cheering, slurping from water pipes.

"What a night, what a *performance*, Brother . . . children dancing, men singing, women clapping . . . and sometimes, everyone crying at the words, the nostalgia of all those songs about a whole way of life drowned out of existence, all beside the Holy River Nile, and underneath an audience of stars."

I'm in awe. I'm transported. I'm en*tranced*.

If she's *not* for real, then she must be some cyborg programmed from memory engrams stolen from me while I was asleep or something, or maybe afterwards my mind was wiped clean of the telecerebral theft so I wouldn't remember. She couldn't have said anything more perfect to me, or for me.

This *can't* be real.

But I gotta say something, even if it *is* to a dream or to a robot.

"I'm . . . wow. Like, you've really . . ." And it hits me: "Sister, I don't even know your name yet!"

She stops. She's been friendly all along, but now she offers her first, though subdued, smile. I feel cool air around my neck, hot air on my cheeks.

"Sheremnefer."

"Sharon Neffer? Pleased to m—"

"Sher*em*nefer. Or just—you can call me *Sherem*."

"Sher*em*? Pleased to meet you, Sister Sherem."

I offer my hand, triple-clasp hers. Her fingers are cool, her palm is dry, her grip firm.

"I'm impressed, Brother Hamza." Still that intense gaze, the subtle, scintillating smile. "Most Brothers won't soul-shake with Sisters."

"Brothers need to do the right thing. Sometimes they just don't know what that is." Glad *I* did. "So, I don't know, maybe it's fate or something that we've run into each other three times."

She looks at me hard now. Her smile is still there, but I don't know if it's suddenly ironic, or three degrees cooler.

"No, naw, I don'mean that like some sorta line. I just meant—"

She tilts her head, and her braids writhe, restless serpents. "How do you know I haven't been *following* you?"

Hot *damn.* "Well maybe that's it." I call out to no one in mock alarm: "Constable—this woman is stalking me!"

We share a laugh, and both of us smile. And when she smiles for real, this time, it's stunning. Her eyes crinkle at the edges, moisten, glint all the more, and her purple-plum lips part to reveal all those teeth again. Her nostrils flare while she breathes and laughs.

I break away from looking at her, aware of how much I'm looking at her. I'm suddenly thinking of Screamin' Jay Hawkins's "I Put a Spell on You." I've got to ask this woman out, but I'm on break, for freaking out loud! I got maybe two more minutes before I get yelled at or fired, and that is *not* the way to make a good impression. Pretext . . . I need a freakin *pre*text!

I've got no choice. I contort my face, screw up my voice, squint. This calls for the big guns.

My De Niro impression.

"So, uh, I know I'm just a humble, whaddayacall, dish-washer, but, still, I can, like, show a lady a delightful palette of whaddayacall activities."

"Oh, really? So whaddayouse think you was thinking about?"

Oh, man, she's playing along. "So, like, I was thinkin. Maybe when I get off work, we could, like, share a slice of cof-fee cake."

"Coffee cake?" Her accent suddenly drops. "Well, see, tonight isn't very good."

No—is this endgame so soon? Can this be the end of Hamza "Coyote King" Senesert?

The room freezes, everything in chiaroscuro, the harsh backlight burning coronas onto everyone's silhouette.

Only I exist in motion, and the ghost of Yehats Past behind me.

> When you ask out a chick, if she says, "I can't make it THAT NIGHT," but offers an alternative, she's genuinely interested. But if she says no, with no qualification at all, you're screwed. She don't wanna go.

Inside Un-Time, beneath darklights, I speak to her, moon to comet.

"Oh," I muster. "Okay."

Her voice echoes from afar: "But maybe tomorrow, around suppertime?"

Yehat flares behind me, a supernova, long enough to yell, "YES!" before fading into the deeps.

I hope my smile isn't making my cheeks bleed. Her expression is almost unreadable, but it's still got hope in it. From the way she talks to me, I almost feel like, not that I know her, but that *she* knows *me*. This is too intense. I've gotta take the edge off it all, get some time to think.

Still in De Niro function: "I know what you're thinking."

She's amused. "What am I thinking?"

"You're thinking, maybe this aint such a good idea—this guy's got a big head."

She smiles crookedly.

"Hey, that's okay, I heard it all my life. 'Hey, Big Head, get off the diving board, no high diving for you. . . . Hey, Big Head, you can't be an astronaut—your skull'd explode in space.' Trust me, I'm familiar with your type of prejudice, and frankly, well, it sickens me."

"You must be scarred."

"Scarred and striped. But hey, I'm okay with it. I've learned to love myself, and *give myself permission* to exist in this magnacephalic mode."

"That was magna-*ce*-phalic, right?"

"Right. *Ce*-phalic." Golly, she's damn near made me blush. She has!

"Actually," she lilts, "I was more thinking, what if we hit it off famously? Then, what, on your birthday, I'd hafta buy you a gift, right?"

"Right . . ."

Her: "And of course, what says friendship better than a hat?"

Me: "And because my head's so big—"

Both of us: "—where you gonna find a big enough hat?"

We laugh. *Delicious.*

"Well," I smooth, "I just happen to have a book on how to make hats."

"So bring the book tomorrow over coffee cake. And don't forget your appetite—I can eat a lotta cakes."

"You can get a big gut to go with my big head."

Suddenly the Zitsack shambles over, snots at me, "Break's over, Holmes."

"*Judgment Day's coming, Sean,*" I call out, then stage-whisper to her, "I told him to try laser treatment to get the 666 off the side of his head, but he doesn't listen."

She's still smiling when she reaches for some cash to pay her bill. I'm just about to offer to pay for her when I see she's paying with a handful of dollar bills—actual DOLLAR BILLS. No one's had dollar bills since the late eighties!

"You *have* been out of the country awhile!"

Her eyes pierce me. "What?"

"Well, it's just that . . . I overheard you at the comic store . . . there aint no more dollar bills, just loonies. You were hoarding these or something?"

She sniffs, waves it away with a weak smile, gets up to leave. I stand quickly. "Wait, Sherem! What about your number?"

"I don't have a phone yet, Brother. Just meet me tomorrow at six."

"Where?"

"Rice Howard Way. *Hotep,* Brother."

"Salaam walaikum, Sister."

I grab her hand as she turns, soul-shake as she makes eye contact. She smiles.

And then her braids are swaying, the doors are opening, her scarves are fluttering. . . .

And she's gone.

And for the first time in I'm-sad-to-think-*how*-many years, I don't feel like a total loser.

Tomorrow night.

At six.

FanBoys Skip Rape, Prepare to Pillage

THE WAITRESS HANDS ME MY FOURTH METAMUCIL TONIGHT. She's dressed like a whore—gets better tips that way. Me, I don't go for all that. Woman's supposed to have a certain decorum, self-respect, you know? But hey, that's free enterprise, and if she can make a bundle by making a club full of tanked blue-ballers fantasize about entering her prize, who am I to say different?

I slip out my bottle of Tums, pour out a fistful, and crush them into my drink, swish it around with the swooshy-stick. Drinking this liquid belch is better than the alternative, but not much better.

That's me: green tea, tofu, sprouts, rose water, dal, soy milk . . . I love all that shit. It sure makes me feel so good, so ass-splittingly good I don't daily ponder ramming my head into an industrial vise and cracking my skull open like a fucking cantaloupe. There are still days I could kill a priest for a steak, but not so much, anymore.

My cell rings. "Allen."

"Mista SuPREME Empra ALLEN, Alpha CAAT hyere," he's yelling, never really believing I can hear above all this exploding ass-music, "mi afi mek a riPOHT—"

"Go, Al."

"Yu were riyyt abou' di sumtin-sumtin comin in di eer tnIYYt. DigAEStus pickittup riyyt quick, once we out deer on di havenue. Wi still tryin fi trak dung di preCIYSE loKAYSHAAN, baat soon wi know, an wi near even NOW, suh."

"Wait a minute—it aint inside the target itself?"

"No suh, di store wuz cleah—di sigNAAL wuzn' comin from inside di Mod—"

"NO FUCKIN NAMES, ASS-FIST!"

"Mi sorry, suh, mi sorry, mi sorry—"

"Enough apologizing! You just find wherever the cache is. Maybe those ass-roaches knew we were listening and that whole phone convo you ass-fish tapped was a red herring, an the package already came in." I chew my Metamucil-flavored lip. "If we can locate an raid their drop point *before* they move—"

"Baat see, suh, dis ere's what mi sayin: it naa HAAVE naa fixed loKAYshaan. It's movin and groovin all ho-ver di neibaHOOD, seen? Like—"

Now this is unexpected. This anomaly is moving? What the hell is it? "Like it's inside a trunk or something?"

"May*be,* suh. Or maybe it's even inna briefKAYSE, or sumtin. Suh, do yu even know what dis ting is or looks liyyke? How else caan wi know even *if* wi fine it?"

"Digaestus. He'll know it when he sees it."

"Oh, yu mean becau' ee—"

"Exactly. So just make sure he's *ready*. And take extra primer, just in case he loses the scent."

I'm just about to send him off, and then I remember how these little ass-dicks can get outta hand. "*And for god's sake, be discreet!* Could be a trap. I can't have any screwups now—

I don'wanna tip off these ass-ports or the cops, not when
we're this close."

"Yes, SUH, Mista Grand Masta CHAMPEEN—"

I snap shut my cell.

Whatever it is, I can practically taste this . . . *this thing.*

And all this hell won't've been for nothing.

Unforeseen Confrontation between Jackal Clan and Ymirist Regime in Parking Lot of ShabbadabbaDoo's

I AINT WALKING ON AIR—I'M WALKING ON THE FRICKIN-FREAKIN-frackin aurora borealis, tap-dancing my way along the ionosphere and doing the finale from *Jesus Christ Superstar* on the Van Allen belts.

Don't matter how many dishes, pots, ladles, gravy boats, strainers, or other crapliments I still hafta wash. Cuz HOT DAMN, it's a good night to be alive, with a gorgeous woman fated to meet me for a date. Too good to be true? Better than a dream? Hell, this's full Hamzaramascope in T-H-freakin-X.

The Zitsack tries to attack, pus-ing his way into the dishatorium: "Good to see you're *finally* back at work. Why, though? Strike out, mack daddy Hammy?"

He can't amaze me and he can't faze me. I don't even bother to look up. Cheerfully, "Eat urinal cakes, sweetboy. I'm the freakin man."

He minces away, out of my peripheral vision. It's a good vibe in here. I activate my belt speakers, groove to the tail end of what I was listening to before I took my break and caught a break: a smooth, slinky, shimmering Congolese love ballad,

"Christine," all echoing guitars and Cubano hand-caress percussion. Kot-TAM.

Suddenly my head feels like the plates of my skull are pulling away from each other, like my brain is shoving away the bone with some kind of somatic countermagnetism. What the hell is it now? I only get this feeling when I . . . when—

"Vut izit, Humzah?" asks Ghalib, my dishwashing comrade. "Vut's di mut-ter?

My skull keeps stretching outwards, my brain ringing and singing alarm, gonging, droning.

My Coyote Sense isn't just tingling, it's going into core meltdown. I'm staring *through* the walls—what the hell is happening?

Oh, no.

"Ghalib, cover me—"

I run, not knowing why, just knowing that whatever it is, it's outside, it's—

—out in the restaurant, snooty customers and waitresses blur past me, past the hostess, through the big wooden doors, outside to the cool night air, cold compared to the tropical steam heat of the dishes area—

—outside darkness, streetlights, cars zooming—

—glancing left, right, downstreet—

—running to the curb, raking the avenue—

—damnit, the *parking lot*—

—some freak is stepping up to Sherem—HE LOOKS LIKE HE'S GONNA TRY TO GRAB HER—

"HEY!" I yell, bolting. Both glance at me, startled. "HEY, MUTHAFUCKA! THERE A PROBLEM HERE?"

This fool is some crazy Whiteboy wrapped up in Jamaican gear, a Shabby Ranks with a *vehicle tow chain in his hand*—

"HAHN? WHAT THE HELL YOU THINK YOU DOIN, YA FREAK?"

This muthafucka actually *smirks* at me, like I'm a freakin *kid* or something. "Dere's NO-O-O problem ere, SEEN?"

Damn, one of them *complete* posers, with the whole phony patois and everything. "Mi jass AKSIN di woman a KWESS-chaan—"

Me, stepping forward again, growling. My heart's pounding so hard it's rattling my shirt—blood's thundering in my ears like cannon fire. "Better *not* be a problem, pal."

Then this greeble actually opens his hands, as in, *hey, my mistake,* and then he freakin *tips his hat* towards Sherem! The freakin *nerve* of this guy! And then he backs up, joins some turd in tweed and a tie standing on the corner.

And they're out.

"Better NOT come back, ya Trinidad an Winnebago muthafucka! Kick ya ass three times, quick!"

I try to get my breathing back to normal, but it's damn hard. I haven't been in a fight since grade seven. And I *lost* that one.

Still, hey, if this isn't a cinematically fantastic way to make a great impression on a woman, I don't know what is—a knight in shining apron, defending the woman's right to walk unmolested through parking lots or preppy restaurants. This is worth fifteen dates on the intimacy boostotron, right here!

And now my imagination is about to smash on the tarmac like dropped dishes.

I get a good look at her for the first time since coming out here. She's wearing some kind of crazy shades—a slit visor, like from Mongolia or something.

And she looks *pissed*.

"I could've . . . ," she ices, "handled that."

I am totally unprepared for this. I'm still in the middle of my adrenaline surge, hot and cold all over. Now this? I feel like someone's taking sandpaper and aftershave to my neck.

What the hell do I say to that?

"Uh . . ."

Spit's collecting at the back of my throat. I have no choice but to swallow. I *hate* that, *swallowing* when I'm trying to keep my cool and look unfazed. Swallowing's like writing *panties* across my forehead in blue lipstick. Ah, hell's bells, got no choice but to swallow—better than drowning.

(Gulp. Damn.)

"Okay."

We stand. She's staring at me. I'm staring past her. I can't freakin believe this. What the hell just happened?

I can't let this go.

"Listen, uh . . . you know"—I try keeping my voice even, failing—"there's worse things than trying to . . . keep a Sister from getting, like, mugged or *raped*."

I can't tell what she's thinking behind that visor. Her face is like a fist.

Then suddenly she softens. As if she's just been replaced by the woman from *inside* the restaurant. A complete switch.

"You're right," she smiles softly. Even her voice is soft. "That was . . . very . . . *gallant* . . . of you."

Am I supposed to believe this?

She steps forward. I fight mighty hard the urge to back up, and quickly at that.

She reaches out jerkily, deciding, changing her mind, committing. Then taking my hand.

And *squeezing*.

"Thank you," she smolders.

She removes the visor with her free hand, and I see streetlights twinkling in the dark lagoons of her eyes. And that smile again, like the first warm breeze in spring, like the first ripe raspberries plucked from July bushes, bright and sharp and tender on the tongue.

"You're welcome," I muster.

She releases my hand.

"Tomorrow at six?" she whispers, glancing away, suddenly shy, another person, a third woman.

I swallow again. "Six, tomorrow."

She waves, turns to walk away. I follow her with my eyes.

And she's gone.

I turn to go back inside to find the entire restaurant, customers and busboys and waitresses and dishwashers alike, all watching me through the window.

Hell, if anyone hassles me, I *was* protecting a customer.

Later on tonight I'll sit in my bedroom, sitting in my night chair, staring in the darkness at the Box on my shelf.

I promised Yehat I wouldn't, so I won't.

Today's . . . tonight's adventures, rather, make it so I don't have to.

In a few days' time, when machetes are pointed at me, when an old, old friend betrays me, when a sharpened ice-cream scoop is poised to scrape out my eyes, I'll be wishing I'd never met this woman.

CHARACTER DATA:

Sheremnefer

NOME: Ash Shabb, twenty days' camel from Abdju.

PRECISE LOCATION OF TEMPLE: Unknown.

CURSES, DISPENSE/ACCEPT: +99/+199.

SPECTRAL AWARENESS, RANGE/DETECT TYPE: Unknown/unknown.

ALTER/MERGE: Uasidi/Ta-Khaibt.

ALIGNMENT: The Jackal.

FULL NAME: Unknown.

LINEAGE: Unknown.

AGE: Unknown.

STRENGTH: Unknown.

WEAKNESS: Unknown.

KILLS: Unknown.

TRAUMAS: Unknown.

RISK EXTENT, OTHERS/SELF: Death.

A Dweller in All the Dark Spaces

I WALK UPON THIS SUNDERED EARTH IN DARKNESS, BENEATH THE dome of distant stars perhaps long dead, beneath the neon glare of artificial spirits pulsing with electron blood. I walk in darkness upon this sundered earth, its schism into soilworld and asphaltworld, my roots in one, my leaves in the other.

I am home, in a home no longer home.

There are fourteen men and seven women upon the street of the four blocks visible to me. Among them, thieves, hustlers, whores, homeless, hopeless.

The very night of my return I bore witness to the blessing of my crusade: seeing *him,* knowing him more than he knows himself, knowing him more than he can dream, knowing him just by being across the street from him but in his presence, knowing him for what he truly is, his nature as surely obvious to me as an arctic owl's to a naturalist . . . or to a hunter.

And he believes me and suspects nothing, not even the simple fox-and-hare ruse of today.

And now I am across the bridge and ancient river, above the million tiny twinkling flashes like the silver scales of a vast serpent. And soon, up the wooden staircase and beyond, soon there, at the gateway of carnivores, to intercept the Interceptor.

Across a world she has come, and me across mine.

And when I have her information and she is gone, I will find the object she has hunted and located, find it and then find him. And he, with his talent, will lead me to the ultimate treasure whose destiny belongs to us.

To me.

There are eighteen men and twelve women upon the street of the six blocks visible to me. Among them, liars, cheats, adulterers, slaves.

My soles feel my shoes feel the asphalt feel the trapped earth feeling its own rage, its imprisonment, its death without air, without sun, without moon. My feet feel from fleshbone through to mantle madness.

I am here, in all my *here*s.

I am in homecity, birthplace, Sanehem. I am in Uxmal, Salt Lake, Nanaimo; I am in Kingston, Harlem, Brixton; I am in Ankara, Jerusalem, Jidda; I am in Delhi, Angkor, Kyoto. . . .

I am in Kigali, Bhopal, Coventry, Dresden, Nagasaki. . . .

I am in Auschwitz, Mukden, Elmina, Gorée. . . .

I am in Abdju. . . .

I am in Edmonton, walking in darkness lit by bright and shining lies.

On 97th Street, with its twin eternal lions guarding the Chinatown Gate ahead.

I scramble for the shadows, wait here for the appointed time, crouched, hidden, ready to spring, for her.

She is not here.

She does not arrive.

Unexpected.

Does this Interceptor suspect our plans? And if she does . . . would she even understand that only we can do this? Would her Hobinarit masters recall their Interceptor and engage our search themselves?

Or would she perhaps in fear or greed of damnable slithering myopia betray our cause herself to any of the legions who dwell in darkness against us?

And if she has betrayed us, how far does she think she can run to evade me?

There are sixteen men and eleven women upon the street of the six blocks visible to me. Among them, valiant, vanquished, victims, vipers.

I emerge from hiding, stand alone here at the gate, and foolish men call out to me, approach me, attempt to engage my . . . services.

I offer them a glimpse of my eyes.

And as I behold them, the cowards dash past me, like hutch-bound hares beneath the shadow of a falcon.

I have waited, still waiting. No signs in stars, no scrawl on walls to signal dangers or expected deeds.

And yet . . . the legend . . .

I will place my hand inside the lions' mouths, and if the myths are true and the lions do not bite, I am to be rewarded with great fortune and great future. But stone lions do not rend flesh, and surely the *definition* of bad luck would be for idols to melt into life and claim the living.

Surely *I* require no lessons in the intersection of myth and damnation.

Everything has changed here. The air has thickened, sickened. . . . Faces are warped with putridity and decay from taste of rancid, rotten crops and swill-fed meat. . . . Choir voices sing no more but only moan and wail, congested with phlegm from throats stoppered by tumors, and eyes that seek to look upon the moon are lidded with maggots.

There are twenty-three men and fifteen women upon the streets of eight blocks radiating from the intersection visible to me.

All of them: killers.

I put my hand inside the first stone lion's mouth.

I count, breathlessly . . . one, two, three . . .

. . . to nine.

I pull back my arm.

My hand remains.

If I *am* to lose it, I know that pain will come later, in a place of rain-ravaged cliffs and thirsty sands, in the presence of a metal man and a seeker with a scepter of fire, and a broken man who breaks men, and a Thing that is shaped like a man that dines upon men's souls.

I open my hand, behold the paper scrap upon my palm. Behold in Senzar script the name of the location.

A note left by the Interceptor, who has failed to appear? A trap laid for me by her, or by our enemies?

And if it *is* a trap, I have no choice but to walk into it.

And if this Hobinarit Interceptor has betrayed me, there is no place on earth where she can hide.

Wherever this place, I will find it, and if the information be true, I will secure from this *Modeus Zokolo* the lens of ecstasy and death that—at the eyes of Hamza Senesert, my *sekht-en-cha*—will lead me to the priceless bounty of the Jar.

I am the only person upon the visible and invisible streets who knows what I know, who has seen what I have seen, who has gone where I have gone, whose hands have done what they have done.

Who will do what I have to do, by any means necessary.

CHARACTER DATA:

Kevlar Meaney

REAL NAME: Kevin Lars Meaney.

STRENGTH: Grooming +19.

WEAKNESS: Crème brûlée.

SMILE: Butter-melting +7.

SHIRT POINTS: Egyptian cotton only, off-the-rack only in wartime or famine, tiepin indispensable to eradicate back-collar escape.

SEXUALITY: Flexible.

STEREO: Bang & Olufsen.

FAVORITE ACTION FIGURE DIORAMA: Handmade "Magus kills Adam Warlock" (comes with removable soul-gems).

CELEBRITY MOST RESEMBLES: Giancarlo Esposito.

MOTHER'S NAME: Marie-Angelique Appollon-Meaney.

FAVORITE CITIES: Bangkok, Bogotá, Seville, Vancouver.

AMBITION: Yes.

SCENT: Vanilla-almond.

TRIVIA DEXTERITY: Surrealist art, 3-D collectibles +199.

GENRE ALIGNMENT: Classic EC, magic-realist metafiction, Godard films.

IMPAIRMENT: Heinz Meaney.

SLOGANS: (1) "Diplomacy is the art of feeding people your feces and having them beg for the recipe"; (2) "Papa was a rolling scone."

The Chalice of Cenozoic Dreams

PICTURE THE STATISTICALLY TYPICAL 2.5 KIDS ON A BETTER-THAN-usual-stack-under-the-tree Christmas morning. Picture the wrapping made out of money. Picture Daddy's home after a long time away, and Mummy has been waiting anxiously for him to stuff her stocking. Calculate that family's *aggregate* emotional sum.

Multiply that times five, and you've got my state of being right now.

And why shouldn't I be like this? The sun is shining—yes, delightful, but hardly unusual on a superlative summer Friday morning; my health and physique are excellent—hardly a sur-prise, given my devotion to jogging and *qi gong* and exqui-sitely crafted meals; and my store, this magnificent intersection of global cultures and crafts and wonders, the gold of old, the Modeus Zokolo, is having a banner month in a banner year.

And my brother, Heinz, and I have just been published, his essays and my photographs, and our launch is tonight. And after the launch, a rendezvous with two of the most delicious women ever to entice our appetites.

And walking into the store even as we speak is destiny.

"You Mr., uh, Meaney?" reads the Canada Post gentleman from the invoice address slip on his package, and my prize. The prize is too valuable to be sent any other way than in the open, so as to distract attention by attracting it.

"One of them, yes, my friend."

"Hahn?"

"There are many Meaneys in the world, chum. I'm the one in front of you."

He looks puzzled; I shouldn't toy with them so. He takes off his blue cap, swabs his sweating forehead, and fingers back the matted remains of that which has so far escaped male-pattern baldness. His grassy blond mustache straggles over his thin upper lip. He was once well built, I can see, perhaps a football or basketball player whose dreams of greatness ended with grade-twelve graduation, but now he has a paunch and a stoop, with small, downcast eyes best suited to a mole, or a vole, or a troll. He looks as if he might've tried to join the police service when he was younger and was rejected on some unalterable basis . . . poor eyesight or dull-wittedness. His shoulders cave in towards the front, ever so slightly; there's a droop to the corners of his mouth that seems to form the syllables of words like *can't* and *not anymore* and *sorry, hon.*

I can't take looking at him anymore. I'd best end this quickly. "I'm *Kevlar* Meaney, yes. My brother is Heinz. I'm not sure to whom the package is addressed, but I'll sign for it."

"Can you sign here?"

"Ye-e-s . . ." I chuckle, mumbling quick-softly, "I believe I just *said* that."

He hands me his miniclipboard, and while I'm signing all the places by which he's placed Xs, he says, "Pretty nasty thing, last night, there, hahn?"

"I'm sorry?" I say, without looking up, signing.

"Oh, yeah, y'know, that killing, eh? Pretty sick and all."

"I really haven't any idea what you're talking about. What—"

"It's all over the news, buddy! You don'listen to the radio or nuthin?"

I try handing him back the clipboard, but he doesn't seem to notice it. "Clearly I haven't. Look, just tell me—"

"Oh, it's awful, guy! This woman, yeah. Police found her this morning after the cleaning crew showed up at a restaurant in Chinatown, Dim Mok, or whatever. Awful—"

"Just—! What . . . *happened*?"

"Yeah, well, she was cut up, can you b'lieve it? Head and arms and legs cut off, organs pulled out. An all of it stuffed in those big Chinese jars they make kimchi in or whatever—"

"Kimchi is Korean. Continue."

"—and this goddam sicko or group of goddam sickos, they even pulled her eyes out. And get this . . . they stuffed her mouth and eye sockets and packed her organs with hair!"

"Hair?"

"Yeah, *donkey* hair, c'n you b'lieve it? I mean, where would you even *find* donkey hair? Must be some goddam loony usedta work on a farm or something, or maybe the zoo. Y'ask me, it's all them movies what gives people these nutty-type ideas. Sick. Still don'know how come you didn'know about it. It's all over the news, been on since—"

"I don't follow the news, friend," I say, handing back the clipboard, holding out my hands expectantly for my package. "Too depressing."

"I mean, how far will some people go to satisfy their sick whatevers? An if you're gonna kill somebody, why take all that time with the body? You'd think you'd worry about getting caught! Unless you were tryin to send somebody a *message*, y'know? That's my theory. Gang war. Tongs from Hong Kong, eh? Or a cult, maybe."

"My package?"

His eyes cross momentarily, as if he were trying to follow the intersecting paths of two flies upon which he intended to dine. Finally, he says, "Oh, yeah," and looks at the package, my package, which he's been holding.

His face seems to snap out of the intoxicating trance of his own ghoulish story, assuming any of it's real. In all likelihood it's simply some *National Enquirer* tale he's heard over a large Sweet'n Low decaf and a pair of chocolate-glazeds at the local Tim Hortons, and in his limited capacities he's confounded the concoction with radio or television coverage.

"Tibetan stamps," he says, examining the package he'd held captive beneath his arm, like a jungle-fresh bunch of bananas. He hands it over, almost jealously, and he takes back his clipboard, jealously. "Nice. You guys're an import-export shop or something, right?"

"Yes, that's it, right. 'The exotic for the psychotic.' " He seems to've forgotten his tale of murderous mayhem and mutilation as abruptly as he remembered it, despite my use of the word "psychotic."

"Hahn?"

"Nothing."

"I brought the wife past here a coupla times, plus I walk here myself every day, obviously." He laughs nervously, looking me in the eye and then away and then back again, as if he's seeking approval for his laughter, even though he didn't actually make a joke.

Oh, it's agonizing. I muster a chuckle, feeling so sad for him, granting him the permission he so evidently needs.

He smiles, apparently as relieved as I am. I grant him, "Tell all your friends about us. Come again soon . . . and bring 'the wife' inside, next time!"

He nods, smiles toothily at my invitation, waves, and exits. Through the glass I see him bound away happily in his oversized blue shorts, with hairy legs, a half-giant-boy, half-postal-puppy centaur.

Oh, *why* did I invite him to return? It'll simply be an embarrassment for him and "the little woman" when he examines our prices, even *if* he finds something here he could actually appreciate.

That's it; I've got to stop letting my awkward anxiety about politeness force me into creating later opportunities for even greater embarrassment for others, not to mention myself.

Well.

Enough waiting.

Time to open my present.

The string resists my blade only a moment, then releases with a soft sigh; the paper falls away, brown and scented like spring's moist soil, full of decay's promise. The inner wooden box is exquisitely carved, revealing the craftwork of nimble Sri Lankan fingers.

And inside the box, wrapped in felt, a device so arcane and legendary I was beginning to think no more existed.

Its wheels still turn easily, perhaps freshly oiled; its scopes' crystals and lenses seem free of fleck, scratch, or fingerprint. The valves and bellows slide and detach and fill as easily as the parchments claimed they should.

A sextant that is not a sextant, for navigation among stars.

This, perhaps one of seven or six zodiascopes remaining, will make the final phase of our project so much easier . . . and through it we'll uncover the greatest prizes in human history. . . .

"Starlight, starbright," I whisper aloud.

The book launch tonight, followed by dinner and dessert with Sophia and Sonia, and then as soon as the stars align, we shall truly begin to dine.

Le Philosophe Grotesque

IT'S SIMPLY GRAND TO BE RELEASED FROM MY STANDARD DUTIES amongst my malodorous miscreant malefactors monikered the FanBoys, in order to engage in something as elegantly stimulating as a book launch. And it is with mixed feeling that I return to my mother school, for my unrequited love for her was the cause of my fall from grace and civil sanity.

How long has it been since I set my soles upon the culti-vated walkways of this campus? A campus replete with its splendid Georgian-style Old Arts Building and its Construc-tivist celebration of that Roman marvel, concrete, in its en-gine-block-like Fine Arts Building and Law Building and, of course, my destination, the Humanities Centre.

Overlooking our magnificent river valley, the black trestle of the High Level Bridge, and the amber cathedralesque dome of the Alberta Legislature, the Humanities Centre, or HC as we call it, is a testimony to all that is noble in the liberal arts.

Ah . . . once, a long time ago, years before I was renamed "Digaestus," I walked the august halls of this noble edifice as one of its finest initiates. Until a Governor General's Award-

winning leviathan of a "professor" relentlessly antagonized
me, despised me, upbraided me, heaped obloquy upon one of
my papers after another after another until he actually—oh,
yes, it's true, I deceive you not—inscribed the oh-so-eloquent
elegy "Six pages of shit!" at the end of what was to become
my final essay.

Ever.

Were it not for the able assistance of one Mr. Alpha Cat
bringing me into Master Dulles Allen's fertile, fiendish fold,
I'd likely have "polished" myself off completely in my bachelor crypt with my drink of choice at that time, Liquid Gold
wood polish cocktailed with the mellow contents of a five-
liter jug of Baby Duck I found laying behind the downtown
Army & Navy Surplus on 97th Street.

Alpha Cat, bless his faux-Jamaican soul, delivered me to
my deliverer. Gave me purpose when my degree and con-
scriptic ambitions were neutralized by a hail of professorial
bulleted notes. Gave me a medicament infinitely more en-
thralling than my furniture-stripping cocktail, or even than
my father's best cognac.

Cream.

Of course, I recognize even in my gratitude that the Master
would never have doled out such a treasure to one as unwor-
thy as myself were it not for the utility of my unique talents.
But he is a fisher of men, and if I am one who is of such abilities as to be worthy of his barbs and hooks, then all praise is
due to the owner, general manager, and exchequer general of
the Inferno Nightclub and Lounge.

But that is neither hare nor th'air. Tonight is the launch of
what promises to be an exquisite collection of ennobling
truths regarding the quasi divinity of the creative human intellect, the comp-relig lit-crit po-mo photo-presto-texto spectacular called *Visage Grotesque: Divine I(mage)ry of the
Obscene in World Literature.*

There are more than two hundred people present this very

early evening in this two-story HC Lecture Theatre 1, and not surprisingly: the young author-and-photographer brother pair who crafted this tome were making a name (singular) for themselves even before the dean granted me permanent liberty.

Heinz Meaney, scribe, was a sought-after graduate student, as I recall flawlessly, and many wondered why he settled for the U of A's (nonetheless prestigious) English department when he was apparently fielding offers from across the United States and even fabled Britain. No one ever knew why he turned them down.

It remains, as one says among the FanBoys, an indefatigable mystery. (Well, at least, I say it.)

Were it not for my superior self-control, I dare say I'd find it excruciatingly difficult to tear my retinas away from the pristine profusion of calves in silk stockings and mammaries bedecked in shimmering gowns and in the increasingly public-sanctioned "dress bustiers." All this for a book launch. What remarkable times in which I am blessed to live!

And now the expensively coiffed and fabulously sartorial-ized are taking their seats, as the Maître-C begins his lumi-nous introduction. Much applause resounds, and then this brilliant young "rock star intellectual," who resembles no one so much as a young Robert Redford—no, a young Sting, but with spectacles—takes the podium.

He accepts the applause graciously, his smiles and winks at-tenuated for the greatest possible effect; women's eyes (and those of many men, apparently) are magnetized upon his vis-age and physique. He is utterly magnificent.

I believe I heard the Master refer to this facility with the masses once, in a wording only he could synthesize: "As smooth as a fistful of K-Y jelly."

". . . and we find that this fascination," he continues, well past the three-quarters-of-an-hour mark, and the audience showing no signs of waning, "with the bizarre, with the obscene, with the horrible, if you will, is quite natural, normal, perhaps even . . . necessary."

He smiles, leans back from his podium microphone slightly, straightens his posture, gestures grandly towards the audience. "Some of you know me not only as member of this English department, but also co-owner, with my brother and co-bookwright—"

And our eyes follow his manual vector until we see his brother, the half-negro, young Belafontine Mr. Kevlar Meaney, seated with a woman on either side of him, one Hindoo lady and one White lady—

"—of the Modeus Zokolo, the city's premiere importer of exotic goods from around the world."

Mr. Kevlar Meaney whispers something into the Caucasian lass's ear, and she visibly suppresses her laughter while playfully hitting him in his shoulder. He smiles demurely. They intoxicate my gaze, almost enough to sever my umbilicus to this lecture.

"We seek out and acquire objects from *every* people on this planet," shape Heinz's lips, his violan voice trembling delicately every so often to punctuate his intensity, "each showing the same fascination: de*cay* and death are as much a part of our collective *psychic* experience as parasitic *in*sects and *soil* are part of the *eco*system."

At the edge of the stage is a standee, a man-sized cardboard cutout, flat and shiny and artificial, nigh indistinguishable from the real Heinz Meaney, save its motionlessness.

"It's the 'obscene,' as codified in fairy stories, myth, tales of the bizarre and the fantastic and the *dread*ful, that *frees* the stable, civilized mind from its 'responsibility' to be rational. The ob*scene,* I argue, is the truest, most fundamental, most pungently fecund core of the human creative drive.

"In the Freudian senses of the term, our libido is only truly activated through Thanatos. Eros and Hades are the perfect lovers, giving our species the glory of free will, intellect, and industry.

Oppenheimer, Goethe, Picasso, Moses, Welles, Luxemburg, Huxley, Galbraith, Peckinpah, Tarantino . . . *Madonna*—" (The assembled adorers rise with the very laughter he'd predicted they would.) "—all the greatest genius is fundamentally obscene to the ordered standards of the 'respectable,' noncreative academy."

He closes his book delicately, clasps it to his heart.

"Allow my book to open your mind. There are worlds beyond of more . . . wonder . . . than you can possibly imagine."

The audience rises as one from its seats, for this darling of the Centre of Humanities, such that he might bow and receive them.

CHARACTER DATA:

Heinz Meaney

STRENGTH: Vision, endurance.

WEAKNESS: None.

CLIT POINTS: Patience and delicacy must surrender finally and briefly to aggression.

UNDERGRADUATE GPA: 9.0, U of A scale; 4.0, standard.

DOCTORAL DISSERTATION TITLE: *Won/drous (Tec)tonics: Metadimensional Analysis of Post-Jungian Attacks on Magic Realist and Speculative Literary Tropes.*

MOTHER'S NAME: Ruth Leslie Conrad-Meaney.

CHARISMA: Superlative +23.

ABANDONED CHILDHOOD PASTIMES: (1) Secret play at family acreage with small animals, (2) Firecraft and amateur pyrotechnics.

FAVOURITE JAZZ ALBUM: Miles Davis's *Bitches Brew.*

REPUTATION: Potent, tireless.

TRIVIA DEXTERITY: Horror text (Poe, Lovecraft, King) +92/film +101.

GENRE ALIGNMENT: DC suspense/adult/horror.

ENCUMBRANCE: Kevlar Meaney.

SLOGAN: "The greatest sin is the concept of sin itself."

Wolf in Sheikh's Clothing

THE SIGNING SESSION IS GOING WELL, ALTHOUGH I'LL ADMIT THE whole experience is a tad strange. Yes, I arranged the thing, and yes, I'm glad the book is out, at last. I think this is the first ever double-author signing I've ever attended, and I'm *in* it.

Nice to see Kev enjoying himself, too, sitting right next to me at the table, at my right *hand,* in fact. I'm glad he's getting his own spotlight time. Hate the thought of him dwelling in my shadow . . . I know how much some people live with resentment of successful elder siblings, and it eats away at their insides like a galloping uterine cancer.

But not Kevlar, not tonight. This is spectacular . . . all our friends, all my former professors, now colleagues . . . a damn good many of my students, and numerous grad students I've lent one form of assistance or comfort to over the years.

I think that was my first sign of unhealthy competitiveness developing between Kev and me, the women here. But he's settled somewhat recently, seems to have lost his anxiety about me, seems to have stopped trying to race me or outpace me. I'm glad. More energy for the Project.

But of course, it was working with me *on* the Project that terminated his rivalry and turned him into my finest collaborator.

Dad would've been proud.

And just down the sign line—oh, good heavens. It's Forrest.

Forrest, one of my most annoying, demanding, and sycophantic students, constantly asking me to read his creative writing, e-mailing me with random thoughts and submissions, pestering me to go to the adjacent campus Hub Mall for one or two beer at Dewey's or over to the Powerplant or RATT.

And I can't even hide in my damn office, because that's the first place he looks for me—so I end up trudging halfway across campus to the Faculty Club for serenity and asylum.

And yes, of course, I knew he'd turn up . . . and now he's in front of me, rocking on his heels, gripping his copy of *Visage Grotesque* in one flailing hand, shaking it in front of me, I suppose, in order to provide oscillating proof that he did, indeed, buy it.

And so it begins. . . .

And after twelve and a half minutes he's *still* here, having held up the line for six minutes until finally I motioned for other people to get their copies signed anyway, so he's simply taken to standing to the side, so I can't even exchange small talk with these good people!

Forrest: ". . . ultimately, Dr. Meaney, a much more visceral approach that informs *you,* or rather *your text,* than anything in either Eliade or, certainly, Campbell—"

I glance rightward, where Kev is unhampered in his chances to interact with our readership, not to mention able to absorb the patient affections of Sophia and Sonia and numerous other alluring admirers. Why, oh, why, Kev, are you not helping me out of this? What the hell kind of brother are you?

He smirks, as if reading my thoughts, or at least my

trapped eyes. I wonder if this is how beavers or wild mink or hares fair in snares? Do they simply *wel*come death, after a while? Oh, I'd simply *love* to process Forrest, but the only thing he's addicted to other than beer is the flavor of the detritus on the posteriors of his superiors.

Finally I've had enough.

Quickly, "You know, Forrest, you're still not getting a nine."

Kevlar and Sophia and Sonia burst out laughing. I hadn't intended them to hear, and Forrest looks crushed. Well, c'est la vie. He really hasn't left me much choice, and he's never been one to take subtle hints. A bank safe dropped on his head might yet be too subtle for him.

Oh, but the look on his mug . . . and with *my* luck, he'll be shining that moon-faced look of shame and approbation at me for the entirety of next year's honors seminar.

But then, I forget . . . if everything works out, I won't be here in the fall. With our most recent acquisition—hard to believe that due to all the preparations for this afternoon and tonight, I haven't even *seen* the zodiascope yet, and it's taken us four years to confirm its existence, negotiate its price, and arrange its purchase and transfer—in the very near future I'll be anywhere and everywhere I want to go.

And be everything I've ever dreamed.

Forrest slinks off. Well, good. Serves him right. At the first quiet moment, after another dozen autographs, I manage to whisper to Kevlar, "Everything ready for tonight? Have you cooked dessert?"

He mouths his response: *The cream is cooked to perfection.* My heart is actually fluttering. Even after all this time, just the thought, the anticipation of dessert stokes all my senses to full heat. I'm flushed—I'm actually flushed. This is utterly Pavlovian, I know. I can see Sophia and Sonia are ready, too—eyes shining, skin glowing, blood pulsing in visible ripples at their necks.

They look absolutely good enough to eat.

Jackal Tracks Coyote Tracks Jackal

I'M ACTUALLY *PANTING* I'M SO NERVOUS, EVEN THOUGH I REALLY
don'wanna be caught doing that, for freakin out loud. Trying
to "cold lamp" down here at Rice Howard Way, what with it
being a pedestrian outdoor mall downtown with the cobble-
stones and whatnot, I should look casual, but I'm anything
but. I'm cobble-hobbled. Lame as a baked duck. Checking my
freakin watch every few seconds.

Kot-*tam* . . . it's, like, 5:59 and eighteen seconds. Damn
Westin Hotel clock tower says the same thing.

Hope she's not one of those freakin chicks who you make a
date with, and then she shows up late and/or hungover. I mean,
that is absolutely galactically tacky and ungrateful. Like this
one time I actually planned a movie and prepared dinner so it'd
be almost ready to go exactly when we got back to my place,
and Ms. Satan's Gift to Man informs me at, like, six P.M. that
she's got a headache and nausea because her "friends" (use finger quotation marks) took her out to the club the night before
for her birthday and she was out *all night,* when she freaking
knew about our date the next day! She wanted to know if she

could come anyway. Like a Cretaceous submoron I agreed, only to have her complain all the way through the film (*Eat Drink Man Woman*) about subtitles, how she always hated Chinese food, her headache, and men. And then when we get back to my place she barely touches the dinner I spent hours preparing! I shoulda destroyed dinner with a flamethrower or a steamroller and sent her packing. But instead she just fell asleep at the table. I shoulda called the cops. But finally I just called her a cab and told her happy birthday and that it was time for her to go home.

Ah, this is freakin crazy of me. *So* I meet this Sherem superchick at ShabbadabbaDoo's, *so* she's reading *Watchmen,* *so* she claims she was noticing me, *so* what? This is all nuts. No way does she show up.

What the hell was I thinking? This's all some big brainscrew. I should just go run into the Toronto Dominion and yell, "I'm here to chew bubble gum, and kick ass—and I'm all outta bubble gum!" and start blasting away with my freakin shotgun. That'd teach everybody, show em all.

Aw, what the hell am I rambling about? Still, *They Live* was a great film. . . . Might's well watch it tonight, seeing's how I won't be goin out on any freakin *dates*—

"Brother Hamza, you're punctual! How refreshing."

I spin. She's here—and I didn't even see her coming! How the hell did she do that? No one can do that!

But she *is* here, in person, fresh as . . . as spring flowers. Glowing like sunrise.

And man! There's a slight breeze, warm, and it catches her scent, gives it to my nostrils, and it's like . . . she smells like tangerines and dates mixed together . . . or maybe with figs . . . and the scent of wet soil, earth kissed by rain.

And again with those shimmering scarves, the exotic snake braids quivering in the same bless-scented breeze.

"What's wrong, Hamza?" she says, noticing my expression. I try to cover, remembering my first reason for being shocked.

No one can sneak up on me. Not since I was a kid!

"Nobody can sneak up on me. Not since I was a kid!"

"Well," she hums and shrugs and eyebrows, "I guess that makes me an anomaly."

Finally I shake my head free of confusion, cast the surprise aside. I'm being rude. I offer my hand . . . soul-shake, of course. "Sister Sherem, it's good to see you again. And you, too, are punctual."

I get an even better look at her now—not as tough-looking as last time. More feminine. No boots, for instance, but sandals, the kind that wrap all the way up the ankle and calf. The skin on her feet and toes looks supple, chocolaty, healthy, unlike my ashy mess. I really should moisturize more often.

Anyway, I was talking about *her*. She's wearing a necklace and a couple of bracelets. . . . The stuff's made out of turquoise and amber—I wonder if she got all that when she was in Egypt?—and it really complements her skin and the river-current flow of greens and reds in her draping shirt and billowing slacks.

The whole effect is . . . well, she looks like a cross between a forest rebel leader and a medicine woman from high along the Blue Nile.

"So, where're we going?" she asks, as we start walking east in the direction of the Centennial Library.

I'd better stop staring and start making with the smart-talk and so forth. "We-e-ell . . . I thought since you're fresh back in town you might wanna walk around a bit first, and then we could have some supper."

"Sounds def," she says.

I stop dead immediately.

" 'Def?' " I laugh. I mean, I don'wanna laugh, but hell's bells. I haven't heard anyone say "def" since, like, 1990. "Man, you *have* been outta the country a long time!"

She looks slightly embarrassed. "Mmm . . . maybe I'd better give the slang a rest while I . . . reac*cli*matize."

"Maybe that would be good."

We head off to 97th Street. I figure we'll maybe go to Chinatown, walk around, grab some Chinese pastries or something, like egg tarts or red-bean buns, maybe, then head over to Kush or maybe back to 109th Street and grab some Ethiopian at Ibex.

While we're crossing 100th Street we pass a car with its windows down. The radio is replaying that totally freaking disturbing story about that ritual killing and dismemberment of that woman. But the look on Sherem's face—I can't say she blanches, but maybe that she *beiges*.

Women aren't good with that kind of stuff. I remember making the brilliant decision to take a Bosnian refugee on a date to see *Reservoir Dogs*. She as*sured* me that she didn't have a problem with watching on-screen violence, but about one and a half seconds into the "ear sequence" she was up and out of the film like freakin *Sputnik*.

That alone makes me think I shouldn't make small talk about this murder with Sherem, but based on her reaction, maybe she needs comforting. Not that I'm so crass that I would exploit a terrible thing like this for my own romantic gain. Seriously! But she looks really, really—ah, hell—*don't* believe me.

"You okay?" I ask.

She swallows, tries clearing her throat. It sounds like she's gargling mud and grasshoppers.

"Sherem?" I try again, stopping. "Are you all right?"

She faces me, her eyes all glassy, her nostrils flared. She's breathing deeply. "Ah . . . I just . . . hadn't heard the news . . . ahm. . . ." She lets out a huge sigh. "The, uh . . . details . . . are shocking."

I nod gravely. "Especially that weird crap with the donkey fur in the woman's mouth? And removing her—" She beiges again, so I keep the recitation of the details to a minimum.

"I mean, it's pretty horrible that things've gotten so bad that we *accept* killing, we even aren't fazed by dismember- ment, but it takes, well, *evisceration* to shock us. And why the hell would some sicko use donkey fur? I mean, what does that even mean? And where the hell would this nut get it?"

"I don't know," she snips, rubbing her eyes and the bridge of her nose, then glancing over her shoulder. "It's pretty sick. Can we change the subject?"

"Oh, sure, sorry." Idiot, Hamza! No more *Reservoir Dates*! "So," I attempt, "you've been away *how* long? And you *are* from E-Town, right?"

"Born and raised, yeah." She perks right up, as if the last few seconds had been wiped clean, like Nixon's tapes. It's like she never even heard about the killing. Bizarre.

"This's only the second time I've been back since 'eighty-six, which was, well, graduation. So now you know, I'm a year older than you."

What an odd thing to say. I wonder if she's still spacey from her horror of a second ago? "How'd you know how old I was?"

She pauses. "Mmm . . . good guess?"

What a strange older woman.

That's three big pluses.

"So why'd you go in the first place?" I ask her, just as a bedraggled, be-denimed, dead-locked hemp-hippie named, no lie, *Potter* walks by.

"Hey, Coyote, dude!"

"Hey, Pot-head."

Sherem watches him go past with a "What the hell was *that* about?" sneer . . . or maybe it's something else in her eyes, something grimmer. Almost violent. For just a second all the relaxedness of her demeanor disappears, and I'm reminded of the woman I saw on the tarmac last night, the one with the crazy slit-visor shades and the attack posture.

And then it's gone, and we're just walking north on 97th. Does she know I saw her switch and back again?

She doesn't seem to.

"Well, Brother," she says, "since I was a little girl, my parents took me around the world. They were both . . . very . . . they stressed *knowledge* and . . . social responsibility. When I finished high school, they encouraged me to study in a mon— uh, *academy* . . . outside Ash Shabb."

"Ash Shabb? In Upper Egypt?"

"That's right, just north of Sudan. So since I was right there, I had the chance to travel all over Alkebu-lan—"

" 'Alkebu-lan?' "

"Afrika."

"What language is that? I've never . . ."

"It's Ge'ez."

"Oh . . . so does that mean you studied in Ethiopia, too?"

"Not as such, no, although I did visit. But ancient languages were part of my studies at . . . in Ash Shabb."

"Wow."

"Yeah."

"So where else'd you go?"

"Around the Middle East, South India, Tibet . . . Vietnam . . ."

"Gee whiz, Sister, you've been everywhere. So just how far would you go . . . for one of your studies?" I hope that didn't sound like I intended it to be lascivious.

"Me? Anywhere. As far as I had to."

"So, what, are you in anthro?"

"Well, religions and ancient civilizations, actually."

"Fascinating." I sincerely cock an eyebrow, or maybe cock a sincere eyebrow. "So, you're an archaeologist?"

"Well, yeah, sorta."

"Well, sometimes . . . at the restaurant? I wash some really old dishes."

She chuckles. "I'll make sure you're on the next dig." She deadpans, "You can be our archaeo-crockeriologist." She smiles again. "So, what do you do now? Other than dishes, I mean."

I've been fighting against myself for the last minute, trying not to tighten up. I mean, shit . . . look at her. She's freakin amazing—world traveler, knows ancient languages, obviously as brilliant as HAL—and here I am . . . washing freakin pots. It's embarrassing.

But something about the *way* she asked. It's not, like, out of desperation, as in *Please don't let this guy be a complete loser,* or competition, like *Here's how I put one more little man toy in its place,* but more like just plain conversation, like she just took it for *granted* that I'd be doing something good. Something important.

Maybe I'm just reading into it too much, but that's what it feels like, to me.

So what the hell do I say?

The truth, I guess.

"Well, I do a bunch of creative projects. Me and my roommate do stuff with neighborhood kids, run summer camps outta our backyard, with, like, science and construction and art and acting and drawing and creative writing and stuff. We call it Coyote Camp." You know, while I'm saying it, it actually sounds pretty good. Hell, it *is* good.

"Was Mr. Pot-head, as you called him, was he one of your students?"

Now *I'm* the one to chuckle. "Naw," I say. "Sjust, well, me an my roommate, Yehat, we kinda made a name for ourselves what with all the things we do in the neighborhood. Folks call us the Coyote Kings."

"Really? As in *King of Kensington*?" She sings, "See them walk down the street. . . . They smile at *e-e-e-ev'ryone.* . . ."

This is *great*. I join in, of course: "Ev'ryone that they meet . . . calls them *Kings of Ed-mon-ton!*"

We both laugh. Kot-tam. This is a hell of a date.

"So that's why they call you Coyote Kings?" she says.

"Naw, not really." We laugh again.

"Why 'Coyote'?"

"Hey, Sister, I can't give away all my secrets at once, knawm sayn?" I slide into De Niro. "Otherwise I'll, like, whaddaya-call, lose my mystique an whatnot."

"I see. You said . . . creative writing? You teach kids that out of your backyard?"

"And inside the house, too. Yeah, in my spare time, I'm a writer."

"Really?" She tilts her head. "Anything I'd know?"

I chew this one a minute. That was stupid of me. I know better. You're only a writer when you get paid to write. Everything up until then is explained by the phrase "I write," like you'd say, "I cook," as opposed to, "I'm a chef." Knucklehead. Knucklehead!

Time to come clean. "To be frank, I'm kinda stalled right now. I had a manuscript, a novel, actually—even had a publisher interested—" (This is true. I'm not exaggerating.) "—as long as I made certain 'changes'—"

"And you didn't want to make em."

"Yeah. Well, not only that. See, I just . . . I had a personal . . . *situation,* you know? An I just couldn't find the . . . soul . . . to finish it."

"What was it about?"

"The novel, or the situation?"

She smiles demurely. *"Yes."*

I laugh. "Ah . . . I think I'd better save some anecdotes for dinner."

She lets it pass.

"So, anyway," she asks, "how long ago was that? That you stalled?"

It hits me like a chair over my spine. Has it really been this long? Have I really been an alderman in Loserville for this long?

I'm embarrassed. I try to chuckle it away, but I'm depressed all of a sudden.

"About," I say, "three years!"

Damn.

This isn't how I wanted it to go.

I wish she were wearing her crazy visor. Then maybe I wouldn't have to look over and see pity in her eyes. More than one way to *Reservoir* a date.

And we haven't even sat down for dinner yet.

The Perfection of Loneliness

EVERYTHING FLOWS LIKE WATER.

The four of us flow towards the doors, laughter bubbling, blood pulsing and surging, anticipation making the tiniest hairs on our skin stand erect, as if we're standing before the gates of an electrical storm.

With our condo doors closed, we slide inside, shedding jackets, shedding hesitations.

Kevlar touches the stereo remote, brings to life inside the darkness his "Night Mix." I know what we'll hear . . . haunting echoes of "Moments in Love" by Art of Noise . . . bass drones and guttural tones from Barry White with "I'm Gonna Love You Just a Little More, Baby" . . . interstellar loneliness in Jean Michel Jarre's *Oxygene*.

That's perfect, really. We're here, right now, in our own cosmos . . . here to experience the perfection of total loneliness. Just the four of us.

Everything flows like water, and Sophia and Sonia light the candles, igniting the stars . . . place candles inside the mouths and bellies of the myriad idols from two dozen centuries we've assembled from across the world . . . set cinnamon incense smoldering, conjuring up our nebulae. . . .

Kevlar gathers up the arcane water pipe as delicately as if he's picking up a sleeping child to take it to bed, brings the sloshing body towards us, its tubes swaying like the snake fetishes they were fashioned to resemble, the mouthpieces like cobra heads . . . our smoke-breathing, hydrological Hydra.

I prepare the dessert.

The tools are before me, the knives and the garlic press that is no longer a garlic press, the Haitian mutebe-mutebe bulbs, gestated specially in our own private hydroponicum.

I snip the mutebe-mutebe from the stalks, peel back the outer skin of each bulb delicately, place each one inside the crusher, squeeze the pulp into the censer.

Sophia springs forward, grasps my busy hands, caresses my palms until they are hers, kisses and licks the mutebe-mutebe juice from my skin.

Her eyes close, and beneath the lids the raised bumps above her irises flick and dart. . . . Her throat can't contain its sighs. And I've barely begun.

Kevlar takes the censer from me, places it inside the entrails of the water pipe, lights the coal beneath the pan. The flues and bellows of the pipe will whisk away the coal smoke, never letting it infect the mutebe-mutebe vapors.

Kevlar closes the body. Through the skin of colored glass we see the mists rise, conjuring our spirit, invoking our botanical magic.

By now Kevlar and the women have discarded their clothes. As they all crowd close to take a cobra head in hand, candlelight spasms and jumps from their body movements, slides through colored glass, writhes and bends and coils on walls, on rugs, on hardwood, on softskin.

We all take snake heads, kiss lips to snake lips, nostril-breathe, suck . . . smoke . . . in . . . side . . .

. . . idol eyes glow from internal candles, and incense hazes room, glazes room, fazes room . . .

. . . *everything flows like water* . . .
. . . *my brother and the women pull off my clothes* . . .

I get up, stretch every muscle,
every muscle crackling, bursting,
energizing, battery-flesh from dynamo pipe . . .
. . . *incensed air mates with air-conditioned breeze*
slides about my naked skin, and mutebe-mutebe phantoms
unfurl inside my blood, my brain, my bones,
my skin, my fingernails, my tongue,
my teeth, the roots of my hair . . .

. . . *the women put down their pipes, remain kneeling*
while Kevlar also stands, flexes, breathes . . .
. . . *the women breathe deeply, and then*
the sounds of their breathing submerge into
closed-mouth moans, rhythmic, wetly consuming . . .

. . . *the white cube melts in the decanter,*
the decanter atop the heater,
the decanter's bottom caressed by low flames . . .

. . . *soon, the* dessert . . .

. . . *light massages through blood-bodies*
of wineglasses, dives inside green bottles, remains . . .
. . . *I grasp a snake head, as does Kevlar,*
and we both suck, and the water-pipe-cooled
essences slide inside us while the pipe rumbles
its belly-deep shrlurshrlururklllll . . .

. . . *there is no more up or down or sideways,*
and inside me Niflheim ice meets

Muspellsheim fire, and I begin to melt,
to puddle, a sea forming inside me, and a being
revealed inside it, an ancient man-thing,
vaster, worldhuge, star-eating . . .
. . . fecund . . . hungry . . .

. . . the women switch places . . . but take up pipes first,
and their mouths tighten, then withdraw,
and smoke escapes their lips, trailing,
the tails of white ghost dragons . . .

. . . Kevlar pulls up Sophia, and they kiss,
and her smoke passes into him . . .
. . . fractured lights, color-burst lights,
luminous blood flows along walls,
crawls on single golden wall, ignites,
shimmers, folds in upon itself . . .

. . . the white cube
in the decanter
is nearly melted . . .

. . . we are all together now on the floor,
continuously . . . unbroken . . .
the circle of life . . .

near perfect
near ultimate
near total
intersected
. . . harmonious . . .

. . . loneliness . . .

. . . a dark hand crawls on a white back . . .
white fingernails draw blood from a dark back . . .

legs and backs arch and bodies shudder . . .
we are colony creature . . .
a great, fleshy crustacean in an ocean of smoke
and everything flows like water. . . .

The white cube is melted.

I sit upright, pour the tiny measure of cream *into the chalice,*
and we sip in turn, and then taste it on each other's lips. . . .

We need this like we need air, like we need heat, like we need
light, like we need space . . . we thirst for it, hunger for it, lust
for it . . . everything outside is pain and bitterness and ugli-
ness, but this is what gods drink, what they slay mortals for
sipping, usurping . . .

this is sound and song inside the infinite silence . . . this is
laughter so perfect and powerful it shreds the body to escape,
tears so potent they inseminate the ground . . .

. . . hardwood becomes soil beneath our legs and bellies and
chests, sprouts grass . . . earthworms worms pulse against
ainst our backs backs acks ksss . . .

flowersss rise ise ise vinezzzz embrace us space us encase us
blossoms blossom petals tendrils sliding inside us us us us us
back again soft scents flow out from nostrils . . . everything
flows flows oze oze oze zz z z . . . like-ike-ike-ike-k-k-k . . .
wa-a-a-a-a-ah-ter-r-r-r—r——r———r . . .

. . . like water . . . black water down inside the veins of the
earth slipping away into terrestrial capillaries and dripping
down from skull-cave roofs dripping, dripping, stalactite fang
to stalagmite horn . . . and the crystalline echoes . . . and the
shrill ringing and the loneliness, the darkness . . .

We are so close, so close, and soon we'll dwell here forever and dance across worlds and sleep inside the hearts of stars . . . and be born as worlds and give birth to moons and live among comets and know the Things that dwell in the deeps. . . .

Infinitely later we wake . . .

. . . and the cream is gone.

And we all hold the water pipe amongst us and press together our cooling bodies and sniff the scent of spent flesh and hold each other closer to treasure the vanishing heat and hush ourselves, and hush our sobs . . . and drink the white tears from each other's faces. . . .

Nothing flows. Everything is still, like ice.

Radiocarbon Dating

BY THE TIME WE MAKE IT TO IBEX ETHIOPIAN RESTAURANT, things are better. Fact is, they never really got bad—I just was really worried they'd nose-dived (nose-dove?) when she asked me about my writing and I was so embarrassed I'd been wasting my time.

But things've picked up. The woman is an anecdote master. Fact, only person who can tell a story better than her would have to be, well . . . well, me, I guess.

(There is a significant, if subtle, difference between arrogance and factuality.)

I signal Wasi, the manager, as we sit down that we'll have a combination plate, and I start to tell Sherem about the place. It's pretty in here in the semidarkness, with shimmering shades of gold and brown, and rainbow Mexican tablecloths that seem perfectly East Afrikan here. A mural of Blue Nile waterfalls gushes beside us, framed by plants that seem to merge into the painting, drink river mists, flourish amid the high jungle. Men sit and drink and smoke (that's pretty much the only thing I *don't* like about this place), pull apart strips of

Ethiopian *injera* bread, scoop up gravied morsels of chicken and egg and minced beef.

"Y'know, Sister Sherem," I say to her, "even though Ibex isn't actually in Kush proper, I think of it more like a border garrison or an outpost."

"Why's that, Brother Hamza?"

"Well, the Ethiopian community is fractured, sure, what with the Eritrean war and all, and people on both sides being nationalists, sympathizers, whatever, but of the three or four Ethiopian and Eritrean—"

"It gets real tiresome having to say that all the time, doesn't it? Ethiopian and Eritrean?"

"Tell me about it, but if you get it wrong when talking to someone, get ready to get blasted."

"True, but when we as a continent of peoples should be aiming at unifying, these guys are fracturing all the more. Even *inside* Ethiopia, same thing. It's depressing sometimes."

"So what'll we call em, then?"

She pauses for a moment, pressing her fingers into a cage. "How's about . . . *Abyssinians*? Historical enough, right? Or no . . . *Axumites*. That's arcane and honest."

"Two qualities I like in anyone," I say, and she smiles at that.

"So, as you were saying . . . ?"

"As I was saying," I say, "proof of this place's quality is that even with four or so Ethi—*Axumite* restaurants in town, it's still, like, half of all the cab drivers come *here*."

"Is the food that good?"

"Well, the food truly is good, yeah. But see, it's that the owners are so damn nice. The Sister who runs the joint most of the time, Rosemary—and here's the kicker—she isn't even Ethiopian. She's from Zanzibar!"

"Well, that *is* significant. *Axumites* do tend to be a pretty closed community."

"Yeah, exactly! I mean, even in music, like, everybody's music on the continent is totally different. There's no such *thing* as 'Afrikan music,' singular, any more than there's 'European music,' singular, or 'Asian music,' singular—"

"I know, that drives me crazy, too! But go on."

"Right, so the Ethiopians, even given that, their music is com*plete*ly different from *everybody* else's, except maybe some women's music from Mali, which is half a continent away—go figure. They got their own churches, they got Coptic Christianity, which is the oldest type, pretty much, they can always speak Amharic or Tigrean or Oromo or any number of other languages that *only* they speak, so . . . what I'm saying is that these guys are some closed-off Brothers, basically."

"So the fact that half the Abyssinians locally come to this place regularly and eat the food of a Tanzanian, well . . . is that because she's 'neutral'? Neither Ethiopian nor Eritrean, and doesn't belong to any of the smaller nationalities inside?"

"That's a good theory. I think that that's part of it, maybe. Or like you said before, that she's just that good a cook, or maybe she's just that wonderful a Sister. Makes you feel at home in, like, two seconds of coming in the place." I stop for a second, feeling like recent events are making me a liar. "I don't think she's working tonight."

"I see."

"An her husband, Derege, who co-owns the place, he's a prince. Usedta feed me for free—no lie—when I was broke. See these murals?"

She looks around, fairly neutrally. "Yes?"

"Well, I painted mosta these."

Her face suddenly glows. "Really? You did?" She examines them more closely now. I don't think she's being phony or anything. . . . I think she really just didn't notice the paintings until I said something. I mean, it's not like they're blending into the wall—they actually *are* the wall. "They're beautiful! I especially love this painting of the Nile falls!"

"Well, thanks, but I didn't do that one."

She laughs, and then I laugh, too, to let her off the hook. "Sorry for my foot in mouth."

"Don'worry about it."

"But I really do like those over there, of the little kids playing with the animals—you *did* do those, right?"

"Yep."

"Well *they're* beautiful, too."

"Thanks. So, anyway, on accounta me doing these, and it's not like he didn't pay me, they were a commission when he opened the place, like, three years ago. And he'll still buy my dinner if I come in broke or with a long face. These people, I swear, they're made out of solid joy."

Just then Wasi, the manager, drops off our combination plate: stewed kale, boiled egg in gravy, gravied chicken called *doro wat,* buttered potato and carrot and broccoli, all served on top of a bedding of *injera* pancake bread, with more bubbled, white, flat, and steaming *injera* served on a side plate.

"Enjoy, Br-r-r-aather Hamza," says Wasi, before departing.

I catch the look on Sherem's face.

She's clearly angry.

A Glimpse into Wet, Dark Jewels

DAMNIT—

"I hope you don't mind, Sister," I stammer, "but I ordered—I don't mean to be presumptuous—I just . . . you're fresh back in town, and I thought—"

The anger passes from her face, first from the slanted eyebrows, then from the pinched corners of her mouth, then from the iron rod of her spine.

At last she summons a small smile.

"I . . . I'm sorry, Brother. It's not . . . it's *not* presumptuous. It's . . . it's charming. I'm not used to . . . to *people* doing little niceties like that. Like when you opened the door, before . . . I mean, you read about that, see it in films, but . . . it's not like that in Ash Shabb."

"What was it like there, Sherem?" I'm so grateful that she's not angry at me, so relieved, and as happy there's somewhere else for the conversation to go.

But she's not answering.

"Sister?"

She's looking down at the food. Biting her upper lip.

Finally, "It was hard." She breathes in, out. "And lonely."

"I don'mean to pry. . . . I'm sorry—if you don'wanna talk about it—"

She looks up at me sharply, and I'm afraid I made her angry again. Then I see it isn't anger at all. It's confusion, like I said something in another language. And then, just for a moment, like a phantom prowling at the edge of dusk, like a rabbit diving inside its hutch, I see—I *think* I see—moistened eyes, dark-glistening, like huge, black jewels.

And then she blinks, and it's gone.

"No, Hamza . . ."

Oh, man. I mean, I love the "Brother/Sister" stuff. . . . It's very elegant, very pro-Black and all . . . but just to hear her say my name alone. It seems so . . . so *in*timate from this mysterious, guarded, cryptic woman.

". . . no," she continues, "it's just that . . . well, I'm sure to you this sounds nuts, but even what you just said . . ."

"What'd I just say?"

She looks down again, focuses on the food.

"Just saying that I don't have to speak about it if I don't want to. I mean, asking me how I felt or saying I don't have to talk . . . it's just . . . at the academy, what *I* wanted or didn't want was never an issue. *Never.* So to have you, who I just met, say that to me, well, it's like . . ."

She sighs.

"Thank you."

She looks up at me, eyes glistening again, and that soft smile, like summer rain while the sun shines on.

I'm flushed. *Man.*

"Don'mention it."

I gesture towards the food, as in, *Dig in.*

"Might we offer thanks, first?" she asks.

I'm a tad embarrassed. What would my dad say? I've fallen so far.

But this's been a tough four years. Nothing's been the same in a long time. So much has fallen away and never grown

back . . . a long, unending fall. "Forever Autumn," isn't that
the song, from *Wayne's Musical Version of "The War of the
Worlds"*? Yeah. "Forever Autumn." Come to think of it, that
is something Dad'd understand.

But maybe autumn doesn't have to be forever.

"Of course, Sister."

We bow our heads. And I hear her whisper something that
sounds like

> *Yi, netjerunebunu hetba*
> *Utchãupet, ta emmaãkhait*
> *Dãdãu katjefa.*
> *Duanu, duarã, duakheperi.*
> *Duasebai yinepu.*

Interesting. Never heard that one before. We raise our
heads. "Thank you," I say. "What language was that?"

"Ren-Kem," she says. "Another ancient language I studied.
Middle Egyptian, from the twelfth dynasty."

This woman is amazing. We dig in. I'm pleased to see she
has an appetite and knows how to use it. Wasi drops off a pot
of tea. . . . I smell cloves and cinnamon.

"You know, this is a delight."

"How's that?" she says, tearing off *injera* and picking up
some *tibs,* popping it into her mouth without getting so much
as a droplet of sauce on her fingers.

"Well, most women—most people—I take here or serve
'desert food' to don't know how to eat it. They get all . . .
un*mut*ual—"

"—and eat with a knife and fork off their own little anal
plates."

I smile and nod, meeting her smile and nod.

"I once saw a guy"—she smiles and sneers at the same time,
which is surprisingly sexy—"serve himself *injera* like it was
dumplings."

"No!"

"Ate it up off his fork, didn't even put any food on it. I almost smacked him one just on principle."

I burst out laughing. She likes that, I can tell.

"You're . . . and I hope you recognize this for the compliment it is, you're a tough broad, d'you know that?"

She nods again, still smiling, and the smile is all for me. "Yeah. Thanks."

Then she pours me tea. Kot-tam. I can't remember the last time a woman poured me a cup of tea. So I tear off *injera,* pull together some *doro wat,* and gesture that I'd like to feed her.

"Oh, Hamza." She seems suddenly mortified. "I couldn't—"

"Come on, Sister, live a little. *Axumites* do this all the time. It's a sign of—" I catch myself—I was about to say *affection,* but I don't want to show *all* of my cards (like you haven't already, freak, is that what you're thinking?) "—compassion." I breathe in. "I mean, *comradeship.*"

She smiles strangely, as if she's trying to figure out what species I am. Then she tilts her jaw, and her scarves slide away, again revealing that luscious neck of hers, and that ominous lizard-tail scar on her neck that writhes with her pulse.

I delicately place the food into her mouth. She chews and—and then this "tough broad" actually giggles. *Giggles.* Her. And she looks embarrassed and happy and embarrassed all over again. This is a far cry from where she was before when we overheard that stuff about that murder. She seems like she's over it now. Over it with a giggle and a smile that could turn concrete to putty and putty to concrete.

Man, is she gorgeous. And intelligent, cultured, but it's like she's barely dated or something. Maybe her parents were real control freaks, or that academy or whatever didn't allow it, which wouldn't be so unusual over there.

A lotta my Muslim friends never dated, unless it was secretly. Dad didn't mind if I did, and I did, a little, but maybe that was just cuz he didn't want me to end up like him.

I really like this woman.

"So, anyway," I say, "I saw you at the comic store. You're into comics. What other genre stuff? Movies? Role-playing games?"

"Oh, RPGs? Yeah. I was into everything my brothers were into. But when I was at Ash Shabb it was murder, because I almost never saw genre stuff, not for years at a time."

"So just how behind are you?"

"Well, I don't know exactly. After 1986 I've only seen about a half dozen major things." She looks into the distance, as if peering through the mists of time. "I hear Spielberg made some sort of dinosaur movie?"

"Oh, man!" I yell. "*Tell* me you have a dog named Toto."

"And there's some sort of space show called *Babylon* something?"

"Hell, yes, *Babylon 5*! You've never seen it? Wow, are you in for a delight. It's amazing . . . wars and legends and myth and religion and politics, really strong women characters—"

"All I know is it was very popular in Iraq, but when I was there I never saw a TV."

"You were in Iraq?"

"Yes, I go there from time to time, mostly dealing with the ancient ruins. Since the war and the embargo they've barely been able to attend to anything historical, so if any foreign experts are willing to work for free or barter—"

"Whoah," I stop. "You're . . . you're an *expert*? I mean, I knew you were studying—"

She shakes her head, tries to wave it away. I can tell she really regrets having said anything. "No, bad choice of words. I just mean anyone who can help, that's all. So this *Babylon 5* is good?"

I let her get away with changing the subject.

"Oh yeah. I'll lend you some tapes. It's the best thing since classic *Trek*."

She pours me more tea. In fact, she drains the pot. That's nice of her. But I reach across and offer for her to drink. She looks embarrassed again. But she looks grateful, too. And she drinks.

"So you and your roommate live around here?"

"Yeah, about a klick north of here, in Kush."

"How'd you two meet?"

"Met Yehat back in high school. Loopier than a snake in a garden hose, but one of the smartest and funniest guys I've ever known. And one of the craziest."

"He always been like that?"

"Pretty much. Crazy, definitely. I remember one time in grade twelve, we were driving around in Ye's dad's boat, a Delta 88 Olds. We were never your typical B-boys. . . . Half the time the music on the deck was Run-DMC or Eric B. and Rakim; the other half it was John Williams, Jerry Goldsmith, or James Horner.

"Anyway, one night we're cruising when for whatever reason some cop stops us. Yehat pulls over, and the cop comes up to the window. He's got one of those little cop mustaches, you know? Real fascist type.

"And he says, 'You boys got some identification?' Now, yeah, I know we were seventeen, but I still don'like being called *boy*, you knawm sayn?

"So Ye says to the cop, no lie, 'You don't need to see our identification.' The cop stops for a second, and Ye says to him again, but this time kinda waving his fingers like a spell, 'These aren't the droids you're looking for.' "

She laughs. "Well, did it work?"

"Naw, he rousted us."

We both laugh. Then she says, "Maybe he should've said, 'I have never seen a more wretched hive of scum and villainy.' "

Aw, damn and a half—the woman is all this *and* she can quote *A New Hope* at will?

And suddenly, like a screeching of birds, there's a man making some ungodly sound at the window by dragging his fingers on the glass. The look on his face, it's like he's a revenant from the crypt or something.

I thumb-point. "Well speak of the Deville."

She seems stunned and amused. "*This* is your roommate? Yehat?"

I wave him in. After he comes in I Coyote-shake with him, then introduce him. "Hey, Coyote! Let me introduce you! Yehat Bartholomew Gerbles, this is Sherem, Sheremnefer . . . uh . . . ?"

"Just *Sheremnefer.*"

"Like Madonna?" snickers Ye.

She pauses. "Who?"

No *way*—she *said* she was outta the country a long time, but—

And then her deadpan slides into a simple, small, and subtle smirk, the edges of her mouth turning up and quivering ever so minutely. She breathes in deeply, chest inflating, lungs expanding, and a fresh flood of blood to her face does something to her cheeks and lips on a subliminal level . . . just enough to cause me to have some redirected blood flow of my own.

Aint many people can deadpan the deadpan master.

I likes. I likes.

Sherem and Ye shake hands. She asks, "So what's with this 'Coyote' business, anyway?"

Ye and me grin at each other, as if we spend our lives setting up new people to tell this tale to. Or at least, *a* tale.

"You wanna tell er?" I ask.

Ye: "It's your story."

Sherem, looking at me: "Well, Coyote?"

"Remember, it's not just 'Coyote.' We're the Coyote *Kings.*"

"I see."

"And it goes a little something like this. . . ."

Night Creatures

THE MASTER HAS GIVEN US OUR SACRAMENT AND CHARGED US with our usefulness, and the prize which we seek for his name's sake will soon be in his massive engine block hands.

And so it is that we, the fabulous, fantastic FanBoys, scouring the grey and ebon asphalt of our capital, approach that elite street boutique for the young and wealthy, the Yuppies and their pseudoliberal enlightenment, their fetishism for the exotic, the foreign, the primitive, the curios of the dark world and the crafty fingers of the noble savage and the benighted non-Western psyche.

We descend, then, this Friday night to the bazaar of the bizarre, as humanoid condors, as vultures of the night who strip and rend and drink as we would, feasting upon the fallen and harvesting flesh already dead and without remorse. What is it, really, to steal from thieves? What is it to take what has already been taken, but a righting of the cosmic balance or a continuation of the flow of matter and energy within a dynamic kleptecology?

We rattle inside our dark-windowed iron vessel, our
FanVan ark which has taken more than two of every kind, my
comrades and me, the Knights of the Surround Sound Fable:
Sir Alpha Cat the Compassionate, Sir Zenko the Pristine, Sir
Frosty the Foul, the Beast of Burden the Mugatu, and I, the
Deacon of Demarcation, the Duke of Detection, the Dark
Knight of Discovery . . . Digaestus Caesar.

For ten minutes there has been no talk amongst us. We are
focused, calibrated, determined.

And then, from inside the throat of Mr. Zenko: "Basically,
boys, I think we need a work song," he hums cheerfully. He is
splendid at all times in his pleats and monograms, his shined
shoes and custom cuff links. "Yes, I think we do. Other people
in other professions've always had work songs, and basically I
think it's time we did. And dudes, I've decided what it'll be."

Such a suggestion is without precedent among us. We are,
figuratively, all ears.

And he intones dramatically:

> *O, cosmonaut, astronaut,*
> *Argonaut, have you got*
> *Ear for the epic*
> *Of Rocket Robin Hood. . . .*

> *His actions will cheer you*
> *Endear you and sear you*
> *With glorious stories*
> *O' the plight of the good*

And without objection or amendment, as one we join him:

> *So now to the most distant reaches we race*
> *With Robin the hero of all outer space. . . .*

> *Merry-Men-brothers, comrades, soldiers,*
> *Each adventure makes us the bolder*

Fighting oppressors and the villains of the stars
Past icy Pluto . . . and back to Mars!

Let the clarion call raise your heart
To the glorious battle as it starts
We'll ever triumph in the skies with
Rocke-e-e-et . . .
RA-A-A-AH, BI-I-I-I-IN, HOO-OO-OO-OOD!"

And now, at the crescendo of our hymn, through the orders of our master, and by the power of the ancient one who freed himself from the primordial Ice, who drank the sacred cream of Audhumla, and whose body was the sacrifice and sacrament of all the worlds, who knew the original Dawn and whose *spiritus mundi* we will employ to become that which destiny holds for us . . .

We, the princes of plunder, are here to wait until all is quiet and still, within striking range of the castle of the new age, the Modeus Zokolo, from which we will procure the dark divining rod—or infernal iris—to become the guardians of all the lost and unnameable Grails.

The Secret Origin of the Coyotes

"My mum, see? She was driving through the desert," I tell Sherem and Ye. "*The* desert. SAHARA. And she's *pregnant*, right? She's supposed to meet my dad back in Abu Hamed, way up the Nile past the fourth cataract.

"The jeep? *Breaks down*. Right out in the middle of eight trillion square kilometers of sand. My mum, she's smart, see? Doesn't lose her head. She's packing a gun in case of bandits, got her water supply, radio. But while she's waiting for the rescue team, suddenly *I* start ringing the alarm. I'm saying, 'It's birthering time!' right there on the open bled.

"So, it's night. She's trying to deliver me, alone, by moonlight.

"Suddenly from outta nowheres she starts hearing howling. Wild dogs, who knows? She's trying to birth a baby and handle a gun at the same time . . . not easy, she told me.

"Well, finally I arrive—beautiful, of course. But the howling's getting closer—and Mum still hasn't even cut the umbilical! Now, Mum doesn't want any wild dogs eating her and her baby, but she's weak, and she got no scissors, see, cuz it's the desert, see? So how's she supposed to run or move when she's got an umbilical cord still, uh, you know . . . connected to the, to her, uh . . ."

Ye: "Apparatus?"

Me: "—apparatus, exactly. I'm mean, it's tied off, but it aint cut yet. So the next thing you know, outta the darkness, Mum's surrounded by *a hundred floating orange eyes*. Now my mum can add. She knows ten bullets don't down fifty coyotes.

"So it's looking freakin grim. A legion of coyotes in the moonlight. One coyote, *huge*, size of a wolf, pads up, slowly, got paws the size of hams, mouth like a row of razors, walks over, leans in, and SNIFFS right near my newborn body.

"My mum's mesmerized with terror, terrorized with Mesmer, holding the gun—forty-nine coyotes and HER, all of em, *waiting* to see what's gonna happen."

I capture Sherem's eyes, magnetizing her with my anecdotal powers. We're in the trench, near the exhaust port. *I have her now.*

I keep waiting, pausing, until at last—

". . . *yes?*" she bursts.

"The coyote leans in," I punch it, "bares his teeth, and NIBBLES the umbilical cord through. Neat as a surgeon. And backs off. And as one, all the coyotes lift their heads to the moon and howl, like a voice outta the Ark of the Covenant."

I lean back, sip my water, put the glass down.

"And right there, Mum knew—a new king had been born. Me. The King of the Coyotes."

Sherem's staring at me. I know I'm a good storyteller, but this . . . I don'know. She seems—I mean, obviously I didn't expect her to be*lieve* this story *as such,* but it's not that. It's not the story, I don't think, but something in the story, or about the story . . . ? I'm not sure. It's like I was typing randomly and accidently got most or all of a password into a web page I didn't even know was there.

Finally she speaks. "You don't ever, uh," she says, mock delicately, "suffer from blackouts, maybe, or have trouble remembering your name?"

I look back with a mock-serious, cocked eyebrow. "Hey . . . don't sass the fates."

She thumb-points to Yehat.

"So why's *he* a Coyote King?"

"We-e-e-ell . . . he pays half the bills, so I figured what the hell."

She smiles. "So why're you *really* called the Coyote Kings?"

"Cuz we got style, baby! Style!"

"I used to order a lot of stuff from Acme," says Ye, "and Hamburg usedta throw himself offa buttes."

She laughs at that one, and Ye trampolines his eyebrows in my direction. Then he glances out the window, suddenly startled.

Sherem picks up on this. "What?"

"Ah, nothing," breezes Ye.

Sherem: "No, what?"

"It's nothing . . . either, one, a false alarm or, two, evidence of a secret cloning program gone horribly awry."

"Meaning *what,* exactly?" she asks.

"I thought I saw one of my disgruntled ex-girlfriends."

She pauses, forms those perfect lips of hers into a wry twist, saying, "Just how many disgruntled ex-girlfriends do you *have*?"

Ye, without skipping a beat: "Standard number."

And suddenly Sherem sits stiffly upright, rakes up her sleeve as if she's felt a scorpion there.

"Good heavens," she squeals, glancing watchward, "it's nine o'clock!"

"What's wrong?"

"I'm still set by desert sunsets! We're so far north and it's still so light out I forgot how late it was!"

I'm about to tell her I'll walk her wherever she's going, but before I can even get a sentence fluffed and folded, she says, "Today was wonderful, Hamza—thank you—Yehat, nice meeting you—I've gotta go!"

And she bolts out the door, leaving me and Ye in stunned silence.

CHARACTER DATA:

The Mugatu

REAL NAME: Robert "Bobby" B. Bee.

STRENGTH: Rib breaking +11/skull mushing +8.

WEAKNESS: Church of Jesus Christ of Latter-Day Saints commercials.

WIT POINTS: 0.3.

CULINARY, INVENT/PRODUCE: High.

WISDOM: Non-.

MUST SHAVE: Hourly.

SCENT: Swamp hog.

WEAPONS: Ridged staff, all kitchen utensils; see *Scent.*

SPEAKS: Sort of.

TRIVIA DEXTERITY: Legion of Substitute Heroes +2, *Jonah Hex* +1, *Family Circle* +8.

GENRE ALIGNMENT: *Battlestar Galactica, Captain Power, ST: Voyager.*

IMPAIRMENT: All of the other FanBoys used to laugh and call him names.

SLOGAN: "Lee me *lone.*"

The FanBoys in
The Mugatu's Big Score

SO WERE INSIED THE PLACE. THE MODAYUSS ZOKLEO. ITS DARK. And now were insied cause mr alin toled us to get the things. Its fun cause we get to brake stuff. Liek we broak the locks but we dint set of no alarm cause we Used these gajits. Liek Diejestuss holded up this thing like a remoat and he pointed it and the Camra lite (the littel red lite that blinks) went of. And smoke comes Out. Of the camra.

So were looking around with our flashlites an its dark. And we haf to hurry cause there mite be alarms we dont no about.

Its my job to covere the front window with bags. You no, garbij bags so nobody dont see what were doin. So I do that. And Zengco helps me for a minit. There all my friends. zengco and Alfacat and Diejastis. And even frossy. But Somtiems he gets mad. But there fun and good.

Were done the windoe so I gard the back dor were we came in. And the gys look For the prize (im a poet and I dont even it).

An they brake sum stuff espshly frossey. an dijassdus clozs his eyes an looks around till he points at a place. an the gys nock over abuncha stuff until the finded a Panil in the wall an theyres a safe behind the panil. An they dril into the safe. With a drile. Untill it opens. (the safe).

Lafa cat takes out the thing were sposed to get mr. Alin. it looks like a vumaster thing what you click when your a kid. Cuase you can look into it. an its gots things that hang of it. like litel toobs. But its dark so I cant see very god. But hes hapy.

But there all loking around cause i think mr alan sed to get somthing els but I dont rimambar. I wonder what it is. and there all yeling at dijettis but he dont no were it is an he loks liek hes gone cry. so I say leve him lone. an they yel at me but thats okay cause there my fiends. but they dont find it an alpa Kat seys we got to go or else batman or battyman I think he means cops wil come.

Everone get thair stuff pact up to goe. And Alaf cat Seys 'hurry'. but i wont to lok around because i never bin here before. so they all yell at me. But I ask them can I stay. and they Yell at me no. And I ask why not. and they say bad words.

But I was looking at a stufft Aminal a tyger an it lokt just like reel. Cause a the eys. And I wannid to keep him. an ditejstus seys tiger tiger tiger bruning brite in the fourest of the nite what a mordel handaryc could fraythic fcar fur simmer cheese. I think Thats what he sed but hes tuf to understnad cause of his studder.

And frosee seys go im worning yoo. but I stil dont wannu. So frossy brakes opan the cash rejisder an shuvs the muny in his Pocits. but there isnte mutch in thair so he swares at me and calls me a dumas moth—(i cant sey the rest) an trise to throe the rajestar at me but its to hevvy so he axidetly drops it on his fote. an its not nice but everyone laffs an even I laf.

than the alorm goze of an he runs out an go an al of them go. And when i hear The van start i start to cri cause im afrade there gon to Leve me. but Aphla cat comes Back an seys keep the tiger buddy. less go. so i goe with him.

hes my Frend

Glass Slippers or the Glass Slip?

*Dementia Five is all illusion! It exists only
in our brains! If we close our minds
and eyes to you, we'll be free!*
—ROCKET ROBIN HOOD

HAMZA, THAT JIMP, RUNS OUT AFTER "MISS TEERIO" INTO THE street. I'm looking at him catch up to her through the window. Pathetic. You know, this is so wrong for at least four reasons.

1. You don't literally *run after* women if you have any hope of them ever respecting you.
2. This woman is obviously a Class-10 Screwball, based on tonight's quick exit and the previous parking lot "How dare you defend me?" incident as described to me by Hamza, not to mention that she must be hiding something or some *things* of a highly disturbing nature to be so flighty.

3. "Wonder" Woman has got an attitude bordering on psychological acromegaly. "Meaning *what* exactly?" "How many disgruntled ex-girlfriends *do you have*?" At first I thought I maybe didn't like her tone or the intermingling of her eyebrows. Then I became *sure* I didn't like her tone or her eyebrow minglification. And finally,

4. Hamza is going to destroy himself once again, like he always does, and I'm going to have to pick up the pieces while Wander Woman zips off back to Paradise Island in her invisible Cadillac or whatever.

I'm drinking Ethiopian coffee—very aromatic, pretty strong stuff, like a firm handshake or a good joke—when Captain Goofus comes back in.

"Well?" I ask.

"Way to show up on my date, Ye."

"Way to invite me inside, Ham."

"Oh, so it's *my* fault?"

"So it's *mine*?"

Silence.

Me: "So what'd she say?"

Hamza looks stunned, as if she's hit him between the eyes with the kind of hammer used to stun cows in abattoirs. Did I mention he's *smiling*? What the hell is wrong with this guy?

"Yeah, well, she said . . . I didn'really get what she said, but she had to go and she didn'realize how late it was." He shrugs as if it's no big deal.

"Yeah, huhn."

"Okay, okay . . . I know what it looks like, but we had a great date. We're going out again tomorrow morning!"

"Oh, joy. So this way, she can disappear even *earlier* in the day. One day you'll be eating breakfast and look up and there'll just be this woman-shaped puff of smoke where she was sitting. And you'll be left holding the bill, just like you are tonight."

His face snaps to at that. I'm not saying Hamza's cheap, but if the only thing standing between our solar system and a fleet of intergalactic enslavers was Hamza's wallet crunched inside his fist, we'd all be drilling methane wells on Pluto right now. So if there's one way to get Captain Jimp T. Kirk to wise up, it's to get him to realize this chick is stiffing him, rather than the other way around.

"But Ye," he says, lifting up her plate. He slides out a wad of two-dollar bills, pink and crumply.

How the hell? I wonder. "How the hell? I didn't see her even—"

"Musta did it when we weren't looking."

We hand over the cash at the till, say goodnight to the owners. There was enough there to pay for Hamza, too, plus tax and tip. Okay, so she's not ripping him off. But I still don't like it. Hamza's into a whole bunch of romantic tah-tah, especially when it comes to women.

By "romantic" I don't necessarily mean lovey-dovey romantic, I mean sweeping-vistas-and-momentous-speeches-and-great-dreams kind of romantic. He thinks people don't see that in him, but I remember him from before he crashed. He's no cynic. He wants to believe again, believe in a woman, believe in him*self*. He craves it like a junkie fiending for crack.

I know Hamza—he thinks that the kind of crap this chick pulls is "exotically enigmatic" or "engagingly mysterious," rather than seeing it for what it is. Manipulative. And disturbing. He's so screwed up he probably thinks that he can get her to "open up," that he can "heal" her, that he can "save" her from whatever her secret is. *Whatever* the hell she's hiding, I can guarantee you two things:

1. It aint good.
2. When he finds out what it is, he's going to be hurt. And bad.

On the way home, walking towards the Rat Hole (what Hamza's dad, Dr. Senesert, calls the Belly of the Whale), I ask Hamza's blissfully moronized face, "So what's with the disappearing act, for real this time?"

"I told you, I don't really know. Look, she's just back in town. Maybe she's got family concerns or something."

"But why wouldn't she just *tell* you that if that's all it is?"

"I don't know, Ye. I'm not a detective. Honestly, it's kind of intriguing . . . sort of, uh, mys*terious*—"

See? "That's bullshit. Chick is weird."

"There's only two types of people in the world, Ye, weird and boring. You and me made our choice a long time ago. Sides, everyone has a right to some privacy—"

"No, they don't—"

"You can't just ask someone you just met everything straight-out like a police interrogation or something—"

"Yes, you *can*—"

"People have *rights*—"

"No, they *don't,* not if they're all screwy and weird and secretive, Hamza. And remember, pal—" And I stop walking so he can see I'm serious, while his shields are still down and I'm locking on with photon torpedoes. "And I don't say this to, like, make you feel bad or disrespect you or be insensitive or anything, but come on! I was there, Ham. With you. When you burned down the last time. Secrecy is exactly why you've been enslaved to that kot-tam *Box* for four years!"

I look at his face to see just how much damage I've done.

Direct hits. Engines down, and I think I've crippled his bridge. His eyes are distress signals . . . fading . . . fading. . . .

But I've got no choice. I have to continue.

"That's why you freakin imploded last time, Hamza—secrets!"

His gaze drops. And he's completely silent. The man can talk nonstop, can blab on about film and literary criticism and international conspiracy theories in his sleep . . . so you know that when *he* shuts up in front of you, either he's furious or his vocal cords have snapped like overloaded elevator cables.

Finally he repairs his impulse engines and starts heading back to base. Silent running.

I hate seeing this guy hurt, but what the hell? Am I supposed to sit back and watch him inevitably self-destruct, *again*?

Eventually I get sick of feeling guilty for water-hosing his parade and so I start asking him about her, getting him to tell me about their "date," talking about how pretty she is (I don't think she's so great), trying to cajole him, pretending that maybe I don't cosmically disapprove.

At this he perks way up, and soon he's going on, blah-blah-blah-yakety-yak, about how she can quote *2001* and *Star Wars* and knows ancient languages and has traveled to blah-blah-blah and she's so-o-o pretty. And so I smile and make nice. I feel like puking, but it'd ruin my cape.

At home we talk some more over a couple of plates of nachos and a few tapes of *Battle of the Planets* (the English version with Casey Kasem voicing Mark, and the abominable 7-Zark-7 voiced by Alan Dinehart [not the original Japanese *Gatchaman* with all the death and sex that is appropriate for anime]). I intentionally select the one where Mark falls in love with the woman who turns out to be a Spectra robot sent to destroy him, but this jimp shoveling corn chips down his chute couldn't detect a hint if you gave him an electron microscope.

Eventually he falls asleep on the couch while I stay up and rewatch the *Six Million Dollar Man* multiparter where Steve Austin goes looking for—get this—the *Sasquatch*, who turns out to be—wait for it—a *robot,* from . . . you guessed it . . . *space*. Tonight's theme apparently is "surprise-bots."

I check up on that moron after he eventually shambles off to bed.

And when I check the Box, amazement of amazements, it hasn't been touched! Has Ham-el finally lost his weakness to the kryptonite inside?

I can only hope so.

My question is, at what cost? His powers? His sanity? Or has he just switched to a new form of radioactivity?

I don't look forward to having to delay finishing the R-Mer because I have to build a cryo-tank for that macrojimp to survive in until I can find a cure. Assuming one is findable.

Hm . . . that's a laugh.

Cry-o.

And So the Poor Jackal Had None

AN OLD, OLD STORY, YES, AND JUST AS BITTER IN MODERNITY AS in ancient times. A grave crime . . . a grave robbing.

Has it been by hours that I've missed my target, or perhaps merely minutes? Have I in personal myopia and juvenile fixation destroyed the impossible blessing—the intersection of a natural disaster with a one-in-a-million contingency actually bearing fruit?

That I should have come this far, halfway round this vast, forbidding stone, tracking a device that has danced from halfway round the direction . . . only to have it end like *this*. . . .

All about me, wreckage, rubble, the vile and violent achievement of vandal-thieves. Leaving me here standing in darkness, holding shadows, clutching half-remembered dreams.

And behold, here, in this self-styled Zokolo smashed and torn open for its greatest treasure, I am alone.

And the prize I sought, stolen before I could steal it, stolen perhaps by fools devoid of faintest concept of their spoils, stolen perhaps by drones whose masters' vicious cravings can be satiated only by the fate we are sworn to deny.

Nineteen ecstatic lenses born in the Hidden Forge. Eighteen of them stolen, traded, melted down, shattered, dead.

And the single celestial sibling to survive . . . for it to slouch forth here . . . only to evade my grasp by *hours*—due to my own corrupt and selfish—

Could the fire monks who made you, lens, ever have dreamed what fates their sooted hands and moon-raged minds would bequeath to us? Could those Angkor exiles working in their lost refuge have known six hundred years ago that six thousand or *sixty* thousand years of dreams and nightmares could be made true by the ones who looked through you?

But now . . .

The trail is cold, indeed, cold even like the flesh of victims abandoned to the river, cold even like the blood of crocodiles.

There can no longer be any doubt. . . . The harbinger sent to show me the path to this place, she who never appeared and left me only a scrap of paper, the Hobinarit Interceptor assigned to meet me, has been slaughtered. And the horrible means of that crime is a warning to me and my Clan and any others who know the encryption of crypts . . . that we are being hunted.

But how many hunt us? And will my comrades overcome the hunters or they, us?

And beyond the threat to me from this unknown running-dagger, there is the more important threat to our imperative. Without possession of the lens I sought here, my *sekht-en-cha* Hamza Senesert will never be able to find the answer to the yearnings of all our lives and deaths . . . the answer that dwells inside the Jar.

But what if, with his ability, he could be quickly trained? But no one could ever learn so much, so soon. . . .

Unless . . .

Unless he were . . . altered.

There is only one way of which I know that he could in days accomplish what it would take decades to learn—the application of the ambrosia of misery, the ichor of our enemies' veins . . . the pustulence that even now enslaves and destroys hundreds of thousands, yes, perhaps millions.

And at the dosage of such a damnable medicament that our search would require, his heart, in fact, his *brain*—

Yet, if we do not . . . if *I* do not . . .

It is decided.

Better that one man only, perhaps, should die.

The Gate has been opened, and the cravers of blood are soon to storm the sanctified chamber. Should they achieve the Jar before we can . . . there will be murder and madness of a magnitude the world has never seen.

Render unto Seizure

That silly man, and his silly cookies.
—DETECTIVE TIM BAYLISS

IT IS A SILENCE AKIN TO THAT OF A MAUSOLEUM IN WHICH WE drive back to our headquarters, our Bat Cave, our Mount Palomar–style observatory owned by Professor Hugo O'Gogo. The invincible Inferno Nightclub. We return in terrified stillness because we bear only one-half of our expected booty. And none of us has any idea how we will explain.

But I suspect that my viperlike henchmen hatchmates will place all blame on me.

Damn their eyes.

We pull into the service entrance driveway, debark, unpack our precious treasure, prepare to offer it in hopes that our lord and master may have mercy on our soles.

That is not a misprint; Casper the Fiendly Goth and Marylin Frankenstein, two extremely former members of our unique organization, felt Mr. Allen's righteous fury in sundry, ghastly manners that rendered walking an impossibility. Of course, walking, like most everything else, was an academic issue after that night.

Poor Marylin; while I have never had the slightest comprehension of the allure of transvestism, I was nevertheless moved to compassionate shudders by the sight of his mascara streaming down his cheeks, his eyes bulging in agony and terror, when Mr. Allen . . . when he made us . . .

Excuse me.

I know that we are all expendable, temporary . . . that as the Master assembles his *archives macabres* of the most fabulous arcane treasures, substances, and devices, we are mere *canon* fodder, if you will.

Yet of course, in any tragedy, all endings come too soon for the protagonist. Unless, perhaps, as cathartic release, the ecstatic departure from the final torturous seconds of life.

We are inside, filing into Mr. Allen's office. The now-empty club is dank with expired smoke, the stale rankness of beer vapor. I have never enjoyed nightclubs—even the name suggests the fate of mugging victims. But in its quiescence and with its whirling lights unignited and still, it takes on an even more dreadful demeanor, the ominous character of a silenced carnival ground.

My compatriots are still silent, long-faced, dour, sour. I am conscious of the near complete shrinkage of my phallus, as a turtle might withdraw its head within its shell, expecting the tortoisian analogue to Robespierre and his gravity-powered hair trimmer.

Mr. Allen intones, "Well?"

Alpha Cat: "Mi swear, wi search di whole—"

Mr. Zenko: "Every last part, basically *everything*—"

Frosty: "If fuckin *Digaestus*'d gotten his fuckin ass in gear we'da—"

The Mugatu, clutching his tiger: "Gruhn . . . gruhn nnnAAHMM—"

And Mr. Allen holds up his hand: *Stop.*

He opens the primary loot box (actually, the *only* loot box, as a result of our failure), takes out the mystical mechanism within. It resembles nothing so much as a sextant, save for its drooping bellows and tubes and pipes, and its inscripted Tibetan. He cradles it, examines it, places its eyepiece up to his eye, sniffs it.

He *kisses* it.

"Boys, boys, BOYS . . . ," says Mr. Allen.

We are all frozen. We have seen this before . . . lulling us into a false sense of security in order to terrify and punish us all the more. It was effective once, long ago . . . but now we are left in a permanent state of insecurity and potential horror. We see the points of his upper teeth, caressing the thinness of his lower lip.

We know that smile. . . . It is that of the Bengal tiger, of the great white.

"A bird in the hand," chuckles Mr. Allen, "is worth a night in the bush."

Alpha Cat checks us each with his peripheral vision; we are all still standing, ungutted, unperforated. He makes subtle sweeping gestures with his lowered palms; as the Master chuckles, so do we all.

"Come on, ya little ass-tarts." He waves dismissingly at our terror, a kind of virtual hug. "Ya did good. Pizza's on me."

We walk, still terrified, towards the pizzas unveiled by Mr. Allen. He will not dine with us, having made clear his dietary superiority over us Dumpster feeders for some time. This heightens our terror as we tentatively place our incisors into the pizzene flesh . . . awaiting the shock of poison, of the whirring death from some implanted rotary blades.

Yet there is no punishment. Only three types of cheese, a selection of the finer sausages, and crumbled tofu.

The Master is happy. He does not care that we did not discover any cache of *cream* or its unrefined ingredients.

For the zodiascope is now his.

Saturday Morning Mission

CUE THEME MUSIC: "KIPENDA ROHO" BY TANZANIA'S REMMY Ongala. Man, now this song is really the bee's cheese. Absolutely splendiferous bouncy Zairean-style guitar, kot-tam-happy-to-be-alive vocals, and a rhythm section potency that says "Jump up and get *down*!"

"Kipenda Roho" is my soundtrack this morning . . . a morning when sunshine woke me up and gave me life and got me packing and got me biking on these gray-tone, deep-moan, raw-funk streets, leaf-shadow-dappled, taste-in-my-mouth-Snappled. It's a bebop/hip-hop/jump shot kinda morning, when the whole world is opening up like a wise man's laughter, like a child's smile.

Because I'm on my way with all ten speeds to meet this knockout amazing funktacular dream girl by the name of Sheremnefer.

You know, I've never taken a woman on a breakfast picnic before, a breaknic or picfast, if you will, and I'm kinda proud. See, Ye and me and—well, a couple of other guys we used to know—we all usedta compare notes on romantic things.

I don'mean vulgar stuff or panty-removing remedies, that kind of thing. I mean storybook kinda stuff, the stuff a girl'll wanna tell her mum or her grandkids about. Like Ye—now, he's all crazy and Mr. Moves and everything, but still, back in the day he could be very romantic.

I remember he took this one woman out for an evening picnic, way out into the country, during a meteor shower, so they could watch the shooting stars to a soundtrack of crickets. And lots of little, simple things, like sending her an envelope in the mail with a single playing card, the ten of hearts, which has the most hearts of any card.

Me, I prefer to send the two of hearts, which says more about monogamous commitment. Or one time I did a whole computer-laid-out laser-printed "bylaw infraction" ticket, telling this one teller at London Drugs about how she was being fined because she was in noncompliance violation of the "Dining Out Code." She laughed, loved it, gave me her number, we traded a few calls. . . . Course, she didn't bother to tell me that she and her boyfriend were moving to Vancouver within the week (I hadda find that out from my buddy Grant, who also worked there).

But the point is, is that doing all that romantic stuff, man, that is just capital-*D* Dynamite. Women, I think, in general, don't know anything about being romantic. Oh, sure, they talk about romance and everything, but it's pure clichés . . . flowers, candles, cards—absolutely no originality. And it's almost all on the receiving end.

But say a woman pours you a cup of tea in a restaurant, or brings you a tin box full of cookies she personally baked, or makes and paints a teapot for you, or sews you some leather-soled socks or knits a sweater for your dog—assuming you have a dog—see, that kind of stuff would just kill me dead with a surge of romanticons, the elementary particles that compose interstellar lovey-doveyness.

Those things are amazing. You *live* for that stuff.

. . . clearing the bridge, coming up on Saskatchewan Drive,

only four blocks from the 105th Street observation deck, our rendezvous point, and I've still got fifteen minutes to spare—

Oh, what the hell? My shortwave radiophone's beeping me. Obviously it can only be Ye, since he's the only one who'd try to reach me. Okay, complain, rag me, hold me up to all the obloquy you want. . . . We just, well, we take these freaking shortwave radiophones with us, okay? When we're gonna be apart. We just do. Shut up.

I pull over.

Me, on the SWR phone: "Landing party. Over."

Ye: "Coyote, this is Space-Age Bachelor Pad. You aint actually meetin this chick with a knapsack, are you? Over?"

Me: "Why not? Over."

Ye: "You wanna look like one of these grunge bastards? You need a picnic basket for a date, Captain Genius! Over!"

"Where'm I sposta get a picnic basket, Bachelor Pad? I'm in transit—I'm almost there! Over!"

"Get it from the Modeus Zokolo, over."

"What the hell are you talking about? I don't even wanna think about those assholes, let alone spend my money there! Over!"

"What money? Think about it: *Kevlar!* I bet his sissy store has a billion picnic baskets. That jimpomatic prick owes you a million times over for his brother. Over!"

Me: "Yeah, and what if General Colon-Power is there, huh? Over?"

Ye: "Then at least you tried, dingwad. *Capiche?* Over!"

I consider it. It's not bad advice. "Good call, Bachelor Pad. Will debrief after return to base. Over."

"Hafta wait until the walk home. I'm at Video Feed Bag tonight, over."

"Then catchya tonight, Batch Pad. Over and ow-oo-OO-oo-oot!"

"Over and ow-oo-OO-oo-oot!"

Damn indeed, Ye's my atheist guardian angel, my Stephen-Hawking-meets-Great-Gazoo. He truly does watch out for

THE COYOTE KINGS OF THE SPACE-AGE BACHELOR PAD   173

me—guy wasn't even awake when I left and here he is, calling me up with . . .

You know, I'm feeling so good I think I can actually do this, go to Scumbag's on Whyte and insist on a picnic basket. It's so freaking weird I think I'll actually enjoy it—I may not even puke. I shove the phone away, pedal off towards 82nd Avenue. I feel absolutely—actually, I'm . . . well—

It's a funny thing, feelings. People think you can only have one emotion at a time, like playing a sport . . . tennis OR soccer. Hockey OR knife ball. But feelings are more like sandwich ingredients. You can have a bunch all at the same time, depending on the size of your bread.

Some people are real mayo-on-white kinda guys or, worse, canapé snackers: simple, easy, no mess, no muss. Me, I've always been pure Dagwood—as many feelings as I can pile on all mashed together and dripping with psychic donair sauce, the runny kind. Amused, bitter, euphoric, vengeful, playful, exasperated, ecstatic . . . people say garbage like "He doesn't feel good about himself" or "He's an angry guy" or some other crap because they see you having a bad day or they only see you in one context or whatever.

But it's more like, you got a bad slice of tomato inside of a great mound of corned beef, or the rye is moldy but the Asiago is super supreme. People are so lazy, they want everything to be simple, but nothing is simple. Nothing.

I'm pulling up towards the freaking Modeus Zokolo. I can't believe I'm actually here. I haven't had more than one word with Heinz and more than a hundred words with Kevlar since four years ago after Heinz—

. . . after he—

What the hell . . .?

Kevlar's outside of his own store, pacing? And the front window has a bunch of black plastic half-taped-up on the inside, like a poor masking job for painting the rim. I've got a bad feeling about this.

Kevlar glances up angrily, but I don't think it's aimed at me.

He looks confused, like he's seeing Jackie Chan dance the *Nutcracker Suite,* or hearing Rakim rapping along to Wagner's *Götterdämmerung.*

"Ha-*Hamza?* Since when do *you* come *here?*"

"Hey, Kev. Just in the neighborhood, an . . . uh . . . how ya doin? What's goin on?"

He throws his hands up in exasperation, shoving towards the store, as if it's obvious.

"Bad renovations? What?"

"We were ripped off!" he bites. He sounds like that old comedy album *You Were Ripped Off.* You put it on, and they start singing, "You were ripped off . . . you were ripped off . . ." and so forth. You skip the needle ahead, and ten minutes later, fifteen, and then the other side, same thing: "You were ripped off. . . ." Makes a great gag gift, I guess. This is really going to complicate getting the picnic basket.

To be honest, I'm having a tough time not bursting out laughing. I wish I could meet the guys who did this and thank them. I choose not to mention this wish and the album to Kevlar.

I'd better say something that sounds sympathetic, but not too forceful. . . . I don'wanna *reveal* my total lack of sympathy.

"No way! Man, I'm sorry—how bad?"

"Float's gone—not much, maybe fifty cash. I did the deposit myself, so . . ." He's looking at the face of the store, as if it'll wink at him or something with some hidden clue as to who did this.

I'm glad he's not looking at me—I have a snicker the power of a seizure creeping up behind my mouth, which, due to the typical disobedience of my own face, is probably smirking.

"What about merchandise? I assume with the fancy stuff you guys sell—"

"*That's* the damage. We lost some very expensive exotic goods we *just got in*!"

"What kinda goods?"

"Just . . . well . . . it's a little difficult to explain." He looks back at me and just in time I get my snicker-smirk under control. "So, really, what in the hell're you doing here? You never come by here."

It's very weird talking with this guy after all this time, and so much pain between his clan and mine. A Saturday morning, me in shorts with a knapsack on a bike, and him in his fancy freakin Hugo Gap Klein or whatever the hell tailored monkey suit he's wearing. He looks like Giancarlo Esposito in *Mo' Better Blues.*

I bet this fascist buys designer toilet paper, made of Egyptian cotton or something, with *CK* printed on each sheet.

Looking at him is like looking into the atavachron, glimpsing past worlds that are long dead, that maybe never even existed. . . .

A billion years ago we sat around the same table, him and me and Ye and H. . . . Kev's brother . . . and also . . . also *she* was there. And we played AD&D and ate souvlakis and Greek salads and laughed about our high school SU president who's now a city councilman and watched VHS tapes of then-brand-new films like *Dune* and *2010* from bootlegs the Wolves had gotten from who-knows-where with their dad's money and their own endlessly fascinating and mysterious connections.

I look at him now and suddenly see myself at a long, long table surrounded by the Wolves and a bunch of people I don't know (and *her*) laughing and eating and drinking and me with nothing on my plate and the only sound from me is my gut grumbling and the gurgling with the hiss of acid chewing through my stomach wall. And I realize, only then, that what they're dining on is my liver, and kidneys, and heart.

Kevlar: "So?"

I kick my own ass back into the present. "Your *brother* aint here," I muster, "is he?"

"No, I just called him about the break-in. He's on his way."

"Well, Kev, it's kind of embarrassing considering what you've just—maybe I should just go—"

"What is it, Hamza?"

"Look, it's stupid. I was in a crunch, and I needed to borrow . . ." I sigh. I'm a grown man, and here I am begging, *begging* this money-loving, coiffed asshole for a damn—hell, I'm here already, it's for a noble cause, I can put my own feelings aside for Sherem's sake.

"I came by to borrow a picnic basket . . . for a date."

He looks at me, suddenly amused, that smug expression I remember on his and his brother's faces only too well, the one they wore only occasionally when we first knew them, aimed at everybody else but our inner circle—the Secret Society, we called it (I even designed a logo)—until the four younger members from grade ten caught up with H. at university and I began to see that fucking look out of my peripheral vision when he thought I didn't notice, and by the time I'd figured out—

If I didn't need this picnic basket, I'd love to find a brick and chuck it right through their window, taped garbage bags and all.

Kevlar wordlessly disappears into his store, then reemerges a minute later with a beautiful cherrywood-looking picnic basket. It's brand-new, and I can smell its earthy resin from here. A scent like campfires and outdoor pools and watermelon. Must be like that new-car scent they spray. New-basket smell.

He hands it to me. "Keep it."

"What? No, I couldn't—" I don'wanna be beholden to this guy, even if he and his crooked brother do owe me my entire life, the alternate world where I don't wash dishes for a living, where there's no Box and I'm not a total freaking loser.

"Go ahead," he shrugs. "I'll just tell the insurance it was stolen."

I don't know what to say. Now I'm *helping* his already extensive corruption. But what the hell. "Thanks, Kev!" I grab the basket handle with both hands, lean the bike against my inside thigh while I lower my body into horse stance, put on my best Chinese movie accent: *"Basket-absorbing stance!"*

He doesn't crack a smile. Good. I don't even know why I did that . . . maybe to take the edge off of having to thank him. Hell, *I* laughed. That's all that matters. I restand up my bike, balance the basket in my left hand, start to pedal off. "Good luck with the police and whatnot, guy," I call. "See you around."

He doesn't even wave. He's already forgotten me. I'm just a plebeian to him and his brother.

Fuck em. I'm on my way to meet the woman of my dreams.

I zip north down 104th, past the beautiful redbrick Old Strathcona Library and ground zero for the Fringe Festival, the world's second-largest theater festival, after the one in Edinburgh. Last year me and Ye put on a science/mythology show for kids, even had a bunch of our Coyote Camp kids come down from Kush with their parents—these are kids who never leave the neighborhood, don't even know there's a place called "Whyte Ave" (and no, I didn't make up that name—it's really called that), and we get em to see stuff they never even imagined.

And then I'm on Saskatchewan Drive and 105th at the observation deck, a full minute to spare, just enough time to lock up my bike and stuff my knapsack contents into the picnic basket.

"*Hotep,* Brother Hamza."

Damnit, she snuck up on me again! I nearly jumped. How the hell does she *do* that?

I turn around, see just how startling she is in the morning sunlight, skin glowing like gilded ebony wood, and drink in her scent, like that of freshly peeled oranges.

I form words to say hello, but I'm sure my face says everything.

The Morning-After Pall

I'D BEEN DREADING HEINZ'S ARRIVAL EVER SINCE I CALLED HIM. And now that he's here my only comfort comes from the acknowledgment that my powers of prognostication haven't dimmed with age or ambition.

The inside of the store is a mess, darker than usual because of the bags taped to the window, and the fact that the bulbs are smashed. When I called Heinz he told me to leave everything as it was. "Told" is perhaps a bit restrained a description, I suppose, but at least my ear has stopped ringing.

When he finds out what he must already know, that the most important acquisition we've ever made is gone . . . that the item that was supposed to lead us to the most sought-after sources of—

"So you didn't call the police?" he snaps at me, sorting through overturned shelves and scattered delicate treasures. He's acting like this is *my* fault. All I did was close the store and activate the security system, close early for the book launch, and make the deposit.

"Heinz, you told me not to and I said I wouldn't. Why

would I then turn around after putting down the phone and call anyway?"

"Don't whine, Kev," he hisses. "It sickens me."

"Well, you don't have to use that *tone*," I insist. "Tisn't my fault that we had a break-in!"

He glowers, sorting for something—clues? I don't know what. He's resourceful, yes, a very strategic thinker, of course, but he's no police investigator.

"Since we can't get the police in on this, should I call a private detective?"

He snorts, throws down a piece of whatever broken exoticum he was handling.

"What's missing?" he commands me to answer.

I bite my lip. We're here sooner than I wanted us to be. I stall stupidly, my craftiness always failing me utterly in the face of my older brother. "Well . . . that tiger-fur stuffed tiger is gone."

He bores into me with his eyes as if I'm the most galactically stupid organism he's ever beheld. "Thieves . . . broke *in* to a store on a busy avenue . . . to steal—a stuffed animal?"

He tilts his head towards me with his "I want all of it, and now" look that he inherited from Dad. Even in the darkness, I see how his always-pale face is flushed hotly pink, and veins radiate and pulsate away from his eyes like the wavy lines on a child's drawing of the sun.

I'm choked.

"They got," he sighs, or perhaps *smolders* is a better word, as I can feel my neck baking and crisping beneath the blast of his breath and its increase of the room's ambient temperature, "the zo*di*ascope, *did*n't they?"

This really wasn't my fault. I didn't do anything wrong!

Knowing I'll have to concede eventually, I surrender now.

I nod.

Instantly he stamps around the room, kicking and screaming, literally. Except that, just like Dad, when Heinz yells, he enunciates with all the verbal alacrity of an Oxfordian, and

when he swears, minus the accent, he sounds like Sir Alec
Guinness.

"Those . . . FUCK-ing"—(kick)—"FIL-thy"—(smash)—
"*BLI-I-I-IND*"—(slapping down a shelf, sending its contents
crashing)—"*VER-R-R-R-min!*"

My brother is truly terrifying when he's like this. I've seen
how far his rage can go. I try to position myself closer to the
front door, but he has me hemmed in behind the counter. "Like
*SIL*verfish"—(smash)—"eating away the Shroud of Turin!"

"Heinz, please—"

He turns on me. "*Four* years . . . four *YEARS* it took me to
get this . . . and it couldn't last ONE FUCK-ING NIGHT in
the god-damned *SAFE*? I DIDN'T EVEN LAY MY HANDS
ON IT BECAUSE OF THE BOOK LAUNCH AND LAST
NIGHT WITH THE *GIRLS!*"

"We've still got the cream," I whimper, and instantly regret
saying anything to try to comfort him.

"WHAT GOOD IS THE *FUCK*-ING *CREAM* WITH-
OUT THE 'SCOPE? YOU THINK I PUT IN YEARS OF
SEARCHING JUST SO I COULD GET A SHIPMENT OF
CREAM? HOW THE FUCK ARE WE SUPPOSED TO LO-
CATE ANY OF THE TERRVICES NOW?"

33

Picnic among Pyramids

He hath granted that I might come forth as a phoenix, that I
*   might speak. . . .*
I have been in the water of the river.
I have made offerings with incense. . . .
I have submerged the boat of my enemies.
I, I have sailed forth upon the Lake in the neshemet boat. . . .
I, I have entered into Per-Usir, and I have draped myself in the
*   apparel of him who is there.*
I have entered into Re-stau, and I have seen the hidden things.
—Per-em-Hru, CXXV

WE'RE AT THE SPECIAL LOCATION I PLANNED, SITTING ON THE
hillside overlooking the five glass pyramids of the Muttart
Conservatory ecogardens, eating olives and feta cheese and
avocados and tangerines and basmati rice with hot morsels of
roasted lamb and chicken and potatoes I got up early to make
this morning and kept hot in the Thermeal kit Ye invented
(patent pending), drinking one-bean cocktails from a chilled
bottle of coconut milk, sweet mung beans, and ice.

There's the bright scent of cut grass, the rough caress beneath our legs and feet of the woven blanket Sherem brought, the hot kiss of sunlight on our exposed skin, the grace and delicacy with which she employs her metal chopsticks to pluck food from the plate and place it in her mouth, only to chew with girlish glee.

And I notice to my delight that she *rocks* when she eats, just like a little kid with a hamburger and a milk shake.

I can't remember a happier morning in the last four years.

We talk about everything—movies, culture, food (she *loves* the food I brought, and we eat off the same plate—can you believe it?), and, of course . . .

". . . so between my studies and my travels, there was almost never much opportunity to get . . . involved." She doesn't look at me while telling me this, instead brushing thin braids from her face, looking at the ground, using her finger to pick up a ladybug that stood out bright red on her chocolate arm, then releasing it gently to the wind.

I'm happy to hear what she's said. I know it's stupid to be jealous of people who came along before I did, but, well, I'm stupid, I guess.

"I aint exactly Casanova myself." I chuckle. "With a face like mine, you know."

I don't know why I do this. Ye made me promise not to talk like that, the fishing business. But . . . well, so long as you don't fish too much or too often, you usually don't end up stinking.

She looks up, her fingers trailing through the grass without pulling out clumps (I'm relieved; I hate it when people do that). "But there was somebody."

I chuckle again, too hard. "Well, *every*body has *some*body."

She's not chuckling or smiling. "But you wear it on your face like a gash."

This woman astounds me sometimes with the things she says. What the hell do you say to that? I always usually think of myself as the Gregory Hines of conversation. But now my verbal feet seem mired in setting concrete.

She reacts to something in my face, looks down, embarrassed again. I think she thinks I'm angry at her remark, but I'm more surprised at its innocent audacity than anything.

But it's so strange, really, seeing the way she shifts among her various selves, her mysterious-traveler persona, her sword-sharp iron woman, her still-surprising awkward schoolgirl.

Some part of me hopes that most guys never get to see these facets, that I'm the only one to examine this jewel this close-up for this long.

She looks worried. "Sorry," she whispers into the grass she's combing with her fingers. "In school, we learned to see a lot of things." She sniffs. "I guess a potential faux pas wasn't one of them."

"Don't worry about it." I smile, trying to ignite one of her own. "Am I that transparent?" She still isn't looking up. "I'll . . . maybe later, another time. I'll tell you. I'd *like* to tell you. In time."

She looks up, hopefully, sunlight dancing on her cheeks, turning her coal eyes into internally lit cocoa gold, like fireflies encased in amber and lit for all eternity. "You said . . . you weren't a Casanova."

"Yeah." I hushed. "I just mean . . . I was never a ladies' man, never could be, never would be even if I could. Jumpin beds, leavin babies, breakin hearts . . . that's not how my daddy raised me." I put on my best Dad accent, his Khartoumi Arabic tinged with Dinka. "Hamza, wimmen arrre nott a *salatt barrr*."

She giggles, delighted by my transformation into something, I guess, more familiar to her overseas life. I feel like I've grown wings . . . in her gaze.

I continue: "The supeeeri'r man dass not *gobble*. He seleketsss carrrf'lly, and tastes eff'ry morrrsull—ant isss enrrriched. He is neither anorekasic nor bulemmmic."

She laughs, claps her hands together as if to seal the imitation and the moment between her clasped palms. I keep going, telling her the truth: what I feel.

"Sherem, I tell you, these, these *bed jumpers* . . . they just don't know what they're missing. It's like when you cook, if you're a novice, or maybe a moron, you just turn the pan up high and zorch everything and wilt the vegetables gray and burn the meat!

"Naw, you gotta use *slow* heat, low heat, let everything cook properly, take your time, so flavors meld and, and un*veil* themselves in their true and proper intensity. Sure, it takes patience, but the reward? A great meal, you knawm sayn?

"Mosta these fools're so busy tearing their pants off, they never know how magnificent that . . . that first touch of a woman's hand in yours is . . . that skin shiver of her neck on your *cheek*. . . ."

She's staring at me. I've gone too far. I can't help it, it's not insincere, I get excited, I start talking the way I truly feel, and—

Me: "I'm sorry—you probably think I'm talkin a lotta crap."

Those amber-fired eyes gaze into mine, ignite me. Knight me.

Sherem, intensely: "No. No."

She leans forward. "You know, it's like—" She breaks off, and her face searches for something. "Hamza, do you believe in God?"

"Do I believe in God?" This is *not* what I expected her to say. Damn. I'm embarrassed to answer. I wonder what my dad would think of my hesitation.

Aw, man, I suppose I could just dodge this or lie but . . . Dad always said that of all the lies you tell, the very worst would be about your beliefs. How about your nonbeliefs? Sometimes I sicken myself by sickening myself.

"Well . . . I . . . I used to have a very strong faith. My whole family was at mosque every Friday. But . . . that was a long time ago. My family, uh . . . my family broke up when I was in junior high. I've barely seen my sister or mum since then . . . they moved to T.O. I guess I stopped going to *Jummah* around then.

"For some reason my dad sent me to a Catholic high school after that, which's where I met Ye, who became an atheist. I guess Dad wanted me to have at least some regular mention of God in my life, at least from another People of the Book."

She smiles softly, and her response would probably sound mean or sharp without that smile. "I notice you didn't answer my question."

This is too much. "Why'd you ask in the first place? We weren't really talking about—"

"You were talking about 'bed jumpers.' And a lotta religious people feel the same way, but I wasn't really sure how religious you were. But just doing something or believing something because you're told to doesn't seem very, well, responsible. You have to have reasons, consequences, for why things are right or wrong.

"Which is why I liked what you said. You talked about what you miss in the lasting long term by going for the fast payoff, short term. In Ash Shabb we learned how much *more* human beings are than just . . . *orgasms*—"

The word sounds utterly bizarre coming out of her mouth, and she flushes when she sees my surprise. I'm not embarrassed, but she is. So strange. We *are* adults.

She tries to continue: "There's a level—"

And then a bright blue butterfly flutters by, so startlingly colorful it's like living neon, like swaying leaves on a planet beneath the Pleiades. Sherem seems enraptured, as if she's just witnessed a miracle. I don't mean her reaction is flaky or anything—it's dignified—but the degree of her response is fascinating.

"Hamza, do you know what a variable caterpillar is?"

"No, tell me."

She leans in, confides solemnly, intensely, "There is a certain kind of caterpillar that, if it can find a certain kind of tree, and if it should spin its chrysalis at a certain time of year, underneath a certain cloud pattern, can *choose* what it'll become.

"Not just butterfly or moth, either, but sparrow, fish, stone, running water, *fire*. In one very ancient legend, this is how all creatures came into being, even people."

It's a great fairy tale, but her eyes tell me she's awaiting a *specific* reaction, like a coded response to a spy check phrase. This really screws me up. I don't wanna disappoint her, but this isn't the first time she's done this since we met, either, with the cryptic phrasing and pregnant pauses.

Aw, hell's bells. What do I say?

"I . . . I wouldn't usually admit this, Sherem, but . . . I know you're trying to tell me something, but I don't think I understand." I wet my lips, try to stall, fail. Confess. "I *want* to."

I study her face, probing for even a flicker of disappointment. If it's there, I'll see it, smell it, like mildew, like the stink of a dirty public washroom.

Instead she smiles innocently, knowingly, invitingly. "You will, Hamza."

I smile, too, and then I'm frozen in slow-motion time awareness that she's . . . hitting me in the face?

No—but close—her hand retracts at glacial speed, and I see her fingers clutching the metal chopsticks, and at the very tip, good ghosts: a *mosquito*. Her fingers tense minutely, and its body swells and shreds, a bright red bubble of blood appearing like a sunrise.

She delicately pushes the chopstick tips into the ground, whispers something that sounds like "*khat emta, en chettah*." Then she looks at me. "It was on your neck. Sorry I didn't get it in time."

What the hell? How did she do that? "How did you do that?"

She shrugs, and anger ripples into her face—but I sense it's not at me, but herself, like she's just given out her PIN in public, or drunkenly blabbered too much about family secrets at a party. I hate seeing her look mad. . . . What it does to her face, it's like . . . like desecration. "Hey, Sherem, thanks and all, but maybe that was one of those, uh, variable caterpillars. You coulda just killed my grampa or something."

She laughs, and the hard face is gone.

"Your father sounds terrific," she says. I have to rewind my mental tape to figure out where that remark came from.

"Yeah, Dad's great. You should meet him—" Stupid, Hamza, stupid! Why not just ask her to *marry* you?

"I'd love that."

Whew. Well, then.

"Do you have a big family?" she asks.

"My parents and my sister and me. But, uh . . . well, my parents are divorced, and my sister lives with my mum in Toronto."

"Ah . . . you go there a lot—or do they come here?"

I gulp. I don't know how to answer this question. Anybody else, I'd just dodge, but I get the sense she'd see right through me. "We're . . . well . . . we're kind of . . . I guess *estranged* is the word."

"Oh . . . sorry." She looks down, up, around . . . strangely shy of my eyes. And then she looks straight into them. "But you know, so long as there's life, Hamza, there's hope. You can't give up, ever. If you even have a chance . . . there's no distance too far to go for something really worth having."

This is *way* too freakin much. She doesn't know the situation. She doesn't know about—

I change the subject. "What about you? Big family?"

"Four brothers, three sisters. I'm number five."

"You all close? I mean, with all your travels, d'you see em often?"

She swallows, glances away. Croaks out, "No. Uh . . . a few . . . you see, they're . . . they're all—"

Whoah. What the hell—is she gonna say they're all *dead*?

"Sherem, don't—we don't have to talk about this. Let's just . . . just walk, okay?"

The haunting departs her face, and a smile appears, I'm assuming solely out of relief. She's a strange mix, for sure. So much inside her, like it's all at war against itself.

We pack silently, shake the blanket free of grass, get up to walk around the pyramids of my beloved E-Town.

On Good, Evil, Invisible Hands, and the Wind

"So what brought you back?"

"To Sanehem?" she says, then, "To Edmonton?"

"What?"

"Edmonton."

"No, what'd you say before that?"

" 'Sanehem.' It means 'City of Grasshoppers.' "

"What language is that, Cree?"

"No, my parents used to call Edmonton that, when we were in Ash Shabb. It's Ren-Kem. Anyway, to answer your question, I'm, I'm sort of doing . . . field research, and skill-testing what I was taught at the academy."

"Oh, like a practicum?"

". . . yeah, pretty much."

"Skill-testing what you were taught. Sounds ominous!"

She chuckles.

Me: "Seriously, what does that mean? What were you taught?"

"Mostly stuff about data collection, archaeological surveys. In Ash Shabb we learn a lot of non-Western archaeological theories and techniques, sort of . . . partly intuitive, partly theoretical. It's kind of difficult to explain."

"Fascinating. So what are you researching?"

"I'm looking for ritual texts and objects that discuss the theory and practice of good and evil."

"That's a hell of a topic."

"Literally."

We laugh. I enjoy her little joke. She hasn't joked much so far today. . . . I guess we've been too intense. It's good to be with a woman who can make you laugh. It's been too long. It's like going outside after being bedridden for months, like seeing home after years of captivity.

I'm not only happy: I *know* I'm happy, I'm outside of myself watching myself be happy, and happy while watching. Like a man having a conversation with his own soul.

"So," I ask, "what're you looking at specifically, I mean, regarding evil? That's pretty broad. You mean, like, vampires, or Rwanda?"

"Sure, any of those," she says. We come to a bench, and I motion to sit down. We do, now on the east side of the pyramids, gazing west at them. I put the picnic basket down beside me.

"But it doesn't have to be so extreme," she continues. "Both monsters and all-out genocide campaigns are pretty rare. Could be about everyday evil, and the legends people invent to avoid confronting the real horror of it all.

"Take vampires, for instance, a legend from Europe. Say you've got a small medieval town, everybody knows each other, more or less, plus the rural areas around. Now say you've got a serial rapist or serial rape-murderer. Or a child rape-killer.

"How do you face the fact that you live with this kind of, of freak? I mean, *that's* a monster, right? Wouldn't it be easier on everyone's psyche, assuming you don't know who the guy actually is, to claim that there's a werewolf or a vampire out there, someone who used to be and look just like the rest of you, but now is an autonomically driven organic killing machine?

"So much easier to say 'The devil made him do it,' rather than face up to something much more horrifying: somebody, a person just like you, *decided to do evil. And enjoys it.*"

"That's interesting. . . . So you're looking into good and evil also from a responsibility perspective?"

"Exactly. Because when you see it like that, you realize that potentially everyone can be a monster."

"Man, that's pretty dark. Is that how you actually see the world?"

"Don't you?"

"Well . . . sorta, I guess . . . but some people seem more evil than others."

"Some have more to gain, or care more about themselves than others. Take tobacco companies, or liquor manufacturers. I mean, I noticed last night, you don't drink. At first I thought it was because you were a Muslim, but based on what you said before, it sounds like you're sort of in-between right now, searching and doubting."

"Yeah, that's as good a description as any. To answer your implied question, I don't drink because . . . I've never had a drink, being raised Muslim and all, but even since I sort of slid away from the mosque . . . well, some things kinda stick, I guess. That's one of them.

"But really, honestly? I don't drink because if there's one thing I hate in life, it's being out of control. And that's what booze does to people. If I look at why people are in pain, or me especially, it has to do with having no control over what's happening to me."

Sherem nods without smiling. I ask her, "Why'd you mention cigarette and alcohol manufacturers?"

"Well . . . you just mentioned being out of control. Think about a husband drunk and beating his wife—"

"Or vice versa—"

"Well, yes, that's true, or a parent beating the kids. Or

drunk drivers crippling or maiming or killing a family. Now multiply that times a thousand, or a million, or ten million or a hundred million across a decade and the planet. Now, what's the hidden factor behind that? *Cash!* Some stockholders and fund managers are making billions off of that. Isn't *that* a holocaust?"

"Well, come on, it's not like they have death camps—"

"They've just decentralized them. Now they're the family homes or the public roads! You know, just before I came back, I was reading this one article that said alcoholics account for forty percent of all alcohol sales, and that that's what shapes the advertising, ads showing how booze puts you in control . . . control at the party, at the business dinner, on the date.

"Isn't that something? These 'people' running these companies, they know exactly what they're doing. Make no mistake. They're a *planetary vampire,* drinking the life and hope and dreams and joy out of hundreds of millions of people and turning them into their living-dead slaves!"

I try to chuckle. *Try.* "That's a bit extreme, Sherem—"

"No!" she barks. "It's not! It's the truth! People get accustomed to evil like they get accustomed to smog or noise or graffiti! But it doesn't change what it is."

Man, the woman is intense. And bordering on rude. I wonder what her problem is. She's barely said word one about her parents. Maybe they were drunks—maybe that's why she has this melodramatic thing about booze. Maybe her parents were drunk drivers and killed off the whole family while she was away traveling? Or maybe they were workaholics, too, just like a lot of alkies, and they just ignored the kids or abused them. Or like a murder-suicide thing?

Cuz I mean, she's pretty over-the-top with her antialcohol thing. I'm not pro-booze, obviously, but still, "planetary vampire" is a bit much.

Then again, maybe I'm playing devil's advocate too much. Maybe I'm even being a freakin hypocrite. Why the hell am I even arguing with her at all? Given the megatonnage of how *I* got galactically screwed, the last thing I can do is even *appear* to be defending any kind of addiction—

I'm living in my head again. Too silent, too long. I'm not sure of the expression she's wearing. . . . What is that, embarrassment? Anger that I'm not more sympathetic to her argument?

I try to snap back, say something, cover.

"I don't know about master-plan evil, Sherem. I guess most people who drink or whatever are just trying to feel good, forget their pain or their loneliness, or overcome their shyness or something. They're not evil, and most of em don't really do any evil to anybody else."

I'm afraid at the sight of her expression: tired, disappointed, like she's waited in a long line only to find out she's in the wrong department.

"Yes, but Hamza," she says slowly, "what if instead of harming their brains, they chose to *work* on their problems? To eliminate their pain, or make friends, or confront their shyness? Most of what's wrong with people, they can change. If they try.

"And you're forgetting how many of them are drinking or getting stoned because they're seeking thrills, what they call a *high*. They want to touch glory. But look at how far they fall. They call it 'getting wasted' or 'getting plastered' or—what's that really awful one?—'getting shit-faced.' I mean, look at that! Really think about what that *means*. They want to feel strong, sexy, attractive . . . happy. They want to stand inside the king's chamber, but they haven't earned the right.

"They're everything that's wrong in this instant-coffee and microwave age. 'I want it now.' There used to be that romantic image of going off to Tibet and climbing the mountain to speak to the wise man. And when you got to the top, he could tell you the truths of the universe. Now people wanna take a helicopter to the top—or *e-mail* him!

"But it's the walk in the cold and almost dying to get

there. . . . That's the only thing that makes the answer *mean* anything!"

Did I say "intense" before? How about thermonuclear? I mean, I like to see that kind of passion, but how far does it go, and where does it *not* go? How much can somebody who sees that much of the big picture—or thinks she does, anyway—how much can somebody that fixated see the little picture? Is there enough room in her world for somebody else, or somebody who doesn't feel exactly the same way?

Is there any room for me?

I've been silent too long again. She whispers, sounding even more defeated than before, just trying to be polite, I guess, to make conversation, "Tell me what *you* think—I'll put it in my sample."

I try, delicately. "Well . . . I agree, sure seems like there's plenty of evil in the world. Sometimes I wonder about how much good. But as to, like, capital-*E* Evil, whether there are any *invisible hands* guiding it . . . I just don't know. Really."

She whispers, and I don't know if it's to me, or to the air, or to something beyond, as if she's sharing a secret: "In the great desert . . . outside our temple in Ash Shabb, trillions and trillions of grains of sand collect together in the form of waves, and they march, unstoppably, over *eons,* guided by an *invisible force* . . . called *wind*."

I nod, and then surprise myself when I smile. I was pretty weirded out by her rant, but this quiet talk . . . I like this much better.

"Hamza," she says softly.

"Yes?"

"If I needed you to help me . . . with a . . . uh . . . a *project* . . . and it were really important . . . would you?"

Her voice, and now her eyes . . . this is no coquettish come-on. Whatever it is she needs sounds serious. I hope she aint gonna ask me for money—I don't have any. And wouldn't wanna give her any, anyway. But what could I possibly help her with? Maybe she needs a research assistant. But I don't know anything about what she's studying.

Wonder if maybe she's in trouble?

"Don't look so aghast, Hamza." She chuckles softly, as if she's trying to figure out what I'm thinking about. "It's nothing bad! I just . . . I'm . . . I'm maybe going to be conducting a dig, and I thought, if you were interested, maybe . . . you could help."

Whoah! Interesting. Good—glad it's none of that, well . . . other stuff. "Cool. Sounds neat. When? What's involved?"

"I've got all the equipment, although I'm still picking up a few supplies over the next couple of days. Would you be able to get time off work?"

"Yeah, I think so." Jeez, what I wouldn't do to make this work! Plus, a dig! C'mon, that's neat in and of itself.

But now her face is all grim again—maybe even worse than before, like behind her eyes there's black-water rapids from underground rivers, and she's caught there, screaming for help, and no one can hear her, or no one can come to help.

I'm glad I can.

Then she sees me seeing her see me see her, and—poof!—her horror mask slips away, turns into mist, and she smiles softly again. "I'm not all doom and gloom, Hamza. You know . . . when we were talking a minute ago, about responsibility?"

I nod, and so does she. She continues. "If anyone can be an autonomous agent of evil, then clearly, anyone can be an autonomous agent of good. Evil isn't always invisible. Sometimes it's as tangible as concrete. As tangible as one person helping a person in need out of the goodness of his heart. As tangible as . . . as goodness."

And then I realize that she's holding my hand.

This isn't the first time I've touched her hand, but it feels like it, since now we've talked so much. I feel the soft skin on top, the callused finger bottoms and pads of her palm . . . the bones beneath cool flesh . . . the warmth when she squeezes, and when I squeeze back. . . .

Ten seconds, no talking . . .

. . . looking at the pyramids, her hand, my own hand, blood pulsing, muscles twitching, heat, electricity . . .

. . . twenty seconds . . . silence, her hand, dry, warmer now . . .

. . . thirty seconds . . .

. . . peripheral vision, and she's looking at me— I'm . . . I'm overwhelmed. . . . It's been too long, four years of loneliness, and I think she wants me to kiss her, but four years, man, four years, *four years*! I want to kiss her, more than anything, but . . .

I take out my camera instead, breaking our clasp.

She squirms away. "No, please don't take my picture—"

But it's too late—*click*—I've already done it. I cajole her. "I've heard this from women before. It's the people who're most vain who say, 'Don't take my picture,' so they can *guarantee* you'll want to—" *Click*.

Her expression turns to stone.

"It isn't vanity, Hamza," she chisels. "*I don't want my photo being taken.*"

I try to laugh it away. "What's the problem, Sherem?"

"Does it matter? *Please give me the film.*"

She's not kidding.

I'm flustered, desperate, begging: "*What?* Sherem, please— I promise I'll ask next time. Don't be mad. I don't often—it's been a long time since I had . . . since any woman . . . I don't wanna spoil today." Ah, this is depressing. Hell's bells. Why . . . why can't things ever work out for me?

"I, I just wanted to have a picture to remember it by, that's all. I'm sorry. Here."

I begin to open my camera.

At the last second she puts her hand on mine.

"No," she says, relenting. "No. But you have to *promise me* you won't show my picture to *anyone*. You promise?"

"Promise," I sigh, smiling my relief. I wonder why she's so paranoid about pictures, for crying out loud.

She withdraws her hand, gesticulates gently, I guess, either to convince me or calm herself. "I know I must seem really strange to you. . . . I'm sorry. I don't want to wreck today, either. Nobody . . . nobody's *ever* done anything like this for me . . . the food, the picnic, the picnic *basket*—"

(Ye, I owe you one.)

"Thank you, Hamza," she whispers, and her eyes are as big and shiny-dark as crescent moons. "Thank you."

I *almost* have the courage to kiss her right then, when I hear the trees rustle and then see her shimmering scarves blow in front of her face. She catches them, tucks them down.

The wind . . .

The Paths of Dragons, or Advanced Counterbanditry with +10 Saving Throw

IT'S EARLY EVENING, AND KEVLAR'S SITTING QUIETLY AT THE piano, not playing, but revising the score of the technoragtime opera he's writing, a Kraftwerk/dystopic version of Scott Joplin's *Treemonisha*. At least, that's his pretext for being there. I suspect he's cowering.

I put a froth-capped cup of cappuccino on the tall tea table next to the baby grand. He looks up at me—shocked, nervous, humble, anxious—and glances at the cup, and his arm jerks as if he wants to reach for the cup but is frozen by fear.

"Go ahead, Kevlar," I attempt to soothe him. His eyes are like groundhogs scanning for falcons. "It's not poisoned. I swear."

He swivels around on the polished bench, sliding his legs over from the business side to the visiting side, and reaches carefully for the cup and saucer, still looking towards me sadly.

I know he feels responsible for the break-in, and I suppose my yelling in his presence for so long probably made him feel worse. That probably wasn't fair.

I *am* still angry, of course—but I probably overreacted at the store earlier today. I can hardly hold him *exclusively* responsible for this fantastically monumental cock-up.

I sit down on the couch, sink into the cool leather and its softly moaning embrace. The Baal idol faces me from across the room, and with no belly candles lighting its eyes, it looks asleep, or maybe fresh out of ideas.

Fortunately, I'm not.

"I just don't get it," whispers Kevlar into his foam. I'm not sure if he's talking to me or to himself.

"Just what is it you don't get?"

"Well, why would burglars steal what looks like a sextant?"

I've never had much patience for disingenuousness. "Don't be coy, Kev. We both know that whoever took the zodiascope wasn't an ordinary burglar."

"But Heinz, who else in town—"

"Who says it's *any*one from in town? It could've been someone tracking the package from overseas for all we know. Or Vancouver, or Seattle, or San Francisco . . . hell, it could've been the Tibetan Star Crane Clan for all we know. Or the Guardians of the Ice Henge."

"But you think you know who, don't you?" he asks, sipping, then wiping away his white mustache. It's so bright on his skin, he looks suddenly very old, like a 1970s Duke Ellington.

"Yes, I have my suspicions."

"Heinz, *please* . . ."

"You *al*ways have to know *ev*erything, don't you? As soon as I've thought of it. For all we know, this room is bugged. That wouldn't be beyond the capability of some of our friends, would it?"

My younger brother places his cup into its saucer, and the clink is punctuation of his resolve. "I'll have the place swept tomor—I mean, I'll get the equipment. I'll do it myself."

This is disgraceful.

"It really wouldn't *do*, now," I lay into him, "to have *people* in here, *would* it?"

"C'mon, Heinz," he whines, his eyes downcast, "it was just a slip of the tongue! You know I wouldn't be so stupid as to—"

"Let's not talk *today* about what you are or are not too *stupid* to allow to happen."

I don't like having to do that to him, but *hon*estly.

Kevlar places the cup and saucer on the tall tea table. He seems to quiver on the piano bench. He's always been too skinny, and now he looks like an immaculately dressed Pinocchio, his spindly wooden legs betrayed by the drape of trouser cloth.

Still, seeing him like this, almost ready to cry . . . I may as well give him a *portion* of the solution.

"At any rate," I grant, "I think posting a reward should get us back our prize."

Kevlar glances up with question marks in his eyes, but his mouth is motionless. He turns back to his musical notation rather than, I suppose, betray too much interest again. But he's hardly writing. In fact, he reaches for his cappuccino.

I check a number on the Rolodex, dial, wait. Speak.

"Paul, it's Heinz."

Paul's sounds of joy at hearing my voice are an impressive simulation. I need to keep this short, though.

"Paul, listen. Something of mine was stolen from the Zokolo. It's worth a lot to me. It looks like an old-fashioned sextant, except . . . yes, that's right, the old navigator's . . . right . . . but with valves and bellows . . . right . . . no, I'm *not* sure who took it, but I have my suspicions. . . . Yes, exactly. And I need it back, and time is of the essence. I'm prepared to offer five hundred milliliters of cream, no questions asked—"

Kevlar's cup and saucer hit the floor—smashing.

"Oh, for god's sake, Kevlar!" I say, shielding the phone. "The Persian!"

He apologizes, scampers to the kitchen for towels. Sometimes . . . I'm just not sure. "I'm sorry, Paul. Had an accident here. Yes, that's right, two cups. If it takes longer than a week, it goes down to one cup. Past ten days, half a cup.

"After that, tell your people that I'll know whoever took it and I'll make sure they're unable to enjoy it. *And* I'll cut off our entire supply of cream to this city. You know what that'll do to the price. Not to mention the effect of the remaining . . . dairies . . . trying to stamp out all competition. Got it? . . . Yes, I'm serious. . . .

"Really? . . . No, that's no good, it's got to be sooner. How about eight thirty? . . . Yes, here's fine. Good man, Paul. And a finder's fee for you, of course. Buh-bye."

I hang up. Kevlar, sopping up his own mess, looks up from the floor. "Heinz, two cups? That's worth—"

"Seventy-five thousand dollars wholesale, yes—"

"And two hundred fifty thousand by the time it's diluted and retailed! A quarter of a million dollars—Heinz, really—"

"Just finish cleaning up, all right? I *offered* the reward. Paying it is a different matter."

His jaw goes slack. "Are these really the people we should be toying with?"

"Don't be so damn timid. Once we have that 'scope back, everything else changes. Assuming our translation of the *Yamayaksha Sutra* is correct, once we sink into total-eclipse cream trance, the zodiascope is going to make every pathway to every terrvix on earth as clear to us as highways on a sunny day.

"And once we start harvesting from the terrvices, these silverfish we're forced to deal with here won't matter a damn. No one will be able to stop us—we'll be the most—"

"But what if we don't live that long? I just don't want to die while trying to recover this thing. Is our life really so bad as it is, right now? I mean, Heinz, really . . . I *care* about Sonia and Sophia. We could be happy here, or anywhere we want! Hong Kong, Paris, Rio, L.A.—"

"Where's this coming from, Kev? I thought you were behind this. I thought you understood this! You really want to live a Salisbury steak existence when it could be filet mignon? You want to be Baby Duck when you could be genuine champagne?"

"Heinz, it's all so . . . ," he says, still kneeling on the rug, "it just seems so theoretical. . . ."

I reach out to him, pull him up, set him down on the piano bench. He studies the sponge in his hand, charged with caffeine and essence of coffee bean. The brew must be seeping into his skin.

"Kevlar, look at me."

He does, after a moment.

"When we're in the cream trance, all four of us . . . you've felt it. You've felt that purity, that perfect loneliness, haven't you?"

He is looking down, *again.*

"Yes," he mumbles.

"Look at me!"

He snaps back up.

"Have you or have you not felt it?"

He nods.

"And what is it like?"

Tears well in his eyes. "It's . . . the most beautiful, awful thing in the world. It's like dying and being born at the same time. It's like . . . like . . ."

"Like the most powerful orgasm you've ever felt, only ten times better, right?"

He nods, but keeps his eyes on me this time. They tremble with the fear of the memory of it . . . of just how intense existence can be, if only for a few moments.

"When we get the 'scope and we see the *lung-mei,*" I whisper, "we'll go straight to the first terrvix, and then follow the *lung-mei* to the next one, and the one after that, and the one after that . . . until we've found all the lost Dreams on the planet that've been hidden away for ten thousand years.

"And then the cream trance will seem like pain compared to what we'll experience. We won't have to leave the king's chamber just as soon as we get there anymore. We'll *live* there."

I wet my lips, breathe, dazzled by all the truth and glory

and wonder of it, of the absurdity of compressing the multi-verse into the syllables of three words:

"We'll be kings."

And to that, Kevlar only sighs, so uninflated, so tiny.

"But why," he cants, "would we be able to find all of the terrvices when ten thousand other searchers have been combing the planet for thousands of years—"

"Because until the fourteenth century none of them had 'scopes—"

"Some of them did—"

"Yes, but none of them had cream—no one'd taken cream past the second stage until twenty years ago! And if anyone who had cream *did* think to combine it with 'scope use, there's no evidence any of them could find a 'scope to try. Until us. Until now."

"So really, this is *all* still theory, Heinz, right? For all you know—"

"*Enough!*" I blister. "What do you think the *last half decade* of research has been about, anyway? Physiology, acupuncture, astronomy, geomancy, archaeology, botany, Sino-organics—do you think I'd've undertaken that much investigation in addition to all my other work unless I was sure? I perfected cream production in this province, didn't I? I know what I'm doing! It *will* work, ALL RIGHT?"

He looks away, and this time I don't want him to look back.

I'm sick of having to justify what we've spent five years preparing for. I get up, go to the kitchen island, pour a glass of wine from the bottle I've been letting respire for the last twenty minutes.

I retire into the deeply reclining chair near the window, letting the red liquid magic seep into my root soil, leaving my brother to deal with his lack of vision on his own. With the press of a button, the curtains retract, reveal a sky breathing its first flames of the imminent end of the day.

Lung-mei.

I wonder if the ancient Chinese looked up into sunset's fire and imagined it as the breath of the dragons they claimed flew upon those *lung-mei* skyways.

Well, regardless, we'll have the zodiascope back soon enough, and then we'll deal with the people who've inconvenienced us.

And soon after . . . my God, I can practically taste it. After such a long time waiting, searching, only to find it and get it and at the last moment lose it—right now I'm craving it, *aching* for it. . . .

And when we have it, we'll become the poetry and passions of dragons.

Vengeance of Yehatotron

IT'S SATURDAY NIGHT, AT VIDYSTOPIA, WHERE ALL THE SCUM OF the earth come seeking their filmic fantasies. I give them their visions, for a price. For I am a knight of the realm returnal.

Sir Yehat the Grave.

Jimps come and jimps go, but I stand bravely, ready to defend my Duke of Dim, John the Vapid, who even now orders me into battle while I grant order unto his archives.

"Aw, crap on crust, Yehat, *NO!* I've told you before, *Jungle Fever* goes in *Comedy*—"

"I accept your argument, John, except for the part where people who've actually *seen* the film realize that it isn't a comedy."

"Who owns this place, Yehat?"

"You do, my liege."

"Just get it done, footface."

It's not important that his remark is meaningless. If I started to understand him, *that's* when I would worry.

And then, as Ignoramus Maximus shambles away from me to attend to whatever he attends to, I look up to see, in slow motion no less, a Gorgeous Sister™ walk into our humble shitopolis.

I dust off my knees and greet her.

Yehat: "Your father."

Chocolate goddess: "Excuse me?"

"Your father . . . he must be a thief."

She looks too stunned to be horrified.

I have her *right* where I want her.

"Well, how else could he've stolen the stars and put them in your eyes?"

I see her estimating me, evaluating my roguish wit, my Han Soloesque charms.

"Now, surely," she says, her lips forming the words so precisely that I'm hypnotized by their fleshy pronouncement, "*no one* would say such an absurd remark and actually *mean* it . . . so I have to assume you said it to make me *laugh*."

"It's good to assume."

I smile, coaxing a chuckle from her. And from those lips.

"Since you're looking through our esteemed collection, madame, may I offer my services to you as your guide towards a piece of quality cinema? Foreign, perhaps? New Wave? Neonoir? Boudoir noir? World oir? Star Oirs?"

"Haar haar. So faar." She smirks. That smirk could sauté butter.

"Ooh, a graduate of the Seuss school. I'm impressed."

"It's good to be impressed."

"I couldn't agree more."

"Actually, I'm looking for a good De Niro. *Deer Hunter* . . . or maybe *Midnight Run*? Charles Grodin digging at De Niro . . . oh, man, it's a scream."

DOING.

Within a few minutes more of this it's time to wrap up my transaction with this fired-bronze succubus, all the better to eat her with, when we end somehow off course and I actually hear her saying the words "I think I'm busy. . . ."

"Vel—" (That's her name.) "It'll be fun. Come *on,* when's the last time you ate seaweed ice cream?"

"Well . . . let me think about it."

"I don't kno-o-o-ow. . . . There's not too many people who are allowed access to knowledge of my secret culinary delights. If you *don't* call, I may have to destroy the city to prevent it from falling into the wrong hands."

"I understand."

"You gonna call me?"

"I'll call you."

"You gonna call me?"

"I'll call you."

"Vel, Velma, Velima, Velocity . . . are you for real, or just a dream so good she can walk outside my sleeping mind?"

She laughs again.

"I'll call, Yehat."

Johnes Simplex: "YEHAT!"

"I guess I'd better go." She smiles, slipping out the door, just as John lames up to the front.

"Yehat, my store isn't your personal pickup pad complete with, with, uh . . . pillows . . . and, uh . . . *pow*der puffs—it's a *bus*iness, for cripes sakes, and I can't have you scaring off every broad who swivels her hips in here lookin for *Dirty Dancing*—"

Explosions cut him off—somewhere outside the store, something major must be transpiring, even as we stand engaging in our fine intellectual dalliance.

John Jacob Jimpleheimer Schmidt: "What in friggin jasmine *is* that?" He pounces over to the window, gawks up towards something distant and evidently huge.

I then hear people screaming, car tires squealing and chewing concrete to speed away from our location. I gaze out into the street.

Towering above us, sundering buildings and snapping power lines, having waited all this time only for my telecyberpathic signal to wreak unholy vengeance upon this city that has spurned my vast and violent technotopic visions, my two-hundred-meter-tall metallic masterpiece is unleashed at last.

A middle-aged Asian customer runs up to the window,

stands beside John—and while his mouth works for ten seconds, I hear only four words come from his mouth entirely out of sync with his lips. "We are doomed!" he cries. He looks upward and points:

"*YEHATOTRON!*"

My invincible Yehatotron stalks above us at last, smashing houses and mashing buses as hundreds of Asian customers run from the store and clamber into tanks and flying cars shaped like moths.

Then the front window and roof smash inward like a matchstick house torn apart by a beagle's snout as the unstoppable omnisteel clenchotronic fist of my Super Sentinel invades the store for its prize—

John: "*NO-O-O-O-O-O-O!*"

The fist withdraws, dropping Johnish gore and limbs as it leaves. Velma runs back into the store, clutching me and my chest.

"You've saved us, Yehat, with that massive brain of yours! And to think you're so good-looking—why haven't you been snatched up a long time ago?"

"Baby," I say, "it's funny you should use that word—"

"YEHAT!"

It's John, rudely still alive, standing in front of me with all of his limbs or reasonable facsimiles thereof intact.

"What in the donkey's balls are you smiling at?" he yells. "Now, pay attention and do like I said!"

And just as John walks away through the sadly undestroyed store, who should place video boxes for *The Hidden* and *They Live* on the counter but Kevlar Meaney of the Wolves? These putrid bastards really never took direct aim at me, but they did blast my partner to smithereens, so I've got a pretty good hate on for them myself. Sharp dresser, Kevlar, just like his brother—sharp enough to slice off human skin. And right here with him, their two ultracoiffed hos, particularly spectacular, veritable aut-ho-mobiles. Shiny chrome and evrathang.

These guys have enough money to buy their *own* video store. . . . Why the hell would he be renting?

Too bad this isn't a restaurant, so I could spit in his food. He preens, pretends, pays, pushes off.

Prick.

Work finally ends just as Hamza walks in to pick me up. We start the long walk home. He's been in a great mood ever since (1) meeting this nutty broad and (2) *dating* this nutty broad. He blabs on and on to me all about his picnic date with her this morning, and he's in such high spirits that he's gone back to carrying his spray paint can.

(Sidebar: Hamza doesn't tag—he just leaves political messages—and right now he's altering a bus bench sign about our premier from HE LISTENS, HE CARES to HE GLISTENS, HE SCARES.)

I notice while we walk away how he's doing his little urine dance. Hamza has a bladder about the size of a shrimp testicle. Weakness . . . I hate it.

"And I started writing again!" he suddenly chirps.

I stop dead.

This is serious.

The man hasn't written in three years, and all he ever wanted to be was a writer.

I don't like the reason . . . but . . . but I have to be grateful for this result. I just hope it doesn't dry up as quickly as it bloomed.

I ask him to tell me about whatever he wrote, and he recites a poem for me, a delicate set of lines about luminous clouds at night over the city.

I . . . I *like* it.

I want to believe that she could be good for him. I *want* to believe it, for his sake.

But I can't.

Excerpts from Heinz Meaney's Visage Grotesque

"CAINTHROPOLOGY:
THE UTILITY OF AGONY"

THE MECHANISM OF UNIVERSAL ADVANCEMENT IS PAIN—THE pain that comes through conflict and, yes, sadly, death. The best (indeed, the only honest) name for this conflict is cannibalism.

The cannibal's comprehension of the transfer of energies from one being to another is primitive, but in its Occam-like unadorned simplicity is elegant. The conqueror captures and consumes the flesh, and most preferably the brain, of the conquered. This Stuff is the recently living repository of the passions, drives, songs, prayers, hopes, glories, and Secrets of death and eternity.

For the conqueror to eat of this Stuff is for the conqueror to imbibe of the organic, somatic truth of existence. It is to celebrate the life of the vanquished, and incorporate his life energy into the never-ending hunt. . . .

· · ·

[F]rom outside the original Indo-European mythic genealogy is the parable that is now at the core of the Western mind, from that Semitic clan of wanderers, mystics, madmen, and warrior-philosopher-kings: the tale of Cain and Abel. This most misunderstood story is key to all, to explaining and expressing the power and the glory of the ascendancy of Man as revealed by the Prophet Darwin (may peace be upon his gametes).

Cain slays Abel, we are told, because YHWH finds Cain's agricultural sacrifice inferior to Abel's offering of meat from his herd. In jealousy, we are told, Cain rises up and destroys the object of his diminution. YHWH, incensed at the world's first documented case of sibling rivalry, banishes Cain from the land to which his parents had already been banished after their own pathetic and transparent attempts to improve their bargaining position with the Almighty. . . .

But what if we've misunderstood the story all along? What if God weren't punishing Cain, *but rewarding him*? What if the contest of sacrifices didn't end at God's acceptance of Abel's mutton or beef, but only after Cain vanquished that offering with an even finer cut—*by sacrificing Abel himself*?

After all, once God affixes his mark (erroneously assumed by European clergy to be a racial signifier, but indicative of something far, far more grand), Cain leaves the presumably unpleasant refugee grounds he shares with his parents for a territory where he fathers a vast dynasty apparently also protected by Divine Immunity and with which he reintroduces cattle herding, but also for whom he invents the tent, the harp, the organ, brass- and ironwork—not to mention the first civilization.

This is the penalty for the world's first murder—and fratricide, no less (not to mention the aforementioned genocide of one-quarter of humanity, whom the Nodites were apparently

created to replace in abundance, or in fear of Cain's proclivities . . . or to feed those proclivities for the Godhead's/Civilization's sake)?

It seems far more logical that this ancient and oft-told but always misunderstood tale is the central revelation of the price of civilization: sacrifice.

Human sacrifice.

CHARACTER DATA:

Frosty Gorkovski

REAL NAME: Robert Frost Gorkovski.

HATES: Digaestus, "that billion-dollar-word-stuttering little puke-stick," not to mention the Mugatu, "that gas-sniffin Sasquatch-stinkin pile of man-crap." Plus everyone else, but especially those two.

DREAM: To beat Digaestus to death with a massive aluminum replica of a feminine-product applicator.

MAGNITUDE OF BITTERNESS: Like unto the Tower of Babel.

ARMOR TYPE: Kessel Run–style victory vest (black).

CAMERA: Minolta.

SCENT: Formaldehyde.

SECRET: As a child, cried during the Bugs Bunny version of Wagner's *Nibelung* when the Bugs Bunny Brünnhilde (or whatever) died.

REPUTATION: A true gentleman, so long as he's asleep.

GENRE ALIGNMENT: *Babylon 5, Hellblazer, Kolchak: The Night Stalker.*

IMPAIRMENT: Enormous contempt for all life.

SLOGAN: "Aw, fuck em. Fuck everybody."

The Milkmen Deliver at Night

I'M WAITING FOR A CLIENT THAT PAUL DAMASK CALLED ME about, some new woman with a whole lotta green, while hanging at one of my usual sales haunts, Club Murder.

That's this fuckin off-Whyte nightclub *that shall remain nameless* that caters to every preppy wipe-ass and jailbait-chasing frat-boy-rat-boy of the greater E-Town area. I swear, these pukes come in on convoys from Stony Plain, Leduc, whatever. All a buncha crotch-rots.

So goddam loud in here, nonstop dance/nineties rock/pop shit, and all these expensive pukes and their money and their hard drinks. So loud I can barely think. Not that that matters to these submorons—not a goddam *one* of these brain-pans has a single neuron firing for any function higher than eating, shitting, fighting, or fucking.

And like I said, the music! The same thud-thud-thud-thud jungle bunny bass and drumbeats again and again and again—I swear, this is what people hear in their heads before they open fire in a post office. Usedta be in this city you could catch punk jams all over the place, almost any night of the goddam week.

That was me, back then, before I grew my hair out and shocked it totally totally white, back when it was red and me and my brother Ted (who also had red hair and was thus called Red Ted, although some shit-stains usedta call him Red-tard-Ted, Uneducate-Ted, ek setchra) usedta be everywhere in the scene, DK shirts on, Mohawks up, and safety pins in and all over.

Best gigs ever were the SNFU ones. Chi Pig, their leader, was, like, my idol. He was, like, the model of what I wanted to be, except he was Chinese. But other than that. He had a pure punkness to him, a perfect punkitude, screaming out primal numbers like "Snapping Turtle." Wasn't all corrupt and faked-out.

Well, not back then, anyway. Now him and his group're total goddam sellouts. Guy I sell to was hawking their concert shirts at this one flea market, had some leftovers from InFest (near Calgary in '93), not the ones with the rotting zombie heads, but the real commercial designy ones. I told him no way. Like they need the fuckin money.

And here I am, still waiting for this new chick to show up while I waste my night in Club Murder in the rectum of Whyte Ave/Old Strathcona.

Shit. Usedta be nice and peaceful, so they say, an "arts district" when in the eighties it was a buncha crummy second-hand bookstores and lotsa comics joints and arcades and Scona Bowl and Wee Book Inn and Sir Donut and whatever and then after theater gets all trendy and takes off around, say, '86? everything began to change. I mean, yeah, the theater boom was good for me, at first. I actually had semisteady work for the first time.

But then Old Strath became a boutique zone, and then a frat hatchery, and everything went to H-E-double dildos.

Paul Damask says this woman wants to score some cream,

a whole bunch. Says she's a new client, a real looker, some black chick. Says he thinks she must be a model or an actress or a football player's wife or something, what with all the money she's flashing.

I don't care who she is or what color she is. Long as she's got the cash. And as long as she shows up soon. I'm getting bored here. Only so many whores you can look at in one night being chased by meatheads. I'm thinking I should hook up with Alpha Cat after everyone's done rounds—I just got a wide-screen version of *Ran,* and the Cat's always talking about how Kurosawa's "the article don" or whatever.

Like I'm saying, the whole Whyte Ave area explodes as hangout supreme after '86, specially with the Fringe Theatre Festival, when, like, a half-billion cheapskate assholes and hangers-on come out here and *don't* go see plays.

Yeah. The eighties: they're *all* assholes, all posing in their fancy fuckin sunglasses and expensive designer watches and Day-Glo colors and upturned collars and shaker knit sweaters. And they come down here faking and phonifying up the whole area and making everything they touch turn to diarrhea.

So this is *my* origin story, just like getting bit by a radioactive spider, but in my case, it's getting the shit kicked outta me by some radioactive frat boys. I'm leaving the sketch comedy show I'm doing at the Chinook with a troupe called Monsters from Space, and I come out wearing this giant lobster costume and as I try to get in my car, my pinchers are so big I can't get my key in the lock.

So I'm taking off my lobster gloves, and these inbred chute-eaters come up hassling me and pushing me around while I'm wearing the goddam costume. There's too many of em for me to fight anyway, and until then I was never much of a fighter, but for fuckin out loud, attacking a guy in a costume? I can't even run away in this thing.

So these beered-up shit-steaks start shoving me around, give me a coupla black eyes, and when they get me on the ground they start kicking me in the ribs and cracking me in the nuts and shouting, "Get the butter, man! Get the *butter*!"

I end up having to go to the hospital on accounta these pubes'd collapsed my left lung. If some customers from the Second Act hadn't seen me lying there I probably woulda died. When they're loading me on the ambulance I hear this one woman on the sidewalk say she and her friends didn't even realize there was a person inside my costume (I was knocked out and lying there for, like, fifteen minutes or something)—she thought I was just some giant foam lobster lying on the street for whateverthefuck reason.

It's their jackets that gives em away, their Gamma Kappa Epsilon GEEK coats. Doesn't take me forever to find out who's saying what at Club Murder, since I know that's where all these tapeworms hang out, and obviously a story about gang-banging a giant lobster is gonna make the rounds.

And it doesn't take much to then arrange to sell em some product. See, that's how I get into the whole trucking business in the first place—until then, I just take a little stuff now and then before a show. But I know some names—in theater, you're never more than two people away from scoring—make some inquiries, get hired. . . . Fuck, it's like the goddam civil service, I guess. Only no union.

And then I—what's the word? I *bide* my time. Find em. Sell to em. More than once. Build a trucker-client relationship—but hush-hush. Without the lobster suit they don't know who the hell I am, anyway. And then when I get the chance, I even arrange to deliver, just like Domino's, just like Lydo's.

Goddam waitress keeps pestering me, like she's gonna get fired if I don't buy more drinks. I order a Trad just to shut her up and get her to leave me alone. At the last second I ask her, even nicely, if she can get the DJ to throw on something from Metallica's *Kill 'Em All*, or maybe the Dead Kennedys' "Too Drunk to Fuck," but she looks at me like I just took a shit on the dance floor. I don't know why whores are never nice to me.

So anyway, after I get to the frat boys' place, somebody's

apartment off campus, I get em juiced up so bad they don't even try to stop me when I duct-tape their wrists together behind their backs and duct-tape their ankles to their chair legs. Just see em noddin off with sick self-satisfied suck-ass smiles on their faces.

So many years of being pushed around by pricks like them. First when I was a kid, then as a comix kid, then as a struggling actor. Always putting up with overgrown rich-prick assholes and the fag jokes and the fag bashings and the preppy scumwad flak-attacks. I aint queer, but my brother Ted was, and on his account alone it's great to score one against the bad guys.

I guess I shoulda called myself Lobster Man—the Invincible Bottom-Feeder on his Crustacean Mission to Pinch Injustice. But what kids usedta call me—*that* had to become my superhero name. That's how I got my revenge on Joe Chill, or the Burglar who killed Uncle Ben, or whoever killed the Punisher's family. Cool, calm, clean. The Ice-Man.

Frosty.

Whenever I feel pushed around or feel like the world's getting outta control, I just remember the looks on those taped-down fuck-holes' faces when I'm cutting off the first one's ball bag and cock and then make the other two eat their buddy's meat.

Man, duct tape is amazing. When I castrate that first cunt, the tape's so strong that all his face can do is sorta stretch out with the eyes all bugging out and shaking like bingo balls in an airstream—but the tape doesn't surrender a goddam millimeter.

And then I duct-tape the other two's mouths after I make em eat their pal's unplugged groin. And while I'm slitting their throats, I'm worried the blood might soak upwards and let the tape slide off like a bib, but naw—it stays in place, even with all their taped-mouth groaning and taped-down shaking in their chairs.

One guy even shakes so much he knocks his chair over and

smashes his head on the floor—but his body keeps the same taped-in posture, just like he's a posed action figure. No—wait—a *no*-action figure.

I swear by duct tape. Still carry at least one roll of that wherever I go.

Waitress brings me my Trad. About goddam time.

Since that showdown with the GEEKs, whatever fear I carried of bullies since I was a kid is gone. Gone for good. I'm cured, permanently. Hell, I should write one of those self-help books. *Bullied No More: Three Fun Steps to Fearlessness.* And taking out a guy what's bigger than me? That's like winning a *platinum* medal at the Olympics.

So when is this bitch I'm supposed to meet gonna show up? I hope Damask hasn't screwed up again. I'm gonna hafta have words with that guy someday.

Bullies, like I was saying, they don't scare me anymore. Not even Mr. Dulles goddam Allen. He thinks he's so big. He's so fuckin full of himself, like he really does got us all locked under with his little Jedi mind tricks. I learned you never let *any*body have anything over you unless you got something under them. Something sharp and long that you're willing to use without blinking an eye.

The boss thinks he calls all the shots? I can live with letting him think that for now. And when the time is right, when he thinks he can snap his fingers and make me do his bidding and send me off to die, he's gonna get the biggest surprise of his life. And the last.

So where's this goddam woman, anyway? Damn club is too packed with idiots—

I nearly shit my pants.

She's right beside me—snuck up on me somehow. That never happens. Swhat I get for drinking on the job. I know better. Mr. Allen'd have my soles if he knew. Fuck it. She's here. Got me penned in, too, me sitting down in the corner, her blocking my way out. She's got a look, like she's completely unsurprised. Like she's been watching me.

Tall—goddam. These black broads, you never know—probably usedta run track or something. Or play basketball, obviously. If her eyes weren't open, I probably wouldn't even be able to *see* her in this place. She's dressed funny—some kinda khaki something or other, boots—only thing dressy on her is her scarves. How the hell she get past the bouncers—doesn't this joint have a dress code? No black-chick survivalist gear or whatever.

Man—check this crazy belt—got these shiny thimble sorta things connected to some metal somethings . . . sorta ethnic looking. Weird.

She sits down. She looks casual, but I seen too many people like this—behind the casual she's keeping eyes on everything, me included. Tough chick.

Damask was right . . . she *is* a looker. Sorta like that Somalian model in *The Undiscovered Country*. But younger.

And here she is, wanting to buy *cream*.

I tell her Damask said she wanted a stick, and she says that's right. I ask her if she knows how much that's worth, and she says she can cover the price Damask said it'd be. I tell her to prove it. She puts her hand palm down on the table, and when she slides it back slightly, I'm seeing enough rims of hundreds to figure it for about the right price.

We go outside to my vehicle. She doesn't get her hand stamped. It's hot out, the streets half in shadow from all the heavy summer leaves blocking the cones of streetlights. It's dark enough in places, you could hide a small army.

We're down the block. She's checking out everybody and everything with those eyes of hers—she's like a . . . I don't know—she looks like she could rip open someone's guts without a blink. Like a jackal—that's what I was trying to say.

I saw this one documentary, with the night-vision animal photography and all, of jackals, which is what got me into taking photos—and the thing's eyes were all distorted, glowing, like demon eyes or something. That's what she looks like.

At my car I take out a metal Thermos, the heavy-duty kind. I wanna just take the cash and hand it over, but she don'wanna do that. She wants me to open it first. What the hell . . . good customer relations, plus, she aint so hard on the eyes. Maybe if this goes well I can clear some punani. I unscrew the Thermos, dribble out the packing foam slowly, take out the stoppered test tube.

"Fifteen mills," I say, holding up the stick. "Smell it if you want—you can't fake that smell, y'know. Even the smell's got a kick."

She does smell it.

She winces, just like they all do.

"Paul said you'd be carrying more, if I wanted it."

"Yeah, I'm always ready. How many sticks you planning on?"

"All of it."

"'Scuse me?"

"Everything you've got."

I snort. Chick has balls like snapping turtles. "It's gonna costja."

"Whatever it is, I've got it."

I keep an eye and a half on her, put one hand on the piece at the small of my back, flex that thing, let it glint, let her know better'n'ta get funny ideas and start goddam fuckin with me, and put the other hand on the handle of a case underneath the passenger seat.

I pull it out, open it, step back, let her look. She's gonna shit her pants when I tell her.

"Twenty-three sticks," I smooth. "Plus the one in your hand." Any second she's gonna shit. "Fifty-five thou."

Goddam if she doesn't reach inside some of her cargo pockets and pull out four bound bricks of bills.

"Actually, fifty-five two," she says. "Imagine you'll throw in the case for free."

Fuck a duck.

She hands me the cash.

I'm actually shivering by the time I hand her the case. What kind of chick walks around with fifty megabones?

"Count it. And I'm going to as*sume*," she says, "you wouldn't risk wrecking your chance for repeat business . . . by selling me diluted stock. Or decoy sticks."

"I'm, I'm, I'm a *bus*inessman," I stumble, trying to flip through the wads. It's all here . . . like she knew exactly how much I'd be carrying. This shit aint right. This shit is insane. Can't let her see me freaking, here! Calm down, Frosty-cakes!

"Bad decisions," I say as slowly and as smoothly as possible, "are bad for business."

"*And bad for your health,*" she rasps, fixing her jackal eyes at me.

And narrowing them.

And then I'm cold, not just shivering, but *really fuckin cold* all of a sudden, like I'm lying naked on ice with a sleet wind raking my whole body. And my guts're all fucky, churning, my head's light, my balls are shrinking—just cuz some chick says to me—

I haven't felt like this since—since way back before the end of the whole lobster incident, before I—

"Be seeing you," she says, her voice sounding all hoarse and smoky and awful, like a goddam furnace or something, "before you see me."

What the fuck? How can anyone—a *chick,* for crap's sakes—make me so—

She retreats, never letting her ice pick eyes off me, until she sinks into the shadows.

I know one thing. Damask is wrong. No way is that bitch a model, and she's no actress, and she's no pro-baller's wife, either.

And one other thing.

Her repeat business, at any price, I don't want. Ever.

Telescope to Avalon

Why, that green-blooded son of a bitch!
—L. McCoy, upon discovering proof of life after death

I KNOW BETTER THAN TO GET MY HOPES UP. I DO, I KNOW better. I aint one of these ass-banks who gets on his helmet and pads and cleats and grease and then runs out and slips on the grass. Comes time for a tackle or a touchdown, I'm ready. For whatever it takes. And I leave my feelings in the goddam locker room.

I'm past city lights, way out west on the highway to Jasper, just dark road, shadow grass, and black sky swallowing my headlights.

And me.

You don't get to where I am in life if all you do is let your expectations hijack you. That's not how you earn three Grey Cups, and that's not how you build an ass-stomping empire, either.

You got your brains, you got your savvy, you got your intimidation factor, and you got your balls, *capiche*? You do what you gotta do, and you just do it—no thinking about it, no despair, and no hope. Cuz once you start hoping, you screw the pooch every time.

My fuckin heart nearly explodes.

There are demons on the road.

I'm speeding down-road straight at em. Flaming-hell eyes, open mouths rowed with fangs, and dripping tongues—

I get ahold of myself. Only cayoats or something. I've dreamed of things like this. Dreamed it a buncha times. Red flaring eyes and fangs and then my neck and cheeks being torn open and my eyes ripped into pieces. And teeth chunking the last bits of meat off my ribs and thighbones. And flapping tongues lapping up my muddy blood puddles.

Just *cayoats*—

I blast the horn, get em outta the way so I don't run em over. They fly off into the darkness. Prairie ghosts. I don't gotta hurt em. You don't get anywhere or at least you don'stay there long by doin that. You put a hurting on someone or something only when you gotta. And then, only as much as you gotta.

Road's clear again.

Like I was saying, you can get your hopes up on things, which then means you destroy yourself by fucking up your morale one organ at a time. You gotta focus, have what the Japanese call "no-mindedness." *Mushin.*

Road sign flares yellow: my turn's coming up.

I read this one book by Sun Tzu—he's *Chi*nese, not Japanese—and in this one part he says (I got this memorized):

> On desperate ground, I would proclaim to my soldiers the hopelessness of saving their lives.
>
> For it is the soldier's disposition to offer an obstinate resistance when surrounded, to fight hard when

he cannot help himself, and to obey promptly when he has fallen into danger. . . .

Forestall your opponent by seizing what he holds dear, and subtly contrive to time his arrival on the ground. Walk in the path defined by rule, and accommodate yourself to the enemy until you can fight a decisive battle.

My life changed after I read that book. I don't live by the fuckin Dow Jones anymore. I live by the Tao, Jones. The balance. The exact agreement of force between the inside and outside of the bubble. Too much force either way, and—

Here's my turn. I hang a hard right north onto a gravel road. SUV handles it okay, but still . . . I don'like all the vibrations. . . . My colon feels like someone's shoving an auger around up in there. My internals've never gone back to what they usedta be. I'd fuckin *kill* someone for a tall, ass-cooling Metamucil right now.

There's this other thing I like that Sun Tzu says—he says, "Exhibit the coyness of a maiden, until the enemy gives you an opening; afterwards emulate the rapidity of a running hare, and it will be too late for the enemy to oppose you."

Y'know, I'm from small-town Alberta, Barrhead, to be specific. And I used to hear all this shit about the Chinese back in the locker room, back when I was in high school, all these asslords always making em out to be stupid crumbums who can't talk straight or do shit right for themselves, but lemme tell you, it's like Richard Pryor says: The Chinese are the most intelligent people on earth. How do I know? he says. Cuz anybody who can eat with two sticks has *got* to be the smartest motherfucker alive.

Even just *thinking* about that fuckin nut Pryor still makes me gut-laugh, even though when I do, it feels like my balls are gonna break off one at a time and roll away. God, makes me laugh so hard I feel like I gotta take a dump.

I'm far enough away from the main road. Even darker out

here now. Might as well stop and get out and try out the 'scope.

All comes down to this. All this waitin and tryin and hurtin and dyin, it's all scrunched into the one second when I put the lens to my eye and look out here, away from all the light pollution under a clear night sky.

Hard to believe I didn't even dream any of this existed—the 'scope, what the 'scope's sposta reveal about any of this before—I didn'about any of it until Mr. Fancy came along with his franchise offer. Not that that ass-badger was ever planning to let me open all the books and learn the eleven secret herbs and spices for myself.

No, only way I learned what I know now was the hard way, callin in every favour, tappin every source, swipin every secret manuscript and scroll, using every bit of brain power and fist power I could muster.

Been hard gettin the marrow stains off my clothes.

But I'm here now.

I don't wanna hope. Because if this doesn't work I don'-know what I'm gonna do. So much ass-breaking pain forced me this far. Just want it over. Don'even wanna break anyone's skull anymore. Just want this ass-grind *done*.

I stop the vehicle, grab the zodiascope, open the door.

Sky's so big and dazzling and buzzing and crackling and moaning with all that black silence, I feel like my skull is open to space, all that way-beyond soaking directly into my brain. Stars and stars and stars . . . some of em planets, some of em satellites. All of em out there, alone, untouchable.

Hell, probably ninety percent of em, light's been traveling so long . . . they coulda been dead burned out for ten thousand years or ten *million* years and we wouldn'know it. I heard my little ass-scrapers talking all about this one time. . . . Space is like a time machine, a time telescope. . . . Everything you see is only as recent as the light that brung it to you.

It's like a letter sent to you by your uncle in World War II, lost in the mail and only gets to you today. In the letter, everything's still happening and he don't even know that Hitler lost. He never even met Auntie Anna yet or had his kids or saw em grow up. It's a brand-new brand-old message trapped in time, like a bright blue butterfly in amber.

Up there, in the darkness, all that space and galaxies and whatnot . . . since so much of it, guaranteed, is long gone, space aint only a time telescope. . . . It's really a death telescope.

You see the dead like they're still living with you.

I bought my own telescope after I heard my little ass-soaps talking all that shit. Got it out on my balcony, too.

But for this, I hadda come out here. With a different kind of 'scope.

It's about three thirty A.M. in the ass-busting morning. I'm in the middle of a field, totally alone in the dark, under about a billion billion stars. If cayoats or badgers or wolves come out here, I'll have to tear em apart with my bare hands.

I did that once, to a wolf.

I'm actually fucking shaking as I bring the 'scope up to my face.

I close my eyes, breathe in deeply, put the eyepiece in place.

Open my eyes.

I see stars.

And nothing else.

I try adjusting some ass-stinking tubes and dials and buttons on this piece of ass-crap, but I don'know what the hell I'm doing—for all I know I could be pushing the settings farther *away* from what I wanted! It's not like it came with an instruction manual—all I thought was I was sposta look up and see the direction up there in the sky with stars or flames or northern lights or whatever pointing the way—

I *told* myself not to—*not to*—

That fuckin bastard. Even when I'm trying to screw him back for all he's done—he screws me again!

"HE'S SCREWED ME *AGAIN*!"

There aint even an echo—my voice is nothing out here, with nothing to bounce back off.

"Screwed me *again*," I whisper, over and over.

I guess if I'm honest, my whisper sounds more like a sob.

But out here, no one hears it anyway. Not even the stars.

Like a Nighthawk Feels Thunder

UPON THESE FILTHY STREETS I WALK, RETURNING TO MY BASE OF operations, once my home, nine lives between me and it. Each step towards it enchants an agonizing-sweet nostalgia I must deny; each step towards it conjures forth a breathless, wonderful horror I have no choice but to embrace.

Here, in a neighborhood called Highlands, I walk with a case of metamorphosis, a case of vials full of destiny.

The darkness clutches at me, but I tremble not. For how few days upon my path even at noontime did I walk in light? I have always trodden the paths in all the lonely spaces, between mountains, in valleys, through caverns.

I will not be deterred.

Yes, I am the woman who lights the darkness, doubly lights it. I will overthrow the destroyers, and make to stand those who weep, who hide their faces, who sink down.

And for the task I have before me, I have assembled enough ichor to transform the *sekht-en-cha* Hamza Senesert.

And yet—

No!

No, not when I am so close—not *now*—

He stands there between me and my home and home-no-more, a Thing built of dynasties' anguish and hatred, a thing counter-Kabbalistically sewn together, a living vengeance in the beats of a dead heart.

The streets that intersect into these crosshairs are empty save him and me.

"You," I whisper at him from half a block away, spitting in the molten-iron speech of Senzar. "I will not stop, not even if I die. And I will not die alone!"

He stands, a thing without meaning except for this encounter, a being without hope except in its craving for my destruction. My bluster is pointless—why threaten death to one who has never believed he was alive?

"Heart-Eater!" I hiss the Senzar curse, approaching him, for there is no retreat, no running. No escape. "Heart-Eater, I defy you! I call you out in your name of 'Despoiler of the Holy River'! I call you out in your name of 'Butcher on the Night Path'!"

Each step I force myself to take towards him consumes whole seconds, the distance closing between us taking minutes.

Yet now, finally, we stand now only a few strides apart.

I taste his breath. I hear his scent. I feel his voice like a nighthawk feels thunder.

For at last, he speaks.

"Arrogance. Delusion!" he rumbles at me in Akkadian. Even in his choice of tongue he is dead . . . and defiant!

"*We* are not deluded, Crocodile," I whisper, putting down the case, letting all my muscles become soft, pliant, letting my breath become as mist about the rain. "We will prevail!"

"Foolish! Vain! Wrong!" he says, not stepping towards me yet, but all his body engorging with his turgid blood, his mouth slavering with frigid venom. "None of *you* is fit to open the Jar! Can't be trusted! Can't be allowed!"

"*Only* we—"

"*You* are defilers! You, with your scum Hobinarit Interceptor, whom *I* intercepted!" He laughs with the mouth of a tiger: he glares with the eyes of eagles. "And we will not let you doom us all!"

" '*Sebi kher, āāui-f qaus,*' " I recite, fighting my terror, willing my hands to become instruments of this destiny, " '*hesq en demt thes-f. . . .*' " *The beast hath fallen. . . . His two hands are hacked off. . . . Cuts asunder the knife his joints. . . .*

"Your death scripture cannot save you, hunting bitch!"

His shoulders twitch.

I reach to my belt, flow forward.

It has begun.

UnenRamaãnefer.

Tracking Coyote, Hidden Jackal

SO, ANYWAY, WHEN I GOT UP THIS MORNING AND FELT ALL THAT sunlight pouring into my room like some solar soul recharger, I said to myself, You're gonna go find Sherem. So what if she doesn't have a phone yet? *You* can find her.

Ye's not even up yet. Usually by eight A.M., even on a Sunday morning, you can find him up, tinkering with the R-Mer. It's actually looking pretty good these days. . . . He's got the gloves wired in, plus the arm controls operational.

I told him I don't want him working with explosives in the house anymore, not since he blew out all the windows and nearly destroyed a whole buncha comics (windows're replaceable, but he could've burnt up a stack of *ROMs* and *Micronauts,* all with Michael Golden covers). So I don't think he's putting the rockets into the arm launchers anymore. Really, it's the most supremely amazing thing he's ever built, but I have no idea if he'll ever finish it.

So, anyway, like I was saying, he's *not* up. I guess he's still sleeping so he can get ready for meeting this Velma woman or whatever tomorrow night. Me, I'm not waiting for tonight.

I'm in and outta the shower splashetty-split, dressed, grabbing some trail mix, and I'm out.

Morning's amazing in Kush. I should be up at this hour more often. If I were up even earlier I'd hear the call to prayer from Masjid Imam al-Mahdi. Man, their *mueddhin* can sing, lemme tell you. He's like Baaba Maal or something. Any other neighborhood in town, that'd be impossible—noise complaints—but when you hear him in the afternoon, fuhgeddaboutit, traffic stops. Seriously, people stop walking, talking, whatever their religion, just to listen to this guy. It's beautiful. So beautiful, makes me wanna believe again.

So I don'know where she lives but that kinda thing never stopped me before. When I hit 107th Ave I sniff the air and just kinda hang there for a bit, eyes closed. The sun's so strong through my lids I can see the veins, snaking purple black on red.

Then everything goes a deep shimmering sapphire, like the wings of an Amazonian morpho butterfly, like the inside of some kinda Neptunian seashell.

Then it fades back to flesh red, and I open my eyes, walking east, to the sun.

An hour or so later I'm somewhere in or near Highlands, and I come upon a bunch of run-down apartments. If not for the effects of this dynamite morning in the youth of a soultacular summer, I'd be tempted to call this couple of blocks the urban-planning equivalent of the lower intestine. But not even metro blight can blunt my mood this morning.

The air is so absolutely pristine . . . musta rained last night, late, and so everything is completely fresh, sparkling, each detail standing out like an F-22 shot with a strobe light. The whole world, even the dirt, is clean, and every color is more intense and true to itself under the early-morning amber gold than it can be at any other time of day, even sunset. Sun's too tired, too red, by that time of day to be completely honest. Right now, everything is spectrally sincere.

I know I'm close.

In fact, I think it's this building right here: *the Mordecai Richler Estates*.

I hearda this place. Man, what a shit-heap disgrace to E-Town—excuse me—what a *gloriously quaint piece of preserved culture. A heritage building, for sure.*

This whole area must be condemned. I know she's here somewhere—my Coyote sense confirms it—but why here? In a condemned building of all places? All the windows boarded up, and the doors boarded and chained, too? How the hell's she get in?

I creep around back. Back door's boarded up, too, but there're no chains. And I can see where the boards are loose, which must be where she gets in. Damn, she is a bizarre chick. Really. I mean, I like bizarre and all, but even for *me*—a condemned building, for crying out loud? What the hell could account for *that*?

Like, I guess I've known she was sorta *off* since I first met her, what with the weird thing in the parking lot, the crazy visor, her micromoodiness and whatnot, and hey, I've always been a sucker for some mystery, y'know? She's an adventure wrapped inside an enigma wrapped up in a dynamite set of flesh and bones.

(I'm *guessing,* anyway. . . . Her clothes aren't exactly revealing or anything, but she's tall, got a *Hel-LO*! face, and underneath all that cloth she *looks* shapely.)

But *still* . . .

Here goes nothing.

I squeeze through. It's dark inside, especially after that iris-slamming intensity outside, and it takes me a minute to adjust, more than long enough to pick up smells in here. Not *so* bad . . . at least not like legions of homeless've been making southern exports here. Mostly dust, rusty water, rain must decay.

But why in the hell would she . . . ?

With the few strands and shafts of light sliding in from dislodged boards at hall windows, I find the stairwell.

On the third floor, what used to be apartment 3, I knock.
Nothing.
I knock again.
Nothing.
I knock a third time. I *know* she must live here, but I can't
be sure she's home at this instant. Then there's faint sounds,
shuffling, clanking, and—I think, yeah, definitely—even more
shuffling. And muttering.

The door opens a crack, and Sherem is on the other side,
wearing massive Nigerian embroidered gold-green pants and
a slim, orange, formfitting top. And *what* a form, lemme tell
you. No skin, but good kot-*tam*!

And she's absolutely astonished to see me.

"*Hamza?*"

The Ancestral Crypt

She's speechless. This is fun. I love doing this.

"Good morning, Sherem."

"Haa . . . how . . . how on earth did you find me?"

"Uh . . . hunch?"

She stares, stunned.

"Why're you staying in this dump, Sherem? The Richler usedta be legendary. Bad wiring, bad smell, death trap. Shoulda been torn down years ago."

She's still teetering on the edge of credulity. "Slong story." She shakes her face, as if to scatter the mist of her disbelief. "Well, Hamza . . . you might as well come on in."

She ushers me in quickly and nervously, checking the hallway before she closes up. She mutters something. "What was that?" I ask.

"Nothing. Just talking to myself."

Inside I notice her face—I didn't notice in the shadows of the hall—she's got a scrape on the right side of her jaw and cuts on the right side of her forehead. And her arm—hell,

she's got a big bandage on her left arm with a huge dark burgundy spot!

"Hey, Sherem, you okay?"

"What, this?" She waves. "I just . . . heh heh . . . fell on the *stairs* last night. Pretty dark, got cut on some old junk. But when you travel as much as I do, you've gotta be part medic, y'know? So I just fixed myself up. It's no big deal."

She says it all way too easily. "Are you sure? Maybe you should see a doctor. You could have tetanus or something."

"Don't worry, Hamza. When you travel as much as I do you're always taking shots for everything."

"Yeah, but still . . . maybe your arm is broken and you need a cast."

"Hamza, when you—"

" 'When you travel as much as I do'—yeah, yeah."

She laughs, too energetically, pulls me towards her half a step and then places me two steps away to check me over. Her deflection of my questions and her shock at me finding her have given way to something else . . . something I'm hoping is appreciation.

"I *am* impressed," she says, smiling, shaking her head. "You're quite the detective. Did you, uh . . . follow me home or something?"

I don't know if this is just her distraction technique to get me to stop pestering her about medical attention, or maybe to prevent me from asking why in the hell she lives in this bizarre condemned crap-hole, or maybe she just can't believe that I could actually find her, but something in her tone says she doesn't believe that I could've followed her even if I would've tried. Like she's asking if I ever surf on top of the space shuttle during reentry.

"Naw, naw." I chuckle. "I aint no stalker. I'm a Coyote King. We specialize in the impossible."

"Apparently." She nods. It's a funny expression she's wear-

ing . . . like she'd rather be furious at someone—me, herself, I don'know—but instead, she's just delighted.

It's a nice look.

I hope to see more of that. Especially when she's dressed like this.

"Come on in, sit down."

I'm thinking maybe I shouldn't take off my shoes, given the condition of this building, but the floor looks clean, and it's mostly covered with . . . bamboo mats? I enter what I realize can only be called the sanctum sanctorum, and I can't believe I'm inside a wrecker. . . . This place is spectacular!

She has all kinda wall hangings up, covering split plaster or exposed brick or whatever, but in, like, a million different scripts: this one here's in Arabic, another in Amharic—then there's one in Sanskrit. . . . Over there's one in those ancient Chinese characters that look a lot more like pictograms than the modern ones do. And . . . I think this one here's called cuneiform, from Babylon . . . but most of em are hieroglyphics.

And beautiful, beautiful . . . venetians slit up the joint with just enough light to ignite gold and silver writing on old parchment, and give glow to paintings of ducks and geese and dogs and fish and wheat and cows, rivers and sphinxes and dragons and giants. . . .

And diagrams of the human body with connecting lines and circles radiating from the brain and below the belly button and all the fingertips and ankles, like some crazy Homo sapiens Van Allen belts.

The woman really *has* traveled, no question. Not a single "I went to Tibet and all I brought back was this lousy llama shirt" kinda thing in sight.

Not a lot of furnishings, though . . . some work shelves suspended from the wall . . . covered in beakers and jars and slides and . . . and a few microscopes? And a scale? And all kindsa bottles and jars?

I gesture. "Are you a chemist or something?"

"Oh, uh . . . with all the archaeological stuff I do . . . I have

to keep up on restoration techniques . . . paper, wood, paint, you know. Even metals. It's also a way to earn money. . . . I restore antiques, heirlooms, museum pieces . . . even classic cars."

"Cars? Really?"

"Uh, yeah."

Other than the shelves and some low, U-shaped bucket seat stools and a coffee table, the only other things I can make out are a whole bunch of plants and a really, really big pumpkin.

"Uh, won't your plants die in here? It's so dark."

"Yeah, well . . . these are special breeds. . . . Too much light'll kill em."

"And the pumpkin?"

"In case Prince Charming invites me to the ball."

I chuckle. She's quick, I'll give her that.

"This is a surprisingly nice place, Sherem."

"Well, in other circumstances I would've said something cheeky like 'I specialize in surprises.' But it seems like you've got me beat in that department."

I wave it off. "I'm good like that."

She arches an eyebrow. "Some trick, finding me. Siddown."

She offers me one of those ultracurved seat stools, and we sit at the low coffee table. She keeps looking at me, like she's trying to find a trap door or a hidden latch. I like the attention, sure, but I feel the sudden urge to pat my back pocket to check on my wallet.

She's so still, sitting there watching me, and with her in only that slim top she's wearing, for the first time ever I can see her muscled yet feminine shoulders beneath the tight cloth . . . but also, where the dance-type top opens at the center, the length of that ominous lizard-tail scar on her neck that writhes with her pulse. The scar continues past her collarbone, as if the lizard—actually, there're no feet marks, so I guess snake is more accurate—had headed straight for her heart.

"So, Sherem, you *live* here?"

"Yep."

Pause.

That's followed by another pause.

"For real?"

"Uh-huh."

A series of pauses erupts.

"Be*cause?*"

"I know it must seem nuts, but . . . well . . . when I was a girl, this was where I lived with my family. We didn't have a lotta money, and it was cramped: Mum and Dad, my four brothers and three sisters. This was the last place we lived together before we moved to Ash-Shabb.

"I don't care it's condemned. I've traveled through places that make this look like a palace."

I was wondering if maybe her being here was some kinda immigration thing, like she's illegal and doesn't wanna be caught, but she was born here, so she must be a citizen. And then I was thinking maybe it was some sorta religious thing, and she's an ascetic or taken a vow of poverty or doing penance or something. But maybe . . .

I mean, she's . . . I'd like to ask her more, but the way she said *This was the last place we lived together* was so . . . there's so much pain fossilized in how she says "Mum and Dad," there's gotta be an entire archaeological dig of trauma in there. . . .

I have no business asking about it . . . at least, not yet, not right now.

Man . . . family's all broken up or in foreign jails or dead or something, and just her here left in the ancestral crypt.

So that's it, then. I mean, it's extreme and all, but what *else* could she possibly be hiding by being here?

Serving Tea and Oracles

WHILE I'M THEORIZING ON HER GENEALOGICAL TRAGEDIES SHE'S been studying me, and openly, a dozen questions on her face and in her eyes. And she's been leafing through a deck of over-sized cards. I can just make out the faces: just like the wall hangings—birds, fishes, mythological beasties.

She shuffles the deck and looks like she's offering me one.

"You . . . you want me to pick a card?"

"No," she says, eyes on me, eyes glowing amber in a single note of light. "*I'm* going to."

She does. I can't see it, but she studies the image, those lit eyes dancing up a melody. She then puts the card back in the deck without showing me and shuffles it.

"Find the card."

"What?"

"Find it."

Strange chick. I pick up the deck, splay it poker-style, concentrate. I close my eyes, blink again, look at the deck. A bird, tall and skinny and angular, like a Ferrari version of a flamingo, catches my eye. I take it out.

"This one."

Her eyes and nostrils flare, like she's breathing in all of me.

This is getting too weird. "Look, I hope I didn't come at a bad time or anything—"

"No, no, Hamza, I'm glad you came, really! Just stunned, of course. Quite the talent you have. You seriously could be a detective. And certainly an archaeologist. Like Indiana Abu-Jones." She chuckles at her own joke. "Listen, I was just about to take tea and meditate. Would you care to share some tea with me?"

"Well . . . so long as I'm not imposing or anything."

She gives me a friendly scowl, like *Stop fishing for yet another invitation*. I smile back: *I guess the jig is up*. Suddenly she grabs a keepsake box, reaches in for something.

"Hey, this is for you."

She hands it to me: it's a turquoise scarab pendant, on a necklace of smaller amber scarabs.

"Really? This is for me?"

She nods.

"Thanks. Thanks a lot!"

"Well . . . I wanted to thank you, for . . ." Her voice trails off, and she looks down, breaking her gaze at me for the first time since I got here. "For being so nice to me and everything since I got back. The work I do, and all the traveling, well . . . it's very lonely, actually, Hamza, and I guess I've been suppressing just how lonely it is, because since meeting you, I just feel so . . . well . . . I just can't stop thinking about you."

Kot-*tam*.

Now there's *really* a pause.

With the hand of her bandaged arm she grabs the necklace out of my hands, saying, "It's called a *tchaua*. Here." She practically pounces on me, too fast for me to react, placing it around my neck.

Man. I never really cared for jewelry before. But no woman has ever given me anything like that before, so . . . this is really special.

I pay close attention to it, cuz I'm too shy all of a sudden to look her in the eye.

"I can't stop thinking about you, either, Sherem."

I still can't look at her, but I can feel her there, waves of heat coming off her, like I'm standing full in the sun on a hot noonday beach.

In my peripheral, I can see *she's* still looking down, too.

Suddenly she zips away to the kitchen.

Thank heaven.

I look around a bit more at the shelves, the calligraphy. I sneak a peak at her in the kitchen. No running water, I see, just big decanters, and no electric kettle . . . she's using a Coleman. Kind of a risk in this place. I jerk away quickly when she looks at me, go around the corner to some shelves of books I didn't see before, check out their moldy spines. And looking up at me from the corner is that crazy pumpkin.

How the hell did she get all this stuff here when she only arrived a few days ago? And why does she have a pumpkin in July? Maybe it's a dried gourd or something. I'm just about to pick it up when she rockets back into the room. "Hamza!"

"What?" Man!

"Please . . . uh . . . you can look at anything here, but please don't touch my pumpkin. It's a rare strain, it's been a real ordeal growing it, and it's *very* delicate—please, please— thank you—"

She loops her arm through mine, pulling me away. She grew it herself? They let her take *foreign produce* through customs? She is crackers, no doubt.

In the kitchen she makes me gather up the tea service, a gorgeous teapot covered in hieroglyphics, two large shot glasses for the tea (just like in the old country), a sugar bowl with a long, thin spoon, and a crystal decanter of milk or maybe cream. In the living room she takes a rolled-up mat from an empty planter and unfurls it on the floor, and we sit.

She places the tea service just off center, and at center she places a small, engraved censer. Then she takes out a lighter, which looks really out of place in her hands, lights a coal, puts it in the burner.

The room looks even darker now, and the coal glowing inside the censer seems all the brighter. She spoons what I had up till now thought was sugar into the censer's top bowl, and it snaps, glows red, gives birth to sweet and bitter drafts of smoke. The scent . . . I can only describe it as nostalgic . . . melancholic.

Out of nowhere, she says, "Tea is the most drunk drink in the world after water—did you know that?"

"I did not know that," I say in my best Carson.

She pours two steaming cups of gritty tea, then stirs in two spoonfuls of what I had thought was powdered incense. Well . . . it aint sugar . . . looks like a mix of salt and pepper. I reach for the milk, but her hand shoots out—

"Ah! Ah . . . Hamza . . . have that in a minute, okay? Try the tea as is for now, okay?"

"Sure," I say. Anxious chick. She picks up her glass. I follow her lead.

> Cast complaint upon the hook
> My comrade and brother.
> Make offering upon the brazier
> And cleave to life, as I have said.

That's nice. Wonder what it's from? "Salaam," I say. "*Shukron.*"

We drink.

"Say, this is actually pretty good. You kinda scared me there for a minute with the incense and whatnot. What kinda tea is this, anyway?"

"My own 'special-ty,' " she hums. "Same way I grew the pumpkin, I grow my own tea."

The woman's something else, no doubt. Tea really is good, too. All warm and evrathang.

"You know," she says, "I was . . . even before your amazing

trick of finding me . . . I knew you'd be great help on the dig . . . but now . . . now I know you definitely will, if you're still interested?"

"Sure, *sure*, Sherem, shu-u-u-ure . . . ," I sing. Can feel every parta me where the tea slides down and touches me and gets all hot and glowing.

Feel like a chimney, fireplace, logs, smoke, whatever.

Sgood tea all right.

"Mm, all done. Cn I hava nuther?"

She pours a glass and smiles. At me.

Man, a pretty smile. Like to kiss that smile, man. Big olteeth and juicy plum lips . . .

Jeez hope I didn'say that out loud.

I ask her why're ya smiling cuz I'm worried I mighta said outloud whatIwasthinking. An she says she's juss happy iz all, happy I came overta visiter.

Hamza you sonuvagun, yold soupdog.

Made a goodimpresshun. *Yeah.*

She asks me to medutate withher and I say shore.

And she says to close all of my eyes but they're so heavy I can'even keepemopen. I can hear her spoonin all that powder stuff and hear it sizzling and there's more smoke and stuff and it smells pretty and I feel real cumftrbull an sleepy and kinda sad but mostly happy like I just ate a big meal.

She tells her to give me my hands so I do.

Mm so sleepytired, all warm and soft and glowing . . .

She mumbles something sounds like "*dattuunyi deggeg shauuf*" or whatever and then her hands are on my neck and shoulders and slipping around my ribs and her fingers're on my skin and are so cool and soft and pure like water from a brook and I can smell her lips and her neck like cinnamon and her hair is flowing all around me like rain and smells like rain-earth smells and her lips are on my earlobes wet and her breath is like the mists of dawn and her chest is against mine and the skin's all hot and soft and tingling. . . .

. . . and we're rolling over and yawning and getting out of

bed and waking up the kids in their sunshining goldandblue
sleeproom and feeding them pieces of mandarin oranges and
peeled lychees and ripe dates and chunks of feta and Asiago
cheese and flatbread with brown gold honey all gooey and
ropey and when we wipe their mouths I look up and she
mouths to me the words *I love you* and there's no sound from
her throat but I can hear the music like kora strings chiming
from her lips. . . .

. . . and I'm on a cliff and we're holding each other and
we're afraid but we're together and our skin is cold and wet
from fog and we hold on to each other, hold each other. . . .

. . . and she's holding me in the dirt and sand in the darkness and she's sobbing and I'm limp and she's sticky darkred-
purple and I'm so tired, so cold, and it's so hard to move or
breathe and it's so dark, so quiet all of a sudden, dark and
silent. . . .

I wake up to find her staring at me, horrified.

Shit—what'd I do? How the hell could I've fallen asleep?
What an idiot I am! So much for good impressions! Can't've
been *too* long, can it? Teapot, sugar bowl, two glasses still
there—but the milk's gone, like maybe she had to put it back
in her fridge or cooler or whatever because I was out that
long? Hell, *look at her face!* Did I *talk in my sleep?* Did I talk
about *her?* Did I talk about—oh, no, man, please *don't* let me
have talked about R—

"Sherem, Sherem," I scramble, "I'm *so* sorry for, like . . .
well . . . but I've pulling some late shifts and I got up really
early this morning and I just . . . I'm sorry—it's so freakin
rude of me to, like, just fall asleep right here with you when
you're meditating. . . . How long was I—I guess it doesn't
matter, just the fact that I—can you forgive me? I—"

"No, no, Hamza," she says with the same expression, horrified.

Aw, *shit.*

"It's okay, honest," she says. "It's not a problem at all—"

She starts collecting the tea service. I shamble up, still sleepy, and she pulls the mat up off the floor where I was sitting.

Oh, damn, great date etiquette, Hamza, you freakin urinal cake! I try to help her with the stuff, but I'm still so groggy I can barely move fast enough to keep up with her.

"Ah, Sherem—jeez—don't be—"

"No, no, Hamza." She rushes around. "Really, it's fine. I'm not mad. I'm just really busy—when you came over I was right in the middle of getting some things ready, and I've gotta get back to work—"

"I hope I didn't offend you or something—"

"No, no, I just have some things to do, you know?"

"You're not upset?"

She's got me at the door, and I struggle to shove my feet back into my shoes. "No, honest, look, I'll call you, but you hafta go!"

I almost fall over. "Whoah!" I yelp, and she grabs me, steadies me with a surprisingly strong grip.

"Well," I say, seeing as how I obviously have absolutely nothing else to lose, "I was hoping we could maybe catch a movie or something, or you could come over and see the Coyote Cave tonight."

I know I'm screwed, but if you're falling off a cliff, you might as well try to fly.

"Tonight's not good, Hamza."

Shit. Damn. Hell.

"But I could come by tomorrow afternoon."

Ye's Date Law #7: The chick proposes an alternate! YES!

Guess maybe I'm *not* in the crap house. Yet.

I'm still muddleheaded, and before I know it I'm asking, "So whatcha doing tonight, anyway?"

"Taking care of some business," she mutters, whispering something I don't hear, opens the door.

"What time Monday?" I step through the doorway.

She glances anxiously out the hall. "Whenever's good for you, Hamza."

I fumble a card out of my pocket, give it to her. "My address. Say, twoish?"

> **HAMZA ACHMED QEBHSENNUF SENESERT**
> The Coyote Kings
> 10821-107A Avenue T5H 4K9
> Edmonton AB coyote@crystalnet.org

"Okay—tomorrow, twoish—now get home safe, Hamza."

She whispers something, closes the door, and I start stumbling down the dark hall. Then I remember to call out, "Sure thing! Thanks again for the necklace!"

Damn dark in here.

Craziest Sunday morning date I ever had.

Craziest dream I ever had, also.

Hope I didn't talk in my sleep. Dream was pretty hot, too, except for the part where I ended up dead.

The Long, Long Drive to Nowhere

WHAT IS IT WITH THINGS YOU LOVE AND HATE AT THE SAME TIME?

Hate—that's the wrong word. Things that tear your guts open, how about that? Never had these kinds of ass-baked feelings up until three years ago. Thought I knew everything there was worth knowing.

In the old days, you get a lineup of inbred small-towners in front of you—you smash em into spareribs and clear a line so the receiver can head for the end zone. You want a business— you demand your loan, you set it up. You wanna expand, you force everyone to take a cut and then with what you save you open up a plant in Mexico or some other ass-world country, then fire everyone at home.

You just do stuff. You want it, you move for it, you get it done. Easy. Lickety-split. *Capiche?*

But *this* . . .

I should just keep heading north up 109th Street and over the river and up 97th until I get to city limits, take Manning until my turnoff. . . .

But hell, I'm here already, still on the south side. Might's well turn into the Garden first.

I pull the SUV into the lot. Sunday afternoon, church is finished for all the Jesus freaks, not that they come here anyway. Morons. Going to some ass-ball building to get their souls tuned up. Whatever you gotta fix, you don't fix it goin to some ass-burnin building.

Cool inside the Garden. Always the first thing to hit you, that kiss of the cool air, and then all the fruit, cut and piled in little pyramids on the trays. All organic. No chemicals here, no way. The red globe grapes, $8.99 a kilo. I take a pawful, pop em, one at a time. They crunch. This is my only wine. This is *my* Sunday sacrament . . . sweet and honest and decent. No lies from chemists, or from priests.

You wanna heal your soul? Step one is healing your soil.

No one's seen me yet . . . all busy with the ass-shaving Yuppies.

Tray to tray . . . Granny Smith slices and giant raisins like soft rubies. Jackfruit and star fruit . . . nectarines and plums . . . kiwi and watermelon and honeydew and papaya. All made by sun and dirt and rain.

"Mr. Allen!"

I look down to my left. A chirpy little black girl with freckles and glasses and bouncy reddish hair tied back into a bundle. Sixteen years old if remember her record. I know her name, but even if I didn't, her tag is right above the *Rachael's Garden* logo on her body apron and says HI MY NAME IS SANDY. And she's written two exclamation points after her name and put a smile underneath the dots. So damn girlie-girlie.

I can't help smiling.

"Mr. Allen, I didn't know you were coming in today, sir," she chirps, and giggles. "Otherwise I would've made up a longan-asparagus-cashew salad for you."

I smile some more. Cute kid—I can't help it. Love to have her myself.

Not like that, ass-beak. Should've had kids of my own by now.

Yeah. Well.

"I would offer you some of the delicious sweet potato samosas I just took outta th'oven," she sings, her tilted head bouncing scoldingly with each phrase, "but I know you're a raw-foodist, so . . . unless I can convert you . . . ?"

I laugh. "If anyone could, Sandy, it'd be you. Anyway, I just . . . stopped in to grab some fruit, see if everyone's okay, make sure everything's going all right."

"You bet, Mr. Allen! Tight ship you own here, Cap'm!"

Before I realize it I'm pinching her smiling cheek. Hell, last thing I need is a young dame hitting me with a sexual harassment suit. But she smiles even more. I let go, even though I don'wanna.

She loops her arm through mine, even though she's wearing those see-through latex gloves, grabs a biodegradable Styro tray, and fills it with fruit slices while she walks me up and down the aisles. "For your road trip, and for your . . . for sharing," she explains softly, even sadly.

I almost start to yell, but before she looks up I've beaten my face into a smirk. Close one. "You, uh . . . you know what I'm doing?"

"Cap'm, anytime you come in and walk around like this without talking with the manager first thing, you always have the same look my dad has when he doesn't wanna do something. And someone mentioned something once about you taking Manning Freeway, and I . . . ."

She looks me right in the eye, and for the first time, her smile shrivels up. "Well," she says, "I understand, okay? Once a month I take Manning, too."

What do I say to that? Anybody else I'd probably wanna smack for getting into my business. Smart kid, Sandy.

There's an older couple, probably professors or something, standing over in the potatoes-and-leeks section, whispering. They don't know I can hear them.

"Isn't he the former Eskimo? A former CFL player owns Rachael's Garden?" says the old woman. Her husband or whatever says, "Not only owns it, he founded it. I hear now he wouldn't *dream* of touching meat. People really can change, I guess."

I take Sandy's snack pack and head out past the farm-fresh organic chicken, lamb, and beef, the vitamins, the energy work and feng shui book rack.

I pull out back onto 109th, head north for 97th, up to Manning, eating the sweetest fruit in town that's one hundred percent flavorless to me right now.

Can people really change? Or do they just postpone the poison catching up with em?

I wish this freeway could be longer.

But just how long would it have to be? How far would I *not* be willing to go?

Before I know it I'm there. For what I love. And what I hate.

Dating Homo Erectus

"YEAH, I STYLED HER. STYLED HER LIKE *GQ*!"

Ye is working on the high-tech bowels of his R-Mer and blathering on again about this broad he met at work yesterday who he says he's seeing tomorrow. He's been going on like this all day, and now it's night! Man, the guy can really freakin fart up the place once you get him started about anything, but especially a chick.

I'm *trying* to write in my journal, but every time I get in a smooth groove he looks up from the entrails of the R-Mer and crashes into me again with some line of high-fat *fromage.*

"Made the impossible *possible,* Ham-cake! Like Schrödinger's Pussy!"

"Good job, Ye."

Jeez, I'm trying to write. After three years of the worst case of writer's block I've ever heard of, I wrote that poem last night about the E-Town night-sky clouds, and I haven't wanted to stop! Could probably write all night, even after I get back from work. Damn fill-ins. Sposta get Sundays off.

Still, don'wanna stay up too late . . . can't be falling asleep again like this morning. Man, that was embarrassing.

In order to shut the freakin guy up, I try turning on the radio, but it's news, not music. I'm just about to switch the station when the anchor says there's been another murder.

And not just another murder, but another one involving *mutilation.*

> . . . the unidentified victim was discovered this afternoon facedown in the sand heap of a Highlands construction lot, legs bound at the knees and ankles, arms bound behind him at the elbows, with his hands cut off. The location of the hands is unknown.
>
> The man, believed to be in his mid-thirties and possibly of Middle Eastern extraction, was also branded on the area of his chest above his heart with the image of a donkey. Preliminary forensics say the victim was stabbed through that branding postmortem.
>
> The mutilation and donkey image have fueled speculation that this killing is connected with the Thursday night mutilation-slaying of a still-unidentified woman whose dismembered body parts were found stuffed into jars full of donkey hair in a Chinatown restaurant.
>
> Police spokesperson Troy Kudawudchuk says it's too early to say one way or the other whether there is a connection between the two homicides, but cautions inner-city residents against panicking over worries about a serial killer. . . .

"Oh, man," I say. "Two in one week? That's bad. And what the hell is up with all this donkey stuff?"

"Talk about killer ass," says Ye, and then he laughs at his own cornification.

"Pretty cold, Ye," I say, turning the station as far left as you can get on the FM dial (and that's no mistake) for some music. "Not to mention crass. Two people killed really horribly and you're making jokes? I bet if it was a coupla kids you wouldn'be talking like that."

"Hey!" he snaps, looking up from adjusting his electro-doohickey-magna-whatsits inside the guts of the R-Mer. "Don'even joke about that."

"Well, *every*body's *some*body's kid."

"You should write show tunes. Way I see it, you got five possibilities," he says, going back to playing with his nuts and bolts and circuits. "One, serial killer; two, copycat killer; three, gang war, probably involving drugs; four, cult ritual slayings, possibly involving drugs and the intelligence community, like in Jonestown; or five, a gang-cult of human-hating, copycat, drugged-out, mutilating super-donkeys.

"Or . . . perhaps even, six, a convergence, or con*spir*acy, if you will, among such forces."

At this point, Ye begins explaining in great detail each of these points. By the time he's spent about ten minutes running down *yet again* the same Jonestown/US Intelligence/British Blackwatch troops/MK-Ultra mind control drugs/mass-murder cover-up/conspiracy spiel I've heard him make at least three times before, I figure the only way to shut him up about *that* and keep him from going nuts—scratch that, nuttier—is to go back to what he was obsessing about in the first place: Miss Super-Hips from the video store.

"So! What—you got her number?"

Ye looks up from examining circuits or whatever.

"Took it off the customer list."

Splutter. "She didn't *give* it to you?" Ye slides what looks like a rocket into a tube on one of the R-arms. "Hey, man, I thought we had an agreement about explosives in the house!"

"Go back to steady state, Herbert—it aint armed! Not even an engine. I'm just checking to see if it slides in."

"Practicing for your date?"

"Exactly. And yeah, I got creative with getting her number. Women like that."

"I think there's a technical term for that. It's called 'abuse of office.' And 'violation of privacy for purposes of sexual harassment.' And 'civil suit.' And 'fired.' And—"

"And 'Yehat Gets Trim, in 3-D!' "

I laugh. "Good one. Anyway, seriously—"

"How's things with you and the Desert Queen?"

"Great, great. She's coming over tomorrow."

"And there were huzzahs, and yea, the people made great acclamations even unto the heavens, singing alleluia."

"Pretty much."

"You're pretty crazy about this egg tart, huh?"

"He was the world's greatest detective, but he had one flaw: he spoke the galactically obvious."

"Just don't get too crazy, Hamite."

He's stopped working on the R-Mer. He's just staring at me now.

I know what he's talking about, but I don't feel like getting guilted right now. "I'm fine, okay? I'm great. Don'worry about it. So what're you gonna do with the video store chick?"

"It's covered, King."

"Covered?"

"Like a pot of rice and peas."

"You know," I say, tilting my head towards him so he knows I'm serious, "if you're gonna be seeing her tomorrow, you can't be jerking off tonight."

"What?"

"They can tell—women can tell."

"What the hell you mean, 'They can tell'? I mean, what makes you think I—"

"Look, a man's testosterone drops below a certain level, his skin heat and respiration change subtly, for about twenty-four hours. Subconsciously, women can see this like a bee sees ultraviolet or a wolf sees infrared. It's an *environmental adaptation*. Homo habilis woman had to know that when she's takin the old seedpod the thing aint unloaded. Modern women don't know"—I tap my skull—"but they *know*."

Ye's frozen, speechless. Could this be *true,* maybe, he's thinking?

Me: "Look, it's all in a May 'ninety-three *Omni* I got if you don't believe me. I can go get the issue for you if you want."

He considers my presentation. "So . . . no predate jerk?"

"No, sir."

"Never stopped *you* before."

"And look where it got me!"

I slam shut my journal. Time for me to get up to go. I was gonna wish him luck on tomorrow's date and shake hands, but I don'think I wanna do that anymore.

Prelude to the Negative Confession

I SIT IN THE DARKNESS OF THIS ROOM, EIGHTEEN HOURS OF shielding myself from the sun, starving for the sun, ravenous, raging, aging, caging my rage. Caged in a house where once a family dwelt . . . a lodging now only a lodge, hodgepodge of a thousand dead scripts, crypts for ideas, ideals, seals of letters never meant to be opened, now torn open, ravaged for treasure secrets eyes were never meant to see.

"I am not dead," I declare unto the darkness, and it answers not.

I wait, in silence.

And when I can wait no longer, I broach what must be broached.

"The matters are few, but grave. The Heart-Eater, probably from the Salt, butchered the emissary from the Hobinarit and sought to stop me. I have brought him to peace. *Ãaui-f qaus.*

"Yet I know not of my eighty comrades, of their plight and progress, and whether other Heart-Eaters have engaged them, and which among them also . . . knows peace."

And still, the darkness gives no speech, no sigh, no moan, no tone.

Finally, I speak and say: "And then there is my pledgeling, the *sekht-en-cha* Senesert. Having lost the ethereal lens to forces unknown, and knowing our divine cause doomed should they reach the Jar before we do, I saw no choice but to . . . to *alter* the pledgeling . . . by use of the enemy's poison."

And there is the tangible trembling of shadows in the anticipation of thunder, and the taste in air of copper, and the scent in air of frost.

"But listen! The pledgeling's *sekhem* is greater than that of any man or woman known to me in all my travels and researches! Indeed he found me from across the vastness of this city of Sanehem solely by his own unprecedented capacity!

"*He* does not need the lens! He does not need the poison! We are not lost!"

And the lightning does not lash. And thunder does not sound.

Yet the threat—

"My conscience bears the press of granite, and withstands," I recite unto the darkness. "I will not have come so far only to fail."

I wait, inhale, ponder, exhale, wonder, breathe again.

I listen, but there is nothing. I breathe and speak, saying: "It is written:

> *All through your earthly life, accomplish*
> *   righteousness*
> *Do not oppress the widow*
> *Do not drive a man from the land of his father*
> *Do not hinder the great from fulfilling their duties*
> *Do not punish people unjustly*
> *The character of a righteous man is more agreeable*
> *   to God*

than the sacrifice of a dozen oxen from an evil
        man.

"And it is written, too, 'For every joy there is a price to be
paid.' "

I fret upon the absence of an answer from the darkness, yet
not wanting it, I summon the power of *nommo,* instanta-
neous, extemporaneous:

"And have the stakes ever been higher? Have we . . . the
right . . . to be constrained by custom, tradition, condition?
Let our mentality be freed of sentimentality."

I do not yell, but my voice is a sword of iron, and my tone
is venom upon the blade.

"And freed," I demand, "of morbid attention to self."

And I say once again unto the shadows, "Or of narcissistic
clairvoyance."

And then there is lightning!

"*It is also written,*" says the Dark Man, and my mind trembles, hearing, fearing, " 'If his heart rules him, his conscience
will soon take the place of the rod.' "

I do not whimper. . . . My mouth gives not utterance to
any moan: my body quivers not in the frailest bone. Yet my
heart . . . my *heart*—

"An outsider, uninitiated?" he demands. "A balm of poison
for this pledgeling, you would have given, perhaps to his
death, yes? Knowing not for certain if even *this* deception, for
deception it must surely be, would bring us to the Jar?"

And the Dark Man speaks again and says:

> " 'It is better not to know and to know that one does
> not know, than presumptuously to attribute some ran-
> dom meaning to symbols.
>   If you search for the laws of harmony, you will find
> knowledge.
>   Exuberance is a good stimulus towards action, but
> the inner light grows in silence and concentration.

> *Not the greatest Master can go even one step for his disciple; in himself he must experience each stage of developing consciousness.*
> *Therefore he will know nothing for which he is not ripe.*
> *The body is the house of God.*
> *That is why it is said, "Human, know thyself." ' "*

The lightning is stilled.

I stand.

The Dark Man speaks. "To keep the fullness of the truth is the necessity of the Way. But to lie? Are we fit to open the Jar if in our methods we are indistinguishable from our foes? Just how far is it that you will go?"

"How far will *I* go? How far have we *all* gone, how much have we all sacrificed, to protect the *Sa-Nekhbut*? I'm not doing—I haven't done *any*thing wrong!"

"Another innocent will die. And *your* hands are to open the Jar? Have you no understanding of what will happen to you when you do?" He breathes out shadows, lungs exhaling, exhuming choking smoke, smoldering. "And after . . . there will be forty-two judges to whom to answer."

I move to leave. I will not be stopped. "My confession . . . is my concern."

"It is all our concern."

I yell: "This is a war!"

My feet force me forward, my hands clasping black air. "And if he dies, he'll die a hero! And I'll die a scoundrel! Are two deaths and one damnation really so high a price to pay . . . to save so many? And maybe *free us all*?"

I lace up my boots, clasp my belt, install my vest and cloak, and whisper my supplication to the doorframe before I grasp the handle, then whisper thanks upon my passing.

"Arrogance destroys!" I hear him moan through shadows, through my skull.

"Is it quotation, or curse?" I demand. "Or *cowardice*?"

The darkness rumbles, silences, rumbles.

"You have waited too long!" I yell. "Hoped for this, prayed for this, paid for this . . . but you will not bleed for this! You will sacrifice anything except that which truly costs!"

And there is silence.

Until finally in that voice, so that even I am shocked, grim surrender.

"The Heart-Eaters have been wiped out. But so," says the man, "has the last of your pack. Of the nine nines sent out, you are now . . . the last."

And I say unto him, "So then there *is* no choice."

He whimpers, begs, in a voice full of aged shame: "The sellers of poison . . . their grim medicament still can aid any of the other vast and hungry legions who seek our prize. You must destroy the roots of that evil tree—"

"Or cut off each and every of its branches."

"Know that there are still vicious ones unknown to us, and close by, and desperate!"

I close the door on the frightened old one in the darkness behind me, and outside in the night I am free in longer chains.

And it is written:

> One does not discover the heart of a man if one has not sent him on a mission.
> One does not discover the heart of a wise man if one has not tested him.
> One does not discover the heart of an honest man if one has not sought something from him.
> One does not discover the heart of a trustworthy man if one has not consulted him in any deliberation.
> One does not discover the heart of a friend if one has not consulted him in anxiety.
> One does not discover the heart of a brother if one has not begged from him in want.

The streets are cobalt, the grass bruised jade beneath the dusk.

There are three women and thirteen men on the crossroads before me, and all of their bodies are soaked with blood.

He is almost ready.

CHARACTER DATA:

Darwin M. Zenko

REAL NAME: Darwin N. Zenko.

CUNNING: Situational politricks +13.

EDUCATION: B. Comm. with distinction, working on MBA.

EATS AT: ShabbadabbaDoo's on Jasper, Earl's Tin Palace, Red Robin, Joey Tomato's, Eddie Bauer Espresso, Gap Pastaccinno.

DRINKS: Perrier, Aquafina, Nostalgia Atlantis.

MOTHER: Psychiatrist.

FATHER: Psychiatrist.

CLEARLY, THEN, SIBLINGS: (*a*) Became addicts and/or (*b*) joined cults and/or (*c*) entered rehab and therefore (*d*) became psychotherapists.

SCENT: Money, by Hugo Boss.

REPUTATION: Good, hardworking boy from a good family.

DECEIT: +99.

TRIVIA DEXTERITY: Roger Corman +21, Sam Raimi +83, Calvin Klein +17.

GENRE ALIGNMENT: *ST: TNG*, *Miami Vice*, *Crime Story*, *Wiseguy*, and *Riptide*.

FAVORITE SONGS: Gary Numan's "Cars" and the Cars' "Drive."

MOST SURPRISING BELOVED BOOK: *Man's Search for Meaning* by Viktor Frankl.

HERO: "Paul Muad'Dib, the biggest player in the universe. The best marketing character in literary history, moved more product than everyone else combined."

MORALE: Spectacular +9.

SLOGAN: "Don't worry, babe. I'll tell you right before I do."

Mr. Self-Improvement,
or I Love My Job

Who's gonna hold you down when you shake?
Who's gonna come around when you break?
—THE CARS

BASICALLY, I CAN NEVER STRESS ENOUGH JUST HOW IMPORTANT
it is to truly love what you do. Some guys go to work every day
for twenty, thirty years, hate the boss, hate the job, come home
and beat the wife and kids, hate themselves, and end up chewing the shotgun ten years before being able to pension out.

Not me. I love my job.

Like putting down scores, for instance. When I was a
teenager I saw Chuck Adamson and Michael Mann's brilliant
serial *Crime Story,* and I basically fell in love with that whole
lifestyle of Ray Luca, the intelligent super-hoodlum, who basically learned the difference between mules and managers
and saw that the mind was the ultimate safecracking tool and
weapon.

That's what I'm pledged to do with my life . . . develop myself so I can crack open any safe, literal or figurative. Like Alexander with the Gordian knot, basically.

Take our score on the Modeus Zokolo last Friday night. I mean, yeah, Alpha Cat's technically in charge, but from Gore-Tex to latex that job was pure Zenkovision all the way. Initial surveillance, final sweep, electronic-security bypass, camera blowout, Czech octopus lock picks—I mean, c'mon, what can I say? I'm the best.

The only thing, and really, I do mean the *only* thing, that grates is going to all that work and then basically not even really getting to see what we boosted.

Hey, I'm a samurai for my shogun and I'll point my katana where I'm told, but still, I like to know the name of the ronin I put in the ground, you know? I don't know what Mr. Allen wants with that thing, and I'm not askin for a cut. All I'd like is to *know* is all, y'know?

Anyway—be in the moment. Beautiful late dusk out here on Whyte. See all the hot cars—what my frat buddy doing an S.O.B. job (south of the border) calls "tricked-out rides"— with the hyperflashy hubcaps or the ultrachrome finish and the subwoofers tearing the night another asshole.

And the *women* inside these cars, let me tell you something—tricked out? Believe it. Best the medical industry's R and D can provide.

Some guys don't go for that, but me? To me it just makes the world more fair for everyone. Usedta be you had to have the right breeding to be beautiful. Now surgery can make the *whole world* more beautiful. Basically, within a couple of generations—not to mention what we can do with gene therapy—we can stamp out ugliness, once and for all!

Imagine that . . . no big noses, no weak chins, no underdeveloped parts north or south . . . just a more beautiful world. Who could be against that? Tell me, honestly, who? I am not being sarcastic.

Me, I love my life, and I love my job. If I can do it into my sixties, I'll be the happiest man alive.

I get out, I get to meet the people, have dinner in nice places, see beautiful women—I mean actual tens, you know, not your everyday chuck roast, but filet mignon—plus, it affords me the lifestyle that I desire in terms of my own tricked-out rides, and, of course, really nice clothes.

Sunday night business is usually pretty slim—even the bars close early, and Whyte Ave is, basically, Baropolis. But over on 104th at Gazebo Park there's always someone looking for a little instant self-improvement.

That's what I'm into. Tony Robbins, Susan Powter, John Stuart Mill—self-improvement. I'm basically a utilitarian, just like Mill. (I did some Victorian philosophy for my arts option—actually, that's where I met Digaestus, but he was called Wilbur back then. I didn't really know him—Alpha Cat recruited him.) Utilitarian, not as in, "Everything has to be practical only," but basically, "Everything you do should maximize happiness."

"Zak, cun I have uh ice cree?"

The Mugatu, the poor thing—always hungry. "Moog," I try to tell him, "there's no ice-cream place open at this hour."

"Whuddabout Basskinnanrons?"

"They're closed, Moog."

"Bout Mudonald's?"

Frosty yells, "They're fuckin closed, ya stack a yak-shit sacks!"

I smile at the Mugatu, pat and rub his shoulder. "We'll find something later, okay Moog? Okay? Okay, Moog?" He pieces together a smile. I reward him, smiling more, scratching his shoulder. "That's a good boy! Good Moog!"

"Ah, ya prep retard, you're gonna fuckin *spoil* im," whines Frosty.

"No-o-o-o, don't say *that*. No one can wreck the Mugatu! Right, boy? Right?"

The Mugatu smiles so broadly his cheeks bunch up, and he shakes his head to agree with me, and the shaking is so violent I can actually hear his brains bouncing back and forth inside his skull like one of those Indian rubber balls.

Stack of yak-shit sacks. You see, that kind of line is not only hard to say, basically you could never just improvise something like that on the spot. That's one of Frosty's problems, and it kinda wrecks his credibility when he tries too hard.

He's so eager to be seen as intelligent, as quick-witted, that he actually takes out time to make *lists* of ideal insults. I've seen him do it, although he denies it. Says he's writing a letter to his girlfriend "who lives in Ottawa," although he never goes there and she's never come here and he's never shown us so much as a picture of her. Whenever he runs into trouble he always makes some reference to Claire coming or him expecting a call from her or something. Pretty pathetic, really.

But with the intelligence thing, yes, he's really nowhere near as smart as he wants to be seen as. He's smart, but he's not *really smart*.

That's another thing that gets me—people trying to take credit where it's not due. I mean, it doesn't really basically *get* me, but I just don't think it's right. Win a trophy, take a trophy. Don't win, don't take. That's my philosophy. But hey, no skin off my fore.

Anyway, as I was saying, Mill was basically like a Victorian Kwisatz Haderach. His dad, James, and his dad's partner, Jeremy Bentham (they had this *J* thing going), built him into a Victorian super-brain while they were working on their theory of universal hedonism. By age three Johnny could speak Greek!

Now, given, not a big deal for Greek kids, but John-boy could *write* it, too. Then he writes about a billion books in his spare time (in English). I mean, how can you not be impressed by that? The man loved his work.

Okay, had its downside: Mill did have a nervous breakdown at age twenty, but seriously, I think if Mill lived today, he'd understand what we're doing right here in Mr. Allen's operation. Might even've bought a piece of it. Because what we do is what he believed in. We bring happiness.

You know, speaking of loving my job, my coworkers are a never-ending source of amusement to me. Take tonight, for instance, out on rounds with Frosty the Angry Snowman and our crew's homage to Wookiedom, the Mugatu.

Individually they're fine—they're even fun. Sure, they have their shortcomings. You can't really blame either one of them. . . . Conditioning and genetics made them what they are and what they aren't. But if you don't look at them for too long, they're really fun guys.

But you put these two into each other's proximity, and, well . . . I remember this one time when Frosty and I were really ripped after pulling a double—I mean, like, projectile puking, you know? *That* kind of ripped—and Frosty swore on his brother's grave that sooner or later he would, quote, shank that land manatee and feed him to the dogs at the SPCA, unquote.

Now, I never really knew how seriously to take that, but there are legends about what Frosty does with knives and tongs. I'd rather not see the Mugatu get shanked—he really can cook. And basically he's just so fucking stupid, you really can't top his comedy, even if it is all accidental.

I remember one time when we—okay, when *I*—got him to eat five cups of flour, raw, no water. Can't even remember how I got him to . . . oh, I know. I said it was a cure for his cold. (What the hell?) But yeah. I almost wet myself. Plus I picked up something like two hundred in cash from the other Fan-Boys who bet that the Mugatu wasn't *that* stupid.

Turns out they're *all* that stupid. But really, good, good guys. I won't take anybody giving my boys a hard time.

Y'know, grabbing this sextant or whatever and not knowing why is basically getting on my nerves. I mean, if I at least knew the angle, like maybe it was something Magellan or Vasco da Gama used and so it's priceless, then I could understand. But it was sitting in a Whyte Ave boutique, not a museum. Why the hell did the boss want it so bad?

"Hey, Frosty."

"Yeah?"

"Any idea what's the deal with that score the other night? How much's that thing we grabbed worth? The boss selling that gizmo, trading it, or is it a bargaining chip?"

"I'ont fuckin know. Whadda*you* care? Always gotta know everybody's business, Zenk. Always askin fuckin questions. I'ont know an I'ont care. Fuckin asshole."

"Frosty, don't pretend you aren't curious. On the way back I heard you whispering on and on to the Cat and basically asking questions about how old it was and how it was gonna be used. And then I heard you say something to the Cat about a . . . a *terrvix*?"

He gulps, and his face basically looks like I've just inserted a frosted catheter inside his unit.

"Well, so what's a terrvix?"

"I'ont fuckin know! Why oncha ask Caesar?"

He's smirking at his own joke. Maybe I can ply him a bit. "Caesar? He's like Bilbo Baggins on heroin. That turd can hardly say his own name. But Frosty, Frost-man, Frostotron, you know the operation better than anyone!"

"Not better than the Cat. Ask him, Polo."

"He isn't here an you are an I'm askin *you*."

"I already tol'you I'ont know, ya goddam asshole."

"Fine."

He knows something. Just hafta ask one of the others, I guess. Anybody but the Cat. I would ask the Moog, but I'd be better off asking a pony. Whatever. Nobody cracks a mystery like me. That oughta be my jingle, like Maaco: *Uh-oh? Better call Zen-ko!* Only a matter of time before I solve this one—this device, and whatever a terrvix is.

I refuse to be shut out on this one. I'm not taking a backseat to that motherfucking wigger anymore.

The FanBoys vs. Cubby

WELL FOR HELL'S SAKES. NOBODY IN GAZEBO PARK. TRY OLD Scona, my alma mater. Always a couple of people needing self-improvement there.

Some people hang their heads in this job, but the way I see it, we're not selling something illegal. Basically, we're selling something *extra*legal—we're selling dreams. You can't put a price on that! Hell, at our prices for dreams, you can't afford *not* to buy.

At the Old Scona parking lot, we run into one of the regulars. But also one of our absolutely least dependable ones, a grown man-boy who actually wears a Cub Scout cap and therefore, not very imaginatively, likes to be called Cubby.

When he sees the three of us, he has at least two expressions vying for control of his face: the look a starving man has before getting a meal, and the look the meal has upon seeing the starving man.

"Cubby, come here, c'mon! We won't hurtcha! C'mon!"

"Like fuck we won't," rumbles Frosty.

"Frosty, c'mon, let's—*Cubby!* Nice to see you again, buddy!

Lost some weight, uhn? Lookin good! You been workin out, too?"

"Uh, naw, well, maybe a little," he says, nervously fondling the Cub Scout logo on his cap as if he's afraid it might've been stolen, or like he might've traded it for some food and forgotten.

"Hey, Zenko . . . uh, look, man, I'm a little short, y'know, but, like . . . fyou could just give me some, like, powdered milk or somethin, man, some 'duds . . . or like a two-liter jugga water with, like, only a *drop* of *cream,* man . . . I'm dying out here, c'mon. . . . Y'know I'm good for it—"

The Mugatu: "Yoo stillowus furrasstine, Cuddy. . . ."

"Uh, 'scuse me?"

Frosty: "The puke-stand is saying that YOU"—and he knuckles on Cubby's head crisply—"still OWE US"—(knock-knock)—"for LAST TIME, CUBBY!" (Open-palm smack-push.)

"I didn'pay you? *Thought* I paid you—"

I laugh a little. "Well, Frosty, maybe you shouldn'go round taking third-party postdated checks."

"Chew my hemorrhoids, pretty boy. He paid in *ice*—said he'd hit some house in Windsor Park."

Cubby: "I thought they were real, man, honest!"

I laugh a little more. "But instead, Cubby, you left Frosty here taking our boss a trio of zirconia."

"Shutthefuckup, Zenko." Frosty reaches out and grabs Cubby's lips, skinning them back like he's inspecting his teeth. At first I'm just shocked that Cubby doesn't pull away or defend himself, but he seems used to this. Then I think Frosty's just doing this to establish dominance. But now I'm pretty sure he's actually looking for gold to take in payment. Ah, Frosty and his tongs!

"Ya get nothin, Ensign Rectum," snaps Frosty. "NOTHIN!"

Cubby looks definitely ready to cry. There's a bright—under these radioactive streetlights—bubble of snot that expands and contracts with his breathing. It's really a Kodak moment.

Or as Frosty proves, a Minolta moment. He's got his camera out, and he's got the Mugatu holding Cubby by the throat, and he's yelling, "Hold him steady, Moog. Cubby, breathe out through your nose . . . yeah, like that . . . an don't break that fuckin bubble, ya tube-jockey, or I'll have the Moog rip your nostrils off!"

(Mr. Allen has no idea Frosty brings it with him and'd probably make him basically regret ever having heard of cameras if he knew. But hell, it's a good extortion chip to have in my pocket against Frosty if I ever need it. And if Mr. Allen asks me why I didn't report Frosty for keeping evidence . . . I'll just tell him that Frosty swore the boss'd given him permission.)

Frosty looks pleased; I guess he got the bubble volume that he wanted for his photo. I'd better wrap this up.

"Moogie, old buddy, let the Cubster go for a minute, okay? That's a good Moog." I stroke his shoulder a second before I turn to our client.

"Cubby, you're a nice guy. We like you. We like doing business with you. You've definitely had your days as a good customer and a valued member of our little community."

"Thuh-thanks, Zenk, man," sobs Cubby.

"So we will give you something."

Frosty: "WHAT?"

Cubby: "THANKS, ZENK!"

"We'll give you two days. Yes, two days, Cubby. And then if our boss doesn't have three *real* diamonds or cash equivalent plus interest for what you still owe us, we're going to track you down, split open your vertebrae, tear out your spinal cords, and strangle you with em. And if they're not strong enough, we'll use your small intestine. Moog, show him we're serious."

The Mugatu grabs Cubby's neck and squeezes. That brings

back memories. On one of our retreats, I remember seeing the
Mugatu kill a pig—I mean, a really large sow—using this
exact same method. It was basically pretty impressive. Then
he bled it and cooked it—I mean, it *was* our dinner and everything.

Still, we'd have to dig a pretty large BBQ pit in the Old
Scona lawn for Cubby, and frankly, we don't have time.

Cubby chokes out, "He'll . . . *huhh*—get it!"

"He'd better."

"HE'LL . . . GAHH—*GET IT*—"

I make a cutting gesture to the Mugatu: *Release him*. But
it's my own fault for crediting the Moog with too much sub-
tlety. I'm frozen-stunned when he whips out a hunting knife
and prepares to slit Cubby open like a bluefish.

"*What tha FUCK are you doing?*" panics Frosty.

"Zak seddta *cuddim*—"

"I said to *let him go!*"

The Mugatu is angry, hurt, confused, indignant. He lets
Cubby go, mumbling to himself, "Fugg, *I* don'know,
jusstryinna do whud they *ast* me—"

"*M-O-O-N* spells *FUCKFACE,* Moog," rips Frosty, poking
Chewie in the chest. The Mugatu could probably snap off
Frosty's arms for toothpicks, but he looks as hurt as if Frosty's
words were a newspaper smacking down on his nose. "Ya
tryinna get us pinched in the middle of the park for murder
one, ya fuckin stack a yak-shit sacks?"

"I believe you already used that one tonight, Frosty."

"Fuck you, Pillsbury!"

"Yes, that's quite a rich, uh, rebuttal. Anyway, Cubby, no
hard feelings, but we don't get paid within forty-seven hours,
I'm fixing up you and the Mugatu on a date. And there won't
be any Vaseline, understand?"

Cubby runs away. I'm almost hoping he *doesn't* pay up.

We clear out of the park, hit 105th Street. Maybe enough
time's past, I can try Frosty again.

"Frosty?"

"*What?*"

"Seriously, c'mon, what's a terrvix?"

"Fuckin drop it, okay?"

"Listen, back at my place I've got that latest Jenna Jameson video you wanted. You understand? *Sperminator 2?*"

"Shit, really?" For the first time he's looking at me while we walk. And I swear, he's actually licking his lips.

"I heard you talking about it, I know some people, so I arranged to get an advance copy."

"Ah, c'mon, Zenk, y'asshole, that aint fair. You're sposta wait, just like everybody else, until you pass the degree. *Then* you get to know. When you're in as long as me, then fine, but if Mr. Allen ever found out—"

"Since when are *you* afraid of authority figures, man? You're Frosty the Killer Snowman!"

"Yeah, but . . ."

"Hey, I've heard a lotta things about you, man, but no one's ever said you were a pussy. And this Jenna Jameson tape, guy, it's so hot it practically melts the VCR!"

And Frosty actually bites his hand, just like Squiggy does when he sees a hot chick during the title sequence of *Laverne & Shirley*. In fact, that's where I think he got it from.

"Ah, hell! Okay, fine! You're not sposta learn this until you do the Applying-Mud-Balm-to-Yggdrasil degree. But, uh . . . a terrvix is like a surge point on a terrestrial artery."

"It's a what on a what, now?"

"Shit, ya fuckin prep dinkweed! How the helldja get *this* far? Didn't you pay attention when you passed the Jotar degree?"

"Oh, right. Right, of course."

Now, this basically is part of the mystery to me of Mr. Allen's whole approach to management. I mean, I like a good dose of mystery and fooling the employees as much as the next guy. Mystification of controlling the means of production is basically basic to keeping the whole pie to eat yourself. Basic lesson in L. Ron–ism right there.

But sometimes it seems that the boss actually be*lieves* all this Aquarian/Ragnarokian serpent-shit. Maybe the only way for me to crack this case and get some straight answers is basically to just break into the boss's safe and see this thing for myself up close. Hell, I set up his whole security system for him—I even bought the safe! Getting in'll be easier than stealing an IV from a veteran.

And if I can't figure it out, maybe one of the boss's books'll explain this thing, or give me a price range, at least.

Anyway, back to Frosty. "So what's this thing we stole got to do with this terrvix whatsits?"

"How can you not fuckin know this?"

"I could just *sell* that tape—"

"Okay, okay! It's like a spectroscope, or whatever. The terrestrial arteries, they bleed some of their energies up into the air, and at night, assuming y'know how to use a zodiascope, you can see the force lines reflected in the ether.

"They say if you're using a 'scope they look like the northern lights, but, like, way better. Chinese call em 'dragon paths' or suh'm."

Gotta remember those names. *Zodiascope. Dragon paths.* "I see," I say, nodding, "and *so-o-o-o* . . ."

"And so, ya goddam moron, you follow the dragon paths to the terrvix!"

" 'Terrvix,' as in . . . 'terrestrial cervix'?"

"No fuckin duh!"

"So what gets born there? Or does someone just get screwed?"

"You wanna know that, you gotta pass the goddam degree."

"Oh, come on! You're gonna hold out on me now? Jenna Jameson! Going once—"

"No way, man. Not for twenty *quadruple*-X Jenna Jameson tapes. Not if you set me up on a *date* with er."

One secret of management is basically knowing how far past somebody's comfort level you can push them, and when to back off from there. And when to go right back to pushing them.

"You better give me that fuckin tape, Zenk."

"Relax, Frosty. I'm good for it."

So we have one more place to go, but we'll have to go back for the car first. I'll need my piece. Don't like to walk around Whyte Ave with it—it's too expensive, and Whyte is clogged with far too many eager police. But for the next stop, it's appropriate.

If the boss really does buy all this hyperdung, there's no way he can hang on to his empire forever. And maybe somebody with basically a little more perspective and a little stronger grip on reality should be in place, with a few allies, to ease it out of his hands.

And then maybe some fucking phony who's about one percent as competent as his reward suggests can get what's coming to him.

God, I love my job.

Night of the Living Cream Puffs

SO, WE'RE THERE ALREADY, THIS NEW PLACE. THEY CLOSED DOWN the other one, the Catacombs, after the stories broke about cannibalism, but this new place—I don't remember if they're calling it the Hostel or the Hospice—but it's not bad. An old abandoned walk-up, like a hotel for the chemically challenged. It's quite nice, actually. If I were a junkie, I think I'd happily live here.

Ah, well, six of one, we're here, I've got my piece, we're fine. The door opens crustily, and all three of us enter.

They could do with some domestic help, honestly. The trash, graffiti, broken vials, cigarette butts, bottles—these I can take. But basically, it's the stench of human waste that flaps my unflappability. Plus, the people don't smile enough. I'd like to see a bit more enthusiasm. We are making their dream come true, after all.

"Moog, say 'Ho-ho-ho.' "

"Har ho HORrr."

"Merry Christmas, ya buncha shit-shakes!" calls Frosty, full of unseasonal cheer.

"Santa's brought some *gi-i-ifts* . . . ," I sing. I even flash a tiny vial, just to lift their spirits a bit.

Their shriveled bodies unravel and rush towards us with surprising speed for people who've lost around forty percent of their body mass. The Mugatu steps forward, his giant chest and arms all the warning we need. They back off pretty quick, basically.

"*That's* so much better," I say, "isn't it?"

A woman (woman?) approaches me. I'm glad she isn't afraid, but lord could she use some Irish Spring and some Scope. Not to gargle with—she'd probably drink it. As perfume.

"Zeng, please, please, drop me some Christmas. I'll Maxwell House you to the last drop—just give me some. . . ."

Where do these junkies get lines like that? Sounds like some corny thing Frosty would write for her. This one . . . I think I remember this one now . . . Sharon, or Sharla or Charlene or something. Maybe Tina. Anyway, we helped her out late last year, October, I think. She looked about twenty-eight years old at the time. Now she looks like a very old sixty. It's kind of nostalgic, actually—given her hair color and her change in build, it's the shift between young, dewy, starlet Rosemary Clooney and old, saggy, postcareer Rosemary Clooney.

I don't think I can take her deal. I'd better let her down easy. "As arousing as the notion of having my cock turn purple and rot off is, basically I'm afraid I'll have to decline. Next."

She sobs and pleads, but I gesture to the Mugatu and he throws her away. I have no idea how this is physically possible, but when she hits the wall, she sounds just like a bag of glass.

"We don't have all day, people," I call out, tapping my Rolex. "We're on a *sche*dule. Who's got real money or quality trade?"

The room is filled with freshly improved clients, Frosty is snapping some photos for his collection or upcoming show or something else that should probably basically be confiscated, obviously, and the Mugatu is relieving himself in the corner.

"Well, gentlemen," I sigh contentedly, "our work here is done!"

This is such a sweet operation Mr. Allen runs. Where he got the formula for cream, I don'know. . . . It's a pretty new zap, as I understand it. I know a guy in New York who's never even heard of it, but everyone I know from Vancouver to San Francisco says they've been doing it for years. Did the boss buy a franchise or something? Whatever.

But basically, seriously, Mr. Allen is a very, very smart man. When I think of all he's accomplished—not just with this here but on the legit side with the club, the stores, getting that city councillor, what's his name, elected, not to mention producing cream itself—I mean, he's like Trump Escobar Kennedy or something.

Still, all these hoo-hah mystical degrees and whatever, that's just ultimately gonna backfire.

Man, I can basically *taste* getting into that safe! The big thing is to make sure I have enough time, unwatched. Gonna need a diversion . . . and I think the Moog is just the right shape and size.

One more look around this shit-hole before we go. You know, basically, for me, doing this whole *Glengarry Glen Ross* thing just never gets tired. We help people find out that they both want and then need something, and then we bring it to them. We don't sell products—we sell futures, help people feel confident, feel good about themselves. We should be on the chamber of commerce.

A hundred years ago we could've been written up in one of your finer Victorian magazines. I'm not kidding—in England, they basically used to rub opium paste on the gums of teething babies to help them *and* their mothers sleep. You can *still* read Sherlock Holmes stories where Watson or somebody gets the girl, but Holmes says, "Well, at least I got the heroin."

And everybody knows about that whole cola thing. Not to mention Britain's *Just Say Yes* policy with China.

I just notice—how odd. The Mugatu's urine is bright purple. I wonder if Frosty slipped him something. No . . . the Moog doesn't seem surprised or scared, so . . . oh, I remember now . . . that carton of grape Freezies I bought him.

Frosty steals the sunglasses from a prone girl, puts them on. I tell him, "You look good, Frosty."

"Really, Zenko? You're not shitting me?"

"No, no, dude, you're totally tricked out in those."

"Testacular! Claire's coming up. . . . I wanna look good for her."

"Totally, guy. She'll, like, *love* em."

Right. "She" will "love" them.

We leave. And I didn't need my piece after all. Ah, well, maybe next time.

Now back to base to face the boss. And me, to face the safe, find out the truth behind "zodiascopes" and "terrvixes," and start the beginning of the complete Zenkification of this operation.

CHARACTER DATA:

Alpha Cat

REAL NAME: Marky Presley Kraal-Snowfinkle.

COMPLEXION: Pale, given to freckles.

STRENGTH: Loyalty.

WEAKNESS: Loyalty.

EATS: "Pa-tty an ro-ti an ting."

DRINKS: Ting (from the bottle).

ARMOR TYPE: Kangol hat, oversized shirt and gaucho combo, shiny red.

SCENT: Collie herb.

TRIVIA DEXTERITY: *Alpha Flight* +28, Alpha Blondy +3, Moonbase Alpha +31.

GENRE ALIGNMENT: *B5, Enemy Mine, Captain Harlock,* and *Battle of the Planets,* English dubbed version (with Casey Kasem as Mark, and Alan Dinehart as 7-Zark-7).

IMPAIRMENT: *Ersatzschwärzen* −12.

SLOGAN: "Too much tiyme inna Babylon amungst di ba-a-ald*heads* for I-an-I, maan. Wi muss do liyke Mahcuss Gahvee say, go bock to Afreeka like wi anSESSta, seen? Nuff respek. Bo-bo-bo!"

The Lame Child and
the Selfish Giant

So yu know mi WOK intu di baas-maan hoffice—di
SitchuWAYshaan Room, ee calls it—fi mek a ripoht on stock-
an-ting, an see if dey is enniting mi can elp out wit, SEEN? An
wenna mi hopen di doh, mi fine di mos riyyychuss empra,
kingakingz, lohd-a-lohds, LIONAJUDAH, Ras Dulles Allen-
I, sittin in his trone widdis BOCK tooned to di doh, which him
ave poosnally tole mi neva fi DO.

"Supa-Don Mista Allen, SUH," mi snappto attenSHAAN
to saloot. Baat im naa even toon arounn. So mi apprOWUCH
im cairful, seen, in case im naa hird mi. Baat mi know im has,
caz no one inna di whola kriAYshaan av betta earin.

"Mista Allen, suh," mi say soffly.

Im naa turn, but iz ledda-boun cheeyr is TREMBLIN, seen?

Mi tink meebeey mi shud jaas LEEV, baat it naa riyt. Mi al-
weez elp di baas whennim liyk dis, yu know?

Mi wok aroun di dess. An liyk evra time befoh, im ava feeyce
fulla teeyz. An it a CROCK mi 'eart riyt downa di SENTA fi
see he liyk dis, a giant uva maan redoos ta cryin liyka beeyby.

Mi kneel in frunta he. "Ey, baas. Fi do?"

Im trya ide iz feeyce, but it naa do naa gud. Mi go fi grabbim sum Kleeynex, an im tek it an blow an snoht tillim betta. Dennee poots iz haan onna mi shoulda, an im sez to I-an-I, *Yu a gud souljah, Cyaat.* Mi say, "Tank yu, suh!" An mi aksim reeyl gentle-liyk, "Whutz WRAANG?"

Im expleeyn howa di whola MISSHAAN fi steayl di 'SKOHP naa profit NO WAN, cuzza di 'scope na even WUK! Tree *yeaz* imma wuk on dis, aan it all come down fi NUTTIN? It naa feeyr, im seey. Im criye an crye, *Ow caan mi end di peeyn an di suffrin when evrating mi du end liyk DIS?*

Mi cyann tek it, caz mi know it troo.

Im try EVRAting im know, an im is a SMAAT maan, despite im avin beena futBAALLa, im reeyd plenti boox, a whole lie-berry—I-an-I seen it miself—at iz man-shaan. Shelf afta shelf onna di daak mystreez uva di yunivirrsal soul-an-ting, di powaz an di prinsiPALLATEEZ uva di whola kingdaam of Jah an iz prophet, di giant Ee-mma, an di wikkid wanz oo ovatroo im. An how di RIYchuss av an inHEERitanss, if only demma WUK fir it, seen?

Baat mi see di man a cryin, anna mi afi deal widdis peeyn.

"Mista Allen, suh, lemme have a crackattit. Lemme look troo di boox miself."

Alpha, im seey. An mi staap. An im sniffle. An im squeeze mi shoulda.

Alpha, im seey, *yu mi numba-waan kwaatabaak, yu know? Yu mi honly frenn.*

Mi aart swellz whennim seey daat. Swell cuz mi appee im see mi azziz frenn. Swell wit peeyn cuz im naa hav naa udda.

"Mi know, baas," mi seey gentlee. "Lemme bi yuh troo frenn in retoon. Lemme check di MAANyoolz miself fi help yu."

Im nod. Mi go to di seeyf, unlokkit, teeyk out di buk written inna di eenchaant langwidge im a teeych mi fi reeyd. Di cuvva so hold anna widdaad, anna di peejaz dem so krummly. Baat di tiytle still cleah whenna mi eyz tchraanzLEEYT:

THE BOOK OF THE LEGACIES AND MYSTERIES
OF THE MURDER OF THE GOD YMIR

Mi reeyd. An mi reeyd agenn. An mi reeyd sum moh, foh an howa-an-ting. Anna Mista Allen naa move di whola tiym.

An mi tink mi foun sumtin.

"Mista Allen," mi seey, "mi tink mi know di praablem."

Im leeyp hout uvviz cheeyr. *Whaat izit?* im seey.

"Peeyple liyk yu oh mi, wi naa haav di riyt talents fi yuze di skohp. Na maatta how haad wi try, it will NEVVA wuk fuh us. Wi cyaan do it, full staap."

Im a curse anna flail an mekafuss, an mi weeyt fah him fi stoppiz mashin anna smashin-an-ting. When im kwiet an cool agenn, mi say a he:

"Baat baas, deer's a soluSHAAN."

Im wiyp iz nose an di cohnaaz uviz mout, an snap at I-an-I, *How much it gonna caast? Ow much wi afi steayl? Ow menny legs wi afi breeyk an nekks wi afi SNAP?*

"No, suh, yu naa ovaSTAAN. Wi naa afi go nowheah, do naattin. Di soluSHAAN is riyt unda wi NOSE."

Im eyz grow bigga daan cup-an-sossa. *Whaat?* im seey.

"Di skohp meeyrly ampliFYYY di eyz uv waan oo alreddy seez into di shadoze an di sheeps uv tings unseen, into whaat di buk sez is 'di kee to di mystreez uv di hevvaLUSHAAN uv maan intu *god*.' Oo wi know who av im di hextra siyt? Oo caan see whaat uddaz cyaan?"

Im eyz open even wiyda.

SEEZA! im seey. *DIY-JESSTAS SEEZA!*

"PreCIYSEly, baas," mi sey. "Mi gettimatwaanse!"

It gud fi help im. At iz hart im is a gud maan.

Baat mi fear it will soon alla be hova. What wi do widdout him?

Baat at least im will sleeyp easy at lass, fo-eva.

Crypt-ography

WE'RE BACK AT THE INFERNO. BASICALLY IT'S ALWAYS COOL returning while the music's still playing—usually we get back after everything's shut down, which is pretty, uh . . . well, basically it just makes me feel lonely.

Frosty and the Moog and I walk in just when the deejay's putting on a torch song . . . must be third-last song of the night. "Drive," by the Cars. They're a bit too jungle bunny for my tastes, but I basically always loved this song. Guy's singing that part where he says, "Who's gonna hold you down when you shake 'n' break?"

For some reason I find myself basically looking at Frosty real close during those words. Huh. Anyway, we gotta go see the boss, make our report.

"Grab some chow, boys." I wave em off. "I'll settle up with the boss-man."

On towards the stairs I grab a waitress, tear a fifty in half, and tuck one part in her halter. "I don't care where you have to go. Get my big friend as much ice cream as you can—two buckets, maybe—and I'll give you the other half. And maybe . . . heh . . . something *else,* too."

I like the kind of smile she gives me. It's the shocked-raunchy kind you get after smacking a chick's ass and she finds out she likes it.

"And be back in ten minutes, juicy."

I stake out the place. I got two doors—the unlocked door to the anteroom in front of the Situation Room, and the door to the Situation Room itself. The Situation Room—that's the boss's office—is locked, and nobody answers when I knock, and I can't hear anything in there, which probably means he's out, but nobody knows where.

I can get through that lock no problem with my Czech octopus tools. And there's no camera inside, which I know since I'm the one who basically set up the boss's security system. Unless he's added something, which I doubt. So the only issue is whether the diversion will work.

Nine minutes're gone and that sweet-ass of a waitress is back with the ice cream. I give her the other half of the fifty and squeeze her produce, just to make sure it's fresh, then send her on her way after I stuff my number in her halter. She'll call. They always do.

I gather my shambling diversion. "Hey, Moogie, ice cream!"

He basically grunts like a water buffalo during mating season, thunders over. "Hey, Moog, c'n ya keep a secret?"

"Shore!"

"You like the boss, doncha, Moog?"

"Course!"

"Well howdja like to help me plan a surprise party for im?"

"Yeah!"

"Great. All you gotta do is this. I'm gonna go into his office, right, to plant some presents and a card. All you gotta do is sit out in front of that little lobby-type room with the door closed behind you eating ice cream. If Mr. Allen or anyone else tries to come in, you just make a big sound and grab em or hug em or something, just long enough for me to finish and keep the party a surprise, okay?"

"Yuhn! But cn I tal Yalpha Cott?"

"No, Moog, it's a surprise, remember?"

"How bout Frossee?"

"No, sur-*prise*!"

"Bout Miss Turallen?"

"No, *defi*nitely not Mr. Allen, Moog! It's *his* surprise party, right?"

"Uh, yeah! Goddit!"

Like teaching calculus to a malamute. Anyway, we're set. Got a spoon and a chair for the Moog. I'm inside the anteroom, my Czech octopus flashing, slipping, sliding . . . and I'm in—

Weird. Never been in the Situation Room alone before.

Feels wrong, somehow.

Like . . . like someone's watching me. But that's crazy. Boss wouldna had a camera installed without me knowing.

Room feels cold, too.

Basically better get started. Gloves're already on (*always* carry gloves), and get to work on the safe. I'm sure he had the digital security codes changed, but the tumblers'll be the same as when I ordered this baby—

Photos on the desk? Eight-by-tens. Screw em. Gotta get this safe cracked, but . . .

Aw, hell. Too damn curious for my own good. Okay, hurry up.

Hm. Looks like Frosty's handiwork, his kind of composition. Did the boss find these, confiscate them? Frosty's gonna be in major trouble when . . .

But maybe . . . now, I never thought of this. Maybe the boss *does* know about Frosty carrying his camera? Maybe he *wants* photos taken? But why?

Flipping through . . . some sort of white room . . . a table with straps . . . and IV bottles and needles . . . beakers . . . hacksaws . . .

Now, what the hell is that? Close-ups, like a bowl of Chinese octopus soup or something . . .

Now the soup meats on a white tabletop . . .

Wait, this is ringing a bell from my lab to Bio 231. Is that a . . . a fucking human brain?

Shuffling outside—

Get back to fucking work. One mystery at a time. Slide the phony air vent off the wall, whip out my google-code input, connect up to the magnetic port. Punch in my parameters. Could take up to an hour if I'm wrong, but basically I shouldn't be too far-off if I know Mr. Allen. . . .

Door's quiet, anteroom's quiet, hall's quiet except for the Moog singing while he slops through eight liters of Neapolitan. . . .

Code input's got the first six numbers. . . . Five more to go . . .

The room's even colder now, and it's like there's two or even three sets of eyes watching me. . . .

Eight numbers down . . . three left . . .

My skin's tingling, and my balls've crept up inside me, like I'm playing the ten-cherry hundred-thousand-dollar slots . . . like I'm hiking Vegas blackjack for millions. . . .

Nine numbers down . . . two left . . .

I'm panting. Can't shake the sense like there's basically someone hiding right above the ceiling tiles—

Ten numbers. One left—

Sweating. Air's all hot up in the top of my lungs. Feel like a lamb walking through a field full of wolves, with a hundred hungry eyes ripping off my flesh before they even reach me—

Code's broken! Outer door clicks open. I swing it wide, hit the dial, spin those tumblers—

Groaning and yelling outside—shit, the Moog's signal! Allen must be on his way back—

Around once and eighteen left . . . around once and fifty-nine right . . . *back around once and ten left*—

Fuck, missed it—spin back, *BACK*—"

On the other side of the doors:

"HABBY BORT-DAY, MISS TURALLEN!"

"STOP HUGGING ME, YOU ASS-CAKE! IT AINT MY BIRTHDAY! AW, YOU GOT ICE CREAM ALL OVER ME—"

Click!

Shit, no fuckin time! Click shut, close the digital door, put back the false air grille—

Slip out into the anteroom, sit down, WIPE THE SWEAT OFF YOUR FACE—

And in comes Mr. Allen (wiping his jacket with a hankie) and the Cat, followed by Digaestus, *who's holding the zodia-scope.*

And I left my google-code input on the boss's desk!

"Zenko, ya lil ass-spill, what're you doin in here?"

"Basically just wanted to see you as soon as you got in to hand over tonight's take."

"Why didncha just wait downstairs?"

"Just eager to give you your money, sir."

He gives me the eye, and then looks at the Cat, who shrugs. Mr. Allen waves me to come inside. "The Moog's carrying the haul," I say. "Better'n a Brink's truck, y'know?"

"Assuming he don'eat it. Let im in."

"Moog!" The Moog shambles into the anteroom.

"An no fuckin huggin!"

I whisper to the Moog that there's more ice cream inside the Situation Room. As soon as Mr. Allen's got the door open, the Moog's all over the place, and Mr. Allen's yelling at him not to touch or eat anything, which is all the commotion time I need to grab my google-coder off the boss's desk.

And I'm slipping it into my pants when I think I see the Cat avert his eyes, like he's just seen me.

Shit!

I get the Moog to hand over tonight's proceeds, and then I

say, "Hey, boss, since I'm gonna be undergoing my next degree soon, any chance I can stay now, help out with whatever you guys're doing?"

Silence.

It's a tense ten seconds while something gets e-mailed from the boss's eyes to the Cat's.

"Sure, Zenko," he finally says. "Nice to see such enthusiasm."

If the Cat *did* see me . . .

They set up, open a laptop and turn on the PC and the projector, take out maps and charts. It's like I'm not even here anymore—no one hardly even notices me. Fine. Whatever. That's good.

Alpha Cat goes straight to whatever they're doing with the laptop. Some kind of program they've got going—I'm not sure—I've never seen it before. Some kind of maps of Alberta, BC, Saskatchewan, the Pacific Northwest . . . and the Cat's typing in stuff that Mr. Allen and Digaestus are feeding him.

The boss and Caesar're working on the charts or whatever. . . . They've got compasses—y'know, the spiky kind, not the Boy Scout kind—and Digaestus's eyes are closed while he mumbles something. As usual.

The Cat's excited, though, pointing to an area on his screen that's just gotten highlighted, a Venn diagram center zone. He taps the keyboard, takes out a disk, puts it in the PC, pulls down the screen on the wall, and then activates the projector.

On the wall screen, the western provinces appear, big as bookcases, and a big eye-shaped bright spot takes in the whole southern border of BC clear across to Saskatchewan.

"What's going on?" I try.

Mr. Allen flashes me a look. I know that look. I don't bother asking any more.

After about twenty more minutes Mr. Allen grumbles something that means the Cat can take a break. Then he takes a stick out of the refrigerator, gives it to Caesar, and starts fiddling with the zodiascope.

And the two of them take the back stairway to the roof, and the clear, starry night out there, leaving me here with the Cat.

I glance at the table and the computers. All kindsa stuff I'm apparently not privy to . . . what the hell? The projection on the wall screen starts tracking along a world map, with some sorta hexagonal grid, and the maps on-screen and the ones on paper are covered in *runes*?

Basically I really think I deserve more than this. I deserve to be on the *inside* of all of this. Don't I do my share? More than my share? I bank more than any of the other FanBoys put *together,* practically. I'm the brains of this whole operation! And yet the Cat's the leader. Oh, yes, the Cat gets all the—

"So, maan," says the Cat, "how wuz tings out deh onna STREEYT tniyyyyt? Gud haul?"

"Yeah, dude, sure. You shoulda seen me simonize. And the Moog, he practically split a guy a open like a lobster."

"Wish I-an-I coulda SYEEN it. Baat wi av wi OWN wuk HEAH, seen?"

"Yeah, I can see that."

I start to glance at a really weathered volume the boss's left open—more runes . . . and diagrams—a skull split open with a globe inside it, veins and arteries and—I know that symbol (Alpha Cat deigned to tell me once) has something to do with magnetism or something—

Alpha Cat snaps shut the book, the book I'm actually fucking reading, like as if he doesn't *know* I'm looking at it, like he's pretending he's not actually shutting me out.

"Mi goin HOUT fi sum gwoat RO-ti, bredda, frommun afta-hhowaz pa-tty SHOP. Yu waan fi commalong? Mi cud yuze di CUMPNY, seen? My *treayyyt.*" He smiles the whole time he says it, that honest, totally open, totally generous smile the Cat's famous for.

That fucking smile.

"So where're the boss and Digasestus goin?" I try as casually as I can.

"Oh, dem juss tek a breeyk. Up onna roof, yu know? Fresh air-an-ting."

"Ahn-huhn."

This's all gotta fuckin stop. The boss's mystical crapfest, the favoritism, and the Cat's super-phony super-shit. This can't be good for business. I'm working on tryin to expand our operation, take us into Winnipeg, Toronto, Chicago . . . a much bigger franchise thing.

I've *tried* to talk to Mr. Allen about it, but so long as— hell—basically for the life of me I have no idea why the boss puts so much faith in this wigger. I mean c'mon! In those huge shorts and the fakin-Jamaican accent? C'mon, guy. You're not foolin anyone. You're whiter than a Finn eating Minute Rice.

"Yeah, sure, Cat."

Soon's I pass that next degree, the Cat's gonna take a little trip to the SPCA.

52

Plan B

I KNOW I SHOULDN'T LET THE TENSION GET TO ME. I'M USUALLY cool in these situations. But I'm excited: a new chick fit for new tricks, summertime ripe for romance and shedding pants, *comprende?*

Still, it's not until tomorrow night. So I should try to be productive. As I see it, my options include (but are not limited to)

1. resuming work on the R-Mer (sidebar: My TEC [time of estimated completion] of Version 1.0 of the R-Mer is now down to ten Ye-hours, at which time I can take it on-line for a preliminary shakedown cruise),

2. reading two books, for instance, Haldeman's *The Forever War* and Ford's *The Final Reflection* (note: no real connection there—I just enjoy them both),

3. getting the hockey gear, model rockets, and scale-trebuchet kits ready for tomorrow, and

4. masturbating.

I review my options and their merits—all fine selections, to be sure. But I decide to leave the R-Mer, novels, activity gear, and Extra Value bottle of Johnson & Johnson's Baby Oil aside and go for a walk to enjoy this fine night.

I get no farther than almost opening the front door when I see through the window our new neighbor across the street and four houses down—a willowy wisp of a man who reminds me of Luke Perry or one of those other 9021-hos.

I turn off the lights and scramble for the R-Mer's telaudiophonic headset, put it on, and plug into the Coyote Cave's exterior audio hookup.

Ah, there is good old Perry, sitting with what must be his girlfriend. She could pass for, say, Sandra Bullock leaving or entering a methadone program.

Based on their angular, cranelike sitting posture on the raggedy wooden steps of that house, my approximation analysis suggests the following likelihoods (L):

> L 45%: *Gyno-ultrascoldification of "male"*
> L 35%: *Gyno-redefinition of relationship*
> L 19.999%: *Outright gyno-termination of relationship*
> L 00.001%: *Gyno-proposal of marriage*

I glance at the glowing blue liquid crystal display on the R-Mer glove, enhance the sound, calibrate gain for distance, and presto:

> **PERRY:** I'm *trying* to understand, but—
> **SANDRA:** No, you obviously *aren't* trying—
> **PERRY:** Then *make* me understand—

I turn up the volume—my own giggling is making this nearly impossible to hear.

> **SANDRA:** You're *crowding* me, okay? Why can't you just give me some space?

> PERRY (*voice cracking*): This is really about *Keith*,
> isn't it?
> SANDRA: Leave Keith out of this—

I up the volume again—man, this is gold! Gold! Hamza'll
love this—am I recording? Yes, coming in clear—

> PERRY: I've never demanded *anything* of you, but
> now I *demand* to know why you don't love me any-
> more!
> SANDRA (*indignant*): What?
> PERRY: *You heard me!*

I can't take any more. . . . I'm gonna explode. I toggle the
R-Mer audio control on the LCD to SEND, speak clearly, Paul
Robeson/Keith David–style into my mic.

> THE VOICE OF GOD: ATTENTION, MAN! YOU
> ARE IN VIOLATION OF SECTION ONE-
> THREE-SEVEN-A OF THE MANLY CODE—
> BEING A BIG PUSSY IN PUBLIC! CEASE AND
> DESIST AT ONCE OR YOUR REMAINING GEN-
> ITALS WILL BE IMPOUNDED!

The guy leaps off the stairs, scanning everywhere in the
night, but of course he doesn't see me. Oh, man . . . I should
take all of these-type recordings and make an album. Like the
Jerky Boys.

Ah, well, fun's done. Might's well grab the novels and some
oil.

No Use Crying over Spilt Cream

I FINISH UP IN THE SHOWER, PULL ON MY DRESSING GOWN, TUCK a comforter around Sonia and Sophia nuzzled sleeping where I left them on my futon, and walk out to the living room, away from the mingled scents of mutebe-mutebe smoke, cream, and the expended perspiration of three bodies.

It's late, and I'm exhausted. And anguished as hell. I'd hoped spending some quality time with them might still me, expend my anxieties, but it hasn't.

I know I must talk with my brother about our affairs. I'm *hoping* his rage has come down, somewhat. I'd really rather not subject myself to more of his . . . exhortations . . . which would also wake the girls.

But far worse is our depleted inventory situation. Since I know almost certainly what it will mean.

"Heinz?" I ask gently, with all the melody and lightness of Debussy in my voice.

He holds his gaze upon his parchments and his maps, a compass in his right hand, and a compass just beyond his left. He has been working here for the last fourteen hours.

He does not look up to address me.

"What is it?"

"I was just wondering how that reward situation was going. If there . . . any *word* . . . or anything."

I realize I'm breathing from the tops of my lungs. I try to settle myself, taking deep, slow breaths, thinking pleasant thoughts of chocolate truffles and silk lingerie and Debussy's *La mer.*

It helps, a little.

"Well," he begins, "I'm sorry to report that so far, nothing has changed. In fact, the very *absence* of news and attempts to scam the reward makes me wonder who it is we are dealing with who can scare off all takers. I've composed a mental list of about, oh, seven local and regional groups who could be responsible . . . but so far my discreet inquiries have gone nowhere."

I pause. I had really hoped he'd have some good news. "Oh."

"You look like you have something else to tell me, Kev."

I try to shrug, but it comes out spasmodically, like a mini-seizure.

"*Well?*"

"Well, the problems—well, maybe not problems so much, really, but the issues, I guess . . ."

"Spit it out!"

"Our middlemen. And inventory. Paul D., Tony the Tiger, and Moon Knight haven't kept their appointments with me, and none of them sent messages, either. I'm worried—what if they've—"

"There'll be others ready to take their places, Kevlar. Next issue."

"But Heinz! They're three of the most dependable movers—if they're betraying us . . . or if someone is . . . well, *getting* to them—"

"Natural selection. A market correction. Next issue."

"—or *killing* them? If our people are now being targeted—"

"*Next* issue."

I sigh deeply, clear my throat. "Inventory. We have only a month stockpiled—past our embargo of the local scene—pending the outcome of the reward situation—and that includes . . . our private stock—"

He looks up for only a moment, from underneath an arched eyebrow. It's a splendid arch, really. But I'd really rather not enter the temple beyond it.

"Yes, I'm aware."

"Oh. Okay." I gulp. "Uh, well then . . . the question becomes one of candidacy, because we'll need at least another three months to cultivate—"

"I've already arranged the purchase of two plane tickets. It's taken care of for tomorrow night. At least you had the chance to spend this evening saying good-bye."

I start to pant, involuntarily glancing back to the bedroom, hoping the girls haven't stirred, haven't heard.

"No, Heinz, please—" I don't want to whine, but I can't help it. "Please . . . let's just ride it out, take a break—we don't need to—how can we just—? Heinz! Don't—"

"No. No, as soon as we recover the 'scope, we're going to need as much cream as possible if we're going to locate the *lung-mei* and all the terrvices. And since we'll be on the road at that point, with no opportunity to come back to the lab, it means having all our supplies in place right now.

"And once we start, we won't be able to stop, anyway. We'll be far too ravenous—you know that."

My knees weaken, and I flail out, clutching the baby grand, lowering myself onto the bench.

I can't stop it—I start to cry. I'm actually blubbering now, softly, so as not to wake the girls—I know Heinz hates crying, but, but—

And to my shock he comes to sit next to me, puts his arm around me, cradles me, clutches me while I—

"Huh-Heinz . . . ," I wheeze, Sonia's face ringing into my mind, her lips, her eyes, her arms, her *taste*. "I . . . I don'*wanna* . . . I'll muh-*miss* them. . . . I'll miss *her*—"

"Sh-sh-shhhh . . . don'worry, Kev. . . . Everything'll be all right. You know, it's actually better this way." I can feel him nodding, the shaking motion transmitted through his chest to where my ear and the side of my face are pressed.

"Relationships come and go all the time, Kev. But she'll always be with you, inside of you, you know? It's *not* really good-bye. . . . It's a better way."

I try to still myself, but it's not working.

"And when we wish upon that star—" He tilts my head up. "C'mon, Kev, what? What'll happen? Tell me."

"All our . . . druh-dreams . . . come true?"

He nods.

There is no rustling, no whispering, no sound at all coming from my bedroom.

I bury myself in Heinz's embrace.

And my tears, my tears . . . I can't stop them. . . .

A Big Girl Visits Coyote Camp

MONDAY AFTERNOON, A GREAT BIG BEAUTIFUL DAY IN KUSH, AND Coyote Camp is humming along as nicely as ever. I was worried, what with this utterly insane news all over radio and TV (the news was too late for the papers), that maybe no parents'd let their kids out of the house.

But hey, (*a*) it's daytime, and (*b*) everyone probably assumes that they're safe or their kids are safe cuz they're not involved in whatever this insanity is. It's something "out there," nothing to do with them.

So anyway, we're safe and sound here. So far today, with twenty-three boys and ten girls (mostly cousins and sisters of the boys), we have:

1. **Built scale-model trebuchets and destroyed sand castles.**
   The kids had to do their own math to calculate mass and distance! (Sidebar: The medieval trebuchet was a gravity-launching catapult in which the payload end of the throwing arm was counterbalanced by massive iron bars or a load box of rubble. The entire assembly was

mounted on wheels so that the descending counterbal-
ance could move directly downward to maximize speed,
and the rocking motion caused forward movement of
the assembly, which increased the momentum of the
missile.)

2. **Launched and recovered model rockets** in the park behind Victoria Composite High, including my own two-
stager complete with camera. (Counterdrift recovery
mechanism, patent pending. This close to the municipal
airport is going to get us into real trouble one day, but
how're we supposed to move all these kids out past city
limits?)

3. **Held Hamza-Tall-Tale Time.** (Note: HTTT is always
hilarious as Hamza intentionally mixes up the stories
so the children rail against him with their "correc-
tions"—kids love being "smarter" than adults. E.g.,
Hamza: "So Cinderella gets into the turnip—" Kids:
"PU-U-UMP-KIN!" Hamza: "Right. And she goes
down to watch the Stanley Cup play-offs—" Kids
demand gigglingly: "The royal *BA*-a-all! Tell it
ri-i-ight!" He can hold fifty kids that way for an hour,
easily.)

4. **Held art, sculpture, and crystal-making craft times.** As
led by the wonderfully skilled Hamza, this is always
great fun. The man can teach anyone how to draw
using basic geometrical/cartooning skills. He'll take a
group of kids—and sometimes even their parents—and
get them to draw a face from a model. Then he'll lead
them through six easy steps using the Hamzamatic Vi-
sual Technique, and zesto-Django! Art!

We take donations and so forth from the few parents in Kush
who can afford it, plus a lot of stuff from the better local busi-
nesses. A few mums and dads bring trays of food for the kids.
But most of our kids attend completely for free. Pretty

much all Somalis, Ethiopians, Sudanese, Pakistanis, Vietnamese . . . plus these days Sierra Leoneans, Bosnians, what have you.

Kids hafta register, so we can at least have *some* discipline, and we only run it two, three days a week, depending. But it's good for Kush, fun for us—plus very occasionally we actually clear a little extra to help pay our own bills. But usually we take a loss.

But that's how come so many people in the street know us, call out, "Hey, Coyotes." Our public service. Well, that and one or two other things, I guess.

Anyway, right now we're in the middle of a field hockey game. Hamza and I usually play in the street, but with kids, safety—and not to mention liability—make us move into the school yard.

Not every kid is playing. Some of the kids are making get-well cards for Sylvia, who aint here today, poor little cutie—her leg's gonna be in a cast for the rest of the summer, but we're all just glad she's alive.

And some of the kids are skipping rope or hopscotching on the tarmac, laughing and singing. . . . A knot of little kids is sitting underneath some leaf-abundant trees eating ice creams the Dickie Dee guy gave them for free. (Buddy of mine who owes me—I whipped him up some nonlethal defensive weapons so he doesn't get robbed cycling his cart around. Mostly using glue, stenches, emetics, and so forth.)

I'm in goal. Hamza takes an assist from the big eleven-year-old Bosnian boy named Hussein, shoots—

I release a catch on my Yehatronic goalie stick, and magnaflaps snap out, tripling the surface area.

The ball hits—and *sticks*.

My team goes crazy, cheering, literally jumping up and down, and chanting my name: "*Yehat! Yehat!*" Although with their little foreign kid accents and pronunciations, it could be "*ski hat*" or "*pee bat*," I'm not sure which.

"Penalty, you cheater!" calls Hamza. "That was a goal!"

I pull off my coyote-image face mask, call back, "You popped it. I stopped it."

"Enough with the gadgets!" he yells. "This is hockey, not *The A-Team*!"

"I pity the fool who say this aint the A-Team!" I laugh. "Actually, I'm more like Howlin' Mad Murdock, but I can't do his voice."

"Ett wass a fairr sayyve, Hamza," calls out a tall, dark man in his late fifties, his Sudanese accent rich like freshly ground coffee, the gray kinks at the temples of his short Afro a badge of his authority.

"Daddy," whines Hamza, "I can't believe you're gonna back this infidel against me!"

"Hey, Dr. Senesert, your son just called me an infidel!"

"Hamza, don't cull Yehaat unn enfuddell. Ett's nutt niyyce."

"Hey, thanks, Dr. S."

Hamza: "I'll just call you a cheater."

"Call me STANLEY CUP—*CHAMPION*!"

My team huddles around me, and we cheer, making hissy high-treble crowd sounds enough to fill the Coliseum.

"Happy about yourr bick dayte, tonight, Yehaat?"

"You got it, Doc! Hamza told you, huh?"

"He sett you werrre exciytet."

Hamza shambles over, tries to pluck the ball from the surface of my Ultrastick (patent pending). "Give me the damn puck."

"It's a ball, Spalding Black."

I peel it off, bat it way, way up and out to the field. The kids scrum for it.

But a woman catches it.

Her.

Crap.

"Hi, Hamza," she sings out, waving. What a phony.

Hamza, the damn jimp, he actually drops his gear and

runs—I mean, that hydrojimp literally *runs*—over to her. Dignity, man! If there's one thing I try to teach him about dealing with fleece, it's dignity!

He trots up to her and then, realizing he doesn't know what the hell next to do, slows down sheepishly and finally just offers his hand. They soul-shake. Real smooth, Denzel.

He walks her back over towards us. He's smiling so widely I'm worried his head is going to crack around the equator and spill out his brains—such as they are.

"Daddy, this is Sheremnefer! Sherem, this is my dad, Tehutmose Senesert."

Oh, and the glad-handing, and the smiley-smiley, and the stomach turning.

"Hamza's tolt me a lott aboutt you," says the doc. Now, this man's tops in my book, wants the best for his son, wants to see his son truly get back on his feet to where he was four years ago—I can understand that. He's hoping—*hoping*—that maybe this chick can make a difference.

But doesn't he see—can't he *see*—what's in front of him?

She smiles some more (can you believe it?). "Really? Well, don't let that worry you—I'm actually a very nice person." They all laugh. Ho-ho-ho, such a canned line. So "witty."

A bunch of kids swarm around us and in a dozen different accents start squealing at Hamza, "Is that your *girlfriend*?" (Sidebar: Some of these little girls look jealous.) Hamza looks so simultaneously embarrassed and delighted, there's an eighty-nine percent likelihood that I'm gonna puke.

"She's my *friend,* you guys," he gushes.

It is only my superhuman will that prevents my gagging from being both visible and audible.

"Hey, you're all better now! And no bandage!" says Hamza. What the hell's that supposed to mean?

"Yeah, well, I wasn't actually hurt that bad," she says, touching her face and arm. I can't see anything. "And besides, I heal pretty quickly."

"That's great. Oh, Sherem, you remember my roommate Yehat?"

"Yes, of course, hi, Yehat!" She offers me her hand, too, smiling while she does it.

I take her hand, and I shake her hand, and I return her hand. And *my* mouth smiles, too.

Phobos vs. Biotron,
or Good-bye, Daddy

BY THREE O'CLOCK WE'VE WRAPPED UP CAMP FOR THE DAY AND
sent the kids home, which gives me the time right now to be
taking Sherem on a tour of the Coyote Cave and the Coyote
Compound, plus give Daddy a chance to suss her out.

I've barely seen Pop this last month, with him busy as ever,
but when I called him the other night all excited, the very first
thing he asked me was, "So, you'ff mutt someone? A
wooomn?"

Daddy, he knows me so well, knows what puts my engine
back in gear. We're so much alike in terms of what gets us
zooming . . . and what puts on the brakes. And what just
plain breaks us.

So, we're on the tour, with Ye hovering behind us, I guess,
just in case Sherem looks like she's gonna break something or
learn any of our sworn secrets or steal any of his pending
patents, and everyone's eating my ice-cream sandwiches,
which is okay, I guess, since I'm feeling so damn good with
everyone I care about in the house at the same time (just so
long as they don't eat too many).

"So, Doctor," says Sherem, "you just *gave* them this house?"

It's great to see her talking directly to Daddy, without me being an intermediary. This is maybe what it could be like in a few years, around the dinner table, you know, with his grandkids and all. I mean, you know. If it worked out and everything. But okay, I'm getting a bit ahead of myself.

So anyway, Pop says, "Beforrre I coott finally gutt perrrmission to prrructusss med'cine in Cunuduh, I worrrktt fixing housssess. Eeffunn whun I gott my licensse here, I kuptt up this on the side. I leassse ett to the boysss . . . whutt they cull 'runt to own.' "

"How long did you have to wait to be recertified, Dr. Senesert?"

"Oh, it wusss . . . too long, dearrr. Farrr too long. Eff I hud come from Engluntt, or Farancce, thun maybeee I wutt have starttet immediately. Buttt . . . it is all in the past. We caan'tt frutt forever abouttt pasttt painsss, cun we?"

Daddy is speaking to Sherem, but I catch his eyes. He's saying it to me. About me. And . . . and I know, with some old tears, about himself.

We continue the tour, and Sherem impresses me once again by correctly naming a slew of my action figure collection: "Oh, man! This is the Hornetroid! And Baron Karza! And wow—*Biotron*? I always *wanted* one of these! And it's in mint condition!"

She turns her eyes on us exasperatedly. "*My* parents gave me a *Phobos unit,* figuring they looked alike—you know, big robot, same body, same brand . . . but the colors, red and black instead of silver, blue, and white . . . and the face, a *fright mask* instead of a serene robot . . . uh . . . *visage*—"

I start to laugh, and I see Daddy rolling his eyes, shaking his head.

"What—Doctor, I know, you think I must be the biggest geek . . . or geek tomboy—"

"No, dearrr. Ett's nutt thattt." He shakes his head more.

"Naw, Sherem, see, my mum did exactly the same thing, got me a Phobos after I'd torn out a picture of Biotron from the Woodward's catalog, and I was all of seven or eight, I guess, and I spent all of the rest of Christmas Day moping. My room was covered with pictures I'd already drawn of Biotron, me and Biotron on adventures, me and Biotron saving Dad—"

"My son hasss a long histry of ensunnutty," chuckles Daddy. And then he adds, with that bittersweet expression of his I know too well, "He gutts it fram hiss muther's siyde, nutt mine."

"And well, back then," I continue, "there was no such thing as Boxing Day sales—nothing was open, since it was, I think, a Sunday—right, Dad?" Dad nods. "So Dad spent Monday lunch from his carpentry job in a long line up at Woodward's, trying to exchange one robot for another for his insane son. How many other parents—"

"Are thutt irrational? Hopefully nutt many, *insha'Allah*."

We laugh, and Daddy's face and smile capture me: the way his eyebrows knot up, the way his smile can be almost six decades old and still snap, crackle, and scat, the way his bright dark eyes dance with joy in celebration of small things, even with all that's . . . with all that's been done to him.

My laughter cools, but only to a warm smile at Dad.

Biotron. Damn. I mean, back then, sure, I was happy with what he did for me.

But now, as a grown man, I'm much more moved *that* he did for me.

"Wow," says Sherem, taking in even more of my old toys, "I haven't seen these since—hey, is that really all *Cerebus*?"

I wave grandly, like a hand model, to a huge comic box marked *Cerebus*. "Yeah—all signed by Sim. And a complete *Big 4* collection behind it—all twelve issues."

She leaps into the books, sifting, selecting. I'm loving this. And a glance behind me shows that Daddy's loving it, too.

Yehat is another story, but hell, he's a big boy, and he's got about ten million more idiosyncrasies than I can deal with right now. Probably sore cuz he figures I won't have enough time to praise his R-Mer anymore or do conceptual sketches for his next model Marsbase or hang glider or listen to his long-winded trebuchet—"Not a catapult!"—tirades or that I won't take an entire Saturday out to watch all the episodes of *The Prisoner* with him cuz I've actually got a girlfriend again.

"Weird shit going on these days," brays Ye. "*Really* weird shit. Ah! Sorry, Dr. S."

Oh, sure, he apologizes for swearing in front of my dad, but not in front of Sherem.

"Oh, you mean thessse terrible killinks?"

"Yeah, Dr. S., maybe with all your medical knowledge or knowledge of the human mind, you can shed some insight into this."

Why the hell's he talking about this grisly stuff now? In front of Sherem? I shoot him a look, but he ignores me.

"Yeah," he shovels on, "first that weird killing a few days ago, with the dismemberment and the donkey fur, then Saturday night that guy with the hands cut off, and Sunday night?"

"Yess." My dad nods, blindly taking Ye's revolting bait. Jeez, Dad! "Fourrr bodies discoverett thisss morningk, four diffruntt locationsss, all four with thro-o-oats cutt. And each hatt a marrrk burntt onto their foreheads—"

"Yeah, a donkey! A donkey brand. Can you believe that? They said they were all drug dealers. But what kind of—I mean, it must be a gang sign or something, tong wars or Yakuza or something. Or maybe a cult? Some of them are neck-deep in drugs, like in Jonestown!"

Oh, great, Ye's on to his Jonestown theories! No stopping him now, not that Dad's helping any: "Ah, butt th'four today could be copycaaatss—the news said these were a diffruntt type of donkey brandt than the one on yesterday's vickatim. Andt thaaat wasss on hisss chest, nutt his forehead."

"Right! Jeez, Dr. S., it usedta be such a safe town, and now, six murders in one week, even if they are drug dealers. . . ."

"Yess . . . it'sss unprece*dent*ed. Ah, butt nutt a-a-all the vickatimsss were druk dealersss. . . . The police dun't know who-o-o the first two were, the woom'n whose mouth wass stufft with th'donkey furrr, andt th'man with his handsss cutt off and the donkey mark burned on his chestt. And the—"

"Hey!" I break in, louder than I intend. This isn't right— it's probably making a pretty terrible impression on Sherem, not to mention disturbing her. She's pretty sensitive about these things. "Thanks for the stimulating conversation, every-one—"

"Hey, Hamza," switches Ye, no segue involved, "I forgot to mention, Swood's coming for a visit next week."

"What!" It's out of me before I can stop it. Pop and Sherem look up, then try to talk to each other and pretend they didn't hear me react. I pull Ye aside, the double-grandstanding bas-tard. "Spotswood's coming *here*? *Again*? *For how long?*"

"Not too long." He smirks. "Maybe only a month this time."

"You freakin guy. Thanks for askin me."

"Oh, I gotta *ask* you if my own brother can visit me? Whaddaya think your father'd say about that? *Oh, Dr. S'n*—"

"All right, all right, ya stinkin monitor lizard!" I hush him down. "How long've you known he was coming, anyway?"

"I've been tryinna tell ya, Hamazon," he whispers, "but you've been so erectile-ga-ga that you haven't heard a damn word I've said in days."

I swear, can't the guy just be happy for a Brother? Does he have to be so freakin particular about everything that he just can't stand *not* to stand in the way?

"Just keep him the hell outta my bed, Ye. I swear, I'll call animal control if I find him there one freakin more time, you understand?"

Ye, whispering, smirking worse than ever: "Maybe if I could get him to quote mumbo jumbo, grow tits, and pull a disappearing act every night, you'd be happier to find him in your bed—"

My whole face snarls in and I know I'm three seconds from a berserker rage.

He makes a cute "bye-bye" wave and ducks out before I can break his balls off.

I'm on the porch with Daddy, and we hug, kiss each other on both cheeks. He hands me a silver dollar, just like he did when I was a kid, for luck. Guess he musta brought it special. I don't think they even make these anymore.

He leans in again just before he walks off. "Don't," he says quietly, "lutt thiss one go withoutt a fiyght, son. *Insha'Allah*."

"I won't, Daddy. And thanks for coming over . . . for the inspection. I really appreciate it."

"I know."

"Love you, Pop."

"*Alhamdulillah*. I luff you too, Hamzibi."

"Give my love to Mum," I call out. He waves, shakes his head.

Our own sick joke, painful as ever after all these years, but what would be worse, I guess, would be the fear of making the joke. And he did already bring her up himself today, anyway.

He walks down the sidewalk, up the street. "Hamzibi"—damn, that's magic. He hasn't called me that in a decade.

It was a sweet visit, a nice good-bye. I don't know it yet, but on account of Sherem, three days from now I will say good-bye to my dad one last time.

And then I will never see him again.

At Last, the Box, Explained

IN MY ROOM (*MY ROOM, SHE'S IN MY ROOM! THAT'S SO INTIMATE!* I don't mean sexually, I mean . . . it should just be obvious what I mean! The place where you sleep! Your nightly crypt, chamber of forever-who-you-were-and-are . . . where all your guard comes down, where you're completely helpless, vulnerable . . . where total trust is an absolute necessity. The place . . . the place where you *dream*) I continue my tour with Sherem, telling her about my fortress of solitude, and my archives of Hamzarchy.

". . . and this, this is the microphone from my high school's PA system."

"Why do you have *that*?"

"Well, it's a funny story, actually. Ye and me were gonna get in trouble for something and get called down to the office, so our theory was that if they couldn't call us, we couldn't get in trouble. So Yehat created a pretty amazing diversion using smoke and buzzers and his dog and while the principal and VPs and secretaries evacuated, I scrambled in and swiped it before the fire department arrived."

She smiles, but confusion twists the edges. "But, like, didn't you still get called down, afterwards?"

"Well, yeah."

We both laugh a good long one. And then . . .

Then Sherem sees it.

My kryptonite container.

The Box.

The Box that due to Yehat's pact, I haven't opened since last Thursday morning when I'd spent another night in the chair from having been on Box watch all night . . . the Box that up until then I had opened every night for the previous four years.

She walks to my shelf, as if she's got a homing beacon planted in her fembot main synergistic analytic module.

"What's in the box?" she says, looking at me neutrally—her hand halfway to touching it, not like she's asking for permission, but more like she's trying to use the power of suggestion to get *me* to open it.

I'm cornered.

That's the absolute last thing I wanted to expose to her.

But maybe . . . Ye once told me the cave with the dragon is the cave you *must* descend to. Figure out what you fear. Then you know what you have to do.

So maybe I should.

Then again, I fear being eaten by wolverines. I fear going to Klan conventions.

But as Galactus probably said, The die is cast, and my fate is sealed.

I take the ornate, carved wooden keepsake Box, still with its sandalwood-scented soul, off the shelf, gently, gently, and I sit, gently, gently, on the edge of the bed. And Sherem, bless her, sits beside me.

It's the first time we've ever sat directly next to each other, our legs . . . touching.

And the sweetness of the heat and gravity of her thigh pressing sideways into mine and the intense bitterness of all the awful, mawfull twisted neuron trail that's stored in this damn creepsake Box . . . hell, it's almost enough to send me reeling, squealing, keeling over, never to wake up from having grabbed these two-thousand-volt cables of joy and pain at the same second.

I hear her breathing softly beside me, and only then am I aware that my eyes are closed.

I breathe, too, at last, realizing I haven't been.

"This," she says, "is your scar."

I feel my own face crinkle in confusion, first aware again of the lizard-tail scar that slithers down her neck, below her collar . . . and then I remember what she said to me on our Saturday morning picnic date, after she asked if there was somebody in my past, and I said that everybody has somebody in their past: *But you wear it on your face like a gash.*

I open the Box, cringes creaking—I mean, hinges creaking . . . and . . . and take out a photo.

The photo.

I don't hand it to her.

"My scar." I breathe softly, softly as I can without being dead. "We were . . . sposta get married."

Sherem says neutrally, "What's her name?"

"Her name . . ." I can't believe I'm going to say it. I never say it. Saying it drains my power. But I have to say it, or I'll look like a freak.

"Ruh—"

Breathe. C'mon, man. Just freakin say it.

Pant.

"Rachael." There. It's done. I did it. "Her name was Rachael."

" 'Was'? Isn't it still?"

I pause a moment, not sure if she's trying to be a smart aleck or if she's just trying to lighten the mood. But my words aren't accidents. My words are *never* accidents.

"I don't know," I say at last. "I haven't seen her in four years."

I'm looking straight at the photo, not at Sherem. I feel the heat and weight of her thigh . . . pull away a millimeter or two. My leg feels suddenly cold, unsupported.

"See, me and Yehat and Rachael went to high school with two guys—Heinz and Kevlar Meaney. Heinz was a couple years older than us, but we all usedta play Dungeons & Dragons together."

"Rachael played D&D, too?"

"Yeah, her an us an the Wolves—that's what we called the Meaneys. We were all friends. Anyway, after we graduated, Kevlar joined his brother studying overseas and traveling. . . . We didn't see em for about three years after that. At university, Rachael and I . . . it was good. We, uh . . ."

I stop for a second, clear my throat, try again.

"See, we had futures, Rachael and me. We connected our plans. She was gonna be an anthropologist. I was gonna be an English prof. It was gonna be good. And then, literally, *one day*—it all ended."

I sigh, shake my head, try to clear my brain.

"I didn't know what was wrong—she wouldn't take my calls. She literally just *stopped* seeing me, altogether, unilaterally—"

"You had *no* idea? None at *all*?"

"No, that's what I'm saying! I *tried* visiting her, but she wouldn't come to the door. After a week, I started cracking up—my work started sliding, which was really bad because you have to maintain a certain average in Honors, especially to get into grad school.

"So now I had to worry I wasn't gonna finish my Honors thesis, and so I was gonna miss all my deadlines and the chance to get into a school somewhere.

"That's where everything gets real cute. *Heinz Meaney* . . . the Wolf.

"By this time he was back in E-Town, at the U of A, and working on a grad-doctoral MA/PhD/SOB program or whatever the hell. . . . So he and I were at the Powerplant one day, me pouring my guts out to him over a milk shake, since he knew Rachael and all . . . and so this guy . . . see, he tells me that if I can't finish my thesis on time, I should just . . . like, *pad it out* . . . with some of my old work.

"He knew my thesis was on depictions of revolution in works by world-African writers, so he said I should just plunder some of my old poli. sci. papers. And since I had, in fact, written two papers for poli. sci. that year, in two separate courses, discussing world-African lit, it seemed like a perfect idea.

"I felt so re*lieved,* so *grate*ful . . . an we just we talked and talked and I idiotically answered all of his questions about my poli. sci. courses that I was taking extra to my Honors degree, which you're not recommended to do but I got permission, and me just thinking that his questions were outta genuine curiosity or compassionate small talk or whatever.

"Well.

"The *hour* I'm supposed to defend my thesis, my adviser stops me before I can enter the room—I mean literally, I'm within ten steps of walking in the door—and says I'm *guilty of cheating.*

"Turns out I'd broken a rule I didn't even know existed: you can't submit your own work twice without permission, and even then you're sposta do radical changes, whereas I just inserted like eighty percent of each paper as chapters of my thesis.

"How was *I* sposta to know? I later on read how their own rule sheet says the profs are sposta explain those rules *out loud* to their classes, not only in writing! Like any of them ever did that, but now *I'm* sposta pay the price!

"These freaks coulda been lenient, but they weren't. They put 'cheating' on my record and kicked me out. Good-bye, scholarships! And with *cheater* on my record, I couldn't even *apply* anywhere else!

"Now, if that isn't bad enough, here's the worst of it.

"I didn't know this at the time, but I found out a couple of months later that people were seeing Rachael *with Heinz* . . .

together! And not only, apparently, were they sleeping together, but some people were also sure *they were doing drugs
together.*"

"She did *drugs*? Well, where were her parents through all of
this? Didn't they seek you out when she changed so drasti-
cally?"

I've been talking so long . . . lost in my old-mold moldy
walkways of memory, of pain-receptor-superstimulation-
nostalgia, the sound of her voice—of Sherem's voice—jolts me.

And the naiveté of her question infuriates me—as if every
junkie in the world simply doesn't have parents, or their parents're all just irresponsible or something. Sometimes . . . some
people just are . . . they just be*come* bad kids.

"Her parents'd moved back to Saskatchewan after she
started university. As far as the drugs, like I said, I had no idea
about any of that at the time. Me, if I'd known . . . lemme tell
you, I hate everything about drugs and that whole lifestyle!

"*Drugs* . . . drugs are about lies—and if there's one thing I
can't stand, it's lies! Users and junkies are the most disloyal
people on earth—the only thing *they* love is their poison. And
if there's one *other* thing I hate as much as lies—it's disloy-
alty . . . and broken trust!

"So.

"Within a month of my adviser tackling me before I can
walk in the door to begin my destiny, Rachael is gone. I mean
gone gone, like apparently out of the city gone. Without a
good-bye, without a trace. So here I am: she's crushed me like
a tick, an I got no idea why. I'm kicked outta school, and I
don'even know how I got caught!

"*Until.* Until I find out that one of the two TAs who'd
marked those earlier poli. sci. papers? Y'know, in courses that
I had so stupidly and carefully identified to oh-so-helpful
Heinz?

"This TA was a *friend* of Heinz. Heinz'd 'arranged' for one
of the younger English profs on my review panel who he *also*
knew to ask *another* buddy of his, *the poli. sci. TA,* some

political question regarding my paper. That's how these freaks connected the dots. That's how they killed Hamza's future.

"Heinz Meaney stole my fiancée, my reputation, my education, my career, and my future. And he left me . . . that son of a bitch left me *washing dishes* while he got his doctorate and traipsed around the world and became a successful freakin businessman an a kot-tam *author*!

"I don't hate many people in the world . . . but I fuckin hate him."

I clear my throat. My dad taught me never to swear in front of a woman, but it's how I feel . . . and if she's gonna know me, and care about me, then she has to understand this . . . and accept my anger on this. As is.

"On, uh, Saturday, when we were at the glass pyramids? You asked me if I believe in God. Threw me for a loop, Sherem. People don't usually ask me that question. They just assume I'm still a good Muslim. But good people get hurt— bad people get ahead, get rich, get your girl. Good doesn't triumph over evil. So, do I believe in God?

"He doesn't believe in *me*."

I sit, looking at the photo of Rachael.

Rachael and her long, dark, curly hair, black locks a locking trap, dark eyes and whimsied smile, the succubus who has haunted my every night for four years minus four days . . . since I met Sherem. I take a last look at her photo, reminded suddenly of just how much Rachael looked like Rae Dawn Chong, and how I used to watch *Quest for Fire* and imagine her and me struggling against all of the forces of the world to survive if we had to, and laughing all the way. Only to wake up one day locked in an ice age with no end in sight, and me without fire, and Rachael with its secret, still a secret, and gone to give it to someone else.

I put the photo back in the Box, shut it closed.

And suddenly I'm aware that Sherem's thigh is nowhere near mine.

I look up.

She's scowling.

"So . . . what you're telling me is that essentially, you got tossed for cheating."

My spine is ice in an instant. "It was *my* paper!"

There's a long, tense silence. I'm totally unsure what to say. Where the hell is *this* coming from? I expected sympathy. . . . Here I am, totally vulnerable, finally revealing to her why my life is a mess . . . and she's driving a Humvee over my heart?

She pushes herself away from me farther on the edge of the bed, targets her eyes on mine, and locks on. "Let me . . . let me tell you something about pain, Hamza. In Ethiopia I saw fields filled with kids whose bellies looked like basketballs due to starvation gas bloating. In Iraq, I saw children without arms and legs by the thousands, born that way because of the 'depleted'-uranium antitank shells the US and allies used over there in the war. I got out of Rwanda just as the mass-murder campaign started. *That's* pain. Pain is being informed by mail that . . . that your parents and, and your siblings have been burned to death. Pain is waking up day after day and wondering whether there's even gonna *be* a world in ten years. *That's* pain. That's *real* pain.

"But pain that terminates in self-pity and wallowing? That's just waste. A waste of your soul. Pain is supposed to be decay, like soil is decay . . . to make the soul of the universe grow. Good triumphs over evil when it's better organized, better trained, better armed, sneakier, and gutsier than evil.

"But you? What are you doing with *your* pain? Crying about it? Throwing away your life? You've got brains, an education, your health—you know how many Iraqi or Rwandese or Sierra Leonean children would like a house or dinner or even legs and arms like yours?

"You *say* you're a writer, but when was the last time you wrote *anything* to maybe try to teach somebody or help somebody or comfort somebody other than yourself? You have no business talking about pain unless you're fucking doing something about it."

That's *it*.

"Who . . . gave you . . . the right to judge me?"

"Non sequitur. Judgment isn't a right—it's an ability. The question is whether one will judge in*tell*igently or *fool*ishly. *I* have judged intelligently. *You* are, right now, judging foolishly, and wasting your life."

I leap off the bed, sickened with the thought of my flesh connecting with hers even only through the convection of the comforter.

"You're some piece of work, lady! Y'know, you're new back in town, I'm nice to you, I make you a picnic, I introduce you to my dad, an you treat me like this? In my own house? What business do you have talking to me like this?"

By now all the air in the room has sunk to zero kelvin. If I've stopped trembling, it's only because my blood is frozen, too.

And her answer to my question:

"Apparently none."

She pushes herself off the bed.

I throw the Box back on the shelf, start to walk ahead of her to let her out of the house, but she's walking too quickly, and she's down the hall, jumping into her boots, and already is out the front door before I can get there.

The door is swinging a good-bye wave on its hinges while she's already at the sidewalk, and just before she right-angles down-street, she takes a second to crisply and decisively slap the dust from the soles of her boots as she steps off the property.

I stumble backward into the room, nauseous, light-headed, and trip and fall on my ass.

Ye, jaw slack, eyes bugged, comes over to me, crouches in front of me.

"Hamza!" He clutches my shoulders. "What the hell just happened?"

Hunter, Hunted

THIS LAST TWENTY-FOUR HOURS WITH THE MASTER HAS BEEN most remarkable. While I have always considered Mr. Allen to be a superb administrator, visionary, and documentarian of the dark metaphysics, I have felt that, perhaps, my own failings as his humble subject and page have meant that my relationship with him has never reached the piquant potency I had always hoped it would.

Yes, Mr. Allen has always made use of my abilities and servitude, based on the inestimable Mr. Alpha Cat's interventions and advocacy of me, as a detector and investigator, as a professional intuitionist.

And he has compensated me generously, despite the aspects of my character that some have described as "off-putting," or what my uniquely depraved colleague Mr. Robert Frost "Frosty" Gorkovski named as "hinkier than a goddamned leech in a condom."

But in the last twenty-four hours, due to Mr. Cat's suggestions, I have been given over ten times my usual dosage of the exquisite nectar and galactic ambrosia that Mr. Allen has, at nigh incalculable price, acquired the methods to produce at modest wholesale scale.

For our genius lord and master, our Sovereign Sublime Ministrant of the Crusader-Templar Order of the Lost Henge, who is the incarnation of the murdered-living god Ymir, Mr. Dulles Innes Allen, demands that my eyes be opened to behold the secret celestial geometry.

The ethereal circulatory system of the world.

I breathe, my mind ignited, my eyes remembering the glories of their bearing witness to the sights behind that sacred lens, the rarefactions of the universe known only through zodiascope.

And with my mind inside that energetic wonder, that Van Allen belt of living cosmoterrestrial ethereal blood, the Aurora Metempsychosis . . .

. . . I flare with the flares and surges of a million million million tonnes of crust-mantle-magma-iron core and its grand expanding, breathing, dark, magnetic respirations . . . as if I were an ingot in an Asgardian foundry . . . as if I were a photon in a celestial diamond. . . .

And I am closer, closer to penetrating the hidden chamber wherein dwells our prize . . . for my mind folds and slithers on the corrugated textures of subterranean memory, yielding synesthetic ecstasies . . .

. . . the ultraviolet scent of cactus and of rattlesnakes . . .

. . . the hypersonic hiss of badlands sands . . .

. . . the piercing, ancient cervical pains of stars aligned above—

—*above the sacred sepulchre*—I'M IN—

And . . .

No, no, not yet, so soon—let me stay in the chamber. . . .

No.

Oh, amid my sobbings . . . the agony to have nearly kissed and then to've lost the unimaginable beauty of what dwells inside . . .

. . . *inside the—the what?*

It's gone.

The weakness of my flesh . . . damnation.

But after rest, after more ambrosial cream, I can return.

But now there is a problem, a danger, a clot, if you will, whose loosening threatens us with imminent death.

It is past dinnertime, and the Master dwells inside his office, eager for the night to fall such that my eyes might employ the zodiascope to behold the veins in the darkness, what the Chinese call *lung-mei,* or "dragon paths," the cosmagnetic force lines whose map invisible links the storehouses of infinity—*the terrvices*—wherein are found the powers and principalities that can make a man a god.

And I, Digaestus Caesar, with my enhanced humagnetic gaze, a Grand Inspector Loki in our Ancient Teutonic Order of the Knights of the Mystic Sepulchre of Ginnungagap, am become the cartographer whose imaging will secure us triumph in the impending darkness of *Götterdämmerung.*

I hear the high whine of his juice-extracting engine, and again and again, its whirring bite turning what I know to be purple cabbage into his preferred beverage, one he has told us many times must be consumed within two minutes of creation in order to enjoy its ulcer-destroying capacities.

Mr. Cat and I approach the Master respectfully, allowing him to recognize us and bid us approach.

The Master, without employing intonation befitting a question mark, speaks: "What."

The captain speaks for me to our supreme general; he knows that because of the superb sacrament our sage has granted me in spades, ten doses in one day, I am finding speech especially difficult. In fact, I am finding standing difficult, and walking difficult, and blinking difficult.

However, I have not felt hungry or thirsty in all this time, and am enamored with the intricacy of creation, the every mote and atom that stands out in my vision, the every symphony that sings in the slightest hiss and crackle in the minutiae of everyday molecular movement.

And so Mr. Cat says, "Mos righteous Super-Don Master Dulles, Digaestus ave ditektid a striykin anOMaly. Sumtin MAYjah."

"Yeah?" says our lord, slurping his Odin tankard of cabbage blood. "Spit it out, ass-beans."

I reach out suddenly for Alpha Cat's hand or arm, and, to my surprise, miss.

When I wake up, I rub my head where I believe it had attempted intimate knowledge of the desktop. My captain and my lord are pulling me up and bringing me to the couch, and Mr. Allen goes to wet a handkerchief with which he now attempts to administer pain relief to me. I am touched by his concern.

"Caesar, what the fuck are you doin, passin out on me like this? You not eatin or something? That's irresponsible an selfish! I need you *alive* to complete this work, ya lil ass-pie!"

"Uh, yes, uh, sir. I'm sorry, sir."

"So what the hell is it you got to tell me?"

Mr. Cat starts to speak, but my head is suddenly superbly clear, as if smashing it somewhat against the desk were an excellent restorative method. I touch his arm to indicate that I wish to try.

"Go head," says Mr. Cat.

"Master Allen, last week, that is to say, Thursday, I believe, when we were doing our final, well, advance work, you know, pre-'scope, that is? Yes, well . . . you recall that Mr. Cat telephoned you to explain that I had picked up a signal, and you asked us to investigate it, remember, sir? You recall, don't you, how—"

"Yeah, yeah! I remember. Hurry up!"

"Yes, well, right. I had picked up the signal which I had thought was connected with the properties unique to the zodiascope itself, but then we found that the signal was moving. Mr. Cat and I tracked it down to a, a trendy restaurant in the neighborhood, and when we locked on, we found that it, well, wasn't a cache of thaumaturgical or geomanciful materials at all, but only a, a couple having coffee, as we reported to you that night—"

"Get to the point, ass-grapes!"

"Yes, well, good shot, sir. I, I assumed it was just another false 'ping' on my perception . . . perhaps the man or woman wearing jewelry from gems or, or minerals quarried from along a *ley-line,* although given the strength of my reaction, I assumed the jewelry to've been mined from a vortex . . . or perhaps even a *terrvix.*"

"AND?"

Alpha Cat cuts me off, just before I can reach my climax and conclusion!

"Ee been a whole twenty-foh ourz inna dis cream TRANCE, Mista Allen, suh, at a DOSage no one eva befoh suhVIYVE, to my knowlijj. Ee pickinnup percepSHAANS an FREquenceez im naa even know exist befoh.

"Five ourz ago, DieyJESStus pickup di SEEYM signal from lass Tursdee niyyt . . . baat now im can reayd it widda clarity im naa ave befoh becozza di intensiTY an durAYshaan uh di TRAANCE.

"Wi tink meeybey deer's a representaTIVE a one a di old, old powaz new in town . . . radiaytin greayt ennajee . . . meeybey also tryin fi traack down di zodiaSCOPE."

"Actually, sir," I manage to squeeze in, "I, I believe I have, well . . . uncovered a potency of signal beyond what a, a, a single warrior or monk could generate. I believe we are, are looking at the presence of some type of, of *templar* . . . attempting to create a Lodge. Or destroy one."

Mr. Allen's eyes focus on me, twin furnaces, and I melt beneath that smelting gaze.

He leaps up, goes to his safe, unlocks it, takes out a giant volume I have never seen before, whose cover reads *Eschatos*

*Historical Ledger of Supreme Thaumaturgy—Recognition,
Composition, and Combat.*

He sits at his desk, demands: "Caesar, tell me everything
you've seen, tasted, smelled, heard, or felt about this man."

"Well, I, you see . . . that's the other thing. The anomaly
isn't, isn't a man at all. It's, it's a woman."

Mr. Allen's mouth opens slowly and then closes slowly
without emitting speech, then repeats this ritual more quickly.

"Tell me everything," he rumbles. "*Ev*erything."

After another hour, Mr. Allen has combed a few hundred en-
tries among the onion skin pages. He keeps his hand on one
page, sits back in his throne, and declares, "This . . . is both
good *and* bad. Assuming your readings are right, ya lil ass-
fruit, we're talking about a member of the Jackal Clan."

I look at Mr. Cat in my peripheral vision. I have only heard
vague legends about the deeds of these fanatics, stories I had
hoped would never be repeated in my presence. But . . .

"Aren't they, they . . . all *dead,* sir?"

"'Parently not. The good news is that we're closer than we
ever guessed. According to the *Ledger,* if one of the Jackals is
looking *here,* and especially if it's a *she,* as soon as Caesar can
finish his calculations with the 'scope, we c'not only track
down a terrvix, but we'll be finding the mother lode of mother
lodes inside."

We wait for the conclusion.

"The *Jar.*"

Once again I examine Captain Cat in my peripheral vision.
He is similarly immobilized with awe.

Of such an opportunity I have never even dreamed.

"*Here,* sir?"

Mr. Allen nods slowly and smugly, like the cat who has just
swallowed the Canary Islands.

"Yu sed deer wuz BAAD nooz, too, suh."

"Yeah, well. The bad news is that obviously now we don't

have as much time as we thought. And . . . and it's a big 'and.' According to the *Ledger*," he recites from his astounding memory, " 'The House of the Jackal is the exalted grand cardinal of infinite agony, the master of murder, and the bringer of damnation eternal.' "

I know what the Master is going to say next, and I think I'm going to be sick.

"Cat—prime Caesar again. Activate the entire crew. And find her. And you can forget about firepower—she's a Jackal. All close-quarter weapons. She'll have range protection.

"Stop her—do whatever you have to—before she reaches the Jar."

My earlier clearheadedness has now completely disappeared, and with it, my lucidity. "Sir, couldn't we, uh, that is to say, well . . . wouldn't it be easier if we, well, just . . . *followed* her? And then . . . well, you know . . . pinched the Jar from her? At that time? More safely?"

I cringe, fearing the worst—and then the Master does something that he has done only once before in my presence.

He laughs.

"Digaestus, m'lil ass-boy," he says, clapping me on the shoulder, "if this Jackal woman reaches the Jar before *we* do, the only thing there'll be left of us you could sift into an ashtray."

The Fall of the House of Yehat, or Hamza Wasn't Kidding

WELL, I WON'T SAY "I TOLD HIM SO."

But I knew it.

The damn jimp had all the signs he needed—erratic moods, mysterious disappearances, cryptic explanations of her past . . . a blueprint for self-destruction. And that pathetic microjimp even has to *work* tonight! I *told* him to call in sick, but he went anyway. I think he was just too ashamed to face me, so he slunk off feeling like a sack of crap from the out-house on death row.

You know, what builds forty-three percent of my disgust about this most recent Hamtastrophe isn't the full range of unbearable self-loathing and interminable autorecrimination to which he will subject me for the foreseeable future, but the fact that this descent into masochomartyrist jimpomania was *totally preventable*. I warned him. I shelled him daily with vol-ley after volley from my hint howitzer. But did he listen?

I know about waste. I know about tragedy. Some people don't have choices.

Take my brother Swood. Please. I know, I shouldn't say

that. But listen, Spotswood is my older brother, but my whole life, he's been more like a younger one. He's got, well, you might call it autism *light*. Swood can no more read social-interaction data than the average jimp can read a menu written in binary. Photographic memory for the most god-awful arcane trivial nonsense, sure, but he can barely remember to zip up his fly. He's out East working on a double doctorate in superstring theory and thirteenth-century Japanese history, assuming he hasn't gotten lost and ended up in the SPCA again.

His whole life people've treated him like a case of eczema, just because he's not normal, like me. He not only's never had a girlfriend and never will—*he's never had a single friend.*

But despite my brother's near total isolation from Homo sapiens *sapiens,* he wouldn't hurt a tick. He wouldn't *cry* on a tick.

Does he complain about his lot in life? Does he find bigger and sharper swords to throw himself on at regular intervals just to make damn sure his scars can never, ever heal? Does he explore strange new wounds, seek out new strife and new traumatizations, and oldly groan where no jimp has groaned before?

(Hint: The above questions are rhetorical.)

I'm glad Swood's coming to visit this week. Glad to see my brother, yes, no matter how much of an imperial pain in the rectum he always is, and glad because maybe, maybe *this* time, Hamza will break the damn shackles he himself forged before his own pet vulture can rip out his liver daily forever. Again. Swood can show him how little a man can have and still not be a total self-whimpering shrimp chip.

Do I feel bad for Hamza and all? Yes. But he's better off, *way* better off without a psycho broad like this. And she wasn't so great looking, anyway. I mean, I wouldn't throw her outta bed for eating curry, but risk my sanity over her? Forget it.

Anyway, the jimp is out washing dishes, and me, I got a date.

THE COYOTE KINGS OF THE SPACE-AGE BACHELOR PAD   331

I wonder how much this woman, Velma, is adventurous. I mean, does she both rock *and* roll? Might she have a friend, for instance, as comely as she is, who would be interested in . . . dancing? It might be very nice to try a little duo-tang.

Well, speak of the deviled egg. The telephone.

"Hello, you've reached the Space-Age Bachelor Pad—all of our astro-operators are busy right now, but if you . . . well, Vel, hel*lo-o-o-o*. So, thanks for returning my call! So, you wanna . . .

"What?

". . . really?

". . . why not?

". . . yeah, okay, I can see how you might see it that way, but . . .

". . . yeah, but . . .

". . . okay, okay, good point, but . . .

"On the other hand, no lie, I know where we can try *garlic ice cream*—

". . . look, once you get to know me—

"Wait, don't hang—"

Well.

This project isn't moving forward at quite the pace I'd expected.

Well . . . *someone's* gonna be receiving a bill for eight hundred dollars in overdues.

Reconciliation and Gifts That Keep On Giving

I'M A FREAKIN MORON.

I know better, I *do,* but . . .

But when you want something so bad . . . when you've been walking through the desert for so long that your tongue's forgotten what water even *feels* like . . . when your irises have lost the ability to open because you've been dwelling in the belly of the cave for a million years, you . . .

You end up back at the freakin sinks of a stink factory for stuck-up preppy pukes called ShabbadabbaDoo's, scraping crud and blasting schmutz with a high-powered nozzle, imagining what it'd be like if you had a napalmer in your hand instead.

The Zitsack is dancing and prancing around me, smelling blood, like a remora on the shark of my life. Whatever he's saying, I don't even have a comeback for him. . . . I can't even hear him. . . . His voice is the fingernails of all the demons of perdition, on a chalkboard eight million light-years long.

To hell with this.

I tell the manager I'm too sick to keep working. It's a slow night anyway, being Monday and all, so she lets me go.

. . .

I don't usually walk home at this hour. . . . It's not even eleven o'clock yet. Whyte Ave should still be packed with losers and knuckle draggers and fake-poor teen beggars wearing three-hundred-dollar boots and smoking six-bucks-a-pack cigarettes, but it's a cool night tonight, cool with a stiletto breeze, cool like maybe it'll rain razor blade drops.

Glad I wore my kaffiyeh and my jacket. Armor against the night.

Light traffic. No one cruising. Just people getting to where they're going.

I slow down suddenly, staggering. Lean against a lamppost, panting, my chest on fire, my head spinning. Am I having a heart attack? Am I? Can I really be twenty-five years old and dying of a heart attack?

Ah, shut up, Hamza, you freakin moron. You're not having a kot-tam heart attack!

Then I think about the phrase.

I decide it's time to keep walking.

Two blocks farther, now in front of Scona Bowl. A man waves to me, calls out, "Hey, Coyote!"

Must be a Kush guy.

"Hey," I wheeze. And walk.

It's dark as I enter the Coyote Cave.

"Yehat?" I call. "Ye?"

No answer. Must be on his date. But his iron engineering ring is on the table . . . and his cape is still hanging next to the door. So—

The phone rings.

Every part of me wants to bolt over to it, pick it up, clutch it, hold it, cradle it, strangle it, confess into it, sob into it, beg into it, pray into it—

Ring . . .

—but hell, no, I should just let it ring, let it starve for attention, cry out its electronic hunger pangs and die its electronic, telephonic death. . . .

Ring . . .

Let it go, Hamza . . . let it go. You know everything you need to know. . . . Don't *debase* yourself. . . . DON'T—

I leap over the debris and collateral damage on the floor, reach the phone just as it sounds like it's giving up the ghost: "Coyote Cave!" I try to still my voice at least a little bit, sound a little less like the pathetic loser I actually of course am.

"Hamza here."

"Hamza?"

Breathe, Hamza.

Breathe.

". . . yes."

"Hamza, this is Sherem."

". . . I know."

"Yeah, I guess that's . . ." Pause. "Listen . . . I'm sorry about . . . about this afternoon."

You're damn right you're sorry—you should be sorry, coming into my house and disrespecting me with my roommate and best friend right down the hall, treating me like a freakin chump! Swearing at me! Judging me, like you're the queen of the universe who's never made a mistake!

Breathe.

Breathe some more.

". . . Hamza?"

"I . . . I've been thinking about it a lot . . . what you said . . . and—"

Go on, tell her, tell her, you freak!

"And . . . to be completely honest . . . you were right. About . . . some of the things you said."

Breathe.

"Well," she says, and I can hear her sighing, and there's . . . a little tiny sob in the back of her breathing, like a camouflaged hare hiding in the brush . . . from wolves.

"See, Hamza . . . it's just that . . . I like so much about you. And I . . . I can see all of the things you're capable of doing. I can see them! To me, they're as real . . . as tomorrow's sunrise. Haven't happened yet, but they *will*. And . . . I've seen too many people who didn't live out their dreams, because they were caught up in pain . . . paying for someone else's mistakes. Living in the chains of bitterness. Crawling like butterflies with their wings torn off.

"And I don't wanna see that happen to you, Hamza. Because I . . . well, just cuz I don't. And when I think of all the good that you can do, and that you're not doing it, because you stopped believing in yourself—"

"Sherem—"

"Wait, please, let me get this out or I won't be able to say it all, Hamza. I was in Ash Shabb too long. My social skills are terrible, and I . . . I was way out of line to talk to you the way I did. I had no right being so rude.

"But if I got you to take another look at how you're living . . . if I shocked you into taking one more step back on the road of becoming the true Hamza, then . . . then I'm *not* sorry I said what I said . . . just the way and the when and the how I did it."

And she sighs deeply, deeply, and then, with a voice as dark as a midnight oasis, as sweet as watermelon on a hot day, she says, "*I believe in you, Hamza.*"

Whoah.

Whoah.

I'm reeling. . . . What do I say to that? My feelings're rocketing back and forth like a kot-tam tennis ball. . . . You always fantasize that the person who hurt you will call you back and apologize and beg for mercy and you'll walk all over em or flash em someone newer and better. . . . I must be crazy. I've only known her for what . . . four days? What the hell am I expecting?

Was it really only eight hours ago I was introducing her to my dad and having fantasies about marriage? Was it only a day ago I was at her abandoned, condemned apartment (!!!) and dreaming of us feeding breakfast to our children? When will I grow the hell up?

"Hamza?"

"Yes, Sherem . . . I'm listening."

"To me, it's just that . . . given what I've seen and lived . . . every day of life is borrowed time. Please, Hamza . . . please have patience with me. Please don't give up on me. Please . . . share more of your time . . . with me."

Shit, shit . . . she knows *exactly* what kinds of things to say to push all of my buttons. . . . I can't stop myself—

"I . . . appreciate your calling, Sherem. It . . . it took a lot of guts."

"Look, Hamza, I know this is crazy, but I got you a gift."

What the hell? "What the hell?"

"A gift."

"What? Why?"

"To say sorry."

"That's not really necess—"

"Check outside your front window."

This is weird. I go to the front window, pull back the curtain. Oh. My. Gourd.

"Sherem, are you serious? I can't accept that!"

"Look, it's a lender, then, okay? If you don't wanna keep it. But I know you need one. And like I told you, I restore em. I was gonna sell it, but . . . it's no problem. Really!"

"Yeah, but . . . it's just . . . my daddy taught me—"

"What, not to accept gifts from women?"

"No, not to take advantage of women. Not even to *look* like it."

"What 'take advantage'? You didn't ask for this—I *offered* it to you. And it barely cost me a thing. Just labor."

"But you've only been in town for five days! How on earth could you've—"

"A girl's gotta have her secrets, doesn't she? Especially a first-rate tradeswoman? Look, have some fun and *write* about it, Hamza. Write about it and I'll love to read every poem, article, and journal entry you write—I'll sit adoringly while you read them to me!"

Every button—she knows every button—

We say our good-byes, after I give my thanks, and before I delicately put down the phone, wondering when all this bubble of dream will burst.

I go to my bedroom, grab the first gift from Sherem, the necklace, the *tchaua* scarab she gave me on Sunday morning for finding her and coming to see her.

I'd put it into the Box after she . . .

I put it on.

I go to Ye's room. "Ye? Ye, you in there?"

I try the knob. It aint locked, so I rattle it a bit in case Johnson & Johnson are meeting their namesake. I wait another half minute, don't hear any shuffling, then open the door and walk in.

Ye is sitting in the darkness in his high-backed bedroom chair, nearly silhouetted by the fractured streetlight splintering in from beyond the window, looking as ominously somber as Vincent Price. Must be trying to scare me.

"Ye, you'll never guess—"

And then, no lie, he says *exactly* these words: "*Leave me. Leave me to my pain.*"

I back away slowly, close the door.

Exactly sixty minutes later I knock on the door again.

"Ye, hey—you okay?"

The door bangs open and Ye springs out like a Pop-Tart. "Rock and roll, baby!"

There's only one Ye.

Outside, on the street in front of the Coyote Cave, is the gift. What looks to me like a '55 Ford Fairlane, a black-and-chrome

winged thing, fully loaded convertible Autosaurus rex. Streetlights praise it glowingly, and it reflects back their praise with
equal intensity.

This is my dream car.

My dream car.

Ye: "The woman has fins? How'd the woman get fins?"

I stroke the Fairlane's fins, the luscious aerodynamoids of
this Dee-troit landspeeder.

"I dunno," I say, "but the woman *has fins.*"

"And she just *gave* it to you?"

"It's a lender, but she says I can keep it if I like it."

"What, she's a car thief?"

"Naw, she told me she restores old cars."

Ye blusters a laugh. "What the hell? And you believe her?"

"No, Ye, it's just like you said. She's a car thief. She speaks
about eight ancient languages and travels the world looking
for classic cars to steal to give to unsuspecting dishwashers."

"I knew it!"

I scowl at him.

"Well," he says, walking around the car and taking it all in,
every moon-silvered, cosmic-blackened, rubber-glass-steeled
atom of it, from eyes to wings, from floor to door and glass to
ass.

"Chick might be crazy," he continues. "But . . . she gots
good taste in mo-*beelz.*"

"Indeed. Let's take er out!"

"Wait, just a sec—"

Ye runs back in the house, and in a moment he reemerges
wearing his cape and the right arm of his R-Mer (so bulky he
looks like a brown fiddler crab), and carrying an envelope or
something in his left hand.

He goes around to the back, slams the envelope on the
back, and it's only then I realize. I walk around, check out the
bumper:

THE COYOTE CAR

"You made *stickers*?"

"Hell, yes!"

"Just now?"

"Naw, years ago! Had em ready. When you made me quit smoking, I thought about what I'd do with the extra money, so I dug em out. Cool, huh?"

"The coyotes wearing sunglasses are a nice touch."

"Thanks!"

"Well, Mr. Scott . . . let's see what's out there."

C.R.E.A.M.

THE RADIO'S ON, ALL THE WAY TO THE LEFT ON THE FM DIAL, and for some reason E-Town's greatest living deejay is gracing us with his sophisticated soultific sensational self on a Monday instead of his usual Saturday slot.

We're powered up with engine running, lights on, blinkers blinking, and system checked when the master man with the master plan intones in a smooth-ass drone:

> *It's twenty-three minutes on the downside of midnight, and the Cruise Master and General Overseer is here with you on a night he usually, positively, absolutely has never been before, a Monday, but that's okay, just this one time, dig it?*
>
> *Riding and sliding with you, guiding you into a summertime glide as you enter the night, with the band called Wu-Tang, reminding you that coffee goes down better with "C.R.E.A.M."—from the man who's always ready to fly. . . .*
>
> *Tee Ee, Dee-Dee, WHY-Y-Y . . .*

Liftoff.

The streets slide beneath us like sheets of slate and silver, the wind coming in through open windows like the sensation of sweet nostalgia. . . .

And we're cruising the avenue called 107th, the main artery of Kush . . . past Axum Restaurant, past Queen of Sheba Restaurant, past Mogadishu Halal Meats, past the Addis Ababa Obelisk illuminated in the night like some midnight arm of a half-buried world clock. . . .

> *And stay awake to the ways of the world cuz shit is*
> *deep . . .*

Top down, midnight's black air roaring inside the cockpit and whispering dreams to us of flying among the moons and stars . . . up north and then southeast back down Kingsway, now *the Coyote Kingsway,* the runway-style avenue lined with red-twinkling sentinels to warn the airplanes passing above us even now to leave this strip to the world of men . . . the world of Kings. . . .

Down 109th now, entering the Belly of the Whale, its long line of spine lights streaking psychedelically upon the hood of this sleek steel machine . . .

Chinatown . . . the neon signs announcing noodles and Triple Happiness and Lucky Heaven Perfection . . .

. . . and then west down

down

Grierson Hill as the valley opens up into four glittering glass pyramids and a sine wave stripe of mercury called the North Saskatchewan River banked on both sides by sensually hugging blackness . . .

. . . and then, then rolling over James MacDonald Bridge . . . and when I feel raindrops, we roll up our windows and pull over as I push a button and the hardtop clambers back into place, a scarab's carapace for the industrial age, and

then out of park and back into space . . . past the Muttart
Conservatory and a big white skeletal bird effigy at the bottom of Folk Fest hill. . . .

We bop heads to the gravitic soulitude of the moment, and
each time the radio unites a Wu-Tang star-sparkling piano
trill with a low-moan, hard-tone, funk-groan bass drone, the
rearview trembles from the auditory passion, and we pass on,
we pass on. . . .

Me: "All right, all right, a-a-all ri-i-ight . . ."
Ye: "What it *is* . . ."

Down 99th, west on Whyte Ave, south down 104th . . .
East on Argyle, back up 103rd through industrial loneliness, a
metallic Jurassic boneyard, brontosaurus crane paused in
midmunch, frozen forever . . .

Cash rules everything around me: C.R.E.A.M. . . .

White van appears outta nowhere, rack of lights blinding
and horns screaming, moving from behind to ram us—
SWERVING—
Me: "*Hell's bells!* WHAT THE HELL ARE YOU DOIN, ya
FREAK?"
—streaking TO OUR SIDE, MY SIDE, trying to RAM US
OFF THE ROAD—
—EVASIVE ACTION—
—cutting us off—CUTS US OFF—
—jumping the curb, ROLLING OVER SOIL AND
GRAVEL, over to the TRAIN TRACKS and a CONCRETE
BARRIER—
—*SCREECH TO A HALT*—
Boxed in.
Frozen—a bunch of White men get out of the van—one of
em's huge—what the hell—rednecks? Skinheads? Neo-Nazis?
Two at each window, one behind—got us surrounded—
A HUGE KNIFE, A KOT-TAM *MACHETE* TAPS on my
WINDOW—

Ye, panicking: "Hamza, what the fuck *is happening?*"

I crack the window half a centimeter—I'm too freakin terrified to talk—

Some crazy Whiteboy in a Shabba Ranks outfit says to me in full Jafaikan accent: "Wheh's di ja-a-ar?"

I blink. Is he mocking us before he's gonna kill us? And what kind of Nazis roll with wiggers?

But before I can make up some smart-mouth thing to bluff our way out of this diaper-filling, throat-slitting horror, a preppy next to him who looks like he's Golden Gloves or something says, in the same freaky robotic tone of voice, "*Where's the jar?*"

The FanBoys vs. the Coyote Kings

WE ARE TOTALLY FREAKIN TERRIFIED NOW.

"Wh-what?"

Shabba taps his machete against the window again. Aw, fuck, I *know* this guy—this is the same freakin weirdo I chased off of Sherem at ShabbadabbaDoo's parking lot last Thursday night! And now he's got his whole gang of drug-dealing murdering freakazoids out for revenge!

"Wheh's di ja-a-ar?"

Tap-tap-tap—

"Where's the jar?"

"What the hell are you talking about?" I belt out.

The wigger: "Wheh's di jar?"

The prep: "*Where's the jar?*"

Ye: "We don't know! You got the wrong fuckin guys! Leave us alone!"

The killer wigger leans in closer, fogging up the glass, and for the first time I see his teeth and all the glamor gold he's got on them, like the skull of some death-cult idol, all horrible and sick and twisted—

I can't believe I'm gonna die like this, carjacked and slaughtered cuz I told some freak to get away from a woman, and four days later he tracks me down in the least likely place and time for me to ever be *anywhere*—

"WHEH'S! DI! *JAR?*"

Rearview mirror—the big guy, must be a freakin *giant,* holding a kot-tam SPEAR—

Glance right . . . two freaks on Ye's side with knives and a fucking *MACE*—

The prep: "Get outta the car, broze."

I slip a glance to Ye. . . . With the subtlest swishing of the fingers of his left hand, he slides my fingers to the waiting end of something cold and heavy—

The wigger: "Ni-i-iyce an slow."

SLAM OUR DOORS OPEN, SMASHING THE PREP INTO THE WIGGER—

Prep LEAPS UP TO RUSH ME—

MY STEEL PUNISHER RIPS INTO HIS FACE and he's DOWN with a stripe of BLOOD and SCREAMING—

Hear scuffling on the other side, just enough time to yell, "YE!" when the wigger SWINGS THE MACHETE DOWN AT MY FACE—

CLANG against it with my iron bar, the impact agony in my elbows and shoulders—KICK OUT and I hear a *POP!* and a SQUEAL as the fucker's kneecap blows out—he's DOWN—

Stomp the prep force-ten in the groin, and AGAIN, zip around the car—a tall skinny totally white-haired freak conked out on the ground just as the BIG FREAKIN GIANT MOVES IN TO CRUSH YE LIKE A PAPER CRANE when Ye flips back his cape and REACHES OUT WITH HIS ARM—

A CRACK and BLINDING ARC leaps out—my eyes slam shut—

Open again, the man-beast is sprawled on the ground, writhing in a seizure, with a couple dozen plastic threads running from Ye's R-Mered right arm and implanted in this

Sasquatch-guy's chest and neck and face and groin—and SMOKE pouring off of his skin and clothes—

One freaking guy left—looks like a homeless librarian—

I scream, "Hey, muthafucka, ya want summa THIS?" and wave the iron bar like Moon-Watcher waving his club.

The freak shakes his head, bolts down the tracks, gone—

I use my club and plow the assholes on the ground right in the nards just to keep em down long enough for us to escape, and then I jump back in the car to try to move around the prone bodies of these twats and get the hell out—

But Yehat is STILL OUT THERE—

"Ye, LET'S FREAKIN *GO!*"

"I—I'm stuck—Hamza—help me—I'm STUCK—"

And that freakin huge muthafucka isn't stroking out anymore, and he's getting up and REACHING FOR YE—

I leap back out, clock him right on the kot-tam brain—hope to hell I haven't freakin killed him in the process. Ye puts his foot on the freak's chest and yanks—the filaments rip free of his R-Mer arm.

We jam in the car, slide out, trying not to run over the skulls of these hyperfreaks, squeal the hell out of there.

"Ye, ya gave me a kot-tam pipe when you had a muthafuckin TASER?"

"HELL, YES, I DID! AND WHAT THE FUCK WAS THAT ABOUT?"

"HOW THE HELL SHOULD I KNOW?"

"Oh, ya DON'T, do ya? Well, who the hell do you THINK they thought they were catching in this GIFT from the girl of your fuckin DREAMS, huh, Hamza?"

I'm speechless, furious—

I get a picture of her in my head, and for a second, everything burns blue in my brain, and when I open my eyes, I gun the accelerator, point the car towards downtown—

Down, over the river, up Grierson—

Up 95th and between two sides of street rimmed with

whores and drunks and plague victims and lepers and bars
with signs screaming NO KNIVES—

I *know* where to find her—

Over the tracks, under the glowing neon Little Italy gate—

Giovanni Caboto Park, clutched in shadowed darkness
from the thick canopy—but not much playground equipment—just a concrete shallow toddler pool, empty at night,
and two figures beside the silhouette of one of the Parks-and-
Rec green crafts shacks—

I pour the car right over the sidewalk and over the grass—

"Hamza," screams Ye, "what the hell you doing?"

I swerve the car to a halt, the headlights capturing this
witch before she can scramble away like a cockroach—cash in
her hands, and some slimy freak dropping Baggies or vials of
something, then scrambling for them to dash away across the
street, between houses—

And she stares at me, frozen—her mouth an O—

I leap out of the car, look at her, too overloaded to form a
sentence, too fucking furious to form a phrase—all I can manage is to shakingly point at her and stutter, bark: "YOU!
YOU!"

She glares back at me, aghast—*caught*—

"No, Hamza, PLEASE—it's NOT WHAT YOU THINK—"

I leap back in the car, gun the engine, rip backwards out—
and the scream, I hear the scream: "*HAMZA, COME
BACK*—"

And then I can only hear two screams—the engine's and
mine. . . .

Can This Be . . . the End
of the Coyote Kings?

WE'RE BACK IN THE CAVE, THAT FUCKIN DRUG CAR OR WHATEVER hidden in the garage, and I've got the R-Mer Taser plugged in and recharging. Hamza hasn't said a word since we ripped outta Giovanni Caboto, and I'm still shaking from that bizarre assault by the Legion of Super-Jimps.

I *knew* something was hinky with being *given* a car, for crying out loud . . . but I had no idea of the full extent of the hinkification going on.

Hamza's walking around the house, storming, slamming things down, slamming doors, not talking to me, gritting his jimp teeth.

I go to the kitchen, put on some coffee, grab a couple of ice-cream sandwiches outta the freezer, tear one open, and tear into it.

I finish it and scarf down the next one, hoping the sugar'll boost me back to the place where I'm not shivering and nauseous from the adrenaline comedown.

Every time Hamza storms past me, stomping and slamming, he glares at me. At *me*!

"Hamza, what the hell is your problem? You're *not talking* to me? *To me?* Am I missing something or have you developed some theory as to how *I* have wounded *you?* Is it not *your* girl-friend who just about got ME killed—and you're busting MY balls?"

I slam open the freezer, grab another couple of ice-cream sandwiches.

Hamza pulls his weird necklace off, jams it in his jacket pocket, while barking at me, "Quit eatin my freakin ice-cream sandwiches. I'm the one who pays for those freaks. You just leave those freaks alone!"

"Oh, okay, sure, let's play games, let's play the Jimp Olympic games, okay? Like this is about ice cream! Like hell!"

"Oh, you want me to apologize to you? I almost got killed, too, you know! Yeah, I specifically took you for a drive not be-cause I wanted to cheer you up but because I WANTED to get us killed so I could at least die with the satisfaction of having revenge on you for mooching my ice-cream sandwiches and everything else!"

"O-o-o-oh, so I'm a mooch now?"

"And *I'm* a danger exposer! I get my friends killed, for kicks! You want an apology, is that it? I'm sorry, okay? I'm sorry that both of us were assaulted! I'm sorry I'm such a crappy friend that when I found you depressed in your bed-room that I thought a car ride might cheer you up—"

"A RIDE IN A DRUG CAR!"

"HOW WAS I SPOSTA TO KNOW THAT? *YOU* STILL GOT IN THE CAR, EINSTEIN!"

"You've really taken the jimp-cake this time, jimpy! You re-alize why we were attacked, don't you?"

"I saw her, too, remember? You don't need to tell me about drugs—"

"A lot worse than drugs, Hamza!"

"Meaning what?"

"Meaning that goddam honey of yours arrived in town at exactly the time that that woman was hacked up in Chinatown! That a coupla days later, a man is dead with his hands cut off, and then four drug dealers are killed? And she's got money to hand out cars as gifts? She aint just neck-freakin-deep in drugs, pal—she's a stone-cold killer!"

"You're freakin outta your mind! Next you'll be saying she's from Jonestown and she's on the payroll of the CIA—"

"Hey, if it walks like a cult and talks like a cult and snorts like a cult—"

"Aw, fer—you got no proof whatsoever she had anything to do with any of those killings—you're freakin paranoid—"

"Whether she personally killed anyone or not, she's involved, Hamza! How can you not see that? Killings and a drug war break out exactly when the ultra-ultra-ultramysterious, Third World–traveling Miss Sherem shows up, and you can't make the connection?

"That damn broad set us up! She gave you a car knowing you'd drive it all over town and be seen—probably her car, probably trying to put her drug-cult-gang enemies, or the police, off her and on to *you*! You're a diversion, Hamza! *She doesn't care about you!* YOU'RE A PATSY—A GODDAM LEE HARVEY OSWALD!"

I'm panting, I'm *shaking,* I'm so angry. I think I'm gonna be sick.

Hamza's immobilized, silent, glaring.

When I get my gorge down, I take a coupla gulps of coffee and grab another ice-cream sandwich and scarf it down.

"Quit—*eating*—MY *SANDWICHES!*"

I munch, whisper to him, "Why don't you fuckin talk about the *real* problem, Hamza?"

"Why don't you tell me? Since you're *going* to, anyway!"

"Look at you!" I rail from the center of the kitchen floor. "I can't believe this! ONCE AGAIN, you're destroying yourself over some BROAD! Look at the choices you make!

"It's like you go out of your way to find the woman who'll do you the most possible damage, like you want a chick whose measurements should be in megatons of TNT! What the hell *is* it with you? You *like* feelin like crap—is that it? You LIKE destroying yourself?"

"Me? You barely wanted to leave your room tonight over some stack!"

"I was bummed for *three hours,* and then I was fine! You're gonna take this an be depressed for the next eight months! An lemme tell ya somethin—when you're like that, you aint exactly Richard Simmons!"

"Look, *my* situation—look—she's—this is not—how was I sposta—"

"How were you sposta know? Cuz you're a *grown man,* Hamza! Cuz you've read this book before, watched the movie, and bought the video game. Because you're NOT an idiot, and you shoulda known better! Look at this freak—takes off without notice, won't give you a phone number, you never *did* tell me where she lives, so I *know* it can't be good—" (Hamza gulps when I say that: bull's-eye!) "And she freaks out over little things and she just *gives* you a muhfuckin *car* all the while that this town's becoming Murder City—and that's just for starters, Hamz!

"You don't learn! You, you *choose* not to grow up! But you should *know* better! So now the bloom's fallen off? O-o-oh, but last week you're a true believer in love at first sight, right?"

"No!" He stomps out of the kitchen. I turn my back on him, too, stuff one of the ice-cream sandwiches in my mouth, grab a replacement out of the freezer.

I follow him out to the living room, chewing and yelling: "Oh, no, hahn? Then"—chew—"how you"—chew—"manage to squeeze three years"—chew—"of Rachael pain all over again"—chew—"into *one week*?" (Swallow, crumple, toss, open.) "You wanna reenact your, your ritual of self-torture? Fine. But don't self-destruct in front of me AGAIN!"

He whirls, points at me and then himself and the walls and floor. "This is my house, Ye! MINE!"

"Naw, it's your DAD'S until you pay it off! Until WE pay it off! And I pay half the bills, jimp-cakes, so this joint is half mine! And that's what your dad told me since the beginning!"

"Yeah, right! You just take over everything! You're the pushiest freakin guy in the universe! This whole house is stuffed with your junk! I can't even walk around here without tripping over your crap! You blew out the kot-tam windows with your stupid R-Mer explosion, you got the backyard filled with dangerous equipment and hazardous chemicals—you move in and the next thing you take over! Maybe you should just rent a warehouse!"

"*Own* HALF, pal! HALF!"

"THE GALACTIC EMPEROR OF MOOCHERY!"

"So I'm a MOOCH, huh? You even know the REAL reason I moved in with you, Hamza? You even know?"

"No, smart guy, why don't you tell me!"

"Because your dad ASKED ME TO, THAT'S WHY!"

That shuts him up. Or at least jams him up—his mouth is open, but nothing's coming out.

Finally, finally, he musters, "Yeah." Swallows. Tries to chuckle. "My dad *asked* you to move in and mooch off of me."

"Your dad . . . asked me to move in . . . cuz he was afraid you were gonna kill yourself."

His face crumples, and he stumbles backward, sags against the wall. "That's freakin nonsense, Ye! How dare you talk about my dad like that—my dad never—"

I whisper: "Why don't you ask him, then?" I pick up the phone, hand it to him. The telephone tone whines at him mockingly.

"It's the middle of the freakin night. Not gonna wake my dad up in the middle of the night just to please you, hotshot."

I just stare at him.

He looks away, down. Doesn't move.

Everything in his crushed posture tells me he knows I'm telling the truth.

He's slid down to the floor by now.

"Look at you—all it takes to bust you up is ONE CHICK. Rachael! That was *four years ago*! She's gone! Get over her already! You ever reconquer your life? You coulda been the best teacher on campus—I've seen you with the kids in our camp, and their parents—but instead you wash dishes!"

"In case you forgot," he mutters toward the floor, "I was expelled. I was white-balled."

"Y'know, I seem to recall there being more than one university on the planet!"

"Yeah, well"—he snaps up a glare at me with heat-vision eyes—"leaving aside the long arm of academic law *and* your omnipresent, omniscient, sarcastic 'wit,' what about you?"

I snort. "What *about* me?"

"You're an *engineer,* for crying out loud, with freakin superhigh marks, you had scholarships, and because you made yourself unhirable, *you* work in a freakin *video store*!"

"Irrelevant—"

" 'Irrelevant'?"

"I don't work for one of these sissy firms *on principle*—"

" 'Principle'—"

"Because these corporate sissies've got no internal brainpower, no vision, no creativity! They don't know what to do with an Imhotep-man. I can't be working for a bunch of pencil-pushing pinheads! I gotta let my intellect *fly*—"

"Yeah, a free-range brain-bird, Ye. Very moving. You can't work for those firms because you're impossible to get along with, you can't take orders, you think you're smarter than everyone there—"

"I *am* smarter—"

"What an ego!"

"—than anybody at any one of those cubicle coliseums, and they can't stand it! Can't stand a Blackman who can orbit intellectual circles around em, conceptually, aesthetically, or mathematically! Go ahead, gimme any three three-digit numbers—"

"Awww—"

"Come *on!*"

"Not this again!"

"Fine! At random, then: two thirty-five, eight twenty-one, seven hundred and seven . . . it's . . . one-point-three-six-four-oh-four times ten to the eighth!"

"Very nice, I've only seen it, what, five-times-eight-times-ninety-five times before! Open the Pod Bay Doors, Ye—I want out!"

I jam a finger at the side of my skull. "The *brain,* man! And *my* brain says you gotta stop acting like Pussysaurus rex and move on with your freakin life!"

"Thanks for the compassion, Brutus!"

Hamza leaps up and storms off to his room, so I yell, "AND DON'T COME BACK UNTIL YOU CAN START ACTING LIKE A MAN, DAMNIT!"

Slam! Through the walls, muffled yelling: "THIS IS *MY* HOUSE, YEHAT!"

"LIKE A FREAKIN MAN!"

"And QUIT EATIN *MY* freakin ICE-CREAM *SAND-WICHES!"*

I snap the two ice-cream bars I got left in my hand in half, eat the pieces in a gulp, open the freakin freezer, and grab the last two freaks in the carton. I'll eat the freakin freaks if I freakin well feel like it.

Freak.

A Bright and Shining
Kind of Discipline

THAT BLACK BASTARD BASICALLY BROKE MY DAMN *TEETH*. I WON'T even be able to see a dentist until tomorrow, and I'm in agony now. Basically we all limp back to the boss's office around three A.M. Well . . . *basically* all of us. One of us is missing.

After we picked ourselves up next to the train tracks and tried to sort out our stories about what we were gonna tell the boss, Frosty started to blame everybody but himself for what went wrong and how those two jungle bunnies kicked our asses, until we all told him to shut the fuck up or we were gonna slit his throat.

I don't know what's worse . . . being smashed in the mouth with an iron pipe, having my nuts smashed with the same pipe, the embarrassment of basically *losing* a five-to-two fight, or putting up with Frosty's bullshit after all of that.

Actually, I know what's worse. Worse by a long shot.

Facing the boss.

Which is what we're doing right now.

Everyone is basically totally motionless. And completely silent.

The boss looms over us like a thunderhead above the open prairies, and I get the feeling we're all wearing metal jock-straps.

He's not saying anything. We're all in a line standing at at-tention—well, basically as best as we can, seeing as how we've all either been canned or kneecapped or electrocuted—and he walks slowly up the line, jamming his face into each one of ours.

Inspection.

I get the feeling this is what cows go through just before they reach the rotating knives on the sluice floor.

Now he's directly in front of me, and we're not allowed to look down, right? Mr. A. takes that as a sign of dishonesty. You basically have to keep looking at him, even when his eyes look like two sunny-up fried eggs and his musk is burning in your nostrils like gasoline.

I never noticed before just how muscular his jaw and neck are. He's like a pit bull in Hugo Boss.

Finally he turns away from me, walks to the center of the room, turns away from us.

Not one of us FanBoys even *glances* at the rest of the line. Just in case he turns around and catches us not standing at at-tention.

"So," he rumbles softly, back still basically turned away, "you not only don't get this Jackal chick," and he flutters his hands, palms up, like he's weighing or maybe shaking really, really light evidence, "you get beaten up by two niggers out lowriding."

He inhale-snorts through his nostrils. It's a real wet sound.

"AND you lose Digaestus."

Tense silence.

Then, real slowly: "*Why* . . . didn'ya just . . . *shoot* them?"

I gasp, stunned, and before I know it I'm spitting out, "We weren't packing—you said—"

"Baat she fraam di Jackal Clan, an yu say di Jackal-dem ave proTECKshaan gainst misSILE attaack—"

Mr. Allen turns his head slightly around and we all shut down in a nanosecond.

"But. It. WASN'T. *Her.* Was it."

We're still shut up.

His head turns another few degrees . . . and now the shoulders . . . aw, shit—

"WAS IT?"

All of us: "No, Mr. Allen, sir."

All two muscle tons of him turn around. "ALWAYS BRING YOUR FUCKING GUNS!"

If my dick still worked, I'd probably basically wet myself right now, but the boss keeps going: "You *lost* Digaestus? How can you LOSE *Digaestus*? I've *seen* him run! He's got the speed an coordination of an epileptic turtle!" He's thrashing his hands at us, still open-palmed, like he's waving down an airplane: *Crash here!*

And now he's jamming his saber-finger at us, and even though he's half a room away, I can see in my peripheral how all of our heads are snapping back with each stab.

"How in the fuck are we supposed to find the Jar without HIM? You *stu*-pid *fu*-ckin ass-drinkers can'even bring down two niggers in a RUST BUCKET?"

And then the shit hits.

Frosty talks.

"Aw, fu-u-u-uck *you,* Mr. Allen."

I can hear all of us basically gasp or pant. All except Frosty. And all except Mr. Allen.

None of us dares break attention. So we can't even look at Frosty to see what the hell has basically taken hold of his face, and his sanity.

"Fer fuck's sakes I'm *sicka* this shit!" he rails. "Dealers being whacked left and right in this town, *we* almost get killed for you by these homeboys from hell tonight, an what are we gettin for it? Grief! You're takin a shit on us when we should probly be in the fuckin hospital right now! An you're worried about the *only* one of us who DIDN'T get hurt!

"Digaestus is probably eating a three A.M. over-easy special at Humpty's right now, just waiting to call us. So don't fuckin panic, *Dulles,* and keep your dick intact, *o-ka-a-a-y?*"

We are all completely horrified.

But Mr. Allen isn't breaking open Frosty's skull. He isn't yelling. He isn't even scowling.

Instead, he looks supremely calm.

And then it's basically the freakiest thing I've ever seen him do—he's still standing halfway across the room and looking at us with his giant fried-egg eyes, but when he does this, it gives me a ripplingly massive sense of déjà vu, so I feel like I've got spiders crawling all over my crotch—*he starts talking to us in German or Swedish or something.*

"*Ther was madma fela . . . of feorwegum . . . fratwa, geladed. . . . Ne hyrde ich chymlichor . . . cheol gegyrwan . . . hildewapnum . . . ond heathowadum . . . billum ond byrnum . . . him on bearme lag . . . madma manigo . . . tha him mid sholdon . . . on flodes aht . . . feor gewitan.*"

Then he walks closer to us. We basically don't understand a word he's saying, but we're magnetic on every syllable. And then he switches to English.

"Many a treasure fetched from far was freighted with him. No ship have I beheld so nobly weighed with weapons of war and weeds of battle, with breastplate and blade.

"On his bosom lay a heaped hoard that hence should go far o'er the flood with him floating away."

I blink, and when I open my eyes, we're standing in a lab.

What the—how the hell did we—?

This must be *the* lab. Glittering white, floor and walls covered in plastic tarps, also white. Except for the drain in the floor. That's black.

Fuck. *I know what's going to happen.*

The Fate of Ungrateful Gods

I KNOW I'VE NEVER BEEN HERE BEFORE, BUT I, I BASICALLY *FEEL* like I have, anyway, like I was here in a dream, or a maybe a nightmare. But why do I feel so much like I have? And how'd we get here?

I'm hoping, *hoping* we're here because tonight I'm gonna go through the next "degree," the "Yggdrasil" one, or maybe even go on to "Bowl of Kvasir." Which means I'll be in all the way . . . no more second-class shit. I'm hoping we're here cuz tonight I'm gonna be *made*.

But I know that's nuts. I know that's not why we're here.

I don'know if I can take this, if I can see this be done. I just wanna leave—but—

I can't move—*I can't move*—

And Frosty is strapped to the table in front of us.

Those knots. Oh, fuck. The knots tying him down. I was the only one of the FanBoys in Scouts. I basically know my own knots like I know my own signature. *I* must've tied him down. Who carried him? How long did this take to set up—is it still night out? Or even the *same* night?

We stand around the table, still as stocks.

Frosty's face—it's all melted into a look of one billion percent surprise, like he's only now figuring out what Mr. Allen can and can't do, after all.

Like me.

And all the time, hell, even tonight, I was so sure Mr. Allen was just manipulating us with his razzle-dazzle gangland mythological infomercial shit . . . and now . . .

It's like being old enough to move out on your own and being in your apartment on the very first night and only *then* does your dad call you at two in the morning to confess that when you were a kid and thought there were monsters under the bed—you were *right*.

Frosty's not even fighting the ropes, but that's maybe only because every single muscle on his body is bulged iron, even his jaw—like he's basically locked into dynamic tension by a remote control switch he can't find to shut off.

Mr. Allen's wearing a vinyl rainsuit and is standing at the head of the table, above Frosty's head with Frosty's neck fitted in a dog collar. And when the boss speaks, everything else is so quiet that the only thing we can hear is his voice, like we're not just out of the city, but maybe like the whole lab has been moved . . . to outer space.

"In the beginning," he says softly, reciting, enticing all our eyes with his dreamy singsong kettledrum voice, "there were only two forces in the universe, two realms. The land of fire, Muspellsheim . . . and the land of ice, Niflheim. In time, the space between them melted into a valley filled with icy waters and fog. And this space was called Ginnungagap.

"And there were only two creatures in this vast place. One was a humanoid so huge that his breathing in and out was all the winds of the world. The supreme sum, the original source, the ultimate man. The cosmic giant . . . Ymir.

"He had children, faithful giants and dwarves . . . and ungrateful sons a bitches called *gods* led by one little pissant named Odin.

"The gods ganged up on their gracious father and slit his throat and stabbed him and gutted him. They turned his flesh into the soil, his bones into the rocks and mountains, his blood into the rivers and seas, and his skull into the dome of the sky.

"But he didn't die.

"He just slept. And in his dreams, he got angrier and angrier.

"And decided that one day he would have to wake up and fuck every one of those ass-spikes who did this to him."

Mr. Allen snorts.

"You might wonder how Ymir survived back before his kids turned on him. The answer is that it was the *other* thing in the universe, before his kids were born, that kept him alive. It was a she. Audhumla. The cosmic cow.

"And you know what she fed him?

"*Cream.*"

Mr. Allen reaches down and then up and there's an awful metal SCREECHING SCREAM—

My face and neck and shirt are wet with hot goo, and flecks of hard shit are pelting my skin like needles, but I can't move—I can't move an inch and can't even blink—

Mr. Allen pulls the chain saw away from Frosty's right arm, which swings on my knotted rope, and the meaty shoulder hits the floor and sounds like a roast dropped into a pan—

Frosty's screaming, but it's an awful scream cuz his mouth's still jammed shut so it's all cramming out of his eyes and nose and ears—

A jet of blood shooting out of the place where his right shoulder used to be, spraying down Alpha Cat's already-red super-shirt and gauchos . . .

And the Cat doesn't move a millimeter.

Mr. Allen says in the same quiet voice, "There was a world-tree that kept all the universe alive. *Yggdrasil,* guarded by three women, the Norns, who nursed it and kept it alive. But there was also a snake at the bottom, a dragon named Nidhog who gnawed Yggdrasil's roots.

"And at the top of the tree was an eagle, and resting on the eagle's beak was a falcon, both there to protect the tree. And the birds and the dragon were enemies, right? But they were separated—so no conflict.

"And they woulda *stayed* that way except for a fuckin squirrel who ran up and down the tree making up insults to make em wanna fight. In *my* opinion, the Norns shoulda just fucked that squirrel right up the ass."

METAL SCREAMING AND WHINING—

And Frosty's left arm hits the floor on the other side of the table.

By now either Frosty's lost consciousness or he's dead.

I get a sudden image of Mr. Allen as a kid, basically plucking the legs, one by one, off a daddy longlegs spider. Or Mr. A. as a grown man, breaking off the limbs of a lobster and sucking out the meat.

I wanna giggle, laugh, howl, scream, split apart. But I can't move, can't smile, can't frown, can't even look away.

Mr. Allen then cuts off Frosty's legs.

The bowling-ball sound from the floor is Frosty's head.

Was.

Mr. Allen drops the chain saw and whispers to us, "The next time I tell you ass-fucks what I want done, I *want* it done, and I want it done *right*. Now you will *clean* this place up, top to bottom, you will *find* Digaestus, you will *find* this phantom Jackal bitch, and you will do all of this within *forty-eight hours*. Am I *clear*?"

We shout as one: "YES, MR. ALLEN, SIR!"

"Alpha Cat. We need reinforcements to take down this Jackal broad. We get back—you get me a list of junior apprentices of the Midgard degree. You'll be their sponsor, you understand?"

"Yes, suh, Mista Allen, suh!"

And then the boss draws in a big breath, sings softly: "*Men ne cunnon . . . sechgan to soothe . . . seleradende. . . . haleth under heofenum . . . hwa tham hlaste onfeng.*

"No man is able to say in sooth, no son of the halls, no hero 'neath heaven, who harbored that freight."

My body suddenly loosens, like some kinda electromagnets holding me in place have been shut off.

Mr. Allen turns and walks away while stripping out of his gore-covered vinyl rainsuit, gestures towards what's left of Frosty, says: "Okay, then, you ass-balls. Drain im, strip im, and grind im. And Cat, you know what to do after that.

"When it's done, you tell em the phrase—you know which one. Then get everyone blindfolded. I'll come get you all at exactly five thirty. So you got until just after sunrise, *capiche*?"

Alpha Cat, the little suck-ass, basically nods like he doesn't have a care in the world.

And then suddenly Mr. Allen turns back and walks straight up to *me*.

"Oh, and Zenko. You told me a lotta things on the way over here, didja know that?"

At this point, with my muscles no longer frozen, I instantly shit my pants.

"You think you're pretty fuckin slick, doncha? I *know* you got plans. An I know those plans involve takin out Alpha Cat."

It feels like hot, steaming mud slopping up against my ass, and it's sagging down my drawers and pants—I can feel it hugging and tugging.

"Well, lemme tell ya suh'm. . . . Alpha Cat's my deputy . . . my *intermediary,* ya hear me?"

In front, my piss is hot and it's sluicing all over my legs and slacks and pouring into my socks and Guccis.

"If anything . . . and I mean ANYthing happens to him— like he catches a cold or skins his knee or gets a hangnail . . . what you heard happened to Marylin or Casper or what you just saw done to Frosty"—and he points to Frosty's pieces—"*that*'ll be like getting a *blow job* compared to what I'll do to *you*."

The Agony of James Brown

EXCERPT FROM H.A.Q.S. JOURNAL ENTRY,
TUESDAY, MIDAFTERNOON

0725.95*15:23

BACK AGAIN AT THIS JOURNAL, THIS WRETCHED TOME, RECORD of my worst defeats. Ignored it for nearly four years because the worst had already happened, and whatever other detail I might enter would seem extraneous, superfluous colorless commentary on the multicar collision that is my life.

Stopped three months, three weeks, and three days after R. severed communication. Couldn't take the strain, the pain, the rain.

Three pots of *pu-ehr* tea, three pots more, three pots after that.

Wish these remarks could be sent back in time, a counterchronistic warning, a disaster forecaster. No use wishing, no use fishing. No payoff in prayers for the impossible.

Vangelis plays behind me, a mixed tape mostly from *Opera*

Sauvage, a title as appropriate as any for what I've just now lived, what I've been living, how I've assembled my life for the last decade. I'm twenty-five years old and a fool. A foppish fool whose life fell off the tracks without an engineer or emergency team to rerail it, left to rot and rust upon desert sands, a grand metallic carcass oxidizing down to dust until only iron bones remain, picked clean by parasites of flying, particulate rock.

Who the hell am I?

Why do I do these things to myself?

Will I ever be better than this?

The phone rings.

I drink tea.

Four years later, and I'm immobile, trapped in a cage, enslaved, enraged, defeated, defunct, dysfunctional.

And Vangelis plays—"Le singe bleu" and "Irlande"—and I'm back on that cliff in my mystical dream, ensconced in the opaque mournful breaths of a vast and restless ocean, the same one moved to ceaseless stirrings by an unrequiting moon.

The phone rings still, but I will not answer it.

I'm enwrapt in that fog, upon the cliff, inside the outcropping, angry waves and crags below, and enemies or endless void above. And holding me, holding me in my cold, cold nakedness . . .

. . . is no one.

The phone is silent.

I drink tea.

Stupid, stupid, STUPID! Idiotic dreams, reams of dreams, reams of screams of dreams. Doing it all over again to myself. Begging for punishment, craving it, scuttling my own engine, blowing up my own tracks. Carrying a tornado around myself like a force field, telling any *sane* woman, "Abandon all hope, ye who enter here." And accepting inside only those who themselves are made of storms.

And now upon my stereo, the Brother, the screamer, not

often known as a dreamer, but nonetheless the one who once sang "If I Ruled the World," the *man,* James Brown . . . but now with a dirge so unlike his usual blithely joyous meaningless nonsense. A song so true it hurts . . . "It's a Man's Man's Man's World":

> *This is a man's world, this is a man's world*
> *But it wouldn't be nothing, NOTHING without a*
> *   woman or a girl*
>
> *Man thinks about a little bitty baby girl . . . and a*
> *   baby boy*
> *Man makes them happy . . . cuz man makes them*
> *   toys*
> *And after man has made everything, everything he*
> *   can*
> *You know that man makes money . . . to buy from*
> *   other men. . . .*

Is that really the line? "Buy *from* other men"? All these years . . . always thought it simply said "to *buy* other men."

Should write to Br. Brown, ask him to change it. More cruel. More honest.

Rachael, damn you, why? After all these years . . . if only you'd told me *why*—but to deny me even this, to keep me from finding out whatever I could've or should've or would've known or done, to stop me from finally reaching the inner chamber to be transformed, instead to keep me here outside perpetually, frozen and frightened and fraught with indecisive, impotent indolence . . . you've thrown me into suspended animation, Rachael! And there's no one, no one who can let me out to live!

The phone begins to ring again.

I draw my last, sip my last.

I make the tenth pot of tea.

Hear him moan, hear him scream, and hear him howl.

That voice more true in this single performance than any other James Brown song anywhere, anywhen.

> *This is a man's, a man's, a man's wo-o-orld*
> *But it wouldn't be nothing, NOTHING . . .*
> *Without a woman or a girl*
>
> *He's lost . . . in the world of men*
> *He's LOST . . . in bitterness . . .*
> *Lost, lost, lost, Lord have mercy. . . .*

The agony of those heart-ripping screams . . . all the pain and misery and fear and loneliness in that voice . . . I'm thinking of Bradbury's brilliant "The Fog Horn," the words of the old lighthouse keeper, how there's always someone alone who loves someone more than that person loves them back . . . always someone crying out *in* the night, *to* the night, forever, like a fog horn. . . .

The phone, the phone—

I await my tea.

Loneliness, that's what Bradbury explained, expounded, exposed. I feel expired. Excommunicated. Exhumed.

Loneliness . . . James Brown's wails, the vicious pain tearing itself out of his throat like the talons of some impossible bird, like the vulture that tore out Prometheus's liver . . . THAT pain, THAT loneliness. Is there anything worse for a man than this?

What is life without even the *possibility* for lasting love? Is it to wake up and walk to bleak and meaningless work, to return home to shove tasteless food down your throat, listen to listless, lying lyrics, exist and subsist for decades, retire to a wifeless, childless, hermetically sealed, heirless environment . . . go to the supermarket to buy ninety-nine cents' worth of anything just for the privilege of having a cashier to talk to for ninety-nine seconds?

And the phone, the phone rings again. . . .

The Tale of Two Brothers

MY SHIFT FINISHED AT 19:00 AND I GET HOME AT 20:27, HAVING had two errands to run and also needing to eat dinner elsewhere. It's still light out, but not *that* light, and the Coyote Cave is dark.

I put down the one bag, go into the kitchen with the other.

That damn jimp must be out somewhere—but I thought I saw his shoes at the entrance . . . ?

I'm about to go into my room when I see Hamza's door open, and him cramped up against the wall beneath the window.

His head snaps towards me.

I look at him.

I want to turn away, give im a "Screw you" turn of my back, but I have a tough time moving, like I'm Iron Man caught halfway between Magneto and Polaris.

Finally Hamza squeaks out, "Hey."

I nod. "Hey."

We stare at each other.

"Just finished work?" he says.

"Yup."

"Good shift?"

"Fair to middlin."

"Yeah."

More staring.

Ah, hell . . . if this's all it's gonna be, I might's well go out again. I restart going into my room.

"Ye—"

"Yeah?"

When I turn back, he's looking at the floor.

"It's okay, y'know, bout those ice-cream sandwiches. I mean, they're there to be eaten, right? What'm I gonna do, horde em until doomsday?"

"Oh. Okay, well, thanks."

I re-restart going back to my room.

"Ye—"

"Yeah, what is it, Hamza?"

"I'm sorry I almost got you killed."

I lean against his doorjamb. Waiting.

"I never meant for anything like that to happen. I . . .- shouldn't be such a freakin moron. An I . . . sometimes I'm too trusting, y'know? Or I . . . I just . . . wanna be*lieve* too much. I think . . . I'm *sure* . . . you're probably right about her—being involved somehow in all this horrible shit, recently. I shoulda listened to common sense. . . . I shoulda listened to *you,* an . . . I mean . . . if anything'd ever *happened* to you—!"

I walk in, sit down against the side of the bed, facing him ninety degrees. He looks at his hands, inside them, as if he's checking cue cards there, and he has to keep fluttering his hands to change them.

"Ye . . . you're, like . . . my oldest friend . . . my *best* friend. You stood by me when practically my whole world fell apart . . . and last night, when I said—"

"It's okay, Hamz."

"No, Brother, lemme finish. I said all that shit about you bein a mooch an all. An that was just completely untrue an unfair an I just . . . I never meant that. I've never felt that way, never wanted you to feel, not for a second, unwelcome here. Sjust me bein angry an selfish an hatin myself an takin it out on you. The one person other than my dad I could always count on, one hundred percent."

Hamza's sniffling now, wiping his palms against the wells of his eyes, biting his lower lip.

I shuffle over next to him, put my arm around him, pull him in to cradle him against my chest. He doesn't fight it, not even for a second. Hell, *I* don't fight it. Is this really *me* doing this? In fact he squeezes himself down, like a squirrel inside the hollow knot of a tree. Before I know what I'm doing, I'm actually stroking his hair.

(Sidebar: It's a strange fuckin thing. You live with a guy for four years, be best friends with him for ten, an yet this simple thing, so natural that little kids do it without thinking, just never happens. We don't even have a word for it that doesn't make a man feel wrong. What do you call this—snuggling? Holding each other? Caressing? We're so—*I'm* so—fucked-up about this. That it's only okay to be like this when my best friend is so depressed from being in the same damn rut he never escaped from that I'm actually in fear for what he might do to himself.

(But I'm here now, holding him and stroking his hair, just like he was my own little kid.

(Self-query: Do I feel like I have to compare it to something else so that I can *think* about it, put it into words in a way that's okay? But it's not true. It's *not* like he was my own little kid.

(Observation: He's still crying. I can feel his tears soaking through my shirt.

(Answer: *He's my friend.*)

"Hamz . . . what is it? You gotta tell me honestly . . . why're you *like* this? Why do you go so heels-over-head for women, especially women who're no good for you? I know this thing here reminds you of Rachael, but why didn'you ever get over Rachael in the first place? I know it was bad, Brother, but you obviously know people've gotten through worse."

I feel him nod. "Yeah, I know," he says. "You're right. It's . . . Ye, did I ever tell you about . . . Leslie Minty?"

"Who's she? Porn star? Breath freshener? Or both?"

I feel him laugh, then hear it, too. "Naw . . . Leslie was this girl I knew in grade seven. She was the first girl I ever slow-danced with. I think it was probably 'Easy Like Sunday Morning' or 'Just the Two of Us'—like, the only two Black songs they ever played at my junior high other than the stuff on *Thriller*.

"But Leslie, she was real cute, y'know? I'd liked her for a long time. An for the life of me, as long as I live I'll never forget this . . . *she* asked me—to dance, I mean . . . an I was really happy about that—but she was so nervous that I could feel, I mean actually *feel* her twelve-year-old heart beating right through her chest and into mine."

"So didja do er?"

"Aw, Ye, you're such a sick man," he chuckle-whimpers. "Naw, see . . . I knew she wanted me to ask her out. Obviously! But I was twelve—I didn'even have the guts to ask a girl to dance, let alone go out on a date! So I just kept on thinkin about what I *could* do, like I could buy her a gift, or I could draw her a picture, or whatever. Instead of acting.

"I feel like, Ye . . . if I'd just asked her out then, if I'd had a girlfriend when I was twelve, instead of waiting until Rachael—maybe I wouldn't be such a freakin coward, so freakin stupid an messed up and afraid to try things. I feel like I've wasted my whole life!"

I shake my head, hearing this sad sadness that's been saddifying Hamza for the last thirteen years.

"Hamz, man . . . you gotta realize . . . you're *not* twelve years old anymore. You gotta let that twelve-year-old boy *you usedta be* off the hook. Stop makin *him* guilty for what you have or haven't done since then. He's just a kid. He didn't know. And . . . and . . . I don'wanna disrespect your family—"

I feel him tense suddenly, so I speed up what I have to say to get it out: "I've never pried about this, Hamz. You've sorta let little things drop here and there, like maybe two a year since I met you. But . . . what happened in your family?"

(Observation: He's been holding his breath for a few seconds, and I've stopped stroking his hair. But now he lets it out in a long breath. I don't stroke his hair anymore, but I let my hand rest on the side of his face. He doesn't struggle. It seems . . . to calm him.)

"Ye . . . it'd take me years to explain it all. I don't think *I* even understand it. Because my dad never really explained it all to me.

"When I was thirteen, my mum and dad split, and my mum took my older sister, Shirley, and moved to Toronto to live near my grandparents. My parents always gave bullshit answers as to why they gave up, but . . . I started to worry like maybe my dad'd had an affair or something, even though that just seemed so not him."

Me: "And? Did he?"

"Naw. I never shoulda doubted him. It was my mum. I don't mean she had an affair—I mean she just left him. I only found this out on my third summer visit to T.O., from Shirley. Said Mum'd told er all about it. Just fell outta love. Daddy just wasn't the kinda man she wannid to be with. An I guess she made Shirley feel the same or something, cuz . . .

"Ye, I mean, what the hell is that? How can somebody just *fall out of love?* If you love somebody, how can you just all of a sudden *not* love them? Isn't love forever, or was it ever even really love at all to begin with, then? An, like, my mum an Shirley . . . it wasn't like they even ever *asked me* to stay with em. I wannid to be with my dad, but still . . . it's like they didn'even want me!

"How is that supposed to make you feel? To know that the two most important women in your life don't give a fuck about you? *What is so fuckin wrong with me that this is the best I can get?*"

"Hamz, c'mon, brother, I'm sure they care, they just . . . they—"

"Ye, in four years, how many times've you heard them call here?"

"C'mon, all the time! A whole buncha—"

"Christmas, my birthday, and Eid al-Fitr! That's it! That's *it*!"

And he's crying freely now, and I hold him, and he squeezes his arms around me, holds on.

And we stay like that for eleven minutes and twenty seconds on the clock in front of me, not moving, not talking.

(Hypertext autopsychologizing: Who is this, sitting here and saying all of this, sitting inside of his own head watching himself hold his friend and saying words to Hamza he's never said to anyone else? Is it possible that *I* am the clueless twelve-year-old?

(So who am I, Ulysses Hatori Bartholomew Gerbles, super-genius? And what unknown syntho-cognitive modulized sub-routine is producing these calming words and phrases? Have I absorbed all of this from living with Hamza's literary gushy-feeliness, a verbal/tactile balm he can't apply to heal himself?

(Enough. All this self-analysis is responsible for eighty-four percent of global jimpification. Stop thinking. Start talking. Use the Force, Yehat.)

"Hamza . . . your problem is that you wanna think that all this is you. All your own fault. You're to blame. I'm not saying you were perfect with Rachael, but you can't blame yourself for your mum an sister leaving you. That's not you, man. You're innocent there.

"This is about ego, in a weird way . . . if *you'd* just done something differently, been a different person. In other words, you make like it's all about *your* power. You wanna be the world-controlling super-jimp who operates the rainmaking machine for storms and growing seasons. But you don'have that kinda power, Hamz. Nobody does. What they did . . . that's somebody else's life. Somebody else's shitty decision.

"But you don'wanna blame Rachael and your mum and your sister, an that's your problem. Cuz if you realize that they *are* to blame, then you can't hold on to your idealized version of who you wish they'd actually be. An you keep clutching on to those idealized versions like a crackhead holding on to his empty pipe cuz you're hoping that one day they'll wake up and see you as a man they can't live without, or that you'll become whoever you think they want you to be, an they'll rush back to E-Town an love you forever.

"So you refuse to hate them or even blame them because if you accepted that *they* fucked up, that *they* made choices that they still deep down believe in and stand by, then you'd hafta admit that they're never coming back."

And I hate having to tell him all this, but at the same time, if someone has to tell him, if he'll believe anyone . . . then . . .

I squeeze him, punctuating what I'm about to say, like the upside-down exclamation mark at the beginning of a Spanish sentence.

"And they aren't, Hamz. *They're never coming back.*

"You're never gonna be twelve again and have another shot with Leslie Mouthwash, you're never gonna get back the happy family you thought you had growing up until the split, and Rachael's never gonna come back here and walk in that door and sit down on your lap and smother you with kisses an say sorry for all the pain she caused you an that she'll love you always and never leave you again.

"Your dad never remarried, right? An you've never told me about him having any girlfriends. So *you're* becoming what he's already living out, like a curse on the second generation, waiting and hoping for someone who's never coming back. And you're so terrified of becoming as lonely as your dad that you're guaranteeing you will be.

"So you got one choice. You gotta bury that Box, and any other box like it.

"And move on."

I sigh deeply, my chest lifting up Hamza's head, then plopping it down again. And I say to him softly, quietly, "You *will* get better. You will. And . . . I know it's not the same, Hamz . . . but . . . *I'll* never leave you. Or at least if I do, I promise to come back."

He whispers, so quietly I can hardly even hear him.

"Ye . . . you've been my best friend for ten years. But . . . I've never loved you more than I do right now."

And I'm glad he can't see my face right now. Bad enough me holding him like this in his *bed*room and all, but to see me get misty and pre-blubbery, well, hell, I'd hafta turn in my Man Card to the Department of Jimpitude and Deballsification.

"Yeah." I sniff. "Well . . . I love you, too, Hamz."

After nine o'clock we get up. Hamza blows his nose and goes to wash his face. When he joins me in the living room, I've got the TV on, watching the original series' "Amok Time." I put it on for a reason: two best friends nearly kill each other over a conniving woman. Maybe Hamza will comment?

He doesn't say anything. I let it soak in and open up one of the bags I came home with.

"Hamza, I boughtcha something." I toss him one of the two items from the bag.

"Hey, damn—a Big 4 jacket! Where'dja get this?"

I slide my own on, a beautiful black blazer with a satin lining and everything. "I went to Value Village after work. Probably the Blues Brothers died or something, and Ma Blues brought their stuff in. Only ten bucks each."

Hamza reaches for his wallet.

Me: "No, I didn't tell you the price so you could—"

He stands right in front of the Big 4 poster on the wall with the Bill Sienkiewicz art, hands me a twenty. "No, Ye. I *want* to."

"*Damn.* Okay." This is really something. I'm not saying

Hamza's cheap, but if generosity were height, Hamza'd be a
Micronaut. I pocket the cash, seeing as how this isn't ever
likely to happen again.

"An I got something else for you, Hamz." I beckon him into
the kitchen, open the freezer.

Inside are two boxes of ice-cream sandwiches, one labeled
HAMZA, the other, YEHAT.

He laughs, and I laugh. And we both laugh together.

"C'mon," I say, "let's rent some pornos or play Sega Gene-
sis or something. Whatever you wanna do."

He looks suddenly sad. "Yeah, thanks, Ye. But . . . I've
been cooped up—I mean, I cooped myself up since last night.
I think I need some air."

"You want some company?"

"Naw, thanks, though. You've already been great.
An . . . you've given me a lot to think about. An I really ap-
preciate it. I think I just need to go for a long walk, y'know?
Sort some things out that're long overdue."

"Well, put on a jacket or something, then. It's kinda cold
tonight, and it was getting foggy when I was walking home."

I think maybe he'll put on his Big 4 coat, but he doesn't, instead reaching for his leather hipster. "In case I get attacked
again by freaks," he says, noticing I noticed, "I don'wanna get
any blood on the B-4 jacket."

"Or so we can bury you in it."

He smirks, slips on his shoes, takes off.

If I could've known the galactic height of stupidity of what
he was actually going out to do, I never would've let him leave.

Novus Ordo Ymirum

SO BASICALLY WE FIND DIGAESTUS EXACTLY WHERE WE THOUGHT we would, eating an over-easy special at Humpty's. He kept drinking from their "bottomless" cup of coffee until they were gonna set the cops on him by the time we got there. He didn't have a dime—he was just waiting for us to find him.

I'm basically still reeling after last night. But the other guys—

Cleaning up was murder . . . and we all had to burn our clothes. And . . . well, it's one thing to . . . process . . . civilians, but when it's one of our own, a full-fledged FanBoy . . . and the Cat, the Moog, it's like they don't even—

No point thinking about it, basically. And whatever thoughts I had about advancement—well, I guess my major goal right now is just to avoid doing *any*thing to get the boss suspicious. To avoid getting Frostified myself.

Speaking of the boss, he was pretty happy to see Digaestus again. He's even letting him sleep, and he told us we're supposed to get the D-man whatever he wants when he wakes up.

That's peachy. We spend all night watching Frosty get . . .

and then have to take him and . . . and then we get to basically clean up after, while Caesar gets a fluffy bed and room service.

Does it *matter* that it was Digaestus's false ID that got us jammed up with those super-jigs or Jackals-in-training or whatever in the first place? Apparently not. "I uh-uh-uh could've been uh-uh-uh thrown off by uh-uh-uh some item she'd stuh-stuh-stowed in the cuh-cuh-car. She ruh-ruh-red-herringed us, Mr. Uh-uh-Allen."

Can't believe the favoritism around here. But what can *I* do? Mr. A. owns me.

Tried asking Digaestus about what he sees when he looks through that thing. He just went on and on about *being* the dew, and *being* the wind, and *being* the stars. . . . It's like asking Shirley MacLaine for directions to the 7-Eleven.

Right now Mr. Allen and the Cat are going over replacements. New blood. New Jackal fodder. And whoever among em *does* survive, well, hell, why not just promote them past me? Does it matter if I've put in three years developing our sales network and guaranteeing a supply of raw material? Guess not, guy! Well, at least I won't have the humiliation of a pink slip and a guarded escort out of the building.

But *the way* I'll leave the building . . . that's the part I . . .

I remember being recruited. I'd heard of the Cat, heard of the product. Got that first taste. Fuckin awesome. I knew this was winner material—whole world market waiting to open up like a hooker's legs for this sweet stuff.

So every time I bought from the Cat, I pressed him for a job. And when I finally met the boss . . . I mean, I had no idea what I know now . . . but it was like meeting a cross between Donald Trump and the Incredible Hulk. Here was a man so obsessed—still don't know why, what his secret is, why he disappears without warning sometimes and comes back looking like he's been driven over with a combine—he was so driven when I met him it was like he had nuclear engines. Thought I was gonna ride this rocket to the moon.

Yeah, but hell, there aint no *air* on the moon.

And look at *these* recruits. Really digging at the bottom of the specimen jar now to fill out the Legion of Substitute Fan-Boys. The Cat was going over a bunch of cutie pies from the Time Lords, the Cylons, and the Tolkien Raiders, but those guys are all losers. So now he's given the short list to Mr. Allen.

How tough could this one chick be, anyway? So we got suckered by two soul brothers. Next time we won't be. Next time we'll be ready. And we don't need a bunch of amateurs basically getting in between us and her neck.

Still . . . if Alpha Cat doesn't make it through the show-down—I mean, my hands'll be clean, right? It'll be this chick, and anything that goes wrong, I can always blame these knobs we're bringing in . . . so maybe this cloud has a platinum lining. And then with Alpha "Mark" Cat gone, Darwin "Jason" Zenko can lead our little G Force the way it's *sposta* be led.

Mr. Allen just got off the phone, and now he's checking over the potentials list the Cat gave him.

" 'Garbage-Man,' huh?" says the boss. "So what does he do?"

The Cat holds his hands open, like he's basically making an offering. "Im trow gahbij-an-ting. Toon enny piece a trash inna weapaan . . . naat so FAN-cy, baat im can wook MAjick inna Dumpsta—"

"Next."

The Cat points at the list. "Atlas S. RAND . . ."

"I know that guy. Guy never shuts up. Always goin on with the, the 'Greed is good' thing. And what the hell kinda haircut is that, anyway? Looks like that woman from, uh . . . *Throw Momma from the Train.* Who else you got?"

They talk over a few names. I've heard of some of these loons: Captain Crunch, Vegi-Might, Imperial Red Guard, Adolf Benito, the Human Torque, and the Shitter.

"What about this guy, Human Torque?"

"Im a SUPA-grappla, baas . . . im praactiss aikiDO, ju-JITsu, JUdo, Graeco-Romaan wresslin, Twista, Dubbaya-Dubbaya-EFF—"

"Okay, bring him in. This guy Cap'n Crunch—he's the guy with jaws like a horse, right?"

"Im caan BIYTE tru a paahkin MEEta, suh."

"In. Vegi-Might?"

"Frum AuSTREEYlya. Im use motoRIZED sliycin weapaans im call *di juicers*."

"Done. How bout this Adolf weirdo?"

"Im creAYTE iz own martial AHT im call 'Goose-Style.' Laats uv 'igh KICKS and *laang* open-hand striykes."

"I dunno. . . ."

"Plus im creAYTE iz own BOOMerangs sheeyped liyke swastikas."

"Boomerangs, huh? That's a nice touch. I like that. Plus they fly on arcs, right, so he might be able to get around her protection against missile attack. Okay, bring him in. *Zenko, ya lil ass-cheese!*" he yells. "Ya hear that? Guy uses boomerangs! Now *that's* the kinda moxie I'm looking for. You should be takin notes!"

The boss laughs. Alpha Cat looks embarrassed—*for me,* can you believe that?

Me: "Right, boss. Whatever you say, I'm down by law!"

Basically? Fuck em all.

I can't wait for this showdown. Then I'll show im who's got moxie, and who doesn't.

Preserve Me on the Righteous Path

Y<small>E WAS RIGHT</small>. I<small>T'S REALLY FREAKIN FOGGY OUT HERE, AND</small> pretty cold, too. E-Town's never foggy—like, maybe three days a year—and not usually in summer, either, so this is weird. Like a veil pulled over "the naked city" for the sake of modesty.

10/th Ave's quiet, but why wouldn't it be on a cold Tuesday night? Nobody out here calling out "Hey, Coyote"—it's so dark upstairs there must be storm clouds above the fog. Like an autumn night, that cold bite in the air that says, like LKJ intones on "Five Nights of Bleeding": "*A bad-bad beat wuz brewing. . . .*"

Suddenly a voice flashes through the darkness like lightning—a mournful wail that comes from desert sands so empty it's a wonder the people who lived in them could believe in anything except pain. I check my watch: 9:17 P.M. And the *mueddhin* from Masjid Imam Al-Mahdi calls out to the neighborhood from the speakers in the minarets:

Allahu-akbaar, Allahu-akbaar
Allahu-akbaar, Allahu-akbaar

Ashhadu an la ilaha illallah
Ashhadu an la ilaha illallah

My dad always took pains to explain that in the usual translation, "God is great" or "God is the greatest" is wrong. Instead it's the comparative: "God is *greater*. . . . There is no god but *the* God. . . ."

And then he'd say how those ancient people looking out on that vast flat land, where the tallest thing was the horizon, they didn't need to use the superlative.

There was everything in the world. And then there was That Which Was Greater.

But all I see is fog and darkness lit by streetlights and neon, with the fog a low ceiling like the sky is within touching distance, and the Addis Obelisk bright engraved stone disappearing into ghost air from the neck up.

And I remember from the Fatihah, the Opening, which my dad would sing to me when I was little, when he was tucking me in:

> *Guide us to the path that is straight*
> *The path of those to whom thy love is great*
> *Not of those in whom there is hate*
> *Nor of those who deviate. . . .*

In the fog I walk down 109th Street, all the way down to the glowing coppery stone of the Legislature, its dome swallowed just like the obelisk . . . over to Constable Ezio Faraone Park at the very edge of the drop into the river valley, with the statue of the slain cop kneeling to guide a little boy forever— ironically, pointing him towards the sunset, and in the direction of the gorge.

And when I look back, the giant spectral eye of the moon, obscured behind the ultraclouds and turned into a blazing cataract, tells me that everything I'm planning to do will be seen, but badly.

So, fine, okay.

So many stupid years of wandering and grieving fruitlessly and being the universe's biggest sap, the designated loser who never fought back. Prince Victim, heir to the throne of all Dorkland.

I close my eyes.

I think about their faces, think about their laughing mouths, think about their turned backs . . . and I don't see blue, but deep bruised purple.

I open my eyes, walk back up to Jasper, along it, until I get to the old Spanish-style villa turned into condos for the nouveau *biche.*

I sniff, smelling indigo, smelling violet, stronger now . . . purple.

Inside the gate, past the fountains in the courtyard, up the exterior stairs, the winding corridors past balconies.

And then I'm at the door.

It's almost ten o'clock, but I'm sure this freak doesn't sleep.

I just hope Heinz "Wolf" Meaney is alone, and that he doesn't have security cameras, so it'll all be finally over when I snap his fuckin neck.

Visions of Blood on White Plush

I HEAR SILENCE, THEN SHUFFLING, THEN SCRAMBLING, THEN stepping—ALL the while my heart's going like a locomotive.

The door opens.

"Hamza? What in the seven hells are *you* doing here?"

Damn it.

Kevlar. He's sweating, and his eyes are glassy.

"It's ten o'clock at night!" he says again. "What, are you here to return the picnic basket?"

I grumble. "Is your brother in?"

That throws him. "You . . . you actually *want* to talk to Heinz? Are you serious? Why?"

"Thought it was time to bury the hatchet, Kev." I don't bother to add *in his rectum*.

"Well . . . this truly is something, isn't it?" he sings. "Cause for celebration, I suppose. Hey, how the hell'd you find where we live? And why tonight? What's really going on?"

"Is that Meaney talk for 'Welcome in'?"

He opens the door more, and I see the getup he's wearing—I can safely say that for the first time in my life I'm seeing someone in person wearing a "smoking jacket." At least he doesn't have on a cravat, or I'd hafta kill *him,* too. He does a little twirly-hand gesture, like a maître d', then says graciously, "I beckon you enter, sahib."

This freak's acting even weirder than I remember. Probably a billion too many double-espresso-crappachino-latte-enemas. Or bad genes. Or both.

I step in, slip off my shoes, leave my coat on. The joint's a freakin palace! Exotic art from around the world, idols, paintings, hoity-toity furniture like out of an art-and-design fair, and, aw, hell, a *staircase?* This condo has *two* floors? Bastards!

"Well, well, well," says Kevlar.

I stifle my look of disgust.

Him, again with *that tone:* "Amazing, really . . . a Coyote King in the Hall of Meaney. Please, sit down. I simply never imagined that there'd *ever* be a rapprochement between our respective factions. And quite the timing, too . . . if you'd come a couple of days later, Heinz and I would've been gone."

"Lucky me, I guess." I sit on his airport-sized white leather couch. I figure somewhere around a ranch's worth of cows must be sewn into this thing. "So where you headed?"

"Oh, uh . . . book tour. You know that we—"

"Yeah, yeah, I heard." I gulp, tasting sour slime: "Congratulations."

"Thanks." He mugs. "You look rather troubled, noble Hamza. I'd say you look like you need a drink, but I know you don't drink. Some tea, perhaps?"

"Sounds like a plan. Say, where the hell's your brother, anyway?"

"Oh, he's out working. Taking care of some details for our trip. He won't be back until tomorrow morning."

What the hell? How the hell can that be? I thought he was here! I've never been wrong, never! Is it cuz I'm so freakin messed up and stressed-out?

But I found that freakin psycho chick last night immediately after we were attacked, and my whole system was in overdrive. Hell, I was shaking so hard from the adrenaline I could barely keep my hands on the steering wheel and I still found her immediately!

How the hell could I've been wrong about where Heinz is? Is it cuz they're brothers? Who knows, maybe being coated in shit is like a cloaking device. Maybe being an asshole from beyond time is like stealth technology. Or maybe he's got some kind of—

Whoops! I'm spacing out here. Kevlar's already gone to the kitchen. Better pay attention. I walk over to glance in, try to figure out if he's been talking to me while I was having deep thoughts.

Their kitchen: pretty freakin fancy. All chrome appliances . . . got one of those "islands." Probably end up on one of those *Celebrity Homes* shows if their whole author-photographer-scumbag thing keeps growing.

Or on *Crime Stoppers,* after I get through with him.

Aw, who'm I kidding here? That I'm really gonna actually kill him? I admit, smashing that freakin weirdo in the face last night was a real stress release, but that was in the heat of battle—we were attacked! Other than that, last fight I had I was twelve, which I lost. I couldn't kill anybody. Not even Heinz, who totally deserves it. Plus he's bigger than me.

But maybe I could really scratch his floor or puncture the shit outta this freakin couch.

I shoulda talked to Ye first. He coulda hooked me up with some kinda gadget that'd straighten these pricks out real good (so to speak, twice).

There's always tomorrow, I guess.

And that thought makes me smile.

"Say, but seriously," calls Kevlar from the kitchen, "how'd you really find us? We're unlisted."

"Just a hunch."

"Still Mr. Mystery, I see. Nothing changes, I guess."

"Or *everything* does."

"What's that?" he calls.

"Nothing."

"Ah, well . . . should've had you over a long time ago." He's spooning tea into some ornate tea ball—looks like a tiny bathyscaphe. "Hamza, my friend, you really do look the wreck tonight. You and Chief Engineer Scott have a tiff?"

I raise an eyebrow. "Not a bad guess, but no, not exactly."

"So don't get me wrong, but it's not as if—" he says as he sets down a plate of baklawa on the mosaic coffee table and sits. "I'm happy to see you of course, but it's been a hell of a long time since we had a sit-down. And I never imagined you'd want to forgive Heinz, or be friends again, or—well, whatever you have in mind."

I sit quietly. Relieved, in a way. I really think that, for about twenty minutes, I'd convinced myself that I was gonna kill him, but that's just completely not me. And I can't really imagine this hardwood here or that creamy rug over there soaked with Heinz's blood. Heinz's ketchup.

That makes me laugh out loud. Old, old joke, one I haven't thought of in years. But Kev must misunderstand. He thinks I'm scoffing.

"I'm not my brother's keeper," he says, tilting his head towards me to show just how much he means it. "I never forgave him for how things worked out between you two. But he's— he's always been so competitive, with such a sense of . . . of entitlement—"

"Yeah . . . well. He aint gonna be back for a while, is he?" I suddenly can't stand the thought of seeing him.

"No. So you've got all the time you need to tell me why you're actually here."

Shit. Again. I forgot his major was psych. He was always good at seeing through people.

The kettle whistle slices through the conversation like a scalpel. Kevlar gets up. "Excuse me for just a second."

I'm wondering what I'm gonna say to him. He's in there, pouring the boiling water into the teapot and swishing it around, then into each of the cups, then pouring it all out and wiping the outsides of the cups. Finally he fills the pot and adds the tea ball.

My dad does all that—"hotting the pot," the Brits say. Except for the tea ball. We like our tea free-leaf. It's not a real cup of tea unless you get some grit in it, some bits of bark and twig and whatnot. But these Meaneys, naw, they all wanna keep their hands clean of everything.

He comes back with the complete tea service, puts it down on the mosaic—what I now see, obscured, is a picture of Janus, the Roman two-faced god who looked back into the old year and forward into the new. "So," he says, "you want to tell me?"

I get up, look through the bookshelves, find myself at a bunch of university psych texts and self-help books. "You, Kevlar? *You* have self-help books?"

"It's a lucrative market." He shrugs. "Heinz and I were thinking of launching a series of self-help books that would combine psychology, literature, and mythology. So I'm studying up the competition."

Before I can stop myself I'm pulling a book on relationships called *Men Who Love Women Who Hate Them* off the shelf.

"Oh, I see," he targets. "Women trouble. Hamza, I'm sorry. If you want to talk about it—"

Fuck, with the amount of pity and condescension in his voice, I'm starting to rethink discarding this whole Kill-a-Meaney plan. I cram the book back on the shelf. Does he *actually* think I'd tell him anyth—

And then I look at him.

He has tears streaming down his face, which he's wiping away with a handkerchief. "I know what it is to love someone . . . and to lose someone . . . when it's not your choice. When you don't want to say good-bye, but someone else is dictating terms."

There's a bitterness in his voice I don't think I've ever heard from him, not in the ten years since we met. And I've heard it all—cockiness, meanness, superiority, arrogance, delight, dandiness, glee, exhaltation . . . but bitterness?

What the hell's wrong with me? Am I actually feeling sorry for this shit-prince?

I go to sit down with him, scarf down some baklawa. And pour tea for us both.

"So I'm not prying, you see?" he sniffles. "Just looking for someone with whom to commiserate."

I can't believe I'm being guilted into this. But what do you say when a grown man's crying in front of you? "You wanna tell me about it?"

He chuckles sadly. "It's so fresh, Hamza. . . . It just happened last night." He breathes in deeply, clearly trying to calm himself. "Besides, I'm the host. You should go first."

"Oh, uh . . . okay."

Damnit.

I clasp my hands together, trying to think of what to say.

I open them, close em again.

How the hell do I get myself into these things?

Finally, "Well . . . I met a, uh, a woman. It looked like, like there was maybe a promise of good things ahead." I sigh, swallow. "The most promise since . . ."

"Since Rachael."

I can't begin to say how much I hate hearing one of them say her name.

I nod.

"I've never forgiven Heinz—"

"Yeah, anyway," I speed on, "*this* woman, she looked . . . I thought she'd be great. Smart, sophisticated, traveled . . ."

"So what's wrong?"

I shake my head, give in to my worst melodrama, say what I probably shouldn't. But when I see somebody cry in front of me, even a Meaney—"I think she's a drug trafficker or something."

He looks indignant and mortified. The prick. I know his brother is some kind of cokehead or something—I'm not sure if Kevlar is, but—

"What? *Why?*"

"Or *something*. I don't know." I should just shut up now.

"Yes, but what's she done that would make you think she's a—"

"She's been traveling all over the Poor World, she got really hostile when I took her photo, and I actually ran into her on the street late last night doing *something,* and . . . she *gave* me a car."

He rubs his head, like I'm a contagious headache. "Oo. *Well*. And how long were you together?"

I wince. "Don't ask."

He nods. We're silent for a moment. I eat some more baklawa.

I'm so freakin tired, so drained, and what with this comfy couch and the sugar of the baklawa, I feel like I could just drift off right here and now.

And in my exhaustion with my inhibitions down, which is maybe why I've been sharing what I shouldn't've so far—I mean, here in the palace of my enemies, ten years after we met, like two ends of a string of time tied up into a totally unjustified friendship bracelet—okay, that was kind of a mess of a metaphor, but I'm exhausted here, and talking too much. "Weird chick," I share. "Had me doing card tricks."

"Card tricks?"

"Yeah, she was shocked I found her place without an address, so she had me pick her card out of a deck."

"And did you?"

"Yeah."

"What, you knew the trick or something?"

"Naw, no trick, I just picked out the right one."

"Just like you found my place."

"I guess."

He perks up considerably, way more than makes sense. "Well, let *me* test you!"

I Put a Spell on You

"I DON'REALLY FREAKIN FEEL LIKE IT, IF IT'S ALL THE SAME, Kev—"

"You think this tea and baklawa's free, Hamza?" He smirks. "*Come* o-o-o-on. Indulge me!"

I shake my head while Kevlar searches through a nearby book, plucks out a postcard of a wolf he's been using as a bookmark.

"Now close your eyes, Hamza. I'm going to hide this postcard somewhere in the room, and you have to find it."

"Fine." Asshole. I'm doing parlor tricks? These freakin Meaneys. Always think the world's their servant. I *should* just freakin leave. But I'm so tired.

I close my eyes, and this freak sings loudly all over the room so I won't know where he's hiding the postcard. I think he's singing some kot-tam Harry Connick song, too, the moron. Could at least throw down a little Al Hibbler or Johnny Hartman for a Brother, but no. Not Kevloreo.

"Oka-ay," he sings, "you can open your eyes now." I do. "Now find it," he says.

"Whatever."

I scan the room a minute, then close my eyes for a couple secs and, when I open em, walk over to the bookshelves, about three columns away from where I was before. Between a copy of Gibran's *The Prophet* and a book on L. Ron Hubbard called *Messiah or Madman?*, I see a book with a turquoise-and-gold spine.

I pull it out—something called *The Nubian Letters* by some woman named Nehassaiu-en-Ibtet. I know she's a woman, an older Sister, because her portrait's reproduced on the inside page, just below an onion skin overleaf.

Hiding behind that is the wolf, waiting for me with diamond death eyes.

I hold it up and Kevlar beams. "*Amazing.* I noticed you closed your eyes a moment. Do you always do that when you're trying to find something?"

"I never thought about it. Sometimes, yeah . . . when it's a tough call."

"What goes through your brain? When you close your eyes?"

"Uh . . . I . . . see *blue.*"

" '*Blue*'?"

"Yeah, and then I know where it is."

"Well, amazing and amazing . . . Hm. I suppose that tea is steep enough to fall down off of by now."

I throw down a buck-twenty-five laugh to cover his little "joke" and drink down the small cup of tea I'd poured before, which's gone cool. Kev goes back to the kitchen. While he searches through some cupboards, he says, "You said you snapped this woman's photo—I, uh . . . don't suppose you have it with you?"

"You're a master of segues, arncha? Yeah, that's how pathetic I am. I did em in the darkroom at my place."

"Oh, you have your own darkroom, do you? That's nice," he smugs. "I'm a photographer myself, you know—oh, well, for our book, *Visage Grotesque,* so—"

These pricks never miss a chance to one-up anybody, even when they already have everything. Except for one thing, I guess—other people's self-respect. I pull an envelope outta my jacket breast pocket, slide a photo out of it, just as Kevlar comes back from the kitchen with a small pitcher of milk and a sugar bowl.

I show him the picture—Sherem, three days ago, in front of the Muttart glass pyramids, those huge eyes and that sunrise smile, and those three huge braids and a dozen minor ones.

He doesn't just look at the picture—it's like he's studying it or something. Jealous, I hope. She might be nuts, but I'll give her this—she's a hell of a looker.

"Nice scarves," he mutters. "She, uh . . . ever travel in Egypt?"

"Oh, you reckonize em? As a matter of fact, she lived in Upper Egypt for about a decade, not too far from where my dad grew up in northern Sudan. Near Ash-Shabb."

"Ash-*Shabb?* Really!"

"You've heard of Ash-Shabb? Aint exactly on all the tourist routes."

"Oh, I've, well, read about it. Camel safaris and all that sort of thing. Well, Hamza, she really is a beautiful woman. I can see why you'd fall for her."

"Yeah, she's pretty, but that wasn't it. She was . . . just so unusual—she knew so much about the world, and ancient stuff. . . . She even gave me a—"

"A car, yes, I remember your saying. How odd—"

"Naw, naw, she gave me a necklace." I realize it's in my pocket, where I left it after I tore it off last night. I take it out, show him the turquoise scarab pendant at the end of a lace of amber scarabs.

This must really trip him up or something, because his eyes turn into goggles at the sight of it. I aint materialistic *or* competitive, but I like the idea of making one of the Wolves jealous.

"She actually *gave* you that?"

"Yeah. It's called a *tchaua*," I deadpan. "You like it?"

His face looks like it's working over a million calculations. Maybe he wants to buy it for his freakin store or something, offer me two hundred bones an then turn around an sell it for ten grand. Freakin jerk.

He downs his cold tea. He's salivating over my necklace so much, I pretty much have to let him fondle it a little bit. He's enraptured when I hand it over. I reach to pour myself some tea, which I usually take straight, but since he brought out milk and sugar and I'm so drowsy anyway, I figure, what the hell.

(You have to pour those in first, you see, cuz that way, the hot tea will dissolve the sugar without agitation, and also the heat of the tea won't scald the milk cuz of the milk-to-tea ratio at first contact. I learned all that from an episode of *The Prisoner*. It wasn't until I saw that that I understood why my dad did it like that.)

I reach for the milk, and Kevlar completely spazzes out.

"NO!" He blocks me. "No! Hamza—sorry . . . ha ha . . . how rude of me. I should be doing that *for* you. Okay?"

"You were afraid I was gonna spill it all over your mosaic or something?"

"No-no-no, not at all," he fake-laughs. "No, it's just, my father raised me to be a proper host, so it's simply terrible for me to be molesting your jewelry and neglecting my duties."

He hands me back the *tchaua* (I guess so that my hands are occupied) and then spoons lots of sugar, without asking me how much I take, into my cup and his. Except it's not only sugar—looks like it's got cinnamon in it or something. And then he pours a tiny stream of milk into each cup.

"Hey, fill er up," I say. "I'm feeling kinda *shai* tonight." A little Arabic joke—shut up.

He shakes his head like a prim and proper ballet teacher.

"Oh, no, Hamza . . . this, uh, milk's very succulent. It's llama milk. Any more than this would be too much. Try it—I'm sure you'll love it."

I pick up the cup and saucer, stir with the sissy spoon, smell it. It does smell good—like almonds and . . . something else I can't put my finger on. *Like barbecue,* I was gonna say, but that doesn't make any sense.

But that's not how it tastes. It hits me right away—it tastes like freakin hot eggnog! "Hey, Kevlar, you were right. This is fantastic!" The heat spreads through me—I can feel my arteries glowing, practically.

Kevlar looks down at the dessert plate, which is empty, and says, "How about a refill? I see Mr. Hungry Giant has polished them all off."

He puts on a disc first, Screamin' Jay Hawkins's "I Put a Spell on You," then takes off for the kitchen. I'd like to have another look at that *Nubian Letters* book, but when Kevlar starts clinking plates I get a sudden ice pick headache and nearly keel over. Then my gut starts swimming. Maybe I'm allergic to llama milk or something.

"Hey, Kev, you got a bathroom around here?"

"Yes, we just had one installed. First door on the hall."

I hope it won't have those little sissy towels and sissy soaps shaped like seashells that you're not sposta use. I try to breathe slowly. When I'm in the john I splash some water on my face, then drink some from my cupped hands.

Damnit—sissy towels.

Then there's a towel on the wall, but is that somebody's body towel? I don't really want to wipe my hands with the Meaneys' bodies. So I just use my pants.

I take a minute, what with my brain still getting charbroiled and my guts still squeezing buffalo juice. Instead of going right back out to the living room, I look at the artwork in the hall. Fancy stuff. Nice—Group of Seven prints . . . and a framed Giger poster—one of the conceptual pieces for

Alien—an early chest burster! Kinda comforting to know these guys haven't lost all their fannish roots.

Aw, hell. This isn't a Giger *poster*—this is an original *painting*! Must be worth ten grand or more! And they've got it up in the *hall*? I feel sick again.

I should go back, but one of the bedroom doors is open. Maybe they've got more supercollectibles in there. Just about murders me to see the kind of supreme stuff they got— probably find original Kirby stuff or Burne Hogarth or a signed Jules Verne or something. Freaks.

I know I shouldn't just walk in here, but when am I ever gonna get another chance? I flick on the light.

The place is surprisingly messy, given that these are the anally retentive Wolves we're talking about. I don'know if this is Heinz's or Kevlar's. Huge room, giant bed, more paintings and sculpture, but clothes strewn everywhere—I guess they're getting ready for this trip Kev was talking about.

Yeah, in fact, here's two of those crummy dot matrix flight itineraries you get stapled to your ticket. Wonder where they're going? Mexico, huh? Oh, wait, these aren't even theirs—Sonia Chatterjee and Sophia Boleyn—must be their girlfriends'. Kinda strange—most people don't detach these sheets.

Okay, no more genre stuff? No original models used in shooting *Star Wars,* no authentic phaser from the original series? Just—panties. Well, I guess those could be from the original series. "Wink of an Eye" or "Elaan of Troyius" or a bunch of others. Must belong to this Sonia and Sophia.

But then again—

Nah. I mean, probably not. Who the hell knows with the Meaneys?

Now, this is weird. I thought this was some kind of furniture at first, covered with clothes. But it's just, what, two huge barrels? What the hell for? Probably hermetically sealed treasure chests filled with diamonds and ancient treasures and *Action Comics #1* and *Amazing Fantasy #15.*

I really shouldn't, but hell, it's easier to ask forgiveness than permission, and it's not like I'm actually gonna be buddies with these freaks again.

I step over a bunch of clothes and just before I reach the first barrel, something shiny catches my eye from one of the dresser drawers. Probably vibrators or something, knowing these guys—

Holy hell. It's a whole bunch of knives an saws an scalpels. Not, like, antiques, but like a surgeon's kit! Why in the hell would they collect this crap?

My heart's jackhammering, and my headache suddenly rips back up to full intensity. Okay, quit it, Melodrama-boy. Stop freakin out, here. Probably for something to do with their store, like faking antiques or something. Probably soak stuff in these barrels to induce faux aging, like in *The Man in the High Castle.*

I glance over my shoulder, still hear Screamin' Jay howling from the living room and Kevlar singing how he put a spell on me because I'm his. Yeah. Right.

First barrel, the cover . . . shit, my hands are *actually shaking—*

See, you big freakin crybaby? Nothing underneath the lid except liquid and some weird stench, probably whatever their aging/weathering chemicals are.

Second barrel's probably got the actual goods. I tug some clothing off it, pull off the top—

—and two fucking half-chewed-up corpses bob up, long hair slicked and floating on the surface—

—some skin still left, dark skin on one, pale on the other—

—eyelids burned off and the fucking eyes STARING UP to the ceiling—

—gut fills with the stink of RAW HAMBURGER—

—aw, fuck, fuck, FUCK—

—screaming, scrambling the fuck outta there, my legs turned to Silly Putty, my feet flopping like flippers—

—*hallway*—*the LIVING ROOM*—
—back of my head EXPLODES—
—FLOOR RUSHING TO MY FACE AND THEN BLOOD
GUSHING ALL OVER MY NECK AND SHOULDERS—
—and I gasp, and my eyes
                    close

The Face of the Wolf

awake
soaked
        head feels like
        a steel drum
        being played by a sledgehammer
        all wet
        look down
                can't
                        head restrained, tugging. barely see.
                sopping. not blood. Dark, thin. Tea maybe.

awake again
get UP
can't . . . restrained . . . wrists . . . ankles . . .

awake again HOW LONG'mIfallinaslpfr?

I'm awake.
    I'm alone in, in the middle of Kevlar's . . . kitchen—I'm

taped down to a chair, duct tape. Head's taped, too, can feel a rod or something at the back of my neck, must be taped to the chair back.

Saw that fucking horror in Kevlar's room. Two dead women half chewed away by acid or something, in that barrel. Never had the foggiest fucking clue just how sick these Meaneys actually are. No idea. No guess.

Why the hell did I have to come here tonight? For my stupid fucking plan to kill Heinz? How's that for lethal freakin irony? WELL, I DIDN'T FREAKIN *MEAN* IT! Please, aw, no, please . . . I was kidding, kidding *myself,* at least. . . . Don't let me die, not like this, cut up and sodomized and eaten or whatever by somebody I actually *know.* . . .

The Meaneys are freakin Homolka and Bernardo and Gacy and Dahmer, all rolled into one. . . . Why me, why the fuck ME?

Kevlar.

He's right in front of me.

Dustpan, bent over his trash can . . . brushing in shards of the teapot he smashed me in the head with. They look like sections of skull.

His face is all waxy, his eyes are glassy . . . and he's changed his clothes. No more smoking jacket. Head to toe in a rain slicker. Had everything ready. These muthafuckas must be experts. . . . How long've they been doing this to people? Why me? Why did I have to come here?

He sees I'm awake—aw, no, no—

"Hamza," he whispers, turning on me.

"Kevlar, hey . . . um . . . y'know, I don'know what's goin on here, but I'm sure . . . there's a simple explanation—you don'hafta tell me—"

can't think say something ANYTHING keep him CALM

"Howzabout y'just let me go, an then you just take off, okay? Plenty of time for you to get a head start—I'm an old friend, you don'wanna—"

"Well, Hamza," he whispers, his face pinched in like a sphincter, "that's very big of you not to patronize me by saying you won't turn me in. I appreciate that."

His face is twitching—the eyes dragging down at the sides, one nostril flaring—he's completely hyped-up on something. "But we both know you aren't in a position to bargain. This . . . certainly isn't anything I'd planned or hoped would happen, Hamza—"

"Well, then, why don'you just—"

"I'M NOT FINISHED TALKING, *HAMZA!"*

His screaming scares the remaining shit outta me.

I have never been so fucking afraid in my entire life.

"Please, Hamza, please." He straightens himself up. "This is hard enough as it is. Please don't interrupt, okay?"

He looks ready to cry, and his lower lip is shaking, too. He bends over me, puts his hand on my shoulder, *like he's trying to comfort me!*

And then he whispers, almost sobbing: "Just . . . for old times' sake, if you tell me what I want to know, maybe I *can* let you go. Maybe I can, honestly.

"But you have to tell me the complete truth, understand? It was very . . . magnanimous for you to say that you'd give us a head start. We are leaving, as I told you. Just tell me what I want to know and it'll all be over, okay?"

I try to nod, nod profusely, but my head's all jammed up with tape and this rod and so it just shakes and strains my neck. "Absolutely, Kev! *Absolutely!* Anything I can tell you— *just name it*—"

"Okay, then. Listen carefully, Hamza. Are you listening?"

"Yes, Kev, yes! Anything! Just ask me!"

"Where's the jar?"

I can't stop myself.

I start to blubber.

Those freaks on the street who attacked us . . . Kevlar . . . is the whole fucking world in a kot-tam conspiracy?

I'm crying, snot running from my nose—I can'even wipe it cuz I'm taped down, bawling: "I don' . . . huh! huh! . . . *know,* Kev . . . *please.* . . ."

"Where's the jar?"

No—no. "You . . . huh! Snuh! Awww . . . please . . . tuh-tell me what you're talking about—"

His face's closer, eyes like gun barrel mouths, trained on my brain: "Where's the *jar*?"

"Why you doin this? Don'do this, man, please. . . . I'm beggin you, PLEASE. . . ."

"WHERE'S *THE JAR*?"

I can't stop my sobbing, can'even talk now—

He leaves, leaves me crying, can't even hang my head—snot running into my mouth, over my chin, on my chest still soaking with tea—

He's back, puts a clanking milk crate on a stool, sorts through it, puts tools on the kitchen island. Then he tears my shirt open.

"Kevlar, please—PLUH-PLEA-EA-EASE."

He keeps ignoring me—that freaking two-face mask of his, one side an ice sculpture, the other side flaring fireworks—

—takes out a small tub, unscrews the top, dips his hand in, then slathers the jelly he just took out over my chest, especially over my nipples, squeezing them—

—and then more jelly on my lips, on the flesh between my nostrils, my ears . . . and then he takes a scalpel and reaches towards my groin—

—cuts open my pants, my shorts—AW, NO, NO—

"Kevlar, NO, MAN—DON'T—"

—and he dunks his hand for more gel, and then reaches down and slathers his hand all over my penis, really reaching and digging, and on my balls—why me, why ME?

And then removes his hand.

He reaches into his crate and takes out a handful of wires and alligator clips.

And he clamps two alligator clips on my nipples.

He takes more clips out of his crate, attaches them to my nose, lower lip, ears, penis. He has to really squirm to reach my nuts. I try to clamp my legs to keep him out, spit the one clamp off my lip, but he pulls out the scalpel again and holds it at my neck.

Then he pulls—my God—*a kot-tam car battery* out of the milk crate and attaches the two poles with wires to a switch box.

And then he connects the switch box to all the wires coming off of me.

He wipes off. Stares me in the eye like he's daring me to say he did something wrong . . .

And finally, "*Where's the jar?*"

"Fuck, come on, Kev, what, WHAT ARE YOU DOING TO ME?"

"Where's the jar?"

"Why're you doin this to me? DON'T DO THIS!"

"Where's the jar?"

"I don't know!"

"Where's the jar?"

"I don't what you're talking about! I DON'T KNOW WHAT THE FUCK YOU'RE TALKING ABOUT!"

His hand—

FIRE, WHOLE BODY AGONY FIRE

I slump back, pain pouring off me like smoke. My fingernails feel like they're gonna split and burst blood, Kevlar's hand on the switch box, threatening to turn AGAIN—

Kev whispering so quietly, so quietly: "Where's. The. Jar?"

"I don't know PLEASE KEV I DON'T KNOW—"

GUTTING EXCRUCIATING BLINDING

Body cracks back against chair—groin, whole lower body, like axes slammed into me—can't TAKE IT—

Whimpering: "Tell me wh-what you're tuh-*talking* about—"

Takes out more tools: *huge* hypodermic needle with a body the size of a test tube, *hacksaw,* what I think must be a rib spreader . . . and an ice-cream scoop. Ice-cream scoop? But the scoop end—the mouth's been filed, sharpened into a single wide fang—

"Please, Kev, PLEASE—"

Takes out more duct tape—tapes shut my mouth—pulls up on my eyelashes and duct-tapes them to my forehead—my eyes feel like they'll pop out—

—takes the hypodermic and the—THE PITCHER OF MILK FROM THE TEA SERVICE?—dunks the needle in, pulls the other end until the chamber fills white—

—places the needle down—

—grabs the ice-cream scoop.

—and I can't scream or scratch him or bite him or run or move or even SHUT MY EYES—

—and he leans in towards my right eye until his face's the only thing I can see—this is IT—this is how I'm gonna DIE—

—and his whole body's shaking, an awful dance—

—and then he crashes to the floor, and standing in front of me with a wire in her hands dripping blood: *Sherem!*

Enter the Jackal

TOO STUNNED TO UNDERSTAND WHAT THE HELL IS HAPPENING— how'd she get in here? How'd she find me? How'd she—

"Don't move!" she barks, and pulls the tape from my eyelids and my mouth, then takes a scalpel to the tape on my wrists, ankles, forehead, neck—

I pull the alligator clips off myself, stagger up with my pants sliced open, my own piss and shit all over me, my shirt soaked with tea. Kevlar's dead on the floor, his eyes rolled up so high they're almost all white, like his eyeballs're filled with milk.

"C'mon!" she says. "Hamza, hurry!"

My muscles are like iron weights, and my head's still hammering, my balance is shot. And my pants are destroyed—I'm covered in filth—

She seems to know what I'm thinking and throws me a kitchen towel and vaults down the hall. I'm practically naked after I yank off my shorts, and I wipe myself off, all the snot on my face and the excrement between my legs. Sherem comes back, throws me a pair of jogging pants.

"Get those on! We're going now!"

I step into the pants, ashamed, humiliated, disgusted, and so desperately, sweetly grateful to be alive.

Sherem has saved my life.

And then I'm into my coat and shoes and we're running, running through the villa's winding staircase, in the darkness past the courtyard pool and then through the main gate, and into Sherem's waiting car, like, a '56 Bel Air, I think, and we're tearing up the street, onto 104th Ave, east—

The lights streak past us, the four angle-topped towers of Grant MacEwan campus like a giant devil's head buried in a postapocalypse beach—this is all a dream—I'm just dreaming—

"Are you okay?" she says.

Me, yelling: "Am I OKAY?"

She doesn't say anything, her eyes straight ahead, like lances—

"What the hell just happened, Sherem, and how the hell did you just appear out of nowhere to 'rescue' me? And no more of your mysterious bullshit! I WANT THE TRUTH!"

She takes her eyes off the road for a second, honing in on my eyes just long enough for me to see their intensity, and her total belief in her words.

"You were about to be cannibalized—"

"What?" I mean, I'd freakin guessed as much, but still, to hear someone else say it—

"—for the contents of your brain."

"My *brain*? He eats brains? *Human brains?*"

"Not just any brains, Hamza. Special brains. And your brain is more special than you can possibly imagine."

She jams the car on a hard right up 97th Street, under the train tracks, through Chinatown, Chinese neon writhing through the night like glowing red demons fleeing the trumpets of Judgment Day.

"It's a very ancient rite—the absorption of an enemy's knowledge, memories, and powers by eating him—"

"You taking the same drugs you sell?"

"You've seen the crocodile's toe, Hamza! Don't mistake *it* for the crocodile."

"What the hell does that mean?"

We're rocketing up 97th, turning east on 118th Ave, over to Highlands. She ignores my question. "He probably would've eaten your brain first, and then your heart. Like flatworms can absorb the memories of trained flatworms ground up and fed to them."

" 'Trained flatworms'? What're you—and what the hell do you mean, 'powers'?"

"Hamza, you are a *sekht-en-cha*. A 'desert hunter.' You can find anything. That's how you picked the card out of my deck, and that's how you found me, *twice,* with an entire city to look through. That man who attacked you wanted to find something—something very important. That's why he needed your brain, and your heart."

" 'That man' is someone I knew since I was a kid—and you just killed him!"

And she doesn't even look at me. "You're welcome."

We're behind the Richler building, in the alley.

Sherem jumps out, races around the car to grab me—and I'm so weak still that she practically has to hold me upright to get me to walk.

"So how the hell'd *you* find me there, in that condo? Were you stalking me?"

"I'm no desert hunter, Hamza. But I can detect people who are. That's why I connected with you in the first place last week. I was letting you think you were finding me. Finding you fifteen minutes ago was different. It was the *tchaua,* the necklace I gave you. It's a beacon."

Man—it was only an accident I still had that necklace in my jacket pocket—I probably would've thrown it away after seeing her in the park like that, if I'd remembered. But if I had, right now, I'd—

I'm still too weak to resist her, the crazy freakin witch—but whatever line of insane schizophrenic bullshit she's peddling, I want to know her full and complete story. If I can just get to a phone, call Ye—if only I had my SWR phone—

We're squeezing through the boards—shit, this place is a hundred million times more creepy at night—

Inside, she pulls me along, holds me. I can't see anything, but she's navigating in the darkness like she's half bat and half mole. We're up the stairs, down the hall, and now at her door. She mumbles something before we enter, and then after the door is closed.

Inside she flicks on portable electric lamps. She sets me down against the wall on a mat, brings blankets, and throws them around me, tucks me in. Like a black widow wrapping up her mate. And I'm so depleted I can't do a damn thing to resist her. Out of the gallows, and into the electric chair.

"So, Sherem—what about the crack or whatever it was I saw you selling? And this freakin car you 'gave' me—that I then get attacked in and almost killed in? Was I a damn decoy in your little drug war or something? And what about all these people killed, hahn? Six bodies? Mutilated and branded? Is that you? Is that *you* doing all that?"

I can see her wincing in the meager light when I say the word "decoy" and when I talk about the killings—oh, shit, is she a killer? All this time, I kept hoping, hoping against hope that Ye was wrong, that she wasn't really connected—

"I didn't kill all those people, Hamza. And it wasn't crack—not what you've been *told* crack is, anyway."

She hoists me up, shoving the air outta my chest at the exact second I was gonna call her on her wording that she didn't kill *all* those people, brings me over to her shelves filled with what I later figured was drug-trafficking gear, the scales, the bags and beakers, the microscopes.

She flicks on the light for one microscope—they're all wired into a car battery on the shelf, and the sight of it and the wires nearly makes me vomit—and motions for me to look through the eyepiece.

I look. Looks like cells.

"So?"

She's very even-toned, businesslike. "That's a sample of so-called crack. But those aren't all plant cells. Some are bone cells. *Human* bone cells."

I pull away, look at her.

"Third-generation *glacier*," she says. "Make it fourth generation, distill it down, and it's the ultimate hallucinogenic and mind control drug—a thousand times more powerful than LSD—called *cream*.

"Users say it's the closest human beings get to telepathy. Magnifies the senses like a nuclear reactor—so for artists, for sex, for people who like to induce pain, or to kill—"

My legs lose their strength, and she catches me, guides me back to the mat, sits in front of me, her hands on the blankets above my knees.

"There's a global network," she says, "of covens . . . cults. Companies. All trying to produce trackers with chemically induced powers to match your naturally occurring ones. Artificial *sekht-en-cha*.

"Street crack was phase one. The most depraved addicts are routinely 'disappeared.' Who'll miss em? They call this 'harvesting.' And they're taken to labs, where they're . . . processed.

"Their spines and spinal fluid are extracted. Refined. And resold as second-generation *glacier* to other addicts. The third generation comes from feeding *their* spinal essence to second-generation addicts and harvesting *their* spines."

"You're saying that crack—or glacier or whatever—is part of a network of, like, freakin cannibals?"

"Essentially, yes. But that's not all. The purpose isn't simple flesh eating, or drinking. Or hallucination."

"Then what is it?"

"To create 'desert hunters' like you, Hamza. To look for the unfindable. There are ten million priceless treasures buried or lost, everything from da Vincis to crates of diamonds the size

of your fist. But the man who was trying to kill you was looking for the same thing that I am. That *we* are."

"Who's 'we'?"

"My Temple. The House of the Jackal."

"The house of the—okay, let me guess. . . . You're looking
for the jar."

Her face springs into temporary surprise. I played my one
card, probably too soon. But I have nothing else, and I have no
idea how else I could've played it, anyway.

She nods, her eyes like icicles.

And I ask her: "So what *is* the jar?"

Prelude to the Badlands

SO IT'S FOUR A.M. AND WE'RE LOADING THE COYOTE CAR WITH shovel, picks, Ye's R-Mer, one of the two shortwave radiophones, food and drink, and a shotgun.

I need a shower to wash all this filth completely off me. But there's no time.

I dressed up a whole thing for Ye about Sherem, how she's not a drug trafficker after all—which she isn't, I know that now for sure—but actually an archaeological bounty hunter, who uses her skills at finding ancient relics and modern lost treasures like Old West caches of gold and diamonds and whatnot. And that the freaks who attacked us were "archaeopirates"—assholes who can't do the locations and acquisitions themselves, but just hijack the finds once the grunts get em outta the ground.

I spin a whole yarn out of it, throw it every gram of Coyote story-making magic I've got, and maybe the fact that it's three forty-five A.M. when I wake him up, which is when the brain is most easily suggestible, maybe that's why he chooses to believe me. Or maybe he doesn't believe a word of it and knows he can't talk me out of it, so he just wants to protect me from whatever he thinks is really gonna happen.

My story sounds like crap even to me, but then, the real story is so much more impossible to believe, and yet . . .

We're headed to southern Alberta, the badlands. Outside a place with the creepiest name in the country.

Drumheller.

Name sounds like the battle themes of doomsday. Which, in a way, it sort of is. At least for our own personal apocalypse.

The R-Mer . . . this is Ye putting his foot down. The way he figures, if we go all the three and a half hours down to the badlands and we don't find this buried booty of an Old Alberta heist of gold and jewels and the lost *Gospel of Louis Riel,* at least he can put his R-Mer on-line for his first test-drive, and even snap off some pictures of it in an alien landscape.

If this is the biggest roadblock Ye can put in the way of getting down there, no problem. But all the pieces—the exoboots and legs and arms and gloves and the central somatic-control module and over-shell helmet . . . it takes up nearly the whole backseat and trunk, with almost no room for the rest of the equipment.

Including the shotgun. I asked Ye for weapons, in case we encounter more archaeo-raiders. And I said I didn't want no freakin iron pipe this time, either. He just grinned and grabbed the shotgun. I didn't even know he had one on the premises, which is illegal anyway, I'm sure.

But when he handed the thing to me, I was surprised and asked him what *he'd* be packing. He grinned again and said, "Don'worry bout it. I'm covered."

And we're out. Out of the city, down the less-traveled Highway 12, nearly straight-line south to the border. Keep following it and you'll end up running over penguins.

Zooming. The headlights swallowed up by the darkness, like snow falling into black arctic waters. And when I glance to my left, from above the rushing rows of wheat to the zenith of the night, ten billion stars, unmoving, so many that to contemplate them would drive you mad.

So I keep my eyes on the road, my hands on the wheel, and try to steady my brain and my guts for what's ahead, the impossible made real and the rush to get there before the men who want to slaughter us do.

The Legacy of Master Yinepu the Embalmer

ONE WEEK AGO I DIDN'T KNOW THE WOMAN. ONE NIGHT AGO I was convinced she was the worst person I'd ever met. One hour ago she was revealing to me a mystery more stunning than anything I ever read or saw in all my years of fannish flights of fancy.

About an ancient dream of spiritual evolution . . . and a seven-thousand-year-old vendetta of blood and horror.

Now I'm in the car, streaking down the darkened highway laid atop the face of rolling prairie, towards the showdown that will end it all.

An hour ago, inside her condemned-building home, Sherem brewed me tea, a special tea to clear my head after Kevlar'd drugged me and tortured me. And she gave me some kind of smelling salts in case I started to fog out again.

I can't even remember how she got me to trust her enough to let her do what she did next. Maybe it was cuz I was still in shock from the attack and all the madness of the last two days, or maybe it was the fanatic conviction in her eyes when she said she would, quote, *reveal to me a wonder and a horror that has been slumbering since before humanity could write*.

It's utterly terrifying and utterly compelling, that kind of total zealous belief. So when she said, "Give me your arm," I couldn't stop myself.

Her fingers slid over my skin like a spider seeking blood. And when she'd found her marks, she pressed five spots like an expert acupressurist would. I winced, then felt tinglingly aware and awake.

She released my arm, gave me more tea, and had me finish it all as quickly as I could, and told me to close my eyes. She sat behind me, almost crouching over me, took both of my arms this time, and put her mouth beside my left ear.

My whole body felt completely aware of her, like every hair on my skin was being magnetically pulled to her, like every muscle was crackling with electricity surging from her. And at my ear, her breath was hot and cold at the same time.

And then she plunged her fingertips into the pressure points in my arms. My body went numb from the shoulders down, so that the only thing I could feel was her breath in my ear and the pressure of where she'd shifted her fingers to the blood vessels of my neck.

And then my eyes snapped open, and I was in the infinite desert.

Hot, dry air, a noonsun like a white-hot hammer was battering the whole of the world.

And her voice . . . I didn't so much hear it as feel it, feel it like nostalgia, feel it like the phantom twinges they say amputees feel from long-gone feet or hands or legs:

> *I tell you now what was told to me, repeated in a chain that leads unbroken back to the time before iron, before paper, before writing, before genocide.*
> *I tell you of a time when* one man *learned what could have led humanity to commune with beings*

*made of light and smoke and let swim our minds
among the rolling deeps of space. To the time that his
killers*—curse them!—*deprived us of his revelations
and thereby ensured that we would dwell in blood and
fear until we destroyed ourselves.*

    *Seven thousand years ago a Sudanese mystic
named Lord Usir realized that he could remember
what the universe itself knew. . . . He could sing the
harmonies of the darkness and describe the jewels
that dwelt inside the hearts of stars.*

And *I* saw him beneath the sun, his blue black skin and obsidian irises, and his fingernails and the whites of his eyes like gold . . . standing at the edge of the pool of an oasis, or maybe on the face of the water. He was holding a shepherd's crook and a flail for wheat, as still as stone, but intimately alive.

And when our eyes met, he smiled at me in a way that made all my pain and sadness and lost dreams and dead hopes drain out of me like swamp water from the lungs of a man who's nearly drowned. . . .

And when I breathed in, all I could feel was astonishing lightness, and delicate moisture, and total, *total, calm.* . . .

    *He taught what he knew, revealing the ever-greater
chambers of Mysteries to his disciples, until he assembled a community around him in the heights of
the desert of nearly perfect compassion and justice.*

    *And from there he went out to the lands beyond, to
teach what he knew to those who did not know . . . to
free the world from viciousness and agony.*

    *But he had not yet revealed all, for such glories
would destroy the unprepared disciples as surely as
unfired bricks would crumble and bring down a temple. Some were angry and some were jealous. And
the worst of these was the Lord's brother,* curse him!
Sutekh . . .

And I saw him, too . . . his skin like two-tone ebony, like vit-iligo that instead of bleaching the skin in splotches had striped him vertically, like the black marks on a white tiger.

His hands were callused, his teeth sharpened, and from his belt hung knives stained with the gore of men. . . .

> *On the day that the Lord returned, the very same day he was to begin to reveal the final Mysteries that would allow all people, everywhere in all the world, to end hatred and pain and slavery, and to love each other . . .*
>
> *And on that very same day, the wicked brother, using his cunning and intrigue, tricked the Lord to lie inside a golden chest prepared for him as a gift. But it was not a gift or a chest—but instead a coffin.*

I saw a banquet at the entrance to a cavern, the fire in the mid-dle of a circle, and the shields and spears arranged as a wall, the glittering robes and the roasting meats, heard the laughter of men and women, saw the dancing girls and boys, listened to their songs.

And I saw the flash of daggers, and the eyes made of coals, and all the people forced to flee or die, even the wife of the Lord. . . .

> *The brother—curse him!—knew that it was said the Lord could send his souls into the bodies of animals and plants and even men if he wished. But it was also known that gold could stop him, for it was said that gold had the power to trap men's souls.*
>
> *When the coffin was unsealed later, the Lord was dead, and the brother had the sacred body chopped into pieces, and scattered it across the lands. By then all the Lord's kingdom was in ruins and all his original followers had been slaughtered . . . all but one—*

I saw a woman, crying and raging, running and falling and running again, a blade in her hand and curses of vengeance on her lips. . . .

> *The Lord's wife, Aset, gathered followers, taught them the Mysteries that she knew, assembled an army, plotted her return and her vengeance. She searched everywhere for the remains of her husband, and wherever she found a body part constructed a shrine. But each sacred piece she placed in jars and secreted these away in the caves.*

I saw her with men and women and spears, axes, torches, slings . . . holing up in hills and caves. I heard her teach them anew and whisper the secrets of time and the wonders of the darkness.

And I witnessed her instruct them in the arts of death.

> *During her lamentations and her pleading with the Glory for deliverance, she was blessed with a miracle of awesome sadness and joy. . . .*

And I saw a series of jars with the heads of animals, and each jar spilling open, and black smoke pour upon the floor like blood in water, drifting towards the center of the cave.

Until a man who was not a man stood there before her . . .

> *The Lord returned to her, for one sacred night, for one sacred wish.*
>   *To lie in passion after the Passion, to make a son . . .*

I saw them holding each other, treasuring each other, memorizing each moment of each other and their final forever kiss . . . and then I saw the jars sealed again, and Aset in the center of the cave alone, holding herself and wailing. . . .

*Many nations claimed their saviors returned from the
dead to save the world, but Lord Usir was their model
and their memory. . . .*

I saw the faces of a thousand idols, a thousand fallen heroes,
a thousand sacrificed champions, men and women and children, and blood and wood and caves and forests and steel and
fire. . . .

*She had become the Avenger who was sworn to de-
feat the Usurper, no matter the cost. She was the true
power, and so her people called her the Throne. And
she gave birth to a son, Heru, whom she raised and
taught so that one day he would know the Mysteries
and lead the world. . . .*

I saw her suckling her child, holding him, singing songs to him
that gurgled like river water, songs that clanged like
swords . . . and his face was sometimes that of a baby boy,
and other times his hair was made of feathers, and his eyes
were like giant gold coins on either side of his head. . . .

*Her army moved against Sutekh's forces, and Sutekh
struck back. For twenty years they waged their civil
war with the people split into two lands, and the boy
Heru each day becoming a man. And a generation
rose and fell knowing only terror and fire.*

*And when the battles knew days of silence, and
with the aid of a mysterious, abandoned boy named
Yinepu, she returned the jars to the shrines she'd built
where she'd found the holy pieces of the body of the
Lord. . . .*

*And Yinepu applied his secret balms to the pieces,
to preserve them and, as Aset wished, to strengthen
the body of the land . . . to bless the soil with the flesh
of the Lord and make the land grow again with more
than steel and stone and foliage of flame.*

I saw Aset, the Throne, sweep three large braids and twelve small ones from her eyes as she buried the jars that contained the pieces of her husband, intoning the verses of the dusk until just before the dawn.

And the two boys singing drones beside her, one with the face of a falcon, and the other with the face of a jackal.

And I saw how after they left each shrine, the red sand would turn to black loam and give birth to wheat that shone like spun gold, and leaves like wafers of emerald, and pomegranates that burst open with seeds that glittered in the tender morning light like the rubies of paradise. . . .

> *But there could be no victory, for the forces were too evenly matched. Sutekh—curse him!—captured young Master Heru and violated him horribly, believing that to let him live thus disgraced would destroy the faith of the legions against him.*
>
> *But the Throne prayed to the Glory . . . and in her anguish offered her own life for the healing of her son and the purification of the land.*
>
> *And the Glory heard the Throne's offer of her sacrifice, and took her and the Usurper from the world to dwell in the Blue, forever. . . .*

And I saw the bloodied boy, the young Master Heru, bathing in the holy river, and dressed in golden garments, and firing four arrows to the four corners of the world, and together with the boy Master Yinepu make pilgrimage to the Place of the Skull of the Lord . . . *Abdju*. . . .

> *The Skull contained the celestial memories of the Lord . . . and the two young masters believed that if they prayed and lived and taught and ruled righteously, the Skull would yield the truths that would free all life. . . .*
>
> *So these two, a master of Instructions for this world and a master of Instructions for the worlds*

beyond . . . these two holy cousins preserved the people until the Skull would give them all the power to come forth by day. . . .

I saw the civilization that rose from them, the crops and the tools, the charts of the body and of the stars, the making of metals and the building in stone, and everywhere the statues of the Throne suckling her child, the young untested Heru.

And the shrine at Abdju where the Skull was kept was fanatically protected by the only priesthood that could be trusted with the task of waiting for the Skull to divulge its Instructions.

That one priesthood was the Embalmers, the Shemsuyinepu—the Followers of Master Yinepu, son of the accursed Usurper Sutekh. It is called the House of the Jackal.

Us.

I saw this civilization rise, fusing mind and stone to make mountains for souls to ascend to the stars . . . and the greed and arrogance of the mighty sickened the body of the two lands so that disasters and upheavals laid them low. Centuries, millennia passed.

The Skull became legendary, knowledge of its dormant powers lost. What powers? To let humans use the eight sealed chambers of the nine rooms of their brains, to become as wise as all the minds that ever lived, to speak a word and have that thing made real, to heal all sickness and hate. To make love universal.

To cleanse the world.

I saw wars, slaughters, the priests fighting with axes as invaders killed all in their paths . . . and the Place of the Skull was about to fall. . . .

> *Two and a half millennia ago, bearded invaders took*
> *the two lands and even Holy Abdju was to be ravaged.*
> *The priests seized the old knowledge that built the*
> *Bronze Empire, and with the aid of the Shemsuptah,*
> *fled with the canopic jar that contained the*
> *Skull . . . "across desert and a great abyss of water."*
> *They never returned.*
>
> *And since that day we have searched for them, to*
> *retrieve the Skull, and with what we have learned*
> *since then . . . to try to use it.*

I saw an earthquake crack the soil and the stone and sands of
dinosaur bones in the dry lands, the quake wound inside the
crust and the mantle, and the pain and ecstasy of it like an
electric arc through the earth's veins to the other side of the
world. . . .

> *Near Ash-Shabb, in the House of the Jackal, we felt it:*
> *the earthquake last week had unsealed a chamber.*
> *The Guardians sent nine times nine of us to locate and*
> *attain the Skull before our enemies did.*
>
> *And they are close, with the use of their poisons*
> *and their wicked machines. But because of you,*
> *Hamza, we still have a chance. . . .*

And then I was awake, back in the darkness of a condemned
E-Town tenement, with Sherem behind me holding her fingers
against my neck, and her lips against my ear, whispering her
final secrets to me before the time of blood and death in the
badlands.

An Infinity of Rape and Murder

I WAS ALL CRAMPED. I HAD TO GET UP. SHEREM RELEASED MY
neck, helped me. I expected to ache all over from Kevlar's torture, but my body . . . instead of pain, I was suddenly crackling with energy, like I was ready to run and fight and climb a
mountain.

"Sherem, I'm—"

"Feeling better?" she whispered. "The 'tea.' The same formula that helped Senwosret's and Shaka's troops. There'll be
time to rest later, Hamza. For now . . . you have to be as
strong as possible."

I wanted to ask her a million questions . . . like how she'd
shown me what she did, what kind of dream transfusion or
telepathy or sympathetic consciousness or whatever it was
that she used.

But I was calm in a way I can still hardly understand and
barely even care to try . . . just completely accepting of how
she'd communicated with me and why . . . the same acceptance and confidence your muscles feel when you jump or

strike, the kind your hand feels when it signs your name or draws, the kind your mouth feels when it talks or sings.

This is impossible, but it's true.

She packed me a case filled with what she called "battle food and drink" and a necklace that looked like a panpipe, filled with powders and "unguents," to keep me ready for what was coming.

And in the here and now, Ye's beside me in the Coyote Car, checking and rechecking the shotgun he brought for me and the arms of his R-Mer and whatever secret surprises he's built into them.

And we're streaking down gaunt dark highways with nothing but shoulder-high stretches of wheat on either side. And the inside of the car's as absolutely, perfectly, impossibly purple as the quasi dawn outside.

Ye asks me suddenly, "So how we gonna find the crate with the cash and diamonds and gold even if we *do* find this abandoned mine?"

I keep my eyes on the purple highway, grit my teeth. "*I* can find it."

And my mind is back in the apartment, with Sherem preparing my panpipe Shaka necklace for battle. I knew I only had time for a few questions.

"So, Sherem," I asked her quietly, like we were in church, or at a grave site, "if this Skull can heal, what the hell do the bad guys want it for?"

"The Skull is more than healing. It's a *conduit* for consciousness. They want access to people's minds."

"Whose?"

"Everyone's."

"Why?"

"Because thought itself is a substance that can be consumed. It can heal . . . or it can become a drug. But it's not easy to harvest. Think of musk. How do you get it? You physically beat an animal until it secretes it. You want a pearl—

how do you get it? You open an oyster's body and stab it with a tiny piece of rock.

"The human brain can radiate *thought* of such intensity that others can taste it. If you accelerate perception enough, the brain can drink in the 'sapphire chimes' and the 'jade echoes' of each mind it encounters . . . soak these radiances in, drink them in, *suck* them in.

"Each emotion and memory the brain experiences carries a *charge,* Hamza, a galvanizing mental charge that an accelerated mind can consume. And pain . . . pain and misery generate some of the highest charges of all.

"So how do you get the brain ready to yield its fruit? Push it. Excite it. *Hurt it*. Prime it with cream. And how do you get your own brain ready to suck in as much as possible?

"*Cream*. Or another conduit that'd make cream unnecessary, one that'd open up the brain past operating at ten percent, past twenty, past seventy-five, to one hundred . . . so it can experience the most intense ecstasy the human brain can tolerate without bursting.

"These . . . *people* . . . they want a never-ending supply of minds to plunder. Human cows to milk."

She placed the Shaka necklace around my neck, handed me my battle rations pouch, and went to the door, her whispering before and after she opened it and we stepped across the threshold.

As we wound our way down the hall's darkness, I asked her, "But . . . why don't they just . . . live off of other people's happiness? Wouldn't that be even better for them?"

"Why? Because they've never drunk the joy of others? Because they don't know how? Because it's easier to cause misery or terror than create happiness? Because someone else's agony has that special rush to it they can't get any other way? Because they don't care?

"Because they're filth. These people, these . . . Things . . . they're the maggots that appeared on the world's first corpse.

They want the ultimate ecstasy, Hamza, and they don't care how they get it."

And we hit outside, and jumped in Sherem's car. And I thought about that word, *ecstasy,* and what it originally meant . . . the unparalleled rapture martyrs feel at the moment of death.

We were back on the road, streaking down empty streets and through red lights to the Coyote Cave, to get Ye, to go to where destiny was buried. Outside Drumheller, the badlands.

The place I didn't even realize I'd named when I was in the Dreamtime with Sherem.

And as we hit 107th Street heading west, I tried to make sense out of it all, struggling to sew words into sentences: "So they . . . basically they plan . . . to rape, and, and . . . torture . . . and mutilate . . . people's minds? And they'll . . . ?"

"They'll *feed* off it, yes. One person after another. Whole families, communities, cities. Maybe they'll form a cult. And they'll take millions. Raping one soul again and again, one after the other . . . and because their appetites will grow, they won't even be *able* to stop. They'll always need more, and more—"

I thought of the two women's bodies I saw in that oil drum in Kevlar's room. Who were they? Customers from the store he'd lured back there? Women he'd met hocking their damn book? Promised them dinner . . . and turned them into it? Hacked up and drained to be turned into cream?

"So . . . the whole world'd be, like, defenseless babies to them . . . and they're . . . planetary mental pedophiles."

"Yes."

I tried to understand it, get my brain to encompass the full horror of it . . . the entire human race turned into a concentration camp without walls, one by one. For an infinity of rape and murder.

We had only two blocks left to the Cave, and she told me how her group, the Jackals, had stopped twelve previous attempts using other conduits to get the same goal. Three of these usurpers had been dictators, she said. One was a Romanian named Vlad Tsepes. Another was a Crusader pope whose men excavated the Temple of Solomon.

"But in twenty-five hundred years, no one has come close to recovering the Jar, Hamza. There're thousands of these . . . *profound* psychopaths, working in secret, working in darkness . . . a network of depravity exchanging clues.

"They want to enslave humanity. Drink all the love and hope and pain and terror from our minds like a . . . tapeworm inside our soul.

"So the stakes are higher now than ever before. This Son of Ãāpep I've been tracking, this man, Heinz Meaney . . . he could be the one to do it, Hamza."

At hearing that name it felt like my headache was coming back, this time with sledgehammers.

"Heinz Meaney? Heinz Meaney?" I swallowed, felt sludge in my stomach. "What'd you call him? Son of—?"

In the present, Ye and I are pulling into the city limits of Drumheller, the sky becoming electric blood above the black silhouette of hills. This is dinosaur country, and the best dig sites in the country are right here. Whole town is covered with giant dinosaur statues . . . used to scare the hell outta me when I was a kid and Dad took us down here to camp.

Sherem pulled up in front of my house, finished what she had to say.

"In the House of the Jackal," she whispered, "some of the deepest Mysteries we're taught are about Ãāpep—curse its name forever. An ancient Thing, a Lie. An enemy of the Glory. A tumor in the body of creation.

"Beings called the Hammemet fought it, eventually destroyed it. But its substance implanted itself like . . . like mitochondrial DNA in all living things . . . waiting to be reactivated, to slouch forth to be reborn."

We can't stop here in Drumheller. We've gotta keep going, on to the badlands, and the destiny buried there under the sands. I glance out of my driver's-side window, see the giant silhouetted, saber-fanged head of a Tyrannosaurus rex, back-lit by hellish red.

"Ããpep," said Sherem, "is what you would call Shai-tan . . . or Satan."

I was past being able to react. It was all too much . . . thousands of years of civilizations and mysticisms and wars and spiritual vampirisms. . . . I stopped even trying to react, to digest, to understand. If we got this Skull, if it was where I'd blue-dreamed it was, there'd be time later.

And this stuff Sherem gave me, the stuff I was breathing in from the Shaka necklace, was giving me tunnel vision, focusing me like a laser. All I could think of was getting to it, and—

"And whatever you do, Hamza, when you find the Jar," she said as we got out of the car, "*don't open it.*"

"Aren't you coming with me?"

"I'll run interference here. Stop our enemies here. You'll have to contact me somehow—"

I dashed inside, returned with one of the SWR phones, handed it to her where she was standing in front of the car. "As soon as I've got it, I'll radio you."

"Hamza," she said, suddenly soft again after all that hardness, after all that history and horror, and for just a moment I glimpsed what I saw in her at the Ibex Restaurant last Friday, or on the picnic on Saturday morning, or at her apartment on Sunday. I saw the fragility in her that I doubt she let anyone else see, the pain in her eyes that looked like buckled bricks on dams holding back a lifetime of tears.

"Hamza," she said softly, taking my hands, "I'm so . . . so sorry . . . you almost got hurt by those men who were looking for me. But I . . . unless we . . . we can't fail in this. I didn't know how else—I didn't know what else to do!"

And then she cleared her throat, and I was afraid she was going to become Iron Sherem again, and I had to hold on to that softness and beauty for just a few more seconds.

So I said, "Did I ever tell you why I'm *really* called Coyote?"

She shook her head, the iron in her face coming back: *There isn't time—*

I clutched her hands, felt the muscles in them, the outlines of the bones, the calluses of her skin, clutched the hands like they were amulets, tried to memorize them in case it was the last time I'd ever have a tender moment, in case I was going to die down there in the badlands.

"They call me Coyote," I whispered, "cuz you can shoot me, push me off a cliff, bust my ass, or break my heart—but you can't kill me. I always walk away. Maybe shaped like an accordion, but I walk away."

Her face was torn, like magnets of fear and guilt were pulling at the muscles from opposite directions.

And I remember how the night was still so foggy, and the headlights were still on and lighting us up in front of them, and for just a second when she looked into my eyes, in my peripheral vision it was like being inside a cloud lit up by the moon.

And in that brief, brief moment of being in the belly of the moon mist, she said to me, "Hamza . . . when this is all over . . . you're . . . you're going to wonder . . . how much of this is real."

And she stepped closer to me. "You have to know." Another step closer, and her nose was almost touching mine, her eyes full of fear and pain and broken dreams.

"All of it's real," she hushed. *"All of me."*

And she kissed me.

And we held each other like that inside the cloud, me feeling her skin against my skin and her braids against my forehead, smelling her scent all mixed with sweat and fear and soil and rain, feeling my fingers in her hair and around her skull and on her neck and on the writhing lizard-tail scar that jumped with each pulse of her blood . . . the two of us holding tight in that fog and feeling arms and lips and warmth, breath passing from her into me into her in the unbroken exchange of breath that went back to the first humans who held each other and, before that, to the first things that breathed. . . .

And wanting never to let go . . . and having to.

"This is it," says Ye, with the sun blinding us above the desolate horizon. "The badlands."

Lung-mei, the Path of the Dragon

I$_T$ WAS NEVER . . .
Never supposed to come to this.

I had to be out. There was no other way. Kevlar and I . . . we were going to have to leave, probably for forever. . . . I had to make sure all our accounts receivable were in.

And with our . . . clientele . . . you can't just . . . expect suitcases full of cash after every delivery. You have to . . . give credit . . . collect in lump sums from news anchors, surgeons, lawyers, music producers, professors. . . .

Had to be out all night, didn't I?

And to come home, to our *home,* and find . . . with the morning sun shining in and what should've been the smells of freshly squeezed orange juice and Kenyan coffee and hot croissants and clotted cream . . .

. . . I find the twisted frame of my poor, dear little brother on the kitchen floor, footprints in the smears of his life on the polished hardwood. . . .

And I had to . . . I had no choice but to—

But now his skull is empty, and I've done what had to be done.

For now, there's a call I have to make.

He answers on the first ring, that same juggernaut voice, that same blunt-force-trauma tone.

And I tell him:

"It's me, Heinz. . . .

"Yes, I agree. We should've had this talk a long time ago. . . .

"You think so, do you? Well, thanks to you jumping the gun, pulling that fucking stunt you did—

"Yes, I'm talking about the Modeus Zokolo! Who else could it've been? And don't fucking deny it. . . .

"Yes, you're right, we do understand each other. . . ."

This son of a bitch wants to Gatling-gun me with his locker-room invective while I've got my dead brother's body lying right here in front of me and I'm trying to explain the gravity of the situation! I'd thought, after the break-in, the disappearances of three of our best movers was just cream racket collateral damage.

But when I saw the photo on the floor, here, the woman, those scarves . . . and that *scar* . . .

"Don't fucking lecture me on what's going on! I know what's going on, and I know who we're dealing with! . . .

"How do *I* know? Don't you forget who introduced you to all this. . . . Yes, yes, for the millionth time I understand what your investment and your overseas contacts have done for this operation. . . . Yes, but . . . listen, I'm not one of your dirtbag flunkies who trembles in fear of you. We're dealing with a Jackal here! If we don't contain this situation, not only will we *not* get to the Jar or any other terrvix, we won't be alive much longer! . . .

"Yes, well . . . something's *already* gone terribly wrong.

"My brother is dead. . . .

"Yes, I know who's guilty."

My hands are still shaking. . . . I'm nauseous—but I had no other choice. There was no other way!

I had to know what Kevlar's last thoughts were before he . . .

And there was only one way.

Seeing what you saw, the pain around your neck, the tightening, the ripping, and the hot slick of your own blood, falling, crashing, gasping bubbles, drowning in blood—and looking up and seeing HER FACE—

But now I know, *now I know,* sitting here in this palace of our ascent and our dreams, this launchpad for what was supposed to be the two of us into a realm of consciousness and actualization that would make Buddha or Christ jealous . . . this stench-pit charnel house where I sit with my brother's gore on the floor, his blood on my clothes and skin, and his brain . . . in my . . .

Kevlar, forgive me!

But at least this way . . . when I disembowel that bitch and that fucking simpleton Hamza . . . it'll be for you.

And now you'll be with me forever.

All four of us will be together, just like you wanted.

"That's what I said, Dulles, isn't it? This is a Jackal. Which means we both know what she's after. Which means if we don't either stop her or get there first—

". . . all right. One hour. The Inferno."

I put down the phone, go to wash and collect my tools.

Before the next sunrise it'll all be over.

The Two Sovereigns

Which of the two sovereigns is imbued with the Moral law?
Which of the two generals has most ability? With whom lie the
advantages derived from Heaven and Earth? . . . In which army is
there the greater constancy both in reward and punishment?
—SUN TZU, *The Art of War,* 1:13

I AM NOW PAST COUNTING THE NUMBER OF HOURS IN WHICH I
have dwelled inside this terrible and glorious phantasmagoria
of cream-induced enlightenment.

Time has become gelid for me, and experience is like ripples in its surface, memories like succulent segments of mandarin and pineapple and bright pink maraschino cherry
suspended inside it. What then is the fluted dollop of whipping cream on top? Delirium. Delirium is a most remarkable
thing, I realize . . . and since I am recognizing and cogitating
upon it, perhaps it is better termed, then, *metadelirium.*

I am no longer entirely aware of what I am perceiving directly and what I am experiencing ethereally. For instance, I

cannot clarify for my own satisfaction whether I am aware that Mr. Alpha Cat ate pizza because I saw him eating slice after slice, if I know he ate pizza because I have assimilated the experience his mind has radiated into the air and the walls around us, or if I know he ate pizza because I can see through his clothing and chest wall into the contents of his primary gizzard.

As well, although I was not present during the moments of Mr. Frosty's . . . culling . . . much of the engrammatic voltage of that experience has been grounded through me as surely as if I were a sapient lightning rod. To witness that psychovicariously, from four points of view, to live inside that polydimensional, multipathic evisceration . . .

I did not *like* Mr. Gorkovski. He was never kind to me. He never missed any opportunity to heap his obloquy or abuse upon me.

But to see him . . . and to *feel* him . . . winding up like *that* . . .

Well.

I for one am grateful, here in the confines of the Inferno on this windowless Wednesday morning, for the distraction provided by the presence of the new candidate apprentices to Team FanBoy. I feel uniquely suited now, in this superior state of perceptual acuity, to evaluate their intellectual and martial acumen.

Such colorful names and weapons and tactics! *Captain Crunch,* demonstrating his legendary mastication for our troops by biting through shot glasses, promotional pucks, and a pair of skates, blades and all, that, for the life of me, I have no idea why have been kept here at the Master's sanctum infernum.

And now, in the pit (although without the fog machines and swirling lights), the *Human Torque* is employing his grappling techniques to toss about Mr. Zenko and even the voluminous Mr. the Mugatu as if they were composed of mere Styrofoam.

Our large vocally challenged teammate seems quite impressed, but I'd describe Mr. Zenko's expression as somewhat less charitable. Nevertheless, even that face masks much. . . . The emanations coming from his id field tear into the gel of my current consciousness like a fork into an eyeball.

In a few seconds the buzzer will ring, and the Master's guest and sometime colleague will arrive.

Mr. *Vegi-Might* has a backpack of some sort—a power supply, I believe. His slicing weapons appear quite formidable, but surely they're for close range only. Still, as our feminine target has protection against missile attack, only close-quarters combat will carry the day, anyway. And I suppose the high-kicking, long-striking Mr. *Adolf Benito* will be of aid in that department, as well—

The buzzer rings.

Mr. Cat rushes out, comes back a moment later with the visiting sovereign, the brilliant, maverick, thaumaturge-entrepreneur who I suddenly understand was the one who sold the Master his franchise de la crème and introduced him to this unique method for human evolution.

Fascinating—I'm realizing all of this in all the time it takes for him to walk along the gantry and breathe the same air as I do—I inhale his awareness and recollection simultaneously as I inhale the molecules of carbon dioxide and oxygen and nitrogen his lungs and nostrils exhale.

He is our master's teacher. . . . *Sigung,* I believe, is the Chinese term.

It was only last Friday that I saw this sovereign lecture on the contents of his book, *Visage Grotesque*—a remarkable text, actually. Especially—oh!—now that I am living what made him write it! What a grim menagerie of glories and grotesqueries! What he did and had done to him in Thailand and Brazil and Haiti and Scotland . . . well. How, then, is the ax blade turned into hardened steel if not through immersion in coal and fire?

Mr. Heinz Meaney, carrying a large expensive-looking duffel bag, looks much less self-assured now than he did last Friday evening, when he was agog with self-congratulation and the crowd's adulation. This morning he looks haunted, in fact. And—

My God.

He actually—

His own *brother?*

I shudder, wondering what the limits are to my intercerebral eavesdropping, hoping I will soon face greater restrictions on my shadow awareness, if the contents of my vicaremembrances are to be of such a nature as *these.* . . .

Mr. Cat shows Mr. Meaney into Master Allen's office. They are beyond my sight—but from my shoulder nearest the wall . . . yes . . . and when I place my hand against the wall's skin . . . ah . . . yes . . .

. . . closely, *closely*—

"Is that what I think it is?"

"What're you talking about, Dulles?"

"In your teeth? You got a chunk of meat there."

I taste Mr. Meaney running his tongue along his front teeth, and when he finds a fatty strand wedged there he sucks it free. His whole mouth tastes like iron. And when he swallows, he has a sudden flush of images and sensations—*a view of his own face,* but younger and from a lower angle . . . *women,* a cascade of women's and young men's faces contorted by carnal joys and horrors . . . and the constriction of his throat into a single, blinding line of agony, and then darkness—

And then the strand is overwhelmed by the burning brine of his stomach.

(I think I've missed something—so hard to filter this storm of recollection during their conversation—)

". . . if you and your crew of dimwit misanthropes hadn't stolen the zodiascope, Dulles, if you'd shared with me this information about a Jackal, I could've found the Canopic Cave days ago—"

"Yeah, yeah, sure, Heinz, you woulda figured it all out on your own little lonesome and shared it all with me freely—"

"—or *found any of thirty-seven other* thaumaturgical sites any number of us have been trying to track down for the last three thousand years! It's not like *you* could've found any of them—"

"Still think you're so fuckin smart, ya pissant little ass-fruit? I got this far, didn't I? *I* knew we were dealing with Jack-als before you did, *I* got the 'scope, *I* made the connection to using cream, *I* got one of my best guys who's *this close* to knowing the exact location—"

"Don't forget who taught you, Dulles! And what would you've done when you got there, hm? It's not a fucking com-puter with a *start* button—"

"You wanna smart-mouth me, ya little ass-pussy? I'll smack the balls off ya—"

"Yes, Dulles, that's right—threaten *me,* the only person who can actually bring this entire project to fruition! Do you *really* think I'd've brought you into this operation with com-plete disclosure, or even pointed you in directions that could ever let you piece it together yourself? You need me. And don't forget it."

(Breath is hot—hairs stand on their necks, faces flushed—teeth grit and grind like industrial files attacking spinning lathes—)

"I've spent a *decade* planning this, Dulles—do you under-stand that? The fact that we were this close to a terrvix of this magnitude is a shocking accident, but no one—*no one* can un-lock it except me! That's why no one else *has.* . . . Only the correct equipment, the correct maps, the correct training, and correctly made cream could lead anyone there. Instead of pre-venting me and stealing from me, you should've been helping me, as we agreed!"

(How odd—disturbing, in fact—to hear someone address a god with such profane irreverence. But I suppose that the his-tory of mythology is nothing if not proof that celestials are the instructors of man's worst sins.

(I taste a rush of wheaty-citrusy water . . . gritty and . . . oh . . . a glass of Metamucil. Master Allen swallows, gulps. His eyes feel ready to burst. He must be issuing one of his legendary napalm stares. I believe he calls it "eye fucking."

(I feel flesh singeing from inside—finger bones crying out to gouge, feet demanding to stomp, to smash—)

"Call it insurance, then, ass-fist. My one guarantee—since ya just *admitted* how much you've been keeping from me, like the fact you'd fuckin *found* the 'scope in the first place—that you couldn't screw me completely. Like you planned. How much've I bankrolled for your search, Heinzy-boy? Lemme tell ya—one-point-one-five mil. A mil for the franchise, and the rest for grease to get the 'scope. I didn'*steal* nothin. I paid fer it already."

"*I* paid for it, Dulles. And my brother paid for it with his life."

(I feel snorting—the mucus travels like a viscous knot, or perhaps a hardened leech, inside Master Allen's sinuses. The telephone is about to ring.)

"Yeah, whatever. Ya might wanna brush your teeth before ya start talkin about him again."

Images, flashes of desire sizzling like hot-pavement phantoms in the air—breaking of teeth, smashing of eyes, snapping of necks—

(The telephone rings.)

"Allen."

(For some reason I can't feel these words—not even through the Master—what's blocking it? What's disintegrating the . . . ? Only fragments . . . I feel rushing land, air-conditioning on full, a high green sign saying MANNING FREEWAY—

(And again, the eyes raping Mr. Meaney's gaze . . .

(Quietly—)

"I understand. I'll be right there."

Silence.

And then—

"Are you serious? You're going somewhere? We don't have *time*—"

"*I* DON'T HAVE TIME, THANKS TO *YOU!*"

(My knees snap like bridge cables at the explosion, and I stagger, fall against the wall, lower myself until I'm on the floor. I touch the floor—try to reconnect—)

"My boys'll take care of you till I'm back. Just in case you get any more of your cute concepts you wanna try out."

"Well, if you'd simply said *where* you were going . . . look, I obviously . . . know the situation, but we don't—"

"*THIS* SITUATION exists *BECAUSE of YOU!* DON'T FUCKIN TELL ME WHAT *WE* DON'T HAVE TIME FOR!"

(Blood engorges internal rivers. Legs fire like pistons—)

The Master bursts from his office like an ICBM from a silo, with our visitor lugging his duffel bag in his train. . . .

And what Master Allen burns with right now—my goodness . . . all of that . . . *that's* been the reason for our war? How many addicts have we culled? . . . How many of we Fan-Boys have perished for this crusade? How many of us more until the Master achieves this one prize? All for the sake of one—

And he's gone, into his vehicle—north, towards Manning Freeway.

The troops, including our novice apprentices, have stopped their training in order to bear witness to the surface level of this conflict, which I alone have remotely assimilated. They now return to their exercises in striking, grappling, tumbling, dodging.

I tell Mr. Meaney how much I enjoyed his book. He smiles minutely . . . but beneath that smile are fangs and maggots.

Mr. Cat calls me over, setting up the *mei* Ouija, the preliminary terrvix map, and our tools, and handing me the zodiascope.

"Mr. Cat, the, uh, zodiascope's no good . . . before, without, well . . . *stars* out. . . ."

Mr. Meaney approaches us, eyes the zodiascope with sudden fury, but makes no move to take it. Astounding! Why not? I listen to the surge of his bile and his blood—but—

Before I can focus he removes a photograph from his breast pocket.

"This is the woman you saw?" he says. His tone matches the acid bog inside him.

"YU don't tell us hour JAAB," snaps Mr. Cat, pulling up his shirt, exposing the custom silvery handle of his erect Glock wedged at the waist of his gauchos.

As lieutenant to the Master, he is truly the peacemaker within our family of fantastic fanatics, but with outsiders, even powerful ones, he knows no mercy.

He takes a step towards Mr. Meaney, fingering his weapon. "Wi know whaa fi do. Fine she an SHE lead us to dem."

Mr. Meaney's eyes narrow.

Mr. Cat addresses me without blinking away from our guest.

"Digaestus, yu get ennytinn yet?"

"Uh, well, no. Not yet . . . she's, uh . . . probably in a *masked,* uh, location, which is why we were never able to get her, uh, before. Until she moves . . . we have to wait."

Mr. Meaney shakes his heads (I mean *head*—that's odd— what made me—?) and turns his back on us, walks to a nearby table. He removes equipment from his duffel bag, piece by piece: a leather case, three bottles of ink, a tiny metal chalice, and a metal bottle, like an army issue flask.

From his leather case he produces Chinese ink brushes and crow quill pens. He sits, rolls up his sleeves, uncaps one bottle of ink. Or what I'd thought was ink . . . I know now it's not ink, but what it *is*—I'm having trouble living him, now that the Master is gone, as Mr. Meaney has become calmer . . . but— could he actually be blocking me? Truly fascinating!

Now he is charging his brush with his ur-ink and is inscribing his palm, his wrist, his forearm . . . a winding maze of black on pink like Tibetan script and Germanic runes writ upon calf's hide.

And he stops, puts down his brushes, unscrews the metal bottle, and fills the tiny chalice with . . .

. . . with the blessed nectar. I can smell it from here. My mind dances in it—my scalp crinkles at the aromatic taste of it in a purity and potency even *I*, over this last twenty-four hours, have yet to experience.

"Shortwave," I announce autonomically.

"What?" says Mr. Cat.

"Shortwave. The, uh . . . *Jackal*. Mr. Cat, she'll be using shortwave."

Mr. Meaney looks startled, then impressed. But I still can't live him.

Mr. Cat looks me over, squeezes my shoulder twice, instructs Messrs. the Mugatu and Zenko to fetch the police scanner from the FanVan and procure shortwave radios, for which he hands them a roll of twenty-dollar bills. While they scramble into action, he wanders over to our guest.

"Whaat in di ell yu doin, Meaney-maan?"

Mr. Meaney returns to his hand painting, but now with a twist—he's produced a razor blade with a dragon tassel on its end. He's cutting a line along his skin inside each of the paths of his ur-ink . . . and now adding new lines, making a greater syllabary, a larger fretwork.

"You prepare your way," he says. "I'll prepare mine."

I walk back to our table, study our work completed thus far, think upon the Master, who even now must be hurtling northward along 97th Ave to his destination in the quiescent countryside, amid the trees and among the buildings that reek of boiled cabbage and cleansing solvents.

And I think upon Marylin and Casper and Frosty and all our clients and us, the as yet living roster of the Modern-Ancient Mystic Teutonic Shrine of Free and Accepted Fan-

Boys . . . and upon the Master himself and what I have only minutes ago learned has been the impetus for all of this chaos and deceit and death.

I think of all of this, and of all of us.

And despite Mr. Cat's attempts to comfort me, I cannot stop the tears.

Silence on Heaven and Earth

[Beowulf's author] is concerned primarily with man on earth,
rehandling in a new perspective an ancient theme: that man,
each man and all men, and all their works shall die. . . .
Surveying the history of kings and warriors in the
old traditions, he sees that all glory (or as we might
say "culture" or "civilization") ends in night.
—J.R.R. TOLKIEN

AS SOON AS I PULL INTO MY PARKING SPOT THESE ASS-FROGS ARE
all over me, showing me to the door, waving down the security
guards, passing me through the gates. I guess when you practically pay for a new fuckin building out here, what the hell
else they gonna do?

Everything about here is *wrong.* Sure, the nice grounds and
all, grass and trees as far as you can see, flowers and grooming
and whatnot. In all the time I ever been here, do I ever hear a
damn bird chirping? Even a magpie screeching and scrawing?
How about see a squirrel dash up a tree to bust a nut? Howz-

about maybe some prairie dogs scrambling for holes? Could I hear maybe a fuckin bee buzz around the flowers? Is everything out here made outta plastic? How can you wipe out all animal life for forty acres?

But this is it. This is the place where they got the professionals, the machines, the experience. If there was any other way . . . but there aint. I paid for every extra thing I could. But this aint the States. These fuckin commies. What the hell kinda country is this where a man can't buy even if he's got the wad?

These same halls. The same walk. Up the stairs, through the doors, right, right again. Elevator. More gates. Another security station my own money paid for.

Hate the smell.

No matter how much they scrub, it's soaked into the damn paint. Boiled potatoes and boiled beef and strained carrots. Piss. Diarrhea. Me, I have food brought up here. Organic. The thought that they'd try to feed this puke to—well, they don't.

They should nuke this place. Nuke the stink, nuke the land that aint got no animals, nuke the pastel paint job that turns the brain into boiled lima beans. And especially nuke the doctors.

More shitty art on the walls painted by the inmates. Sposta to be happy. Sposta be cheerful. Can't the doctors see through this? Don't they know anything? These educated ass-rakes can't see the skulls underneath every smiling face?

And now here's the head ass-rake himself. Dr. Sheldon Philbin. How the hell can a man live on this planet for fifty years with a name like Sheldon Philbin?

"Mr. Allen," he says, all hunnert 'n' thirty pounds of him, branches and twigs, offering his little dry-leaf hand to me. Every time I shake with this guy I figure I'm gonna smash him into kindling. "I'm so glad you were able to make it so quickly."

"Since when've I *not* made it out quickly when you called?"

The little ass-cube turns white, and he's staring right at my hands, then glancing at my mouth. Maybe around here they hafta do that all the time, to protect themselves.

"Ah . . . of course, you've always been excellent, sir, at coming out here at the drop of a dime. Everyone, I mean, everyone, sir, speaks of your devotion to your . . . that is—"

"Sheldon!" I bark. He shuts up. "Sheldon, I'm on a schedule, here. You said there's been a change since Sunday?"

"Yes, yes," he squeaks, and he grips his clipboard in front of him like body armor, "an excellent change. After that violent . . . well . . . the outburst, last week, and Dr. Asdaghi and Nurse Murdoch being injured, we had no choice but to use restraints. We'd've preferred to use antipsychotics, but—"

"But you know what I'd do if I ever even *thought* you were using drugs for this treatment."

"Yes, of course, Mr. Allen! I wouldn't—*nobody* around would *dream* of violating your—"

"Fine, Sheldon! So tell me more about the, uh, the changes. In her condition."

"Well . . . late last night her screaming stopped. At first we thought it was just exhaustion—after all, many times she has, uh, literally . . . screamed herself to sleep. And as per your orders, since we can't use sedatives, we don't have many options.

"Over the last two years the periods of lucidity have been growing shorter and shorter in duration, with greater intervals in between of mania, depression, psychosis, paranoid delusion, extraordinary physical strength—well, you know the list. She hasn't been truly clearheaded in well over three months.

"And, frankly, Mr. Allen," he says, cringing, like he's afraid I'm gonna snap off his arms and beat him with em—which I might still do, "we'd been fearing that her most recent descent might be the last one—one from which she wouldn't return. But, but she's been calm and collected since she woke this morning.

"And she's been asking for you."

It's like my legs are made of pudding. I hafta brace myself

against the wall. The little ass-toad jumps outta the way, like if I fall, I'll mush him. Some doctor. What'd I hear Digaestus calling the doctors who usedta treat him? Hippocratic oafs?

Asking for me?

"I have to warn you, though, Mr. Allen: her physical condition hasn't improved. She's in a better state of mind, yes, but . . . that doesn't affect her prognosis, I'm afraid. Her . . . her appearance, Mr. Allen . . . even since Sunday—" He sighs, fiddles with his chart, like something there is sposta excuse him breakin the news, or'll stop me from breakin his back. "Well . . . I just want you to be prepared."

When I'm steady, the doc shows me in.

Almost blinded when I walk in. Sunlight's streaming in through the ice-block windows I had installed. And I had nice colors painted in here, too. None of that muted crap like everywhere else. How you sposta get better when nuthin around you has any life in it?

I had this room muraled up like a garden, with animal and nature sounds playing on the sound system. I wonder if these ass-chokes turn it off when I aint here? If only I could ask her. But whatever she'd tell me . . .

My eyes adjust.

She aint got the straps on.

First time in a year and a half I seen her like this.

And she's . . . she's *smilin* at me.

That gentle, beautiful, sweet smile, like a sunrise, like dew, like raspberries picked off the bush. So innocent, like nuthin else has happened, like this's all been a dream an I'm the prince what woke her up with a kiss.

I tell the four guards and the doc to get the fuck out.

I sit down next to her. She sits up weakly.

The doc was right. Her hair's—what's left of it—it's completely white. And it's falling out, in patches. I can see right through to her fuckin scalp in places.

And the skin. Looks like scales.

Her forearms, her arms . . . they're like chicken boiled

down to tendons and bones. Ropy lines stick outta her throat, worse than ever before. And there's more lesions. And those . . . those growths or boils or whatever . . . now they're *all over* her chest, where her gown's open.

They look like sleepin fuckin eyes. Like if I talk too loud, they'll wake up, snap open and stare at me.

Accuse me.

It's all I can do to not scream, to not just put her outta her misery and then go and finish off everyone who's seen her like this, just to protect her memory, and then eat my own gun.

She was so pretty. Seems like a billion years ago, but she was.

And when she smiles at me, even with her skull teeth and her sunken eyes, I still see summa that.

With every ounce of strength I got, I hang on to that to keep me from bawling, so I don't scare her to death. So I don't face this thing for what it is and hafta kill myself.

And that's when she touches my cheek.

Her fingers feel like breadsticks, but my brain connects it back to what it usedta feel like, so long ago, so clear. When there was all the softness and compassion and lightness in those fingers on my cheek, when her touch was like rain on cropsoil, like a goose's belly warm on top of her nested eggs.

When I feel this touch it's almost like none of this war ever happened. Like if I could just close my eyes and keep em shut and breathe this in and never exhale, we'd be back to like it was before, forever, and we—

"Dulles, sweetie," she croaks, and my eyes pounce open before I can stop em.

This is the first time in eight months she's said my name in my presence.

I blink away my tears, and she's haloed in my wet eyes and the sunlight.

"You came," she rasps. And that smile. Like a rainbow.

"Course I came. I always come. I told the doctors, no matter what, any change, call me—I'll drop everything, be right there."

"I was . . . asking for you."

"I know." I smile. "And taa-daa—you got me."

She smiles softly, lies quietly again. I can see how much it's takin outta her to talk. "Don't exhaust yourself—I can stay here as long as you need. Forever, if I gotta."

She smiles again at that, while the machines beep away, and all her tubes shift with her every time she breathes or moves. I always hate seeing her in this getup, like she's a fly caught in a spiderweb, waiting for the widow to close in, suck the life outta her until she's nuthin but a shell.

But right now, with her all calm and soft and herself again . . . with the sunlight shimmerin in through the ice block and the garden mural glowin around us and the piped-in bird and honeybee and cricket orchestra chirpin and buzzin and hummin . . . even the tubes and the liquids inside em are glinting with the light, and for just a second it aint like she's *caught* in a web—it's like she's some kinda spider goddess, dark and beautiful with her royal robes made of beamin sun-silk she spun herself.

And then all of a sudden the glow from the glass wall fades, like a cloud's choked us out on the other side, and her smile shrivels into a dead flower.

No, please—just a few more minutes—long enough for me to tell her—maybe if she knows we still have a chance, her morale could—

I gotta struggle—keep her with me in the here and now, not in that icy hell she sinks into—

"Babe . . . I'm closin in on suh'm major. My boys are putting their all into this. We're so goddam close. . . . We're maybe twenty-four hours away from the big one. The real deal. Then . . . you'll be good again." I swallow. "*We'll* be good. Together, back at the house. Healthy." I snort a big breath in through my nostrils, cobble up the biggest smile I can. "You can work in the garden again! Outside, for real!"

She's still fading—her eyes have gone all far away, like giant black pearls sinking to the bottom of the ocean—

"I . . . used to be," she says, her voice all husky and cracked, "so pretty . . . but now—"

"Ah, jeez, honey . . . you're still gorgeous. You'll *always* be gorgeous—"

"Dully, who'd you say . . . I looked like?"

"What're you talkin about, babe?"

"When we were first introduced. You . . . told me . . . that later on . . . you'd told Heinz—"

I wince hard enough to bleed—to hear *her* say *his* name—

"—that I looked like . . . some actress. Who . . . was it, again?"

I try to remember back a billion years ago. I got a face in mind, I think, but I can't remember the name. They did look alike, but my wife's much prettier. But they got the same dark loose curly hair, the same kinda beautiful coffee skin, same eyes like sunrise.

"Uh, that broad from that singin movie. You know . . . the school-of-the-arts one?"

"Oh, *Fame*? Irene . . . *Cara*." She's smiling again—right on the money. " '*I'm gonna live forever . . . ,*' " she sings, but it squeaks out wrong like a kid fooling around on a clarinet. Outta her line of sight I hafta grab and twist the flesh of my leg, just so the pain can keep me too focused to cry.

But I can't stop myself, and I lean into her, put my head on her chest that's become a tin birdcage with a fluttering canary heart inside, trying not to crush her to death. She's twenty-five, got the body of an eighty-year-old. And to think that I . . . that I—

"I'm sorry, babe. . . . I'm . . . so, so sorry!"

She strokes my face again with that miracle touch, like that woman Wealtheow, the peacemaker, King Hrothgar's war wife. She could make a whole room full of berserker bone-brains shut the hell up with a single word.

But she couldn't stop a monster from comin into her family's life, could she?

Dulles, you ass-bastard, how far've you gone to get what

you wanted, huh, and where'd it get you? How much total fuckin misery did you cause this woman? That she would be better off if you'd never laid eyes on her?

Fuck—why'd I ever get involved with that ass-shank? Why didn'I find out *how* he could surefire guarantee he could deliver her? Why didn'I find out what'd be the long term of his methods?

Why'd I ever let him get her turned on to this fuckin cream?

"Dully, darling . . . it'll be okay," she hushes me, with my face pressed against her cardboard ribs. "Your men'll . . . find the cure, like you said . . . and everything'll be fine. I'll get out of here . . . and we'll raise a family, sweetheart. Have babies. Grow old together."

And I fuckin hate myself more every time she strokes my face and talks so nice to me, hate myself cuz I know that when I sob out loud how sorry I am, that she thinks I mean I'm sorry she's sick, not that I'm sorry that I'm the one who killed her.

And I can never tell her. Never. And I gotta carry what I done with me for the rest of my life.

"Dulles, sh . . . sh. . . . It'll all be over soon, darling."

"I swear, babe—in two days, I'm coming back here with your cure, and we're gonna walk outta here forever, together. You hear me, Rachael? *Forever.*"

The Badlands

Look over yonder! Hot sun turning over . . .
And it won't go down, Lord, Lord, Lord!
Did you ever hear cuckoo bird a-calling?
Sure sign of rain . . .
I've been a-wondering, yes, if anybody wondered . . .
About poor old me, Lord, Lord, Lord . . .
—African American spiritual

DRUMHELLER. LITTLE'S OLD, AND EVEN LESS IS NEW. BUT NOW
we're past the Drum, out in the pure badlands. Hell of a place.
Like a giant took a dagger and stabbed it into the earth,
dragged it in a long and winding gash, and the scar just never
healed—instead became red, ragged, and jagged.

Up above the canyon, it's all green-and-yellow scrub, almost no trees. You can see clear into Saskatchewan and Montana. Down in the valley it's purple sage and, when the purple
sage gives out, low cacti covering ground crawling with scorpions, spiders, rattlers.

And when the cacti give out, then it's nothing but dust and

sand and hoodoos—man-sized minibuttes, look sorta like rock men missing their arms, or like Lot's wife turned into sandstone instead of salt. If so, that'd explain what happened to Sodom and Gomorrah's taxpayers. They're all here, in these hoodoos . . . thousands and thousands and thousands of em, frozen forever.

Somewhere in this part of the province there's a place called Head-Smashed-in-Buffalo Jump. No kidding. Names you've known your whole life—they creep up on you at a time like this.

Ye's been pelting me with questions since sunrise. He mostly slept on the way down here, off and on, but ever since he woke up completely he's been giving me his full-out Skeptitron attack. I'm having a hard time keeping my cover story from blowing off.

It's hot and dry, late afternoon. We've been in the car since four A.M., got to the badlands around eight and been driving around here slowly ever since, me trying to get a taste for where we're sposta stop. And now we're exhausted and thirsty and hungry.

We stop at the edge of the canyon, break out the food and drink. Ye eats ice-cream sandwiches (that freakin guy— always with the sandwiches!) he's kept frozen in his patent-pending CoolMeal box, and I eat from the provisions kit Sherem gave me . . . dates, figs, apricots, and something that must be lamb jerky. Everything has a whisper of cinnamon to it.

And the iced tea . . . oh . . . underneath this furnace sun, I can feel every millisecond of caress from the frosted tea in my mouth, sliding around my tongue until my teeth clink like ice cubes . . . down my throat and falling into my gut like water trickling into an echoing underground cave. These moments of relief beneath the sun.

And before what's going to come.

I close my eyes.

All I knew before we left was that this was the general

place. But since we got here . . . I don't know if maybe constantly moving is what was throwing me off, or maybe it's
being inside a machine or something? I don'know. Something's been interfering with my Coyote sense.

But sitting here in the dust with my eyes shut . . .

My eyelid flesh glows red when I turn my closed eyes to the
sun.

But this time something's different.

Usually I get that quick shift into blue, like a blink, like
someone changed the channel. But now I'm getting a shimmering, like sheets of color or tides of hue are sloshing on top
of each other . . . hard orange in granules . . . packed yellow . . . silting gray . . . winding milky brown . . . sun-fired
red . . . then black . . . black . . . black . . .

. . . and then it's full of stars, stars in perfect rows, each
twinkling with five perfect points of light like tiny, lumines-
cent starfish . . . until, finally, the glowing blue. . . .

My eyes snap open.

My hands have dug deep into the dust, and when I pull
them out, I find a stone. No, not just a stone. It's a fossil. Of a
trilobite.

This whole place used to be under the sea.

I wonder what kind of creature will be pulling *my* bones
outta this badlands dust a hundred million years from now?
What'll *it* look like? And what kinda Thing will it be fighting
against for its life?

"There." I point across the canyon, down into the floor
about five kilometers away.

Ye pauses in midsandwich munch.

"Whuh?"

"That's where it is. Let's go."

Cars aren't allowed in here—this is a protected zone of a
provincial park . . . but between my Coyote sense and Ye's

detecto-gear, and a *whole* lotta waiting, we manage to steer clear of park rangers. But it costs us a few hours.

I check in the rearview. The Coyote Car's kicking up a horizontal tornado of badlands silt as we descend into the valley. No, not a tornado. We're a comet. Returning to the star.

Southern part of the province . . . sun goes down a lot earlier. All the sandstone down here's turned a deeper shade of red, baking into coals in the face of the sunset. Looks like freakin Mars.

We come to rest way past the sage, in the sand, among the hoodoos.

Dry cliff walls, scarred with ancient rain channels that taste water now maybe once a year. The skull of the prairies.

We get out, and a wind, a cool wind, plays with my kaffiyeh, flaps it around my face until I tuck it under. Ye's cape flutters. We're like gunfighters in the Old West, waiting for the shooting to start.

South, a couple of hundred meters away. There. The ground's too treacherous, so we'll hafta walk for sure. Ye trots to catch up.

We're at the base of the cliff wall, down where the ancient rain channels converge into the ground, these vertical gashes like ritual scarification on the face of a buried titan. But this cliff's damaged beyond the rain gouge.

The face of the cliff has a giant slit-crack at the base. There's empty darkness below visible even from here. This gash is far too harsh, too stark, to be old. There's no weathering, no curve to it, just the sharp edges of wounded rock without the time to heal.

The earthquake last week.

I was busting Ye's balls because we were so clued-out we'd barely even realized it'd happened, and Ye was the one saying to me that maybe someone'd find undiscovered fossils down in dinosaur country, or antiquities from ancient Cree. And I just scoffed at him.

"Let's get the stuff," I say.

Ye sniffs, doesn't say anything else. If he knew what I was thinking, his eyes would e-mail me an "I told you so." But if he knew what Sherem's revealed to me, he'd—

We walk back, pop open the trunk. Yehat has to unload his camera junk and R-Mer first for us to get at the excavation gear—ropes and picks and shovel and sledgehammer and flashlights and flares. We leave the R-Mer and everything else we brought on the ground, since it'll be easier to repack everything once we know how much space our prize is gonna take up, and then we put our tools into packsacks and head back.

At the slit-crack, Ye points a flashlight down into the darkness. We both look: there's a floor. It even looks smooth. Heads down at a forty-five-degree angle.

"This is a mighty strange coal shaft," says Ye. He doesn't use the words *Your story's full of shit, Hamza,* but with his tone, he doesn't need to.

"*Tell* me about it," I chuckle, I'm afraid too phonily.

He glares at me in my peripheral, like I was actually gonna give him the straight answer he deserves. Instead I take out my SWR phone.

"Sherem, come in. Come in, Sherem. This is Hamza. Over."

Burst of static. Then: "Hamza, I'm here. Over."

"We found the cave. Over."

Even with the tinny flatness of the SWR earpiece, there's no mistaking the excitement and fear in her voice.

"Good, Hamza! Just remember what I passed on to you. And whatever you do, *don't open the canopic jar*—"

"Don't worry, don't worry, Sherem. I understand. But how're you gonna find us down here? It's gonna be a hell of a time finding us at all, let alone with the darkness—"

"The *tchaua* I gave you, remember? I'm no desert hunter, but I can track that. Over."

"All right. We're proceeding into the cave. I'll contact you when we're back out. Over."

"I'll be there as fast as I can, Hamza," she says. "May the Glory guide you through the darkness, and stand between you and all the powers of Ãápep."

You know, it just occurs to me now—Sherem said she'd hook up with us by honing in on the *tchaua* she gave me—but isn't that how those freakin freaks found us when we were driving the other night? If she can track us down here, can't they?

Hell's freakin bells. I can't throw it away now—she'll never find us here without it and if the bad guys are on the way already, I've just gotta hope she gets here before they do.

Nothing like hope to doom you.

A cold wind blows through the canyon. There are clouds coming up where the moon should be. Clouds, out here in the most arid zone of the entire country.

I put on my jacket, pick up the shotgun, strap on the bandolier. Ye checks two gadgets strapped to his thighs that probably launch nuclear weapons.

The sun crashes into the cliff walls and dies as we walk back to descend to the cave of infinity.

Prelude to Slaughter

*All warfare is based on deception. . . . Hold out baits to
entice the enemy. Feign disorder, and crush him. . . .
If he is in superior strength, evade him. If your
opponent is of choleric temper, seek to irritate him.
Pretend to be weak, that he may grow arrogant. If he is
taking his ease, give him no rest. If his forces are
united, separate them. Attack him where he is
unprepared; appear where you are not expected.*
Sun Tzu, *The Art of War*, 1:18–24

" 'The *tchaua* I gave you, remember? I'm no desert hunter,
but I can track that. Over.' "

" 'All right. We're proceeding into the cave. I'll contact you
when we're back out. Over.' "

" 'I'll be there as fast as I can, Hamza. May the Glory guide
you through the darkness, and stand between you and all the
powers of Ããpep.' "

I practically leap outta my chair at the sound pourin outta

the speakers. All my lil ass-toads cringe like I'm gonna stomp em into paste, but I'm ecstatic.

"Great work, ya lil ass-monkeys!" I yell. Before I know what I'm doin I'm actually slappin em all on the backs an even givin em bear hugs around their necks. For once, for cryin out loud, for *once* things are actually goin my way.

And my boys, no question, they done good. Alpha Cat and the Moog slap hands. Zenko smiles like it was all his idea.

"All right, everybody, we are now at Def Con One. Caesar, what're ya getting?"

"She's, uh . . . she's definitely, uh . . . still in shadow. Definitely, certainly still in shadow, Master, uh, Allen."

"All right, all right. Shoulda expected this. You're sure, though—she aint just screwin witcha?"

"No, sir. I'm sure I would be able to . . . in my, uh, current state—"

"All right, all right. You keep your brain out. Even a blip, even a half a blip, you tell me, unnerstan?"

"Yes, sir."

"Can you show me on the map where she was talking to?"

"Yes, sir."

"And I," says that ass-crammer Meaney, "can guide us once we're within a few kilometers of the terrvix, using the zodiascope on the *lung-mei*. And if their forces are using countermeasures against the 'scope at close range, well, I can hone in on that *tchaua* once we're that close."

"ALL RIGHT, THEN!" I shout. "Okay . . . everybody— you're gonna stay here an wait for that broad to move outta hiding. When she does, you take er out. Me an ass-Meaney here're gonna head down now, get the jump on whoever she's working with an grab the score."

Alpha Cat pounces over to me, takes me aside, whispers. "Baat Mos Riychuss Mista Allen, suh—dese two bwaaays she wuk wit—dem nearly tek wi all out. Yu shud tek summa wi along fi yu proTEKshaan."

"Cat," I tell him quietly, "if it was anybody but you sayin it, I'd put a smack on em just for doubtin me. But I know where you're comin from. Don'worry. I got a few things even *you* don'know about. Plus Meaney . . . he might be a piece a shit with eyes and a slick suit, but in a fight, lemme tell you—"

"*Daat's* whut mi MEAN, suh."

I can feel my eyebrows sliding my forehead almost off my skull. I'm so set on this thing I'm ignoring the obvious. The Cat's right.

"Okay, I hear ya. I'll watch my back. I got a few things *he* doesn'know about, either. You just get this broad, okay? Can ya do that for me?"

"Yes, suh!"

I put a hand on the side of his neck, give him a gentle squeeze. "Cat, we make this score, I'm getting outta this whole racket. It's yours, y'unnerstan me? I'll induct you into the final degree, an then it's *all* yours."

He breathes in deep, an his eyes glisten at the rims of the bottom lids. "Mi tenk yu, suh," he whispers, sniffling, "baat . . . Mista SuPREME Baas, suh . . . mi nah WOOTHY."

"Fuck 'worthy,' Cat. It's yours." I pat him, let him go. "Call me when you're finished."

I go to my safe, get out a pewter box the size of an old-fashioned pistol case, open it up on my desk, unwrap the Sif scarf from the contents.

Hard to believe that even four years ago I didn't know things like these existed. That back then, I couldn't read the angled scratches in each one's surface. I musta been like a caveman shivering in the cold, holding a flamethrower, wondering if it was something I could eat.

I slip one of the two fist-sized Lokistones in my pocket, palm the other one to Digaestus while he's showing me the map.

"You won't know how until you're in the moment, Caesar," I whisper, "but if things go bad with the Jackal . . . use this."

He locks eyes with me. "Yes, Master."

"Okay, ass-pukes," I say in my best Churchill-whipping-up-the-troops, "this is not a drill. We got one shot only. No matter what happens tonight, nuthin's gonna be the same ever again."

The Descent

THE CRACK IN THE CLIFF WALL IS JUST BIG ENOUGH FOR A MAN to put his shoulders through without turning. Hamza adjusts his pack, slings my Ye-gun over his shoulder, turns his flashlight on, aims it down.

He's been lying to me since he woke me up at three forty-five A.M. Abandoned coal mine and hundred-year-old buried heist, my ass. There was never any coal mining in this part of the badlands. Only reason I'm here is to keep Hamza from getting killed thanks to whatever lies this Sherem nutcase fed him. And he was gonna go no matter what I said, so here I am.

But I am left wondering what really *is* going on.

We both slide through.

I train my own flashlight down the shaft. The floor slopes down at a forty-five-degree angle. And it is a shaft: the walls are smooth—the ceiling is smooth. Whoever dug this thing out spent a lot of time and did it with real expertise. But why the hell would anyone do this in the badlands? If you wanted to hide something, why go to all this trouble?

Walking down this is tough. We both have to brace ourselves against the walls to avoid slipping. The air's dead. This place's been sealed for a long time, no question. Dry, dry, dry. Can't even smell mildew or soil.

And these walls—they're not just carved out, they seem to be finished in something—plaster? Why the hell? Was this some visionary homesteader's attempt to make some sorta H. G. Wells underground quarter section?

All this heavy gear on this dusty slope—I slip—Hamza catches me, braces us both. When we're steady again, we keep on going.

Down, down, down . . . hell, we must've gone forty meters, which means we've dropped twenty-eight. This is stunning. Why the hell would anyone build this? Why would anyone go to such lengths? And depths?

And now we're at a barrier?

And it's covered in red writing?

At first I think the low light is playing tricks with my eyes, but then I train the flash beam directly on the wall.

"Hamza, what the hell's going on? Why is there Arabic written down here? Is this some kinda underground Taj Mahal or something? Or a Lebanese survivalist enclave?"

"That's not Arabic, Ye," he mutters, distracted, like he's trying to read it. "It's older. Ancient. It's called *hieratic*."

"Oh yeah, Captain Genius? So what's it say?"

He strains his eyes, plucks meanings out of the red splashings. " 'Not . . . shalt thou . . . tread upon me . . . saith the floor of hall this . . . except . . . thou . . . sayest my name.' "

This is too weird. Is he shitting me?

"Since when do you read ancient languages?"

He doesn't say anything.

Okay, I'm now aware of a progression of states within me:

1. calm, clear-thinking concern for the jimp under my protection

2. anxious concern over possible intervention by Sherem's rivals in the drug trade or

  international jewel thievery or chemical-
  weapons market
 3. distinct uneasiness over an increasing collection of data that makes no sense together, viz., the nature of workmanship
  on this shaft, the ancient writing, and
  Hamza's ability to read thereof

Hamza looks frozen. I'd better say something.

"So, what're we gonna do, Indi?"

"Well, we hafta answer its question."

"What? Answer whose question?"

"The next hallway's. Speak its name before we can walk upon it."

"Or what?"

"Or I don'know." He waits. "But probably something bad."

"Great." This is all getting too spooky for me. "Like, spears'll shoot outta the walls and a boulder'll crush us?"

"Oh, no, Ye. I don'think we'll get off that easy."

"So what's the answer, tough guy?"

He closes his eyes, breathes in deeply . . . exhales slowly. Opens his eyes again. *"Nuk Ur, se Ur . . . Nesert, Senesert."*

We hear rumbling—is this shaft gonna cave in?

"Hamza, you shit-hog, I want you to tell me what's going on."

He ignores me, the ultrajimp, but takes off his pack, un-straps the sledgehammer, hands me his flashlight, and then plows right into the wall.

"Hamza, you fuckin idiot! You wanna get us killed? You could make this whole thing cave in an crush us!"

He puts the hammer into the wall again before I can stop him. Dust rains on me. There's a big crack in the wall. "Hamza, stop it!"

And then his hammer breaks through and his unexpected forward momentum carries him with it—the whole wall crumbles and falls almost straight down, and Hamza nearly goes with it.

"HAMZA!"

I grab him at the last second before he pitches into the blackness completely.

By the time we've finally defibrillated and stopped gasping, I practically squeeze Hamza's shoulders off to get a straight answer. *"What the hell is going on here?"*

"What's going on here is I'm going down there."

"Down there? How?"

"The rope."

"What're we sposta anchor it to, spelunkotron? Or did you not notice how smooth this shaft is?"

It's like the spell breaks—for a second. He picks up his flashlight, aims it down into the abyss. "Look!"

Below, we can see the debris from the collapsed wall. It's only a couple of meters down. We can jump. Assuming *that* floor or the ceiling above doesn't give way. "Look, we'll move some of the rubble once we're down there to make a ramp, okay, Ye?"

Shit. Why the hell'd I hafta come along? Couldn't I've just sent flowers to his funeral? I'm too young to become the late Yehat.

I pop out a flare, ignite it, toss it down there.

We jump down gently, one at a time, and before the flare runs out we've made the ramp Hamza suggested. I sweep this new place with my flashlight—it's just a featureless box. A dead end.

Hamza catches my expression before I can say anything, then points to a tiny opening I missed, about three-quarters of a meter high set in the wall.

"Oh, hell . . . you're not serious?"

He moves straight towards it, takes off his pack, keeps the gun, gets on his hands and knees, starts crawling with his flashlight ahead of him like a light saber.

I follow him, of course, like the magna-jimp I am.

It's pretty damn claustrophobic in here. At least it's not hot. But the air is so dry and dead it's all I can do to breathe. I stop, reach into my utility belt, pop a Life Savers into my mouth, hoping it's not my last meal.

We've gone around twenty meters. When Hamza gets to the end, he crawls into the next chamber, and the light dies. He must be aiming it somewhere else. He calls my name, panic in his voice. So now I'm in total darkness, crawling for all I'm worth and needing new underwear, fast.

When I get out, I realize Hamza's flashlight isn't pointed elsewhere, it's just dead. I take out my own flashlight, click it.

Nothing.

"Hamza," I say slowly, so as not to scream, "this is too much of a coincidence."

Our eyes start to adjust. But that should be impossible—adjust to what? We're in a completely sealed underground chamber. Unless we're now in a cave open to the night sky—but then we'd see the hole in the roof.

And then I notice how the walls are glowing.

It's so faint I can't even focus my eyes, but there it is—not an eye phantom, but a definite glow.

"Hamza, you see that?"

"Yeah, Ye! What is it, some sorta fluorescent mold or something?"

I try to work up some bluster in order to calm myself. "Well, unless this place isn't sealed at the other end, I don't see how anything, even mold, could be growing down here. Just breathe in. Even *mold* needs moisture. It's drier than camel pussy down here.

"Plus I get the feeling that this place's been sealed a long time . . . longer than that bullshit story you've been feeding me."

To this, he says nothing. Although he does ask, "Okay, Spock, so why *are* the walls glowing, then?"

I clear my throat. "Unknown, Captain."

"You have any more flares, Ye?"

Man, I *am* rattled. That's the first thing I should've thought of.

"Yeah, course I got more flares. I just wannid to investigate this glow while our pupils were at maximum dilation."

"Uhn-huhn."

I snap open another flare.

We're not in a cave, no. We're in a rectangular room, I'd say about four by six meters, about two and a half meters tall.

And the walls are covered with ancient Egyptian hiero-glyphics.

The Terrestrial Womb

I'M HOLDING THE FLARE LIKE AN AMULET IN FRONT OF ME, TO ward off what, I'm not sure. Credulity? Insanity?

"Hell, Hamz, what is this? Some kinda . . . abandoned movie set or something? Or a cult's . . . I dunno . . . secret . . . like . . . bunker or something? For doomsday?"

He's right beside me, not saying anything, looking all over the walls like he's reading these words, too.

Whoever built this, well . . . this is pretty amazing, for sure. I'm no Egyptologist, but yeah, this place looks pretty authentic. The ceiling—oh, man—it's a painting of a goddess or something, stretching across the entire "sky" of the room. . . . She's swallowing the sun . . . but then giving birth to it at the other end—

"Hamza, look at this!"

But he's magnetized on the wall script and doesn't even bother with the ceiling. It's got pictures, too, full-sized ones, not just the glyphs . . . vignettes surrounded by text.

But this is the weirdest thing I've ever seen. . . . Instead of the animals you'd expect to find in Egypt, all the images show animals like beavers, mooses, grizzlies, ptarmigans . . . and . . . hell . . . *coyotes*. All drawn in that crazy Egyptian-style flat profile.

All animals you'd find right here in Alberta, and nowhere near Egypt.

This is the most amazing and idiosyncratic forgery I've ever seen. I'd love to meet whoever built this place.

The walls are like a giant comic book, a story I can figure out at least partly with just the vignettes: Black folks—Egyptians, I guess—wearing important clothing and getting into boats . . . a long journey over the seas? . . . Then a long, long walk through forests and over flat spaces . . . hiding from lighter brown men with straight hair . . . and are those people sposta be Mohawks? . . . And then . . . I think this is sposta be the badlands.

The flare dies.

I scramble, light another one. We've got only one left after this.

Hamza grabs my arm, points to the far end of the room.

Oh, shit . . . how could I not have seen this to begin with?

There's a small doorway at the far end.

We crouch down, scramble through, stand up into a small room, and I nearly scream when I see what's waiting for us.

Two giant black jackals.

Statues, that is, with golden eyes and claws.

Guarding the doorway into what I'm guessing is the final chamber.

And when we're inside there, oh, man . . . the ceiling is pointed, two huge panels at an acute angle reaching heavenward into each other, covered with row upon row upon row of five-pointed stars, each star looking like a starfish. Like the night sky is the sea, or vice versa.

But there's no mistaking what's at the end of the room.

A statue of a *black* Black man seated in a throne, eye whites and fingernails made of gold, holding a shepherd's crook in one hand and a wheat flail in the other, a tall crown on his head shaped like a smooth ear of corn, and feathers and wheat forming a shield growing out of his back.

I know who this is sposta be.

Osiris.

I realize I've been holding my breath since we got in here. I let it out. I don't know what all this is for, but my usual instinct to joke or analyze seems shut off. I never bought into that church stuff, even when I was a kid, but right now, whatever kind of cult HQ or hoax this place is, I feel what church people must feel when they enter the sanctum sanctorum— what I'd feel if I visited a superaccelerator, or stepped on board Mir.

Hamza walks over to the statue and kneels.

In the lap of the statue is a box.

He whispers . . . something that sounds like *"Dãtunyi khu, oos emmaãkheru."*

"What? Hamza, what're you saying?"

Still kneeling, he takes the box off the statue's lap, opens it, removes a spectacular turquoise-and-golden jar.

I'm completely caught up in this. Before I can stop myself, I ask him, "Hamz, how old is that thing?"

He looks it over, holding it like he was holding somebody else's baby, and clears his throat. "I'd say . . . about seven thousand years."

I shake my head.

I'm getting sucked down into something illogical, and that means we're in danger. "That's impossible, Hamz," I try. "For a whole buncha reasons I'll be happy to detail as soon as we get outta here. Look, you found this . . . this whatever it is. Just grab what's inside it and let's go."

"This jar alone is priceless, Ye!"

"Yeah, some hoax jar is priceless. Whatever. Let's go, before this whole place crumbles in and we die down here."

He doesn't say anything, but cradles the jar like he was transporting transplant organs, sets it down. He takes off his kaffiyeh, wraps his prize up in it.

"Let's get out of here, Ye."

"What'd I just *say*, Hamza?" I try not to let all my panic and unexplainable terror soak into my voice, but whoever went to the trouble to make this place, whatever freakazoids or cultists or people planning to earn a hundred million dollars from a hoax to set up Geraldo or whatever—they're gonna be mighty pissed to find two Brothers in here playing grave robber.

The flare dies.

I light the last one, and we get the hell out, crawling and more crawling, until the last flare goes and we hafta feel our way through the rubble room and hoist ourselves into the angled shaft, jar and all.

It's not the shaft that's going to crumble, but in about ten minutes, my entire world.

The Elegant Application of Death

UPON ALPHA CAT'S ORDERS, WE SCRAMBLED THE ENTIRE TEAM into the FanVan and took to the streets, Mr. Zenko behind the wheel, me at his side to navigate towards our feminine foe, Mr. Alpha Cat issuing commands and clarifying battle strategy behind us, Mr. the Mugatu sharpening the spearhead of his staff with a stone he found, and Messrs. Vegi-Might, Adolf Benito, Human Torque, and Captain Crunch all readying their various weapons.

We moved to the center of the city so as to be equidistant to any point from which our prey might emerge, when she emerges.

She has emerged.

Mr. Zenko crushes the accelerator against the floor of the cabin, and we hurtle towards the location I call out, in Highlands.

I fondle in my pocket the stone that the Master has given me. I tasted his thoughts as he granted me this blessing—a Lokistone, he thought it.

It's cold, far colder than ambient temperature, like a fist made of ice. And covered in runes.

We're closing in—passing directly beside the stadium, heading for the LRT tracks.

"That's her!" I cry out, pointing towards an oncoming vintage automobile, circa 1955—

Mr. Zenko cranks the wheel hard to the left and we smash headlong into her.

Everyone in the compartment behind us crashes about, and my own neck snaps back agonizingly upon impact. But we don't stop.

The mass and momentum of the FanVan and its crew easily overcomes that of even a 1950s-era steel chariot, and we plow her forward over the LRT tracks, until her car rolls down the tracks' embankment.

We jump out of the FanVan, its lights trained upon the dead woman's vehicle, overturned like the carcass of some Ice Age monstrosity brought low by brave Cro-Magnons and their spears.

And then we see a shadow slip from the far side of the vehicle, ascend to the middle of the tracks.

Mr. Zenko immediately aims his pistol, then staggers, waving his chrome-plated skull opener as if he is overcome with vertigo.

"Zenko, she av proteckSHAAN gains misSILE atTAAK, rimemmBA?"

Mr. Zenko puts away his gun, regains his balance, takes out a hammer and a hunting knife.

"Betta," says Mr. Cat, whistling two short, sharp tweets. Our team vaults through the dusk, surrounds her.

"Mugatu," calls our squad leader, "she's yohze."

The Mugatu grips his spear in two hands, runs straight at her as if he were holding a battering ram. Despite his bulk he is astonishingly fast, like a grizzly.

And then the impossible happens.

She sidesteps him at the last moment, trips him, and snatches the spear from his hands as he hits the tracks face first. Before his minute brain can reassess his situation, his leg muscles have already launched him forward to fall upon and crush her. But she has braced the butt of his spear against a rail tie, and the Mugatu rams himself down upon it with such force that it emerges from his back.

And then the spear snaps, and our largest FanBoy hits the long metal line of the track, his head drawing forth a ring from the rail as if his last mortal deed had been to toll his own bell.

The mighty Mugatu, without even so much as a death grunt soliloquy, is no more.

She stands up, not even panting, surveying us surrounding her.

Alpha Cat is clearly unsettled by this development, and he stands in what I take to be a mixture of regret for the loss of our comrade and indecision over how to proceed.

And then, "Cap'm Crunch . . . Vegi-MIYYT . . . move in."

Vegi-Might activates his battery-backpack-powered hand-mounted slicing weapons. Fascinating—rather than a high-pitched whine, they emit a sound like a didgeridoo.

That should not be possible, but this appears to be the night of the impossible. And the Captain—he is snapping his equine jaws open and shut with a sound like the moment that a rack of snooker balls is broken with the first strike.

Having seen how she sidestepped the Mugatu, I'm sure Alpha Cat chose them for the next wave since they are on opposite sides of the circle.

They run at her.

Captain Crunch jumps with his open mouth headed straight at her neck. She flinches away, leaving him to snap off one of her thick braids, and in my heightened perceptual state, perhaps I am subject to hallucination as well, for while I observe the combat, I also clearly observe the severed braid writhing upon the ground like a half snake that doesn't know it's dead.

But I am too distracted for my own and my own team's good. It appears this Jackal woman has managed to ram one of Vegi-Might's juicers into Captain Crunch's face. Teeth—an astonishingly nonhuman number of them—ricochet off the blades towards us at the periphery of the now ragged circle. And Vegi-Might, apparently incapacitated by his unwitting paring of our ranks, is immobilized long enough for her to side-kick him down the slope and jump after him, the arc of which terminates with her left bootheel on his neck.

His juicers continue to make their didgeridoo noise, shooting the occasional clump of gravel or flock of pebbles skittering across the ground.

The remaining crew position themselves for weaknesses, openings—or in Mr. Benito's case, a clear shot with his swastikular boomerangs. I hope the Master's theory bears out that the boomerangs' curvilinear flight paths will evade the Jackal's protection against missile attack.

The Human Torque is next, leaping towards her, spinning and carouselling and somersaulting—his feet hit her full in the chest, and she is blasted backward. He runs straight at where she's fallen, and she staggers up on the uneven pebbled slope, tries to punch him, but the Torque intercepts her arm with inhuman speed, forces it backward to an angle it cannot accept, and the woman's entire body spins against its will, heels over head, and she crashes into the ground.

I feel very confident that this young man will make a fine replacement for Mr. Frosty Gorkovski. Hopefully he will also treat me with the respect of which my enormous abilities are so obviously deserving.

The Torque reaches down to administer his coup de grâce, his legendary one-armed neck snap.

She spits into his face, and he staggers backward screaming.

What on earth?

And now she's standing, her fingers plunging towards her belt, then streaking upward. She spins towards the still-staggering Human Torque, and when her whipping fingers rotate towards his neck, even in the darkness beneath distant streetlights, the plumes of blood—geysers, more accurately—from the Torque's throat are obvious.

He moves one of his hands from his eyes, which seemed to be the source of his agony a moment ago, to clutch his throat, but blood gushes out despite his efforts.

She front-kicks him in the solar plexus and he drops, and she dances over him, raking him with her fingers again.

When she lands, I can see two things clearly: one, that she is bleeding from her head, perhaps due to the initial impact of our FanVan, and two, that each of her eight fingers is encased in a metallic cover, like a long thimble, and from each radiates a ten-centimeter blade. The gesture to her belt—I understand now. Arming herself. With her Jackal claws.

We began combat less than five minutes ago, including the time it took to ram this woman's vehicle and roll her in it like a log down a hill. In that interval, the Mugatu, Captain Crunch, Vegi-Might, and the Human Torque have joined the ranks of Custer's men.

Adolf shrieks out, "*Sieg Heil!*" and launches the first of his two boomerangs at her. He slices off two more of her braids. Then he fires his second swastika.

And with a clang, *she catches it*.

The surviving FanBoys, including myself and Mr. Benito, are so shocked by this turn that we are all frozen. This is particularly unfortunate for Mr. Benito, since when the rest of us turn to see what he will do next, we bear witness to the first metal swastika he threw resting firmly inside our fast-fobbing fascist friend's forehead.

All our candidate apprentices are now dead.

I run at this woman from behind, press the Lokistone into her back—and she screams a sound like a horse might make while being pulled apart by chains, and crumples forward. Her cloak ignites, and she rolls around to try to snuff the flames before she shakes her way out of it—

And I become aware that the entire world is upside-down, my feet and legs rotating towards the stars, and my head exploding into brilliant pinpricks of light. I land with enough force to vacate my lungs of air.

I try to make out what is happening—

Messrs. Cat and Zenko are now in simultaneous attack against her, the former with his machete, and the latter with his hammer and dagger. I can make out only a swirl of near misses and contact and grunting and swearing and screaming and tearing of cloth. I roll out of the way, amble up, and run. I am not a soldier—I'm an *explorer*.

I run for the FanVan.

Only when I am locked inside do I turn back to regard the melee.

From a distance, with my life in less jeopardy, I bring my full sensory cognition to bear, enough to feel the TNT impact of her foot into Mr. Zenko's abdomen and his hyperventilation as his diaphragm spasms—a deliriously frightening evacuation of air I experienced directly only a moment ago myself.

Mr. Cat kicks her heavily in the groin and she collapses, and he brings his machete down straight at her skull.

Two things happen next that, were it not for my hyperception, I would either not detect or not believe. She yells out words that sound like "*Khepernyi smu*," and then, when she raises her arms against the onrushing machete in a vain attempt to block her neck and face, the machete stops.

The blade does not sever her arms or sunder her head. It stops with a distinct *clang*—the same clang I heard a few minutes before when she caught the late Mr. Benito's boomerang.

And then she shoves her flattened, shining hands into Mr. Cat's face. He screams out, "RAAS CLAAT!" and hits the gound.

She is no longer wearing her claws, apparently, but in light of Mr. Cat's massive cranial bleeding, that seems difficult to accept. But her hands—shining like chrome—

Mr. Zenko tackles her from behind, and they roll over top each other. He is clutching her from behind, his arms and legs wrapped around her in a hold I'm sure would have made the Human Torque proud. And now—good heavens, the train is coming!

I scream, foolishly, impotently, "Mr. Zenko—look out!"

But he can't hear me, of course, and apparently the driver can't see them or the Jackal's vehicle in the ditch, and therefore doesn't slow down while the last two moving combatants struggle on the rail ties, walled in by the rails.

And then the Jackal manages to spin her torso and her head just enough, and I live Mr. Zenko hearing her whisper, "*Geryi shemmetem iar*" as she expectorates onto the side of his head, just as she did to Mr. Human Torque a few FanBoys ago. And as Mr. Torque did, so too does Mr. Zenko scream.

But unlike before, this time I myself experience the burning agony of his face smokingly ripping itself apart molecule by molecule beneath satanic saliva.

She breaks his hold completely, rolls off the track—and then the train fills the panoramic windshield view of the Fan-Van.

Mr. Zenko must surely have been turned into pemmican by our fair city's mass transit.

Oh, no—she's running towards the FanVan—her own vehicle destroyed—but I locked the doors—

Her hand crashes through the driver's-side window. I hide myself beneath a tarp. But she doesn't have the keys—they would've been crushed along with Mr. Zenko—

That's the engine—why am I surprised?

Wait—I can still live one more of us, like a beacon burning in a dark forest: Mr. Zenko—he's alive! On the other side of the tracks! He rolled out of the way in time! He's standing, Mr. Cat's machete in hand, ready to launch his last, desperate, heroic, final—

The FanVan lurches forward and bumps up, then down.

Oh, no.

Save for myself, my clan is extinct.

I am the last FanBoy.

I have no choice. I know what I must do.

I must take the Lokistone and press it against the back of her skull. But I shall have only one chance. I have less than two meters to cross, but I must do so silently. One creak and she will certainly disassemble my brains.

I must avenge my comrades. Complete our mission. Protect the Master.

I am terrified into complete immobility.

We drive . . . for I am not sure how long. My hyperception is currently able to receive only the unique depths and intensities of my terror itself. Therefore I can no more plumb the mind and emotions of this ministress of murder than I can read the inscriptions upon the rings of Saturn.

I need only scramble up and throw myself at her back while she pilots this vehicle, press the Lokistone against her neck. And watch while her head bursts like an overripe melon hitting pavement.

Yet when I have done so, will not this very vehicle crash? Might it perhaps catch aflame, leaving me trapped inside to burn to death?

The Master would be safe, but I would—

And then, as the words *The Master would be safe* echo and reecho and build and achieve the zenith of a crashing, smashing, orchestral crescendo in my brain, gravitizing my body against self-preservation to become a human missile against this Lilithian messenger of death—

I hear a gasping metallic *pop,* and the vehicle instantly begins to slow.

We must be out of gas.

I feel the vehicle change course slightly, then the speckle of gravel against the belly of this beast. We are in a ditch or on a shoulder—we must have been on the highway. When the vehicle stops, I hear her grab something metallic from the cabin, open the door, and run.

I throw off my tarp, glance out. In the headlight glare, I see her clutching her side, as close as her hand can get to where I touched her with the Lokistone.

I take it with me, run after her.

She's in a wheat field. I move as silently as I can to find her. This may be a trap. I clutch the stone in my fist. But now I hear her. She's *digging*—apparently she grabbed a shovel from the FanVan. I crouch at the edge of a wall of wheat, see the shallow trench—or a grave?—she has prepared, the mound of dirt next to it.

And she lies down in it, wincing when her back touches the ground, and begins to pull earth down upon herself.

What in the universe is she doing?

She whispers to herself, mutters to herself, sings to herself:

> *Imma sahi kheper sahqeb . . . imma redyi kheper redqeb . . . imma khatyi kheper khatqeb . . . imma āāuinyi kheper āāuiqeb. . . .*

And then she pours dirt over her face and somehow manages to pull her arms beneath the soil until she is completely covered.

This is either a primitive and futile and delirious attempt to hide or a trap to lure me towards her so that she can spring forth from the ground like a trapdoor spider to eviscerate me.

So I wait. Very soon she will have to come out for air. Either way, what a pathetic plan she has devised in her wounded-animal state!

I wait longer, stone ready.

I continue to wait.

And then the mound of earth above her crumbles. Not slipping away to reveal her—rather, the mound itself collapses.

I bolt towards her, stone before me like the head of a mace—

But clearly there is nothing there, even with the minimal illumination provided by cloud-obscured moon and stars.

This trench is empty.

She could not have escaped without my notice or without my hyperception—even with only five senses I would have heard and seen her get up!

I dig my hands through that ground, feel only the warmth of where her body *was*.

This, like so much I have beheld, is impossible.

Perhaps she has been recalled by Hel. But I fear I cannot be so lucky.

I pick up the shovel, walk back to the gasless FanVan.

There is nothing else I can do.

We have failed the Master, and now he is on his own.

Through a Glass Brightly

—STREAKING DOWN HIGHWAY 2 AT A SPEED THAT DURING THE onset of a fog even Dulles must see as reckless, but no, on this night, on this precipice, at the awe of this impending birth, I can voice no objections to him—yes, in this fog, our headlights can probe only a dozen meters ahead of us while we hurtle forward at over 200 kilometers an hour, and yet, there's a craving in me, a yearning in me, a burning in me, a thirsting in me, an unfurling in me, like wings straining to emerge from egg or from cocoon, wings soaking, sopping with natal moisture, and bursting with pent-up exultant raging joy to taste the air and bring the eye above the tops of mountains and commune with moons and stars, that at this proximity to the Jar if we hit an onrushing Mack truck, we'd be propelled through glass and steel and into air and transfigured by our mere closeness to the Jar into silent, shifting shadows like black auroras or dark-matter nebulae and cleave towards our fate, and now, at 240 kilometers an hour, my window electronically sliding down, I push myself up, UP and OUT, until the headlight-bright mists course over me like a comet's veil, and the roar of wind obliterates Dulles's howling furies while I bring my enhanced eye to the sacred zodiascopic astronomicon and draw its tubes into my mouth and breathe and salivate and secrete the substances of my new blood until the chambers of the 'scope fill with the internal reflections-refractions-rarefactions and yield their truth through fog, through darkness, through surly terrestrial bonds, the flaming dragonical cosmagnetic pathway ahead, ahead, ahead, ahead, ahead, AHEAD, TO THE THRONE, THE ZONE, THE CYCLONE OF SOULS, THE UTERUS OF INFINITY—

The Old, Old Dream

BY THE TIME YE AN ME ARE SQUEEZING OUTTA THE CAVE IT'S completely dark out, except for a moon haze caused by a fog that just no way belongs in the badlands. It only rains here once a year, and now all of a sudden there's fog? I don't like this one bit.

But I'm practically ecstatic compared to Ye.

"How come you didn't tell me what we were really coming after?"

No point in denying it anymore. "I didn't think you'd believe me. . . . I was dazed, I was . . . I don'know—"

"What in the hell happened last night? For *real*, this time!"

The Jar's really heavy, and with all the tension in my arms from trying to get through the passageways and up the forty-five-degree slope and then out here without dropping it, well—I gotta rest for a minute. I put the kaffiyeh-wrapped Jar down next to a hoodoo, sit down with it, my arm still around it for safekeeping.

Ye stands, glaring at me in the dark.

"Okay, Ye. All right. I went to Kevlar's last night."

"Kevlar *Meaney*?"

"You know any other Kevlars?"

"Move on."

". . . he tried to kill me."

"WHAT?"

"Dahmer-style."

Ye shakes his head like in a cartoon, like he could shoo away the tweety birds and whirling stars of confusion. "Kill you? Dahmer-style? You serious? Why?"

"Look, you're not gonna believe this, Ye, but him and Heinz, they were in some sorta cult, or actually *heading* it. Like Jonestown run by Hannibal Lecter. I found two women's bodies half chewed up in oil drums in Kev's bedroom."

Ye staggers back, like if he could step away from me, he could step away from what I'm telling him, too. "You're fuckin with me."

"No. I wish." I tell him what Kevlar asked about my finding ability, asked about Sherem, about his test for me, and what he did to me after I found his bedroom surprise.

And then I tell him everything else. From Sherem rescuing me, to what she revealed to me, and how.

"So that's everything, Ye—those freakin freaks attacking us in the car the other night, all her mysteriousness. . . ."

Ye's completely silent.

I pick up the Jar, stand up. Ye's still sayin nothin. I walk. He walks beside me.

"Ye," I finally say, "it's not *like* you to be this quiet. Look, I understand this is hard to believe, but with what you saw in this cave down there . . . c'mon, Vikings, Phoenicians, Chinese . . . people've been coming to the New World since, like, forever. Is it so hard to believe that Egyptians—"

He breaks the silence with a laugh ripped out of a psych ward. "Did the Vikings practice *magic,* Hamza?" He howls after his napalm sarcasm. "Did the Phoenicians do hocus-pocus? ARE WE LEVITATING YET?"

"Ye, calm down! I know it's—"

"Calm down? Calm *down?* You're saying that every rational, scientific thing in the world isn't worth two kumquats
because"—and he switches into the high, singsong, talking-
to-morons voice he uses whenever he wants someone to know
how stupid he thinks they are—"*a-a-all* the little *fairies* and
elves and *sphinxes* and *jimps* are eating Frosted Lucky Charms
and *yogically flying* with Doug Henning and NOSTRA-
*freakin-*DAMUS—"

"Ye, shut up a minute and quit freakin ravin! This's as hard
for me to believe as it is for you—"

"NOT LIKELY, HAMZA!"

And then we stop dead.

Ahead of us is the R-Mer, disassembled like we left it; our
cooler, half full of food and drink; the camera bag; and all our
other stuff, exactly where we dropped it all after we unloaded
the car.

In fact, only one thing is missing.

The car.

Naw, man, NAW, not NOW—

"This chick set us up, Hamza," Ye seethes quietly, viciously.
"She's got us to get whatever the hell this thing is from that
cave and she's abandonded us in the badlands in the middle of
summer.

"No one knows we're here, plus we're trespassing—in tomorrow's heat we're gonna fry, and the only things anyone's
gonna find are two dead Brothers covered in scorpions and
ants."

I whip out my flashlight, hoping to find something, *anything* to save us and shut Ye the hell up. It only occurs to me a
second after I've already snapped on the beam that down in
the cave, the light'd stopped working. But then again . . . that
probably wasn't cuz of the batteries.

And then I find something we *didn't* leave, orange and
round—run over to see it, pick it up.

Ye's not gonna like this.

"What is it, Hamza?"

I hold it up as he flicks on his own beam.

He's looking at a huge, ripe pumpkin with a bumper sticker half peeling off that reads THE COYOTE CAR.

Ye starts scatting. As in, scatologically. At a scream level.

And then he takes off his pack and starts getting into his freakin R-Mer!

"Ye, what the hell're you doin?"

"When in Rome, man, do like the barbarians!"

"Ye, c'mon, calm down—"

He's got his shoes off now and is sliding each of the leg units on, then stepping into his R-Mered boots. He takes out four seconds to look at me and says, "Ham, you tell me to calm down one more time an I'll smack your balls off!"

Snap, snap-snap—boots are in place and locked in, and now he's hefting the somatic unit over his head and wriggling into it. It looks like he's wearing a high-tech safe. Then the arms, the gloves, the underhelmet, and finally the head enclosure.

Even with everything that's happened in the last forty-eight hours, I'm still impressed at the sight. He's been building this thing for two years, but this's the first time I've seen him with the whole thing on. Straight outta Robotech or *The Transformers.*

He presses some buttons on his arms, and tiny lights flick on all over the shell, and then the thing hums and whines with a sound like a jet engine warming up. Headlights snap on and blind me.

And then he turns to walk away.

"Ye, where the hell're you going?"

His amplified voice hits me, echoes against all the hoodoos and cliff walls in this silent, fog-choked valley.

"This is all bullshit. Crazy jimp-broad steals our car an leaves us stranded out here or . . . or is this all some monu-freakin-mental practical joke you been savin up for *years,* Hamza?"

"Ye, man, this aint a joke—you gotta stay here, PLEASE—

we're safer TOGETHER, and those freaks who came after us in the car, they're probly on their way RIGHT NOW—"

"IT'S BULLSHIT!"

The cliff walls: *SHITBULL SHITBULL shitbull itbull* . . .

I'm so panicky now that I get thrown off for a second by what I see underneath the running lights on the back of his chest unit: a sticker that reads IF THIS VEHICLE IS BEING DRIVEN IN AN UNSAFE MANNER, PLEASE CALL . . .

I run in front of him to block his path, grab his R-Mered shoulders. For the first time in his life, he's taller than me.

"Ye, you said you'd never LEAVE me—"

"I CHANGED MY FREAKIN MIND!"

He bats me away like I was made of Rice Krispies squares, and he mechanostomps off into the fog and the darkness, his lights and his jet engine sounds growing fainter with every step.

I could chase him, but I've gotta protect the Jar. If there's one thing I know now, it's that.

I run back with the flashlight to try to avoid rattlers, hoping like hell the Jar's still there, which it is, then get the shotgun, practice aiming. I've never fired one of these things before! Hell, I don't even know where the safety is! What if I can't find it? What if—oh, there it is. Okay, now all I hafta do is not blow my own nuts off.

I look around, try to see anything I can. Moon aint much help under this fog, and I don'wanna use the flashlight too much so I don'give away my location in case Heinz or those freaks are on the way.

Crack—

Whip around AIM THE SHOTGUN but I can't see anything. Fumble with the flashlight, but it's too late. Whatever was there's gone now. Hell's bells, I can't take this—stress like this for much longer and I'm likely to start attackin the hoodoos.

Okay, now there's that sound again. Probly nothin, don't

overreact. Stay calm. Probably a coyote or a raccoon or something. Stay calm, Hamza. Don't go freakin fusion.

It's louder now. Okay, panic time. Sounds like someone diggin a freakin grave, or breakin bones or stuffin skulls in a sack! Animals don't sound like that, all right? ANIMALS DON'T SOUND LIKE THAT—

I've got no choice. I don't take care of this now, whatever it is is just gonna kill me later. If this's some kinda, like, *monster* or something, maybe I can kill it before it's finished doing whatever it's doing, *mu*tating or whatever—

I scramble out into the dark with my shotgun in fronta me, tryin to remember everything they taught us in Scouts and Venturers about tracking animals silently, making enough noise to cause an avalanche, and now I'm just running forward, my whole body shaking and quivering, and I'm squeaking out, "*Shi-I-I-I-T!*" about a million octaves higher than a successful puberty should've let me—

AND THERE'S A FREAKIN THING STAGGERING FORWARD, A KOT-TAM MUMMY OR ZOMBIE OR SOMETHING SHAMBLIN RIGHT AT ME—

"WHO THE FUCK ARE YOU? STAY BACK OR I'LL BLAST YOUR FUCKIN CHEST OFF!"

And then it freakin hisses my name!

"Ha-a-am . . . za-a-a—"

Oh my lord—it's *Sherem!*

I put the gun down, run straight for her. In the darkness I can barely see her, and it's only when I get right up to her that I realize she's totally naked, and even her hair's different, unbraided, and she's wounded, bleeding, covered in sand and dust caked up with her blood.

"Sherem, what the hell happened?"

I hold her tightly, and she squeezes me back weakly. I take off my hipster leather coat, wrap it around her, pick Sherem up in my arms, and run for safety, holding this naked, wounded woman in the fog while we huddle in a cranny in the side of the cliff, her holding on to me and me holding on to her for sweet, sweet life, inside a madness like a nightmare, or an old, old dream. . . .

"Sherem, what happened? How'd you get here? Where're your clothes?"

She's barely breathing, has to pant out each syllable: "Fought them . . . they had . . . a *weapon*. . . . Took . . . all my . . . strength . . . *everything* . . . to get here . . ."

"Sherem, the car—I think it turned into a pumpkin! Is that possible?"

"Pumpkin's . . . just . . . a placeholder. . . . *Did you . . . find . . . the Jar?*"

"Yes!"

"Take me!"

I pick her up to take her back just as headlights cut through the night and train themselves on us. And I know—*I know*—it's Heinz!

Engineering Meets Ignominy

Fᴜᴄᴋɪɴ Hᴀᴍᴢᴀ:

1. tired of his bullshit
2. got us into this insanity
3. get us killed out in the ass-end of nowhere
4. badlands mystery bullshit
5. religionistic crapfest
6. cheap asshole
7. jimp

ABORT LIST—REPEAT, ABORT LIST—

Status: new view, vertical into starless night sky.
   New subject. Record:
   YBG Somatic Armored Combat-Encounter-Environment Unit Version 1.0 needs redesign. Should terrain prove unstable, as in case of cracked, arid landscape, pilot may lose atti-

tudinal control and encounter horizontal displacement leading to immobility. Shape and mass of chest unit effectively prevents rocking motion necessary for remobilization if pilot lands on back.

Endnote: shit.

Coming Forth by Day vs.
Götterdämmerung

I'M RUNNING WITH SHEREM IN MY ARMS THROUGH THE DARK-
ness over crazy ground, then having to stop to pick up and
strap on the shotgun, then grabbing her again and trying to
keep running all the while the car that I'm sure has Heinz in it
is barreling straight at the Jar.

We're coming at it from opposite sides, and when I know
I'm not gonna make it there before they do, I put Sherem
down, drop to one knee, and aim the shotgun right at them.

They screech to a halt, their headlights on me, not knowing
what I'm gonna do next. I run for the Jar, and Heinz and some
other man scramble outta their car or SUV or whatever. They
run in front of their headlights, turn into silhouettes.

The other man's big, huge even, and he's got a big handgun,
which he's aiming at me, and something else in his other hand,
maybe a cell phone. Heinz has a bottle in one hand and I think
a pair of binoculars in the other.

We stop, equidistant from the Jar.

They got their gun, I got mine. Two against two. Two big
guys who're probably stone-cold killers, and us, a wounded

naked woman in a leather coat, and a dishwasher with a gun he doesn't even necessarily know how to fire.

This is a Western. That's how I'm gonna die, in a Medicine Hat standoff.

The headlights turn the fog into a specter, the ghost of a blue whale swimming through the prairies that used to be an ocean long ago.

Nobody's talking.

Until finally Heinz calls my name.

"Hamza!"

Even with all this madness, this fantastical horror swirling around, even *now,* the sound of his voice, of *him* saying *my name,* makes me wanna puke.

I wanna say something really vicious, really clever, but with the freight-train load of terror and confusion I'm hauling, the best I can muster is, "Whaddaya want, Heinz?" Genius. Pure genius.

"This whole situation is out of control." Silhouette Heinz wags its arms, as if to prove its helplessness, its innocence. "There's been . . . too much death already."

"What 'situation' are you talking about, *Heinz*?"

He sighs, as if I'm a burden on his oh-so-precious patience. And then, as if to prove what a good freakin guy he is, he touches the gun arm of his giant buddy softly, nods gently.

The guy doesn't do anything but keep his weapon aimed at my head. Then Heinz gets firmer, but still gentle, with the touching of the arm. Finally the Unfriendly Giant reluctantly crooks his gun arm so that the steel is pointed at heaven instead of me.

"Hamza . . . let's not play dumb now, shall we? If you're crouching here with *that woman*"—the silhouette points with its tilting chin—"then you obviously have some perspective on why we're all here. Even if she's given you a totally biased and distorted and self-serving explanation—"

He takes another step towards the midground between us

and the Jar that's waiting for someone to open it, still fluttering his palms-up hands as if I'm gonna fall for his line of crap.

"We're all in pain, Hamza. All of us here."

Before I know it he's baited me: "What the hell do *you*
know about pain, you son of a bitch?"

"My brother," he blisters. "You and that lady friend of
yours . . . I know what you did, y'know."

The gall of this asshole! His tone makes us out like *we* were
trying to hurt *him*!

"A big part of me, Hamza, would love . . . to make you suffer for my brother." He clears his throat. "But there's still
time."

"Time for *what*?"

"For you to walk away."

Heinz inches forward again and I brace the shotgun against
my shoulder, aiming right at his chest.

"Number one, you freak: I'm not goin anywhere. Number
two: I didn'kill your brother—he tried to kill me! Number
three: I know all about your—this—"

"You don't have the dimmest notion. You think you can
trust this woman? She's not what you think she is, Hamza. No
matter what you might *think* happened between you and me
in the past, if you were to trust me on only one thing for the
rest of your life, trust me on this—that woman is not what she
seems!

"I *guarantee* you she's been lying to you since the first
minute you met her, and just when you think she's told you the
whole story, all she's done is simply told you her *next* set of
lies!"

"YOU," I yell, "are the PRINCE of lies!" But it's bluster—
what he's saying to me—how the hell does he—no, he can't—
but—how could he? No, he's—

"I don't," he says softly, stage-whispering so I can hear him,
"want anyone else to get hurt. Too much blood on all sides,
Hamza. I've been searching for this object—" And he points

to the Jar with the thing I thought was binoculars, but I now see is something else entirely, like a bizarre camera or even a sextant.

"It's part of the cultural-archaeological heritage of humanity, Hamza. You know me—you know I'm a writer and researcher on mythology! This object . . . it has long-lost information. It could hold the secrets to heal people of physical and even psychological illnesses, Hamza, you understand?

"There's information inside that Jar that's been lost since the Christians burned the library of Alexandria and destroyed the greatest repository of knowledge in the history of the human race!

"The Egyptians didn't suffer from schizophrenia or cystic fibrosis or *cancer*, Hamza! Do you understand where I'm going with this? They built pyramids with technology that we don't have even today—super-concrete or controlled magnetism or telekinesis—and that Jar contains scrolls that—"

"That Jar doesn't have any scrolls in it!"

"What're you talking about?" He stops, seems genuinely shocked. "What do you mean?"

It hits me: what *do* I mean? I haven't opened it—Sherem told me *not* to. How *do* I know for sure what's in there? But everything she told me, showed me—

"Hamza, we can share the discovery together, do you hear me? Imagine how many lives we could save! How humanity could leapfrog ahead with advanced science the world hasn't seen in thousands of years, synergized with modern technology!

"But *this woman* doesn't want anyone but her own cult to get it! Why not? To control people! To have the world come begging to them! For their own stupid, vicious, selfish profit! Is that really what you want? The Hamza I remember would never've—"

"SHUT UP!" I scream. He's talking a mile a minute, and I can't think—

"Don't let her *control* you, Hamza—"

He steps forward again. I've had it. "You take one more step and I'll blow your fuckin face off."

He tucks the bottle he's got in his hand into his breast pocket, then breathes in through his nostrils, spreads his arms wide and clearly, obviously, grandly—

TAKES A STEP.

Okay, my bluff is a puff. Now what?

"Hamza," he says in his murdering, soothing voice, "*killing* . . . is not an easy thing."

I'm getting sick of him saying my name—he's saying it every sentence, like he's trying to hypnotize me or something—

"You've never fired a shotgun before in your life, have you, Hamza? Aiming's difficult—and in the dark? And by the looks of you . . . when'd you sleep last—two days ago?"

I crinkle my finger around the trigger—

"You are *not* GETTING *THIS JAR!*"

—steps forward AGAIN—

—aim way above his head, squeeze the trigger—

—CONE OF FIRE EXPLODES FROM THE BARREL OF THE SHOTGUN, FLAMES RIPPLING INTO THE FOG LIKE A DRAGON'S TAIL, ORANGE AND WHITE—

—gun's searing hot in my hands—think my eyebrows are burned—

—fucking YEHAT coulda TOLD me what kinda SHOTGUN he was giving me, a Yehat brand PLANET KILLER—

I reaim the shotgun at Heinz and his giant buddy, try to look like I intended for that to happen, pretty much figure I'm failing.

Heinz's close enough now I can see his facial expression, with the headlights' illumination sliding around the sides of his skull. Him and his partner look as freaked-out as I feel—guess they didn't expect Ye's tricks any more than I did.

Heinz tries to chuckle one of his ultraphony smug chuckles—a *smuggle:* "That's . . . huh-huh . . . im*press*ive, Hamza, but, uh . . . pretty hard to aim. Short range. No guarantee you'd, heh-heh, actually *hit* me. Without burning yourself up in the process."

And then I figure out how to shut him the fuck up.

"I don't *have* to hit you," I say, and I can't keep the smirk from seizing control of my face. "I only have to hit the Jar."

Suddenly I hear three voices screaming over top of each other—

Sherem: "Hamza, NO—"

Heinz: "Hamza, let's DISCUSS this—"

The Giant: "Like HELL you will, ASS-PORK—"

And the Giant aims his gun at my head again and I aim at him—he's gonna fire for sure—

And then he staggers, looks like he's gonna throw up, actually sinks to one knee. Sherem's right beside me in nothing but my coat, and she's staring straight at him, her hair all matted with sweat and blood and dirt, and more sweat pouring down her face like she's been caught in a rainstorm.

She's staring at him so hard it's like she's buckling his knees with just the force of thought. I look back at the man, and he tucks his gun away, and just like that, it's like the nausea goes away and he stands up.

And the Giant belches at me, "For all I know, ya lil assbunny, your gun'll explode the next time ya try to fire it! I see how you're holding it, like it's burnin your skin off! Maybe you're even outta ammo already!"

At the best of times my face is an open book, but when I'm panicked it's more like e-mail. I know what my expression is telling him: I have no idea whether there are any more shells in this thing!

"So, Kunta," he rumbles, "ya think you can stop me from rippin yer arms off an beatin ya with em before I get that Jar?"

"*Dulles . . .*"

It's Sherem. What the hell does that mean, "dulles"? But by the looks of his face, it must be his name—but how does she know—and what's wrong with her voice?

"He wasn't going to share it, you know."

The Giant looks frozen in midstep, like he was gonna advance on us and now his brain can't send the rest of the signal, or the signal to change course and target.

"What're ya talkin about?"

"Dulles, don't listen to her—she's a Jackal!"

"SHUT UP, YOU! Whaddaya mean, he wasn't gonna share it?"

"He was going to keep it for himself—you've never really been able to trust him, have you?"

"Dulles, don't be an idiot!"

"Dulles, has he ever hurt anyone you loved?"

The Giant's face yanks tight like someone jerked a cord at the back of his skull, and he turns on Heinz, grabs at him like Benjamin Grimm. "Heinz, you fuckin ASS-STABBER—"

He's choking Heinz and I'm frozen watchin it all happen, and Heinz is trying to scream out, "Don't—LISTEN—to her—can't you—*hear*—what—she's doing? BLOCK IT OUT—"

"This is FOR MY WIFE—"

And the Giant pushes down on Heinz, driving him to his knees, to snap his neck and rip off his skull—

And Heinz reaches up with both hands for the Giant's neck and eyes, and then the big man shudders and shakes like he's having a seizure, and he lets go of Heinz and falls back, his big meaty frame trembling and jerking with blood spurting out blackly in pale headlight from his eyes and neck, and even though the man clamps his hands over the bleeding, he can't stop it, and then Heinz gets up and crouches over him and reaches down towards his chest, and I hear a sound like a melon being squashed.

And then the giant man stops moving, except for his fingers and shoes, which twitch another few seconds, until they stop, too.

And then Heinz stands to face me, his hands palms up

again in pleading, but it's all wrong: his fingers are covered in gore, but they're three times longer than they should be, and his nails are like talons.

"*See what kind of woman she is?*" he says, as if I'm sposta not notice how he's changed physically, as if his appearance is no more unusual than that of a man who's just changed into a smoking jacket or a dinner vest.

Meanwhile I check in my peripheral: Sherem's too weak to stand, and she collapses, but never takes her eyes off of my good old buddy.

"That man," rasps Heinz, pointing with fingers way too long for the job, "was my friend. *She* did that to him! She left me no choice! I would've shared the Jar with him! He wanted me to cure his sick wife, which I would've *thought* YOU'D—" and then he stops, eyes bugged, like he's lost track of what he was gonna say, until his eyes narrow again and he yells, "BUT THAT MANIPULATIVE *WITCH*—"

I've been inching forward, and so now we're both closer to the Jar, maybe five meters on either side.

"How much money, Heinz?" I spit. "How much fame? How many hoes? How much power and pain? *How much is enough?* How many people do you have to smash before guilt stops you, you sick fuck?"

"You are so BLIND, aren't you, Hamza?" he yells. "After all these years? How could you not have grown up at least a little?"

He exhales furiously, then changes his voice to a tone at the Lagrange point between condemnation and inspiration. And I'm still trying to keep my eyes on those Nosferatu hands of his.

"Imagine, Hamza . . . imagine. We're on the verge of a spiritual evolution that makes Golgotha or the Kaaba look like a pitcher's mound. Imagine your most brilliant insight and your most intense orgasm rolled into one, then multiplied by a million. *That* would be like *pain* compared to the ecstasy of what the contents of this Jar can do for the human race."

"Since when do you care about the human race, Heinz?"

"With everything I've seen in my travels, Hamza? You want to think me nothing but selfish? Fine. But it doesn't take a genius to see that this planet's doomed, and obviously I can't survive alone in a destroyed world with a dead human race. That Jar holds the secrets to all our survival—no matter what that witch told you I wanted it for."

I've got the shotgun trained on the Jar, but Heinz, I don't know what he's doing. He takes the bottle out of his breast pocket and unscrews it—not an easy task with those superlong fingers of his—and upends it, drinking everything inside. He throws the bottle down.

He opens his mouth to gasp, drink in the air, I'm not sure—and his mouth and tongue are all white, viscous, with ropy spit like stalactites in his maw.

And then he tears off his shirt, and his entire chest is covered with some freaky black-and-white mehndi labyrinth of tattoos that look like Sanskrit or something.

I can't take my eyes off his chest, not even when he takes two more steps towards the Jar. I advance, too, gun squared on the ultimate prize. He stops.

I muster everything I can for my final words. I aint gonna go out like a punk. "I know how you make your drug, Heinz! I know what you do to those people, your victims!

"You take other people's misery and, and, and *death* for your foreplay? Always looking for the bigger high, the bigger big O? That's not Golgotha, Heinz, and it's not the Kaaba! That's Gehenna, you freak! That's the pit!"

"Evolution is change, Hamza," he lilts with that "Grow up" tone he mastered a lifetime ago, "and change is pain. Human history is nothing but a pyramid of pain, topped with the capstone of ecstasy and epiphany for the most highly evolved.

"Those 'people' harvested for cream . . . they led unreflective lives, barely worth living. They were dead before they ever even heard of cream. Lice, compared to butterflies. To eagles.

"Not like you or me, Hamza, people like *us,* who *think* and *dream* and *wonder.* Besides," he says, like he's taking me into his confidence, like he's including me in his sick little group, like I could actually sit at his table without breakin the freakin legs off, "beneath the flowery words, this is all it's ever been about. The food chain, human history, the whole universe. This is childhood's end, Hamza. Time to grow up. No reason you can't come with me."

He steps again.

"That's close enough, asshole. I will fire, this time, and destroy you or the Jar or both, an I'm not freakin kiddin—"

"You still have a choice, Hamza! *That* can make you . . . into whatever you want to be, like a caterpillar that can turn into *any*thing—"

"Heinz," I say slowly, tightening my grip on the gun, which I don't even know if it's loaded, holding on to it like it's my anchor to reality, to the most important instant of my life, the whole reason I was put on earth, to be here, at this place, on this night, at this moment, against this man:

"*You* have taken from me . . . nearly everything that ever mattered. What I *wanted* to be—I *would've* been, if not for you!"

"Don't fool yourself, Hamza," he drips. "Rachael didn't love you! Time to stop blaming me for that, hm? If she did, why'd she leave you so easily, eh? I didn't 'do' anything to her, except give her a taste of *real life*—"

"YOU'VE PLUNGED ME INTO THIS!" I scream. "Whatever I want? That's what you said the Jar can give me? This gun, Heinz, aimed at your heart. This is all I'll ever need again. *This.*"

He glares at me, and I glare back.

"This is it!" I snap. "COME ON!"

His shoulders twitch—

And THE HOODOO BEHIND HEINZ EXPLODES, FIRE AND CONCUSSION, and rock RAINING DOWN ON US—

But I didn't fire! What the hell?

And a voice rips echoingly into the canyon:

"*SURRENDER*-ender-der, *ASSHOLE*-sole-ole!"

Glance behind, up—YE! On a plateau, with smoke pouring out of one of the rocket launchers on his R-Mered arms—

Turn back as HEINZ LEAPS, squeeze the trigger—

My ears feel the thunderclap, the light brighter than the headlights, so the whole thing's in freeze-frame: Heinz's chest blasted apart into flaming chunks instantly, arms and legs and head flying away—

And Sherem bolts from behind me, leaps for the still undestroyed Jar, flings off the lid, and yells, "*Khepernyi yirkhut— Glory FORGIVE ME*—" and plunges her hand inside—

Everything turns white and my eyes slam shut—

Sound like a bomb exploding—

Open my eyes, and, and . . .

I stagger forward.

My jacket is on the ground, on fire. Empty.

Where Sherem used to be is nothing but ash and red embers in the chalk outline shape of a woman.

The Ascent

BUT THERE'S NO TIME TO FEEL IT, THINK IT, KNOW IT, GRIEVE IT, sob it, scream it—above the crackling sounds of brush on fire, I hear a rasping. What *now*? I get my flashlight out again, train it on where the sound's coming from.

There. On the dirt, beside a cactus.

Heinz's head.

It's *moving.*

The eyes are rolling and lolling, but when they steady, they glare at me. And the mouth—the lips are skinned back, and the tongue is way too long, like a snake or a giant leech or a huge penis, twitching, writhing . . . and then it slurps back inside.

And the teeth, oh, the gums . . . hell, the opening in his face is like a fuckin hole. Like the mouth of a lamprey . . . or a rectum lined with razors.

And the eyes—the *eyes*—accusing me, cursing me.

I remember reading somewhere about the guillotine, probly in an old EC, that the brain can live for a few minutes in total shock after decapitation.

It can't talk—no lungs for breath—but I can clearly see the

lips trying to mouth something. . . . Maybe it's *Fuck you forever* or *I'll get you* or maybe it's something else completely, something in some ancient language I've never heard of that was spoken by Things that weren't even human, Things that live off hate and death like piranhas in the river of souls. I don't know what the hell he's—it's—saying.

I stifle the impulse to kick it away so it can't look at me anymore. I don't wanna touch it, not even with my shoe, for fear of what it could still do to me, how it could infect me.

I step back, way back, slide a shell out of the bandolier, figure out how to snap open Yehat's little toy, insert, close, aim. Squeeze.

The desert floor lights up.

There's the sound of crackling, and the sight of a flaming bowling ball, and the smell of barbecue.

I hear the jet aircraft sound behind me, see the headlights play over the floor of the badlands, know that Ye's walked up behind me now. The jet sound whines down into a moan, then shuts off, and I can hear Ye pulling off his R-Mer in pieces.

I turn around, and we throw ourselves at each other, hold on, crushing each other, two best friends two minutes after—after . . .

"You okay?" he begs.

"Yeah, Ye. You?"

"Nearly blew my arm off with that rocket, but—"

"Thanks for the save."

I'm making this inane small talk because I can't bear to look. But I have to look.

I have no choice.

I stumble back, guts full of brine, full of swamp stew and broken glass, see the Jar and my empty jacket surrounded by ash and embers.

I fall, my knees hitting the dust.

Even though it could cost me my life, I have to know, hoping maybe there's some clue, some reason to believe she's survived.

I look inside the Jar.

It's empty.

What the hell did she do to herself? What'd she mean, "*Forgive me*"? Forgive her for what? Is this what she planned to do all along? Did she touch that thing knowing it was going to destroy her and itself, just so no one else could get it and use it? Did she even know that by touching it she would destroy herself?

Or did she?

Could she've changed, become . . .

But all that's left is ashes, bits of bone, the smell of sulfur. . . . Did she change her mind at the end? Was this a miscalculation . . . an accident?

Probably never know.

I can't hold back my moaning. I sound like a motor caught on something, the metal straining and groaning while the gears try to shred the system, the keening and lowing and the gasping and hiccuping, and the tears that give more rain to this earth than it's known in ten years or maybe ten thousand.

That's all I have left.

Ye's at my side, and he holds me. No R-Mer, just him, the real man.

He holds me and we both cry.

Him, for maybe just the release from all this horror, for having survived. And me . . .

Well, I've killed a man. No matter what kind of a man he was or what he became, he's someone I knew since I was fifteen. We had good history, then bad history, and finally worst history.

But I've still taken a life.

And I'm also crying because, because . . .

Because no matter what she was or wasn't, Sherem . . .

Finally Ye releases me, walks away, comes back with the shovel we brought, starts to spade up Sherem's remains.

"No, Ye," I rasp between tears, "I'll do it."

He nods, hands it to me, takes the shotgun, walks toward the still-running SUV Heinz drove up in, checking the backseat just in case there are any more surprises, then popping the trunk. When he gives me an all-clear wave and shout, I take the shovel and sift Sherem into the Jar.

When I'm done, Ye asks me, pointing to the dead Giant, "This guy's as big as a planet, Hamz. What're we gonna do with his body?"

Wow. Not a question you hear every day.

We debate whether we should dig a grave or try burning it, too. But neither one of us wants to risk a brush fire with any more pyrotechnics, and we don't know if we can dig a grave deep enough before sunrise.

Then we think about throwing him down in the cave, but not only don't we think we can lift him, the thought of putting this guy, whoever he is, down there—to me it seems like desecration.

So we dig a really shallow trench next to him, roll him into it, and put Heinz's limbs next to him. After I've shoveled all of Heinz's scattered hunks and chunks, I nearly go nuclear with insane giggling. Ye gazes at me in horror, me sputtering and stuttering out loud in gallows humor, "Heinz's pieces . . . Heinz's 57 pieces!"

Ye and me both laugh a gut-shuddering posttraumatic stress disorder howl, then cover the titan and the singed limbs with sand and rocks.

And then we load up the Giant's or Heinz's SUV with all our stuff. Including the Jar. And the pumpkin with the peeling-off bumper sticker.

And it's me and Ye on the road, in the fog, beneath the darkness.

So much swirling in me right now, so much fighting and forces not igniting but negating each other. How are you sposta feel at a time like this? My brain is strained, flattened, taut. I'm in the node where two waves from opposite directions cancel each other out.

There's only one thing I can think of through all of this numbness and dumbness and deafness and deathness.

Ye.

There's that old phrase, the old question: *You got my back?*

You never know, no matter how much you *think* you know, who's really got your back. Cuz when the shit starts pouring and Zeus's thunderbolts start firing, most fools're gonna run and then some, maybe take your wallet on the way out or use your chest as a raft to ride out the tidal wave.

But Ye. Ye's the man. Ulysses Hatori Bartholomew Gerbles. Roommate, engineer, mad scientist, trickster, fool, ladies' man, guardian, brother to my soul, *Coyote King* . . . he had and has had and continues to have my back, my front, my brain, my guts.

I don't know anything else for sure right now, and maybe I never will again. But I know that he stood with me on dooms-day night. And because of him we both walked outta hell so we could come forth by day.

Together.

The Time for *Wudu*

IT'S A LONG DRIVE BACK TO E-TOWN IN THE FOG AND IN THE dark, and we have to stop for gas once along the way in Red Deer. Good thing there's a credit card in the glove compartment— I pop it into the machine above the pump, fill er up.

Good thing because not only can I not find any cash in the car, but we either lost our wallets down there with all the evidence that connects us to what looks like ritual killings, or they're inside the pumpkin, and I don't want to try cutting it open for fear of who-knows-what-in-the-hell could pop out with em.

And another thing is, I don't relish having some late-night clerk get a good look at me with what's probly written all over my face. I know I'm covered in sweat and dirt and dust, and I've probly got blood spattered all over my face and clothes, too.

Driving with my guts getting more knotted every minute, stoking themselves with painful flame, eating themselves, digesting myself away.

By the time we're fifty klicks north of Red Deer, the fog has disappeared. Soon we're passing the international airport, fifteen minutes outside of city limits. The sky's lit up in that bizarre period of protodawn, when up above looks like a primordial solar system a-borning: ropy, lumpy clouds, black clots strewn across a field of inky indigo that will soon give birth to fire.

And then we're passing the outer membrane, the WELCOME TO THE CITY OF CHAMPIONS sign and the decorative oil derrick and the grain elevators that stand in silhouette like temples . . . or monoliths.

Up Calgary Trail North, flanked by lights, floating over highway-becoming-freeway . . . speeding on copless streets until we're zipping over Whyte Ave, then down into the river valley, up 109th until we're downtown, then through the Belly of the Whale, and into Kush, and past the Addis Ababa Obelisk lit up and announcing the coming of the sun.

And then we're home, at the Coyote Cave, which I thought I would never see again.

We unload the car, take everything inside.

And I change my mind, and take one thing back.

The pumpkin, which I put in the driveway.

Just in case.

I leave Ye inside, drive the SUV down to 107th Ave, look for the first roughneck I can find. I figure I'm gonna hafta do some fast talking.

At thug number one, I roll down the windows on this tank, call out, "Hey buddy, you want a free set of wheels?"

He looks back at me with a face I can't read. I hope he doesn't try to kill me. "What's the catch?"

"No catch. Take it, drive it, trade it, strip it, blow it up—do whatcha want—but make up your mind right now!"

"Yeah, dude, sure!"

I get out, leave the engine running. He hops in, peels away.

That went way better than I expected it to.

I walk home, not even trying to think about tonight, about yesterday, about the last week. Just trying to memorize everything I'm seeing in Kush right now . . . the faces of the Ethiopian restaurants . . . the way the obelisk looks with dawn's light turning its gray face pink . . . the Mac's Store with cabs in the parking lot and their Ethiopian drivers inside scarfing coffee and Danish . . . the way weeds press their way up through cracks in the sidewalk, insisting upon their right to live.

I've killed a man.

And I've lost the most remarkable woman I could ever meet.

I get home, go to the john, look at myself in the mirror. My cheeks and forehead're scarred, my goatee's matted, my hair's burned and messy, my clothes're dusty and bloody.

I wash myself completely. Do full *wudu*—complete Muslim cleansing from scalp to toenails, nostrils to anus—shower, shave off my goatee and my hair and even my eyebrows.

Sun'll be up soon, and the house is turning into delicate panes of pastels.

I put on a white shirt and fresh black pants and socks, tie a black tie, pull on the Big 4 jacket Ye bought me.

I unfurl the prayer rug my dad brought me from Mecca, perform *fajr*.

I get up, get my sunglasses.

Unfurl the Sails, Speak the Names of the Stars

THE SONG ECHOES THROUGH MY HEAD, "DAANDE LENOL" BY Baaba Maal, a song that sounds like rushing rivers, like the flutter of capes and scarves and sails in the wind, like torches crackling, like the building of temples, like the forging of bronze.

This is the song I feel and breathe when I call my dad to wake him out of bed. I tell him I'll be right there, but he hears the echoes in my voice and tells me to wait right where I am—he's coming for me.

I go to wait for my daddy on the porch.

The Coyote Car glistens in the driveway beneath the morning light.

The bumper sticker has fallen off, so I go to pick it up. It's a reflex to crumple it up, but I stop and fold it neatly, put it into my jacket breast pocket like it was a handkerchief.

Dad's there in a few minutes and when he sees how I'm groomed, he knows something has gone really bad. We go inside, and I tell him everything as best as I can, and I'm braced for him to think I'm insane, that I've gone nuts, that I've been drugged or I've joined a cult. Maybe I have. But . . . but I hafta tell him everything. Everything.

He's my dad.

There's no point in explaining how he takes it or how I get him to believe me. Suffice to say he *does* take it and he *does* believe me. And Ye sits in on the end, just to confirm everything I've said, and to show the few physical pieces of evidence we have. Like the canopic jar.

When he sees that, touches its body . . . whatever doubt I had about him believing me . . . it's clear by something that passes into his face that he has accepted enough of this string of impossibilities to not need to ask any more questions.

And then I hafta tell Daddy how I can't stay. How who knows what kind of trouble is gonna come looking for me and Ye now that we've been dipped into this stuff up to our necks.

It's not easy for anyone here. Something Ye only just reminded me about this morning was that his brother's supposed to be coming to stay with us, his brother with a genius IQ who can barely dress himself or buy groceries. I've only been thinking of me, of my departure, of having to leave my pop. But Ye's gonna bleed through this, too. And no matter how much I've heard him make fun of his brother over the years, he at least *has* a brother.

Well, I guess I do, too, but you know what I mean.

And then there's the Coyote Camp. We've spent years building that up. Doesn't seem right just to leave all the kids and their parents hanging like that, even if it is only a few irregularly scheduled afternoons a week during the summer.

But Dad's basically retired, and he loves kids, and even though Ye's brother, Spotswood, is nuts, he's gentle, at least. And he needs a place to stay while he's out here. So Ye and me lead Pop through all the camp stuff, while Ye briefs him on Swood, and we try to figure it all out.

So then Ye goes off to type a letter for his brother so Daddy and me can—

So we have a whole lotta tears together, Daddy and me, and we hold each other tight and then he helps me pack the car with clothes, the R-Mer, the Jar, whatever gear we can fit, and a few extras we figure we'll need. And then we hug some more.

It's a special kind of hugging, the kind where deep down you're facing the unspoken fact that this's the last time you're gonna hold somebody, and so you make your cells hold on, make em drink in somebody's scent and texture, so you can keep em with you after the world has taken em away.

My throat's knotting, cracking, and neither of us can talk anymore. And we only let go to wipe our noses and eyes on our sleeves.

Finally we release when Ye comes out. He's shaved his own head, too, and's dressed up exactly like me, except that he throws his cape on over top his Big 4 jacket. He hands Pop an envelope marked "Spotswood."

"Take care of him for me, will ya, Doc?" says Ye. "He's a good man, smart, but he's got the sense of a minijimp."

Daddy musters a smile. "Dun't worry, Yehaat. I cunn alwayce yusse anaather sonn. You'ff been a gudt one yourselef."

Ye looks down, away. Daddy reaches out, holds him. Ye holds him, too.

Then they release, and Ye fumbles with some Kleenex. Turns his back and fumbles some more.

When he turns back around he's got his Big 4 sunglasses on, and his cheeks are glistening in the morning light.

It's time to go, "Daande Lenol" still playing on my internal stereo, the song of the open road calling me. Dad and me say our finals on the porch, and I try not to sob too hard when I hold him one last time and say, "Dad . . . promise me . . . promise me you'll date again, okay? And maybe even get married?"

He tells me he will, and I hope he's not just saying that.

And we tell each other how much we love each other, and then I'm in the car, backing up to pull away, looking at my dad the whole time, until I can only follow him in the rearview mirror as he shrinks away to nothing but a Dad-shaped dot.

We speed down 107th in the morning sun until we get to Highlands and the condemned Richler building. Ye and me squeeze inside with our flashlights, go up to Sherem's apartment, ready to break the door down.

But the door's open a crack. Before and after we step over the threshold I whisper some words I think I remember her saying and then we search the place.

All the maps and diagrams and charts and microscopes and scales and everything else are gone. All of it, like it was all a dream, like she never lived here, like she never existed at all. For a minute I wonder if I got the wrong apartment, and I'm all set to check next door.

But then in the corner I spy a small book leaned up against the wall. I leap over, open it up—page after page of hieroglyphics. And on the cover, more glyphs. And just like down in the cave, like déjà vu, like a geyser of memory . . . I can *read* all this. These are formulas, instructions. For awareness . . . and transformation.

And I know what these figures on the cover mean.

Se-Nesert.

Son of the Fire.

There's one other thing I find after we search the entire place top to bottom—inside a kitchen cabinet there's a leather satchel with four necklaces in it, three bronze rings, eleven multicolored gourds varying in size and ranging from tomato- to banana-shapes, a dozen small tubes of various ointments like the kind Sherem put into the panpipe necklace she gave me. I can't begin to imagine what all this stuff can do . . . and what those gourds can turn into.

And a photograph:

An apartment full of Christmas decorations, with decor

that speaks of the 1970s. Maybe this very apartment, but in much better shape. A Black family: Daddy, Mommy, four brothers, and four sisters, all of them smiling.

Ah, Sherem. You, just a little kid, with a toothy smile and bunched-up cheeks and your legs tucked underneath you just like a puppy dog's . . . so innocent and so untouched. Before all this horror.

There's one other thing inside the satchel, something I almost didn't notice because it was tucked inside a hidden pocket.

A notebook the size of my palm, but thicker.

Inside, onion skin pages covered with the tiniest writing I've ever seen . . . and also in hieroglyphics. There's gotta be five hundred pages in this thing.

It's a diary. With writing this size, it could cover her entire life.

I flip, stop at random, stop and flip and read, and again, through the ancient, alienating grammar and script that so awkwardly describes the feelings of a girl, a teenager, a young woman . . .

> *Parents-my do not understand. . . . Brothers-my and sisters-my and I chose not this life-death-mission. . . . Chose it for us they did . . . asked us not what wells make us thirst, ask us not which breads and meats make us slaver. . . . Do they care or even see how deep is the canyon of my loneliness and agony? How can they demand I give away everything that anyone should want . . . for a long-dead dream?*

> *Childhood a sacrifice, but sacrifice for what? Will road-my ever be walked on by Joy? By Hope? By Love? Will children ever laugh and dance to call me in my name of "Protector of Small Ones"? Will a man ever embrace me and kiss me and call me in my name of "She Who Lights the Darkness"? Or will I only ever be the huntress, feared stalker in shadows, forever alone, in an ancient war I did not make and cannot win? . . .*

*All of them slaughtered . . . never again to hear their
laughter . . . never again to hear them call me in my
name of "Daughter Who Holds the Fire" or "Sister
Who Guards the Books." How can I study and train
when grief clutches me like a panther's jaws? Death is
in my sight today, like a man waiting to be released
from jail, like a rivercraft at full sail on a windy
night. . . . I crave to die almost as much as I crave to
kill. . . .*

*Through horrors of deaths-their and pondering death-
mine, through dwelling on the truths about me, told
and taught but never truly understood . . . the double
being of Religion and Gnosis . . . the outer, beautiful,
glowing, inedible, bitter rind for public palate . . . and
the inner fruit of slaking sustenance and delicious
strength, for the few, the Initiated . . . and so is all of
Was, and so is all of Is, and so is all of To Be . . . and the
Instructions are true, and parents-my were right, and I
am the last of us . . . and the War is just . . . and I will
not fall, but I will stand to come forth on that day. . . .*

*And if I am to be the one to uncover the sacred
Canopic Jar of the Beautiful Being, the Lord of the
Limits, can I, with all of comrades-my being dead, return to the Black Land with the Jar to my masters who
will Open the Way for all our race to leave this world
of tears and know perpetual peace and joy and light of
perfect Knowledge and eternal discovery?*
    *Yet such a journey, when so many other enemies
remain, is dangerous and may lead to murder-mine
and theft again of object of ancient yearning-ours, and
doom, doom doubled, doom made infinite.*
    *So if I, encircled by enemies, cannot return, what
am I to do? Dare I attempt to Open the Way when
hands-my are soaked in blood, and souls-my know
rage and viciousness and hate? Could such sinning
hands and souls succeed? Would I be transfigured
here, or sail along the Star-Nile to reach the Duat and*

*commune with Lord Usir Himself, or be annihilated in
the mere touching?*

*Yet if I do not dare this deed, enemies-our will drain
the celestial powers for themselves. No—better that I
should court death or worse than that. Perhaps let my
body be destroyed and open a Gate so that my souls
might take the divine vessel . . . even though they
would be scattered and wandering-lost inside the
rolling deeps of space, where dwell only the echoes
between the stars.*

*Yet the Jar would be safe. And humanity would be
safe.*

*Better that I suffer endless and eternal night of lone-
liness than for the world to have the Jar possessed and
perverted by the wicked and the vicious . . .*

*A hesitation I have not felt in years . . . when drew
forth from future-mists the shape of fate-his this morning . . . and saw children-our, and life-our . . . and saw
that love could belong to me, or me to it . . .*

*Have I not been faithful? How far will You all have
me go?*

*Eternal Ra, Lord Usir, Throne Aset, Master
Yinepu . . . take this Jar away from me. . . .*

I close the diary, put it back gently in the satchel, put all the
stuff back in, shoulder the kit. Put my palms to my eyes, press.
Wipe my palms on my black jacket.

What could've changed for everyone if there'd been time? If
Sherem hadn't been too wounded or too desperate or too
afraid at the end to finish what she started out to do? If she or
the people who sent her could've used the contents of the Jar,
instead of her destroying them along with herself . . . or taking them with her to wherever she's gone?

What have we as a species lost? Do we have to wait another
thousand years for a second chance?

How do your words in "Natural Mystic" go, Marley? Asking how many more will have to suffer . . . and to die?

Me, to Ye, to myself, to the shadows in the fossilized living room of this extinct family: "Let's get the hell out of here."

It's a little after eight fifteen A.M. when I finish spray-painting the final giant backward *S* across the glass patio wall of Shab-badabbaDoo's.

"Think they'll see it?" I ask Ye.

He nods, standing there in his magnificent cape, a black phantom in the glory of the morning sun. "I think they'll see it."

We get back in the car, pull away. The lunch crew'll read it easily from the inside, stretching from east side to west: *I Quit, Assholes.*

Ye opens his CoolMeal box, takes out an ice-cream sandwich, waits to see my reaction. I shake my head. And grin. He takes out another one and unwraps it, hands it to me. This time we both smile, and we both munch.

At the Super Video 82, Ye dashes inside, holds the door open while he talks to his boss. I hear the whole thing from the car.

"John," he speeds, "you have the personality of a colostomy bag. Working for someone as dumb as you has been hell. Thanks for direct depositing my last check. Try not to go out of business without me."

He's back in the car, and I see John's mouth hanging open, maybe even swaying in the air-conditioned breeze.

Soon we're zooming down Calgary Trail South, then zipping down Whitemud Freeway over to 91st Street for even more southwardly zooming until we hit 23rd Ave so we can head east to the great beyond. Something pinches my brain all of a sudden and I say to Ye, "You know, I probably should've mentioned this before, but I brought my passport."

Without a word, Ye reaches into his jacket and slides out his own. I smile again.

"Any thoughts," he asks, "on how we're gonna survive?"

I glance to my left, the east and the sun, check out all the high-tension-wire towers rimming 91st, trying to memorize em.

Probly never see em again.

Most people think they're ugly. But to me, well . . . they're like giant, man-shaped wire outlines . . . man-shaped except they have six or eight limbs. And for kilometer after kilometer, they're all connected by wires, like they're holding giant rosaries or lifelines that stretch across an entire country, surging with power that makes our whole world run.

Ten thousand years from now, if these towers are still standing and everything's switched to cold fusion or nebula power or whatever, these towers'll be as mysterious as the heads on Easter Island.

I try to move back to Ye's question on how we're gonna survive. On a self-dare, I say, "Check the glove compartment."

He does.

It's crammed full of cash.

Ye leaps to a fast count. "Hammy, this is, like, ten thousand dollars! And that doesn't include all the foreign currency!"

I nod my head, keep my eyes on the road.

"Shit better not turn into spinach when we're paying the freakin tab," he mutters.

That makes me think of something else, and when I spot it, I tap the dashboard glass in front of me, show Ye.

Drove all the way to Drumheller, 350 klicks, easy, and now we've put another 10 klicks on this morning.

And that gas gauge hasn't budged.

We smile.

When we're outside of the city, streaking eastward towards the rising sun, Ye asks me something that punches me right in the gut.

"You ever tell her why we're really called the Coyote Kings?"

I try to digest that one for a while, finally spit up an answer. "Naw."

Burying Cocoons and Bursting Forth from Them

WE FIND THE KIND OF FIELD I'VE BEEN LOOKING FOR AROUND high noon past the border with Saskatchewan, a field with knobby hills and flattened trees on rolling prairie, like we're on savannah. We pull off the road, drive as far as the land'll let us, get out.

We're underneath the dome of the sky, shock blue with white gold at the zenith, and it's like everything I see is through polarized lenses, clean and crisp and atom-clear.

I dig the shovel into the earth, again and again until the tiny grave is ready, put the shovel down. Wipe my hands on my pants.

Ye hands me the Box.

I open it, take one last look at Rachael's beautiful face.

Rachael, I don't know what happened. I don't know the why. Ye said I should blame you, that that'd make everything better. But if that sack of filth Heinz was involved, I know now better than I ever could've before . . . it wasn't your fault.

I shouldn't've doubted you, darling.

Given what Heinz was doing, I guess I have to face up to the fact that you're dead. It's time for you to rest, my sweetness, free from being haunted by all the pain I carried around inside me.

I put the picture back inside the Box.

And then I slip out one of the pictures I took of Sherem.

Sherem . . . maybe I'll never know what happened to you. But I pray to . . . to Whatever That Is . . . that you're not in pain anymore. That you don't have to run, or hurt, or be hurt, or hide.

That you can just do what you were born to do. Learn everything there is to know . . . out there.

And delight in it.

I put Sherem's picture in with Rachael's, close the Box, put it into the earth, put the soil back where it belongs.

"Good-bye," I say out loud. "To both of you."

We keep moving east in our black Coyote Car, the sun now at our backs, with the roads ahead and what lies beckoning beyond.

The Jar may be empty now.

But the world is full.

"So where're we headed?" asks Ye.

"Out there," I say without even having to think about it, "to find . . . find whatever we find."

"Anywhere in particular?"

I nod. "She said she came from a temple outside Ash Shabb, in Upper Egypt."

"And based on *that,* you think you can find this place?"

I tilt my head towards him, look at him above the rims of my sunglasses.

"Okay . . . forgot," he begs off, and I look back to the road. He goes on. "So, what, we're gonna drive across the Atlantic, or does this thing turn into a boat, too?"

That one makes me laugh. He goes on.

"Y'know, Hamza . . . you *know* me. I'm a man of science,

of technology. And thanks to our little adventure, like, my whole understanding of the world has been totally turned upside down." He takes a breath, like he's preparing for a marathon. "And you're asking me to take on *even more* on faith." I take my eyes off the road, catch him pursing his lips. "And *faith's* never been my strong suit."

I tilt my chin towards him for the punctuation to what I'm gonna say. "You always believed in *me*."

We drive in silence.

"It's good . . . to have a friend you can love forever, and . . . who you always know'll love you. And believe in you."

It sounds like something I'd say, and the way I'd say it. But I didn't say it. Ye did.

"Yes, indeed, Brother," I tell him, offering him my right hand, and we soul-shake down the open skyway.

"So whaddawe do when we get there?" he asks.

"Learn. Train. I dunno . . . protect?"

" 'Protect'?" He chews on that. *"Protect."* Again. "Hm. I like that. The Coyote Kings, Protectors of the World. Okay, I'm in."

"I thought you were already in, man. We're like halfway across the freakin world already!"

"Don'take me for granted, jimpy."

We laugh.

"Look!" Ye squeals, long-arm points past my face to the northeast.

And there they are, nearly hidden amid the golden grasses. *Coyotes.*

Prologue

I FEEL LIKE I SHOULD HAVE SOMETHING POETICAL TO SAY, Y'KNOW? Some great wonderful momentous thing to quote or whatever. But really, I don'have any words right now. I don'know what's gonna happen next, or when, or why. But all I know is, is now . . .

Now I believe again.

I don't even know all of *what* I believe, but just the simple fact that I *can*.

I know I'm not the same man I was eight days ago.

And I know it's time to find out who I am.

Appendix

EXCERPTS FROM CHAPTER ONE
OF HEINZ MEANEY'S *VISAGE GROTESQUE*

"Cainthropology: The Utility of Agony"

THE CENTRAL CONCERNS OF THE PRESENT WORK INCLUDE THE EX-
ploration of not only the archetypal architecture of primordial-
through-nuclear-epoch literary tropes regarding the struggle of
"good" against "evil," but the root of those thematic appari-
tions within the wellspring of human consciousness, the neu-
ropolis itself, from reptilian id to cerebral superego.

That uncountable myths and legends and ecclesiastical operas and dirges have at their core, if not in their trappings, near
identical mechanisms, performances, and outcomes is proof
most solid of the centrality of the panhuman subconscious—
or superconscious—experience of the myriad and manifold
wonders and terrors of the cosmos.

Simply put, *spiritus mundi* is neither phantasmagorical myth nor primitive amusement for misguided, "slumming" intellectuals in the humanities devoid of a special relativity or a superstring with which to amuse themselves, but rather a functional, measurable, experimentally verifiable reality.

But perhaps the major reason why this discourse has been so absent from polite literary and mythopoetic interlocution is that its living, breathing, smoldering heart is such a terrifying sight to behold. And this dark, cardiacal engine, of course, is the grotesque. It is this grim machine that is not only the binding force of the human, animal, and vegetable worlds, but the Overmind whose existence permeates the physical terrestrium.

Contained within the quasi-misanthropic rantings of the econuminous movement in this ever-dwindling century—and perhaps best expressed by its greatest prophet, who has no idea how close to the perpetual truth he actually resides, Dr. David Suzuki—is the dawning scientific comprehension that the earth is literally *alive*. Not as metaphor, not as simple sum of component life-forms, but as supersystem body to the distinct cells that are all of us.

And as this planet is clearly body, so too must it be *mind*.

What vast, impenetrable dreams must this Titan have! What nightmares! Cast from parent Sol and locked in dance eternal with barren, loveless Luna, its myriad children so many scaled and feathered beasts inside its lungs, so many scrabbling arthropods upon its skin, so many burrowing things inside its flesh and cascading through its unknown subterranean web of arteries and veins. How unimaginably long ago did this Creature fall to slumber? Can It awaken? And if so, who will be Its prince? Who will dare assume that mantle, and what vast price will that prince pay and what vast distance will that prince go to fashion a kiss with which to draw It forth from slumbering . . . to be reborn?

And when reborn, what ancient verses will it pronounce?

What secrets and blessings will It bestow upon Its children—
Its foolish, lost, suffering, pathetic, neglected children? . . .

Much has been dissected from among the myths to explore
the significance of the mortal endurance and experience of
pain. Pain, we are told, purifies the body, expands the mind,
prepares the novice for the tests of life and therefore for initi-
ation into the clan, the sect, the tribe, the gang, the squadron,
the priesthood, the academy, the coven, or the board. It is clear
that such suppositions regarding physical or emotional pain
are true; little more need be said on such matters.

It is the far more disquieting issue to which we now turn
our attention, that is, the utility of agony, not for the novice,
but rather for the initiator—the harvest and consumption of
the victim's misery by the praetor of sacrifice himself.

The history of human development can neatly be divided
into two epochs: (1) the feminine, yin, agro-sedentary pastoral
idyll of the old-to-late Paleolithic Mother-Earth-Goddess religions and (2) the masculine, yang, technomobile hunter-
gatherer-warrior field effect of urbanized, late-Neolithic-to-
modern Father-Sky-God religions.

That humanity owes a great debt to the craftwork of wom-
ankind is indisputable; the surplus product that women's in-
vention of agriculture created made possible nothing less than
the triumphant masculine revolution and the impetus towards
armies, cities, and academies to produce the priesthood/
philosophers/warlords/administrators.

But that alone makes clear, it is only within the ascendant
yang or phallic imperative that humanity can begin its separa-
tion from infancy and total reliance on the (even neglectful or
comatose) parent. It is only now, therefore, that humanity can
take the next step into our mass adolescence: to separate from
parent completely, but only after confrontation with that parent, mastery of Its secrets and knowledge wilfully held by

force of Its suspicion, cowardice, and venality . . . or simple sleep.

The mythic record left by the Hellenic fathers of our Mind makes this clear: Uranus and Gaea had to yield to the castrating sickle revolution of Chronos; Chronos had to yield to the cosmic army of Zeus, Poseidon, and Hades. Sky-Earth fell to Time; Time, too, fell to the Electron, to Water, and to Death.

The mechanism of universal advancement is pain—the pain that comes through conflict and, yes, sadly, death. The best (indeed, the only honest) name for this conflict is cannibalism.

The cannibal's comprehension of the transfer of energies from one being to another is primitive, but in its Occam-like unadorned simplicity is elegant. The conqueror captures and consumes the flesh, and most preferably the brain, of the conquered. This Stuff is the recently living repository of the passions, drives, songs, prayers, hopes, glories, and Secrets of death and eternity.

For the conqueror to eat of this Stuff is for the conqueror to imbibe of the organic, somatic truth of existence. It is to celebrate the life of the vanquished, and incorporate his life energy into the never-ending hunt.

Prey lives on inside of hunter, informing him, infusing his unfolding acquisition, and thereby gaining everlasting life, so long as the cannibalistic chain is not broken. And Earth itself, the ultimate conqueror, even in Its deathlike sleep, consumes us all. This transference of energies is present still in any of the human enterprises of competition and exchange, and no less is it found within the institution of the production of literature and its taskmaster—or vulture—literary criticism.

And from outside the original Indo-European mythic genealogy is the parable that is now at the core of the Western mind, from that Semitic clan of wanderers, mystics, madmen, and warrior-philosopher-kings: the tale of Cain and Abel. This most misunderstood story is key to all, to explaining and expressing the power and the glory of the ascendancy of Man as revealed by the Prophet Darwin (may peace be upon his gametes).

Cain slays Abel, we are told, because YHWH finds Cain's agricultural sacrifice inferior to Abel's offering of meat from his herd. In jealousy, we are told, Cain rises up and destroys the object of his diminution. YHWH, incensed at the world's first documented case of sibling rivalry, banishes Cain from the land to which his parents had already been banished after their own pathetic and transparent attempts to improve their bargaining position with the Almighty.

But blubbering, soft-shelled Cain then begs God for mercy, and God, mysteriously (or perhaps not?), grants Cain a mark, a warning to all the angry public (who apparently at this point is only Adam and Eve, yet there are others later created by YHWH even if the text is silent upon their inception; is it after Cain's crime?) that any who harm Cain will pay a price. Cain then is exiled off to the land of Nod, where he presumably mates with apes, wolves, and boars while avoiding punishment at the hands of a populace that must be appalled at immigration of the greatest criminal alive: Cain did, after all, murder one-quarter of humanity, a slaughterfest statistic that only the Creator of the Universe would be able to surpass, as in a few centuries' time Noah would discover.

But what if we've misunderstood the story all along? What if God weren't punishing Cain, *but rewarding him*? What if the contest of sacrifices didn't end at God's acceptance of Abel's mutton or beef, but only after Cain vanquished that offering with an even finer cut—*by sacrificing Abel himself*?

After all, once God affixes his mark (erroneously assumed by European clergy to be a racial signifier, but indicative of something far, far more grand), Cain leaves the presumably unpleasant refugee grounds he shares with his parents for a territory where he fathers a vast dynasty apparently also protected by Divine Immunity and with which he reintroduces cattle herding, but also for whom he invents the tent, the harp, the organ, brass- and ironwork—not to mention the first civilization.

This is the penalty for the world's first murder—and fratricide, no less (not to mention the aforementioned genocide of one-quarter of humanity, whom the Nodites were apparently created to replace in abundance, or in fear of Cain's proclivities . . . or to feed those proclivities for the Godhead's/civilization's sake)?

It seems far more logical that this ancient and oft-told but always misunderstood tale is the central revelation of the price of civilization: sacrifice.

Human sacrifice.

Not only does the social institution of scapegoating allow for a vast populace to avoid the rather destablizing influence of frequent, decentralized bloodletting, and allow for the culling of cancerous protuberances for the betterment of the body, but through the mythology that is secreted around it, like a pearl formed around the agonizing micrometeor of a sand granule in an oyster's tender flesh, humanity may, through this bloodletting, move psychically closer to the terrestrial Dream itself, to the dark wonders and primordial secrets we need if we are to scale to the next level of human evolution.

The World Man whose skull becomes sky and whose bones become mountains after he is murdered by his children—the Green Man whose body is seed becoming spring growth and summer harvest after assassination at the hands of his brother—the Sacrifice Man made of flesh but who is a *woodworker nailed directly onto wood* (as if the ancient code makers could not have been more clear) and whose followers wear a model of the device that murdered Him like a talisman (only incomprehensible if one neglects the core revelation)—is the earth-god who must die so that Its children may live upon Its flesh: "Eat . . . this is My body . . . drink . . . this is My blood; whosoever partake of Me shall have everlasting life."

The Cannibalism Divine.

Whether Osiris, Prometheus, Hercules, Dionysus, Odin, Krishna, or any of a hundred others, it is clear: the murder of Abel made able the fusion of Technology and Man. Christ did not die for our sins, but for our synergies. Cain, Father of Cities, Master of Arts and Crafts, Convener of the Ceremony that Sacrifice Man must face, Lord of the Grotesque, renews and advances the world.

As terrible a moral conundrum as it is to contemplate, can anyone seriously consider abandoning and destroying the medical knowledge compiled by any of today's animal researchers who have saved millions of human lives? Or eliminating the too-high-a-price-but-paid-for-nonetheless terrible knowledge of the body's mysteries revealed by the *Volksgesundheit* researchers at Auschwitz, or by Imperial Nippon's biochemical-torture-and-warfare Unit 731, or by da Vinci's rarely admitted but groundbreaking live dissections, or by innumerable Chinese torture chambers that three thousand years ago began compiling that unspeakably great corpus called acupunctural medicine?

Yesterday, the grotesque was the gateway out of interminable millennia of mere subsistence. Today, the grotesque is the portal towards the next evolutionary staircase of the individual mind, of the terrestrial consciousness, and of Man's ascension to the stars. Gloriously, "Forgive them, Father, for they know not what they do" may not be merciful pleading on behalf of Christicidal transgressors, but rather, an acknowledgment: "Excuse their ignorance, Cosmos—they have no idea they're activating the universe-gestation machine."

Acknowledgments

MY VERY SINCERE THANKS:

To my friends Mike Cherry, Fish Griwkowsky, and Trevor Russell for having read the first draft of the manuscript and given me very helpful feedback and encouragement,

To my editor, Betsy Mitchell, whose editorial guidance has helped me to make this novel more of what I wanted it to be in the first place,

To my superb agent Marie Brown, who is a wise, wonderful miracle-worker, and a true friend (in an industry in which numerous sources warned me that "no one is your friend"),

To Charles Jordan and Warren Burdine, whose generous words and advocacy lifted me to Cloud 9.1,

To my many friends and teachers who encouraged me over the years to pursue my writing, but especially Prof. Daphne Read, who gave me the advice, "If you want to write, then write!"

To my many friends in drama who participated in the *Coyote Kings* screenplay workshop in 1996 and in the video shoot in 1997 (here's hoping we'll make a movie after all, now!),

To all of my ancestors, may they have triumph and peace,

Most of all to my first and best teacher, my hero: my mum.

Finally, I must say that all splendour, all power, and all triumph radiates alone from the one God, who is the great hope of the universe, the maker and master of the stars, and the love of all the worlds.

Only the mistakes have been mine.

MINISTER FAUST is a high school English teacher, broadcaster, community activist, writer, actor, sketch comic (*The 11:02 Show* and *Gordon's Big Bald Head*), and poet who has performed his verse across Canada and on national television, and has won every poetry slam he entered. He wrote and directed his first play for Montreal's Creations, Etc., when he was seventeen. A community broadcaster beginning in 1989, Minister Faust has, since 1991, produced and hosted the NCRC Award–winning radio show *The Terrordome: The Afrika All-World News Service* (http://www.cjsr.com), a weekly program of Afrocentric and progressive news, politics, culture, history, religion, and the arts. Minister Faust is also the producer and host of *The Phantom Pyramid: Global Afrikan Musics Led by a Headcharge of Hip-Hop*. He currently freelances for *Vue Weekly* and CBC's *Definitely Not the Opera*. Minister Faust lives in Edmonton (E-Town Supreme) and can be reached via e-mail at ministerfaust@cjsr.com.